"Amazing series. ... only a small part of what makes these books great. I can't wait for the next one!!"
—*Amazon reviewer*

"This is my favorite book so far of the Alastair Stone Chronicles, and that's saying something, since I adore the series and its protagonist."
—*Shawna Reppert, award-winning author of* the Ravensblood *series*

"There are few books that strike a chord. This is one of them."
—*Jim, Amazon reviewer*

"Great series, awesome characters and can't wait to see where the story will go from here."
—*Amazon reviewer*

Praise for *Blood and Stone*

"I have read every book in this series and loved them all...this one is no exception."
—*Soozers, Amazon reviewer*

"The writing is extremely good, and the plot and characters engaging. Closest author comparison probably Benedict Jacka and the Alex Verus series."
—*MB, Amazon reviewer*

"The books keep getting better and better."
—*Jim P. Ziller, Amazon reviewer*

"Have followed our expat mage from the beginning and this time around, it's a home run."
—*Amazon reviewer*

"I highly recommend the entire Alastair Stone Chronicles and this latest installment does not disappoint!"
—*Wendy S., Amazon reviewer*

Praise for *Core of Stone*

"Once again R. L. King has come up with another great story for Alastair Stone. I enjoyed this as thoroughly as all the others and look forward to more."
—*Tahlia Newland, Amazon reviewer*

"I love it when a writer starts out strong in her career and just gets stronger. I have loved The Alastair Stone Chronicles from the beginning, but this one just blew me away."
—*Shawna Reppert, award-winning author of* the *Ravensblood* series

"I have loved the series as a whole but have to say this is a favorite just for the character growth."
—*Amazon reviewer*

"The Alastair Stone Chronicles is one of the best series I have read in years…"
—*Judith A. Slover, Amazon reviewer*

Praise for *The Source*

"Perhaps the best addition yet to an already amazing series."
—*Greenlite350, Amazon reviewer*

"A continued thrill to the urban fantasy reader…"
—*Dominic, Amazon reviewer*

"I consumed the four pack in less than a week. This a great series and one of the best ones I have had the pleasure to read in a long time."
—*Skywalker, Amazon reviewer*

"If you like Harry Dresden and The Dresden files, or Nate Garrett in the Hellequin series than this series is for you."
—*Amazon reviewer*

Praise for *The Threshold*

"Once you enter the world of Alastair Stone, you won't want to leave."
—*Awesome Indies*

"Excellent story as are all the others in this series."
—*Tahlia Newland, Amazon reviewer*

"I LOVE THIS BOOK!"
—*Claryn M. Heath, Amazon reviewer*

Praise for *The Forgotten*

"Alastair Stone is like Harry Potter meets Harry Dresden with a bit of Indiana Jones!"
—*Randler, Amazon reviewer*

"I loved the first book in the series, but this book is even better! ... I didn't think I could be any more in love with the protagonist than I was in the first book ...My only hesitation in giving it five stars is that, if the next one is even better (as I suspect it may be) I won't have anywhere to go with the rating."
—*Shawna Reppert, award-winning author of* The Stolen Luck, Ravensblood, *and* Raven's Wing

"This is actually an original idea - such a rare thing these days. Well written too."
—*Tahlia Newland, Amazon reviewer*

"From the first paragraph I knew I was in the hands of a competent writer, and from the second paragraph I was hooked to read on…a novel deserving of the full 5 star rating."
—*Awesome Indies*

Praise for *Stone and a Hard Place*

"The magic is believable, the characters could be people you know, and the twists, turns and mysteries to be solved glue your eyes to the page. You will never forget these characters or their world."
—*Jacqueline Lichtenberg, Hugo-nominated author of the* Sime~Gen *series and* Star Trek Lives!

"Somewhat reminiscent of the Dresden Files but with its own distinct style."
—*John W. Ranken, Amazon reviewer*

"I am reminded of Jim Butcher here…Darker than most Urban Fantasy, not quite horror, but with a touch of Lovecraftian."
—*Wulfstan, Amazon Top 500 reviewer*

"Dramatic protagonist sucked me right in…I instantly wanted to spend more time with Alastair Stone…I definitely want to see more from this author!"
—*Shawna Reppert, award-winning author of* The Stolen Luck, Ravensblood, *and* Raven's Wing

"Fast-moving fun!...[t]he book is full of the things I like in a book, and they are presented in a clean, brisk style. This is a book well worth checking out.."
—*Jason M. Hardy, author of* Hell on Water, Drops of Corruption, *and* The Last Prophecies

"Stone is a completely believable protagonist, and, frankly, damned likeable. We all wish we had college profs as engaging as he is!"
—*Silas Sparkhammer, Amazon reviewer*

ALSO BY R. L. KING

The Alastair Stone Chronicles
Stone and a Hard Place
The Forgotten
The Threshold
The Source
Core of Stone
Blood and Stone
Heart of Stone
Shadows and Stone (novella)

Shadowrun
Shadowrun: Borrowed Time
Shadowrun: Wolf and Buffalo (novella)
Shadowrun: Big Dreams (novella)
Shadowrun: Veiled Extraction (coming in 2017)
(published by Catalyst Game Labs)

ALASTAIR STONE CHRONICLES: BOOK EIGHT

FLESH AND STONE

R.L. KING

MAGESPACE PRESS

Copyright ©2016, R. L. King

Flesh and Stone
First Edition, December 2016
Magespace Press
Edited by John Helfers
Cover Art by Streetlight Graphics

All rights reserved. No part of this book may be reproduced or transmitted in any form or by any means, electronic or mechanical, including photocopying, recording, or by any information storage and retrieval system without the written permission of the author, except where permitted by law.

This book is a work of fiction. Names, characters, places, and incidents either are products of the author's imagination or are used fictitiously. Any resemblance to actual persons, living or dead, events, or locales is entirely coincidental.

To my instructors and fellow students at the Stanford Online
Novel Writing Certificate program.
It's been a helluva ride!

ACKNOWLEDGMENTS

First and foremost, many thanks to my wonderful instructors and fellow students in the Stanford Online Novel Writing Certificate program for comments, critiques, suggestions, and general all-around awesomeness. Special thanks to Helena Echlin, my one-on-one advisor, for final comments and lots of help with the perspective of a Brit moving to Northern California; Deborah Munro, a solid and consistent critique partner throughout the whole program (and a darn good writer herself!); and instructors Stacey Swann, Malena Watrous, Thomas McNeely, Joshua Mohr, Wendy Nelson Tokunaga, and Seth Harwood. That's a huge collection of talent right there, and I'm honored to have had the chance to study with and learn from them.

As always, thanks to my ever-patient spouse, Dan; to my fantastic editor, John Helfers; and to Glendon at Streetlight Graphics for another amazing cover. Also Steven Rosenau for being the body model for the cover, and Taggart Gorman for taking the photo.

And, as always, thanks to everybody who's bought, read, and enjoyed the books.

| PROLOGUE

THE PREY SLEPT, with no idea how quickly his death would come.

The homeless man huddled on a bench at the far side of the park, hidden by overhanging trees and a burned-out streetlight, snoring away in alcoholic slumber. It was a mild night in late summer, but the air still held a hint of bite. The man's knees were drawn up, his ragged coat covering him, his arms wrapped around a battered pack he was using as a pillow.

They moved in stealthy silence, two from the side, two from the back. Their clothes were dark and nondescript; hoods obscured their features. They didn't speak to each other.

One of the two coming in from the side nodded to the other one. His eyes gleamed from within the shadows of his hood. At a signal from the other pair they all moved as one, crossing the grass and the damp carpet of leaves with almost no sound.

The homeless man died in less than five seconds. He probably didn't feel any pain; there was no reason for his attackers to cause him pain. That wasn't what they were after.

Each had his or her job: one sliced the man's neck with a razor-sharp knife, one went for his abdomen, and two pulled his legs out straight and slashed with unerring precision at his femoral arteries. Before the prey had any idea what was going on, he had drained out, plumes of blood fountaining upward and outward, bathing his four assailants in hot liquid. They made no effort to get out of the way.

When the body stopped moving, they fell with enthusiasm to their purpose. One ripped the man's coat and shirt open to expose his abdomen, and then all of them plunged gory, clawed hands into the cavity. They huddled around the body, making the sort of small snuffling noises one might hear from a happy dog attacking a bowl of food. They remained there for perhaps a minute or two, stuffing gobbets and chunks into their mouths as fast as they could, swallowing, licking lips. The meat was always best when it was freshly killed, hot and steaming and slick with blood.

"That's it," one of them said under his breath at last, a mouthful of meat muffling his voice. "Pack it up."

"Ain't nobody here," another protested. "Can't we just—"

"Pack it *up*," the first one said again, more emphatic this time.

Reluctantly, the others unslung empty backpacks and unzipped them. With the skill of butchers they sliced chunks from the man's body, stowing them in plastic bags and nestling them into the backpacks along with their knives. Before two minutes had passed, the old vagrant was missing most of his organs and several large pieces from his legs and arms.

"There," the leader said, zipping his backpack. "Let's go."

The others didn't argue this time. They slung their own packs on their backs while the leader covered the vagrant's body with his coat. From a distance, he would simply look like he was sleeping, at least until it grew light and somebody spotted the blood pooling beneath him.

They would be long gone by then, of course. Gone, with enough food in their larders to keep them going for at least another month before they would have to hunt again.

| CHAPTER ONE

ALASTAIR STONE never could sleep on planes; it was one of the many reasons he disliked air travel. His window seat in business class meant that he didn't have to deal with screaming babies or juvenile seat-kickers, but it did nothing to insulate him from his seatmate, a chatty American cougar who had clearly begun her airborne adventure in some bar back at Heathrow, and who had been giving the flight attendants a workout to keep her topped up ever since.

Stone had long ago given up trying to pretend he was asleep; since he couldn't manage the real thing, all he got by faking it was periodic unexpected billows of forty-proof breath when the woman cast hopeful glances his way every five minutes or so. The last straw had been when her red-nailed hand had "accidentally" landed on his thigh about an hour into the flight. He contemplated a surreptitious stunning spell to put her out for the rest of the trip, but decided against it since he couldn't determine how it would affect someone at her level of inebriation.

He wanted to shut her up, not kill her.

He could dream, though. He settled for a pointed glare, first at her hand, then at her face. She wasn't unattractive, but the characteristic whiff of "trying too hard" surrounded her like a cloud. He'd seen the type plenty of times before—for whatever reason, he seemed to be a magnet for them. Even if he weren't currently uninterested in female companionship, middle-aged divorcees with heavy makeup and way too much visible cleavage didn't flip any of his switches.

"Oh!" She giggled and snatched her hand back, clearly delighted that she'd succeeded in capturing his attention. "I'm sorry!"

Of course you are. It was such a pity that current circumstances made traveling by portal impractical. It would have made all of this so much easier.

She eyed him, her bloodshot green gaze traveling up and down his body, hovering a bit too long on his lap, and finally settling on his face. "I hope I didn't disturb you."

"Oh, I'm quite disturbed enough as it is," he said with an arch smile. She had to be in her late forties, a good twenty years older than he was; it was hard to tell for sure under all that makeup. Her jeans and low-cut T-shirt clung to her like a second skin, hugging the curves of a figure currently doing a pretty good job fighting off the ravages of time—but judging by the number of drinks she'd been downing, continued success was by no means a given. Stone nodded politely to her and pulled out the paperback he'd stashed in the seat back. Maybe she'd take a hint.

"You're from *England*," she said, sounding even more delighted. "I thought you were a tourist, like me. I just *love* a man with an British accent." She studied him again, with a frank lack of self-consciousness and a salacious smile. "Especially one as attractive as you are. Did anyone ever tell you that you look like that young man on that British show? …oh, what was his name…?"

So much for hints.

"Sorry," he said, shaking his head and shrugging.

"I think it's the hair," she went on, oblivious to his discomfort.

For one terrifying moment, Stone thought she was going to reach out and ruffle the front of his hair. He didn't lean back away from her, but it took an effort of will not to.

She didn't, thank the gods. "What brings you to San Francisco?" she continued instead, and took another gulp of her drink. Her lips left bright red impressions on the glass.

He supposed that 'this plane, obviously' wasn't an appropriate answer, and sighed. "I'm starting a new position."

She giggled, waggling her eyebrows. "New positions are always fun." She twisted in her seat, spotted the flight attendant, and waved for another drink, then turned back toward Stone. "What sort of position?"

"Teaching," he said, forcing himself not to sigh. "At Stanford."

Her eyes widened; the effect, combined with the rise of sculpted brows hovering a half-inch or so above their natural location, made her resemble a clown who'd just received a particularly exciting bit of news. "Really?" Her gaze traced him yet another time. "Oh, you'll do fine there," she said. "You'll have the girls falling all over you. Probably all the other professors' wives, too."

Because that's exactly why I accepted this position, of course.

She pointed at his black T-shirt. "Pink Floyd fan, I see. Me too." She leaned in a little more; if she got any closer, Stone wouldn't need his own drink—the fumes of hers would be sufficient to give him a respectable buzz. Her impressive cleavage quivered only an inch or two from his arm. "I noticed you right away when you came on board. 'He's something different,' I told myself. Really, I did! I can tell these things. I think it was the coat." She nodded toward the overhead bin, where Stone had stowed his overcoat. "Though you won't want to wear a long black coat like that in California. Trust me. It gets *hot*, especially in the summer." She attempted to fan herself with her napkin. "Where *is* that stewardess?"

The flight attendant chose that moment to turn up. She set another drink silently in front of the woman, then smiled with more animation at Stone. "Anything for you, sir?"

A different seat, perhaps? "No…thank you. I'm fine."

The cougar patted his leg after the attendant moved on. "You should have one, honey. Loosens you up. Makes the flight go faster."

Stone closed his eyes briefly. Of all the people he could be stuck sitting next to for the next ten or eleven hours, he had to get this one. The babies were starting to look good by comparison. "I'm terribly sorry to be rude," he said, even though he wasn't, "but I'm a bit tired, and I need to finish some work before we land." He held up the book.

She glanced at it. Stone watched her eyes slide over it, then stop and widen, just as he had expected. He'd brought this particular book on purpose: its cover, with its pentagram and ominous-looking hermetic symbols, rarely failed to make mundanes think twice about starting conversations with him. Normally, he wouldn't have minded a chat, even with Madame Inebria von Cleavage here—it would pass the time, if nothing else.

Today, though, all he wanted was for the plane to land so he could get on with it before he changed his mind about the whole business and caught the next flight home.

Okay, so maybe he wasn't over getting dumped by his fiancée yet.

Almost-fiancée, to be fair.

But still.

"Um," the woman said. She glanced at the book cover again, and subtly (no doubt *she* thought she was being subtle, at any rate) shifted away from him. "I'm—sorry. I didn't mean to bother you. I'll let you get back to your…um…work."

Stone flashed her his best charming smile, slouched back in his seat, and opened the book. It didn't matter which page he was on: he wasn't going to read it. His thoughts were already far away, back home.

On Imogen.

CHAPTER TWO

One month earlier: Holmbury St. Mary, Surrey, England

IMOGEN DIDN'T TELL STONE she was coming; she just showed up at the house one afternoon in that silly little car of hers, red-cheeked and a bit flushed from the heat. "Surprised to see me?" she asked when he met her at the door.

"Well—yes," he admitted. They were both so busy these days, their schedules so rarely coinciding between work and studies and simple geographic distance. She hadn't said a word about coming down. "But it's a lovely surprise," he added, smiling. "I'm just glad I hadn't left yet. I was off to do some work with your father later today."

She kissed him and took his arm. "You can call him later. Let's go for a walk. I've been cooped up in that car too long."

They set off together, out through the front gate and up one of the uneven little lanes that dotted the area.

"You look good," he said. She did: there was a new animation to her wind-flushed face, something in her smile that he didn't remember seeing there before.

"So do you," she said, standing on tiptoes to brush another quick kiss across his lips. "Buckingham must be good for you. How's the job?"

He shrugged. "It's all right."

"Just all right?" Her lips quirked. "I remember you were so happy to get it. Jaded already?"

He shrugged, then reached out to take her hand. "Let's not talk about me. I want to hear about you. It's so rare I get to see you these days. We should do something about that. Especially since we should probably be getting on with making plans one of these days."

She didn't look at him. "Alastair, I—I wanted to talk to you about something. That's why I came down to see you."

He tilted his head, unsure of where she was going.

She took a deep breath. "This isn't easy for me, okay? So if you could just sort of—let me get it out, I'd appreciate it." She squeezed his hand, then let loose of it and started walking again.

He quickly caught up with her, matching his long strides to her shorter ones along the rutted road. It was a beautiful day: this kind of bright blue sky broken only by a few fluffy white clouds was uncommon even in midsummer around here. He glanced at her, but said nothing. If she had something to say and wanted him to shut up so she could say it, he could manage that.

She walked in silence for almost a full minute, her fashionable leather booties crunching in the dirt. "We've…known each other a long time," she said at last.

"Nine years," he agreed.

"Almost ten." She smiled then, a faraway little thing that made her eyes shine. "Do you remember when I met you? I had such a crush, and you didn't even act like I existed."

"You were fifteen," he pointed out. "*And* the daughter of my master. Even if you weren't too young for me, that would have been—awkward."

She chuckled. "Yeah, that's true. I suppose if you'd tried anything with me back then, Dad wouldn't have approved."

"Oh, let's not dance around it: he'd have flayed me alive and turfed my carcass out a third-story window." He, too, chuckled as he remembered. Had it really been almost ten years already?

"I don't think he would have done. You know he likes you. He always has. His prized apprentice. His favorite project. The son he never had."

He glanced at her, raising an eyebrow, unsure if he'd heard the odd bitter undercurrent in her voice or just imagined it. "I suppose so. It was hard to tell with him back then—whether he pushed me that hard because he thought I could handle it, or whether he just enjoyed making me suffer."

"I remember." There was the faraway smile again. "I think it was a bit of both. But he does like you. He just doesn't know how to tell you that. Sort of like—" She trailed off.

"Sort of like what?"

She shrugged. "Sort of like—you, I guess."

"What do you mean by that?" he asked, frowning.

She took his hand in both of hers, then looked away. "Nothing. Sorry. I shouldn't have said that. It's not fair."

Turning to her, he gently disengaged one of her hands and held it in his other one. "Moggy, you know how I feel about you."

She nodded, looking down at their clasped hands.

He studied the top of her head for a moment. Her curtain of rich brown hair hung down over her face, hiding her eyes. "This was what you wanted to talk about, wasn't it?" he asked softly.

She reclaimed her hands, pushing her hair back off her shoulder. "Did you ever wonder why I didn't come home often, when I was in school? Why I didn't visit Dad more often than I did, even after you and I had started—seeing each other?"

"I thought you were busy with your studies," he said. "If they were anything like mine, you barely had time to get away, even during holidays."

"That was part of it," she said, resuming her pace along the road. "I missed you so much, but—"

"But—?"

"But," she said, and took a deep breath. The next words came out in a rush, as if something was trying to catch them before they hit the air. "It was Dad. I didn't want to see him."

He stared at her. "Why not? Moggy, your father adores you. You must know that."

She made a sound that might have been a snort. "That's what you saw. Of course you did."

He stopped, turning to her again. "Are you saying he didn't—?"

"No, no. Nothing like that." She shook her head, impatient. "He always made sure I had everything I needed. Well, almost everything." The bitterness was obvious now.

This whole exchange was taking a turn that Stone had not anticipated. He waited, silent and still, for her to continue.

She licked her lips, brushing at her hair again. "You didn't see it, did you? You still don't."

"See *what*?" He wished he had some idea where she was going with this. Usually he was pretty good at picking up her moods, at figuring out what was bothering her, but this time he felt adrift, as if he'd somehow blundered into a completely different conversation. He shifted to his magical senses, just for a few seconds: her strong blue aura seemed clouded, uneasy.

"You don't see it because you're part of it," she said, shaking her head. "And *I* didn't see it because I didn't know any better."

"Moggy—"

She put her hand on his arm. "No. Please. Don't. Just—let me say this."

He nodded, looking down at her hand. She had small hands, slim and pale, her fingers tipped with red polish applied with her usual care.

She started walking again. "I've been thinking a lot over the last few months. It was easy to avoid it while I was in school, while I was living with Mum. After she died and I had to come and stay with Dad I could still mostly avoid it, because I was away all the time."

"Avoid—"

She smiled a brittle smile. Her eyes shone oddly in the late afternoon sunlight. "And then I met you. And even when you didn't notice me the way I wanted you to, you were always kind to me. Funny. Charming. A gentleman. That's not very common, Alastair. I found that out when I got away from the girls' schools and into University. And when I came home that summer and you finally saw me as a woman instead of a girl—" She took his hand again. "I thought I was the luckiest person in the world. "

He shook his head. "You weren't. I was. I am." Moments passed. He spoke in a monotone as a sudden flash of insight hit him: "You've met someone, haven't you?"

Her eyes widened. She drew quick breath as if preparing to say something, but then let it out. Shoulders slumping, she stared down at her feet again.

Stone froze. Suddenly he felt disembodied, as if none of the frenetic collection of thoughts zipping around his head was reaching the rest of his body.

Her eyes came up, and tears glittered in their corners. "Alastair, it's—it's not that I don't love you. I do. I'll always love you. But—there's no place for me in this life. In *your* life. I didn't want to see it, but it's true."

"What do you mean?" he asked, stunned. "Of course there is. I thought we were going to wait for you to finish at University and find a position, and then we'd be married. Wasn't that the plan?"

"It was," she said sadly. "I think we just sort of—assumed it would happen that way, so much that we never really talked properly about it. But—" She looked away again.

"I don't understand," he said. His tone was still calm, still quiet, betraying no hint of the sudden storm raging in his head. "What do you mean, there's no place for you in my life? There's *every* place for you. You *are* my life."

"Really?" She sounded sad and bitter in equal measure. "What part? Your magical studies? Your experiments with Dad? Everything that's so important in your life that I can't share with you?"

"Moggy—"

"Please…don't call me that. It's a childish nickname. We're not children anymore, Alastair."

He nodded. "So," he said after a pause, "that's it, then. The magic."

"You don't know what it was *like*, growing up with that," she said, her voice taking on a strange edge. "Knowing your father never thought you were good enough because of something that you couldn't even help. Oh, sure, he loves me. I know he does. But I saw the way he looked at me—and the way he looked at *you*. And I saw how you were becoming more like him every day." When he started to speak she held up her hands. "I don't blame you for it. How could I? It must be wonderful to be able to do magic. If I could, it would probably be the most important thing in my life too."

"Why didn't you ever tell me this before?" he asked softly, thinking back to all the hours he'd spent in study, between his University coursework and his magical research. How many all-nighters he and Desmond had spent when they were on the trail of some new spell or discovery. How many times he'd had to beg off spending time with Imogen because he was in the middle of something that couldn't be interrupted. *You shouldn't have had to tell me.*

She shook her head. "It's like I said—I didn't even notice it for the longest time. At the beginning I was just so happy that you were interested in me at all that it just didn't bother me. But then after Mum died, after I got out in the real world and away from Dad's influence—I guess I just realized that there was a lot of life out there that *didn't* involve musty old books and ritual circles and conjuring up fireballs with your mind. And that maybe that was where I belonged."

They were passing a low rock wall that separated the road from an overgrown field; Stone moved to it and sat down, still processing her words. "Who is he?" he asked. His voice was dead in his ears. "Do I know him?"

She came over and sat down next to him, staring out across the road toward the sheep grazing in the field on the other side. "No. I met him six months ago, in London. He owns a restaurant."

"And you've been—?" His tone held no accusation or anger. How could he be angry with her, when everything she'd said had been true?

"No. Nothing like that. I promise. But we've been talking a lot, " She took his hand again. Hers was cold, and trembled a little, but her expression was resolute. "I'm sorry, Alastair. I really am. I tried to think of a better way to tell you, but I thought I owed you doing it in person."

He examined their hands together: her shiny blood-red nails, his silver ring with its blocky purple stone. "Does your father know?"

"No. It's really none of his business, is it?" She held up a hand as he started to speak. "I'll tell him. But I wanted to talk to you first." She turned toward him. "Are you—all right?"

He smiled, and if it was a bit manic around the edges, she didn't comment. "Of course I am," he said, gently squeezing her upper arm in what he hoped was a bracing manner. "I want you to be happy, Mo—Imogen." He stood up. "Come on—I'll walk you back to the house."

"It's all right," she said. "I think I just want to be alone for a bit, if you don't mind. You go on."

He nodded wordlessly. For a moment he stood, his gaze lingering on her as if he expected never to see her again. Then he turned and slowly started walking back toward the house.

After a few steps he turned back. She was still standing where he'd left her, watching him. "Imogen?"

"Yes?"

He paused, struggling with the words. "If I—if I had offered to give it all up, to be with you—the magic, I mean—would you have changed your mind?"

Several seconds passed. "Does it matter? Would you have done?" Her voice was so soft it barely carried to him.

He closed his eyes, and hated himself. "No," he whispered. And then he turned again and resumed his pace toward the house.

CHAPTER THREE

STONE DIDN'T REMEMBER MUCH about the walk back to the house. His mind refused to engage, skittering off to focus on some triviality every time he tried to think about what had happened. Even though a part of him wasn't surprised—and had actually wondered deep down why this hadn't happened a long time ago—it was a very small part. The rest of him simply rebelled against coming to terms with it.

As was always the case when he was troubled about something, he eventually ended up in his cluttered study. He threw himself into his desk chair, pulled the heavy drapes closed with a flick of magical power, and closed his eyes.

It was too early to drink until he couldn't remember it anymore, so instead he glanced with no interest at the pile of post that he'd banished to the far corner of his desk.

The letter on top wasn't the first of its kind, but it was the latest. It had arrived only a few days ago, and he'd tossed it on the stack with the others while barely looking at it. Stanford University over in the States was still trying to get him to talk to them about a position in their Occult Studies department. They weren't the first by any means to court him for such a job, but they were certainly the most persistent over the last year.

This time the communication was more urgent: it seemed that they thought they'd filled the position, only to have their candidate, a Dr. Conley, become seriously ill and thus forced to withdraw. Now, with the fall quarter beginning in only a couple of short months, they were not only willing to sweeten their offer and fast-track the visa process, but they were even prepared to sweep aside most of the roadblocks that normally made this sort of thing drag on in an endless tedium of interviews, meetings, and negotiations. They suggested that he give the job a try for a year as a visiting professor if he preferred, and if things worked out, they could both consider their respective next moves.

All of this was the trouble with being an expert in a subject that almost nobody in the world was an expert in: everyone else who was interested in it wanted you for something. If it wasn't a position, it was collaboration on a paper, an interview for some academic publication, or some sort of presentation. Admittedly, the occult wasn't as bad as some subjects, since there weren't that many universities with programs in that kind of thing. Most of them still considered it vaguely disreputable, akin to having a department for studying the history of prostitution, or examining the effects of gambling through the ages. In truth, Stone had fielded more requests for interviews from dodgy tabloids and sensationalistic television shows than from academic sources, but even so.

Stanford, in northern California, was a notable exception. Most of the attempts to lure Stone away were in western Europe, at small, specialized universities that nobody except their alumni had ever heard of. Potentially interesting, certainly, but not interesting enough to dislodge him from his current position. His employer was yet another small, specialized university that nobody had heard of, but it also happened to be within reasonable commute distance of his home in Surrey. That counted for a lot. His ancestral home might be too big, too drafty, and in a perpetual race with his caretaker to fall apart before it could be patched up, but it had been in his family for a couple of centuries, it was his, and he was used to its quirks.

He glanced at the letter again. He hadn't answered it yet; they'd invited him to give them a call if their offer was sufficiently interesting, and they'd discuss details further. This morning, he would have tossed it in the rubbish bin along with the pizza adverts. Now, though...

"Dr. Stone?"

He looked up. Aubrey Townes, the caretaker, stood in the doorway. His lined face was troubled, his gnarled hands clutching at his battered old cap. Stone hadn't heard him approaching, which said a lot about his state of mind. "Aubrey. Is something wrong?"

The old man hesitated. "I...just saw Miss Desmond's car leaving a while ago."

Stone nodded.

"She...I saw her arrive earlier. I thought she was going to be staying with us."

"So did I." Stone regarded him without expression.

Aubrey opened his mouth, closed it again, and swallowed.

"Listen, Aubrey. It's not something I want to discuss right now, all right?" He shuffled the papers on his desk and tried to think of something else to say. Hiding things from Aubrey was something he'd never been very good at.

Long pause. "Yes, sir." He made as if to leave.

If Stone didn't know the old man as well as he did, he wouldn't have noticed the slight stiffness in his voice. "Aubrey?"

"Yes, sir?"

"Imogen and I—well, we've decided to...call it off."

Aubrey's eyes, normally held in an amiable squint, widened. "No."

Stone nodded. "And I don't really want to go on about it. Nor do I want to talk to Desmond about it, so if he calls, tell him I'm not here."

Once again Aubrey looked as if he wanted to say something, and once again he didn't. His gaze held Stone's for a few seconds. Then he nodded, turned away, and was gone.

Stone slumped in his chair, only now realizing he'd been holding himself stiffly upright the whole time Aubrey had been there. He thought about Imogen, picturing that ridiculous little red convertible of hers trundling its way out through his front gate for the last time. Picturing the way she used to look at him. Imagining all the questions her father—his old master—would ask him when he found out.

Suddenly the study, which had always been a place of refuge for him, felt stifling, oppressive.

Before he could change his mind, he shook open the letter from Stanford and picked up the phone.

CHAPTER FOUR

STONE MADE A CONSCIOUS EFFORT to put his mind on hold from the time the plane touched down in San Francisco and he unfolded his tall, thin frame from the torture rack of a seat. Tired, stiff, and stressed, all he wanted to do was pick up his rental car and somehow figure out how to make it down to Palo Alto without getting lost or inadvertently driving the wrong way on the carriageway. *Freeway. They call them freeways here.*

At least he didn't have to deal with Madame Inebria on his way out. Over the course of the flight, she had morphed from drunken to drooling. Aside from random mutterings when he had to gently shove her off his shoulder, she'd spent the last leg fast asleep.

Stone had been to America a few brief times in the past, but always for some magical function, and always by way of the portals. There had always been someone to meet him, to drive him around, to provide a buffer against the majority of the culture shock. This time he was alone, with a pair of suitcases (the rest of the items he'd chosen to bring with him would be arriving in the next few days), an unfamiliar car, and a map full of towns he'd never heard of between San Francisco and his destination.

He made it, somehow. Looking back he wasn't entirely sure how: the steering wheel was on the wrong side of the car, he kept triggering the windscreen wipers when trying to signal a turn, and twice he nearly made right turns into the wrong lane while attempting to find the freeway entrance. At least the freeway itself wasn't bad: everyone was going the same direction, so all he had to do was temper his usual bat-out-of-hell driving style and poke along in the slow lane, keeping a close eye out for his exit.

He reached Palo Alto in less than an hour; they'd warned him about horrific traffic, but since it was midday (thanks to the time difference between England and California), it wasn't as bad as he'd feared. Since he routinely drove the M25 at rush hour, he suspected that the people who'd given him advice simply lacked perspective on the matter. Now all he had to do was locate the place he'd rented long-distance on the recommendation of a current Stanford professor's estate agent and the strength of a few photographs. If he could do that, everything else could wait.

He'd been lucky to find the place, they'd told him: rentals in that part of the downtown Palo Alto area were hard to come by at any price, and the fact that one like this had come on the market just as he was looking seemed as if someone was trying to send him a message.

Even so, he'd have to dip into his savings to afford this one, since there was no way a visiting professor's salary—or even an associate professor's if he decided to stay on—would begin to cover the monthly rent along with the rest of the living costs around this affluent area. Fortunately, one of the few things working in his favor was that he had enough money put away from his father's estate and various investments that he didn't strictly *need* to work—he did so because he couldn't imagine doing anything else, and because idleness would no doubt push his already overactive mind over the edge into insanity, not because he had to worry about where his next meal was coming from.

He could have chosen a cheaper place, perhaps one of the many flats (*apartments*) in the area, or found lodgings in the South Bay that would have necessitated a longer daily commute, but as it was, moving from his rambling old place back in Holmbury was going to be shock enough without forcing himself into a place that would make him miserable. He'd signed a lease for a year, confident that if he decided to give up on the whole idea and return home early, he'd have no trouble finding someone else willing to take the place off his hands for the remainder of the period.

The two-story townhouse, though small by neighborhood standards, turned out to fit Stone's needs nicely. It even had a basement, rare in California because of the earthquakes, which would make an ideal place for his magical lab once he'd replaced the door with something more substantial.

Right now, though, as he contemplated it several hours later through the zombified fog of jet lag, it was nothing but a big empty space. He wandered without aim from room to room, plotting out where he would put his books and his collection of magical items when they arrived. The second largest of the three bedrooms would make a good study, leaving the smallest one as a guest room.

That assumed he would ever have guests—or at least ones who'd need to use the guest room. Not bloody likely. He wondered if it would even be likely that he'd have guests at all—while Imogen had been in the picture, it hadn't been an option, of course. But now—one never knew. That was for later, though. He had far too many things to occupy his mind for the foreseeable future without thinking about looking for eligible women. Especially since he had no idea how long he'd be staying.

It was almost nine o'clock by now; he was dead tired, but couldn't sleep. He threw himself down with a sigh into one of the overstuffed living room chairs and stared with disconsolate apathy out into the darkness. He couldn't shake the feeling that everything felt wrong here. His house back in England, with its drafty halls, untidy grounds and ramshackle roof, had never seemed more like home to him than now, after he had left it behind.

Why had he done this, anyway? What the hell had possessed him to take a position halfway around the world on such short notice? Just so he could get away from the memory of Imogen? People got dumped all the time—they put it behind them and got on with life. Usually, they did it in the same general geographical location. What had he been thinking?

Everything about this area was wrong, from the way the wall plugs worked to the taps to the way people drove on the wrong side of the road and dressed like they'd just got out of bed. He didn't even have anyone he could call to go out for a beer or a chat: Aubrey back home would be asleep, and he hadn't gotten the impression from the brief correspondences he'd had with his two fellow Occult Studies colleagues prior to his arrival that they would be interested in hearing from him in a nonprofessional capacity.

He flipped on the television, clicked through channels without really seeing them, then went out to the kitchen. There was next to nothing in the refrigerator or any of the cabinets, but he grabbed a Guinness and a pack of digestive biscuits he'd been surprised to find in the tiny British-food section of the local supermarket on his recon trip earlier in the day.

He clicked through a few more channels, paused at the familiar logo on a channel called BBC America, and left it there, settling back on the couch. He hardly ever watched television back home, but, like the biscuits, the familiar voices and topics made him feel, if just for a brief time, that he wasn't thousands of miles from home.

He figured the first night would be the hardest. Tomorrow morning he'd have to buck up and get on with it. He only had a week before the quarter started, and a lot that needed doing before that.

It was well after midnight before he finally fell asleep on the couch, lulled by the familiar tones of the BBC News presenter.

| CHAPTER FIVE

Some things, Stone found out the next day, never changed.

It didn't matter whether he was teaching at a small university nobody had ever heard of in England, or a massive one everyone had heard of in the United States—no matter where he was, the bureaucracy of orientation bore depressing similarities.

As part of his uncharacteristically fast-tracked journey through the hiring process, the university had taken care of many of his requirements in advance, including handling any immigration visa necessities that didn't require his actual presence. That was a relief, though he suspected he would have to spend more time than he preferred filling out papers and waiting in government offices to finish up the process and make sure all his ducks were in a row. If the immigration department in the US was even close to as draconian as some of his British colleagues had painted it, they had no sense of humor whatsoever, and Stone had no desire for any of his errant ducks to end up in their gun sights.

When he arrived on campus early the next morning, the first thing that struck him was how large the place was. He'd seen it on the map he had currently spread out on the passenger seat of his rented Ford, but it didn't sink in until he encountered it in person.

The campus was enormous, with dozens of buildings, acres of land, and miles of roads and paths—after seeing it, he could believe the figure of over eight thousand acres that he'd boggled at a bit when skimming the orientation packet they'd sent him. He was glad he'd arrived early, since odds were good he'd make at least one wrong turn trying to find where he was supposed to park or locating the building they'd told him to report to.

He spent most of the rest of the day dealing with various bits of administrivia: filling out papers, sorting out health insurance choices (he hadn't quite gotten his mind around the fact that you had to sign up for private insurance here, since the USA didn't have the NHS), and being issued his various ID cards, keys, and other required items. By the time they let him go after the first part of the orientation, his briefcase was stuffed full of papers he'd have to take an evening to read.

Occult Studies was a tiny subset of the Cultural Anthropology department, which itself was under the umbrella of the school of Humanities and Sciences. The deputy department head of Cultural Anthropology, a cheerful African-American man named Dr. Darius Farley, took him to lunch at one of the nicer of the campus eateries (where he was struck by the sheer *variety* of foods offered, compared to the rather lackluster choices he remembered at universities back home). Farley apologized for the fact that the other two Occult Studies faculty members had been unavoidably detained and thus unable to join them. He promised to introduce Stone to them during the campus tour after lunch.

The meal itself went well. Farley, it turned out, had studied a year abroad in England when he was at university, and the two chatted amiably for nearly an hour. Stone answered Farley's questions about his life in England, and Farley answered Stone's about living in the Palo Alto area before Farley got called away and had to hand him off to one of the department admin aides for his tour.

"So," the aide, a smartly dressed blonde woman in her mid-thirties named Sue Dawes, asked as she drove him around and pointed out the various buildings, restaurants, offices, and dormitories on the campus proper, "How do you like it here so far? Overwhelmed yet?"

He chuckled. "A bit, yes. I just got here yesterday, so the culture shock is still fresh."

"I'll bet the jet lag is too," she said with a grin. "I hope you like walking—wait until you see where your office is. I saved that for last."

Stone didn't quite know what to make of that, but it soon became obvious when Sue Dawes stopped her car in front of a buff-colored, ivy-draped building nearly half a mile from the center of campus.

"I'm afraid Occult Studies is kind of a small department," she said with an apologetic smile. "They didn't really get first pick of locations. "

She led him inside and indicated a door at the end of the hall. "We don't have your nametag yet—they moved faster on you than anybody I've seen since I got here. You can be flattered about that, anyway, when you're hiking back to your office in the rain."

Stone tried out his key and opened the door onto a tiny office with an even tinier window. The little room contained a desk with a phone and no chair, a bookshelf stacked with several binders, a whiteboard, and a single guest chair.

"Well," he said when he saw the desk, "I suppose I'll be spending all my time walking back and forth, so I won't be needing to sit down often."

Ms. Dawes winced. "Ooh...somebody took your chair. It was here this morning. Hang on a minute."

Stone, curious, followed her out and down the hall, where she knocked on the frame of another open door. "Dr. Hubbard? Have you seen Dr. Stone's desk chair?"

An unintelligible male voice said something from inside, and after a moment Ms. Dawes was wheeling the chair out into the hall. "He got used to borrowing it sometimes," she said. "Your office has been empty for a long time. Come on, I'll introduce you."

When Stone appeared in the doorway, he got a brief impression of a cluttered space and a sandy-haired, mustachioed man in his fifties, wearing a brown cardigan sweater and rumpled slacks. The man was heading out of the office, carrying a briefcase.

"Afternoon." He nodded to Stone. "You must be Stone. Good to meet you, but I have to run—class soon, and it's a long walk. We'll talk later." And then he was past and gone.

"Sorry," Ms. Dawes said. "Let me introduce you to your other colleague and then we'll head back and I'll give you your schedules." She walked to the next office, which also had its door open, but she didn't say anything or knock. Instead, she just nodded and raised her hand in an "okay, I see" gesture.

Stone came up behind her. The tag on the door here read "Dr. Edwina Mortenson." The gray-haired woman behind the desk was turned half away from them, talking fast on the phone. She waved a voluminous sleeve at them, covered the receiver, and said, "I'm so sorry, but I need to finish this call. Been trying to get through to them all day." And then she turned back to her conversation.

Dr. Edwina Mortenson's office was neater than Dr. Hubbard's; her bookshelf was packed with books, and she had two framed prints of Tarot cards (the classic Ryder versions of *The*

Moon and *The High Priestess*) on the wall behind her desk, along with an elegant crystal ball in an elaborate stand. These were all Stone noticed before Ms. Dawes touched his arm. "Let's go," she whispered. "I'm guessing she won't be done any time soon."

Once again, he followed her out of the building and back to her car. "Auspicious start," he said when they were on the road.

Ms. Dawes gave him a conspiratorial sideways glance. "They're...an interesting pair. Kind of an acquired taste. But trust me, they're both glad you're here. They've had to take on the extra course load until we got somebody new in." She grinned. "They've also offloaded as much of their committee work as they could on you. New guy and all. I'll give you all the details when we get back to the department office."

This didn't surprise Stone in the slightest—in fact, he'd expected it. He'd also expected his two fellow professors to be unusual. It kind of went with the job description: the study of the occult didn't tend to attract the straight-and-narrow type.

He'd read a few of their papers before leaving England. Hubbard's he'd found to be unimaginative and lacking in any kind of daring, while Mortenson's were well researched but showed definite indications of someone who might be drinking the supernatural Kool-Aid a little more than was strictly approved of for someone at her level. At least someone who wasn't a mage, he'd thought wryly. He'd encountered the type before, but Mortenson, at least at first glance, had more of the classic California "hippie" vibe than he'd expected to see in an academic.

They got back to the main office, and Ms. Dawes gave Stone another packet of papers. "These are your class schedules, maps of where the classes are, parking map and permit, that kind of thing. I also put some fliers in there for some local restaurants off campus, if you're interested. All the new professors want to know where the good restaurants are." She flashed him a grin.

"Anything else I can do for you before I get back to my usual drudgery?"

"Not at the moment. Unless you can tell me a good place to find a car. I'm still driving my rental from the airport."

She pulled a copy of the *Mercury News* from her top drawer. "Here you go. Should be able to find something in there. And welcome. It'll be good to work with you."

"Thank you. I just hope the students feel the same way."

She grinned. "Trust me, they will."

Ms. Dawes glanced around as if checking to see if anyone was listening, then leaned toward him. "I'll never admit to saying this if you tell them, but Dr. Hubbard and Dr. Mortenson have the reputation for being…well…a bit on the dry side. That's part of why they're not as…er…welcoming as you might expect. They're not used to somebody like you. You'll have those kids eating out of your hand, take it from me."

CHAPTER SIX

THE LECTURE HALL where Stone's first class was scheduled was nowhere near his office. He walked there, setting off across campus a little early in case he took a wrong turn. He didn't, so he had a few minutes to kill in the corridor leading into the hall. He had no idea how things would go, how these American students would react to him. His students back home in England loved his style—his consistently high instructor ratings gave credence to that. But who knew if that would translate?

Today was when he'd find out. He glanced down at his watch—right now, in fact.

Showtime.

Before entering the room, he used a flick of his mind to magically switch off the lights inside the lecture hall. He'd scoped it out the previous day: it was an interior hall, with no windows to the outside world. He gave the students in the room beyond a few seconds to mutter in confusion, then faded to invisibility, opened the door, and crossed to the desk at the front. He dropped his old leather briefcase down upon it with a *smack* that resounded through the cavernous space.

Someone gasped. Someone else made a muffled little shriek of fear.

Stone dropped the spell and turned the lights back on.

All their eyes were on him, just as he knew they'd be. "Morning!" he said cheerfully, sweeping his gaze over the rows.

Around thirty students, about a sixty-forty split between women and men. A couple of the men were standing, as if he'd caught them in the act of going in search of the light switches. Others looked perplexed: none of them could have seen him use magic to turn the lights on in the darkness, and he'd been nowhere near the switches when they'd come up. It was exactly as he'd choreographed it: get things rolling with a little mystery to pique their interest. Worked every time. And since nobody—certainly nobody in an undergraduate course, even one with a focus on the occult—knew anything about real magic or believed it existed, he could get away with quite a lot.

Hell, even if they actually saw him doing it, their minds wouldn't allow them to believe it. It was a consistent source of amusement for him, hiding in plain sight like this. In a way, it made things easier: everybody *expected* a professor of the occult to be at least a bit odd. They'd probably have been disappointed it he wasn't. He wondered what his students would think if they knew what he was truly capable of.

"I'd apologize for that little fright," Stone said, coming out around the front of the desk and leaning casually against it, "but I'm not sorry. That's why you're all here, isn't it? To be a little bit frightened? The occult is all about fear. All about what scares us. About what lives in the dark, in the cracks between the worlds." He began to pace, well aware of how impressively his long black overcoat swept behind him when he turned. "And do you know what else it's about?"

He zeroed his laser-focused gaze in on a young woman in the front row. "You. Do you know?"

"Uh—monsters?" she ventured. "Ghosts? Vampires?"

He resumed his pacing. "Well, yes, but those are only window dressing. Don't worry—I've got plenty of ghosts, vampires, werewolves, Satanic rituals, hauntings, and all sorts of stuff like that on my list of things to show you this quarter. But that's not what I was after."

He wheeled on another student, this one a young man with long, stringy hair and a Slayer T-shirt. "You there. What do you think it's about?"

He shifted in his chair; clearly he hadn't expected to be called on. "Um...sorry, I—"

Stone spun away from him, stalking back toward the whiteboard behind the desk. He picked up a marker and wrote POWER in large letters, then underlined it. "Power," he repeated, nodding toward it. "The occult is about power—and not just the power the ghouls and ghosts have to frighten us. If that were all it was, we'd still be shivering in caves, terrified of our own shadows."

He pointed at yet another student, a young woman in pale goth makeup and a leather jacket. "You. What other kind of power do you think I'm talking about?"

She thought a moment, then said, "Do you mean the power we have over the darkness? Like, if we know what we're facing, we can deal with it better?"

"Brilliant!" he said, grinning. "Exactly!" He took in the rest of the class with a wave of his hand. "Listen to this one—she knows what she's talking about."

Back to the front again, he perched on the edge of the desk. "Exactly right. We have two choices when faced with the unknown: we can hide from it, or we can confront it. Shine a light on it. Or at the very least, try to make a bit of sense out of it. Understanding gives us the power to be a little bit less afraid of what's out there. A better idea about what makes the darker side of the universe tick. Knowledge is its own kind of power—and ultimately a far stronger one than anything that might be lurking in the night."

He went to the board again and grabbed the marker. "I'm Alastair Stone. I just started my employment here a month ago, so like most of you, this is my very first Occult Studies course at Stanford." He wrote his name up in the corner of the board, taking care to make it legible (which it usually wasn't). "I'll be your tour guide into the dark corners of the world. As long as everyone keeps their arms and legs inside the car at all times during the ride, I promise you that you'll all arrive safely back in the land of the mundane in ten weeks' time. But until then..." He smiled, raised an eyebrow, and pulled something from his briefcase. "Until then, we're going to have some fun, you and I."

He held up the item he'd pulled out. "Anyone care to take a guess at what this is?"

They all leaned in, craning their necks to get a better look. The boy with the stringy hair, perhaps trying to redeem his previous lack of performance, said, "It's...a tennis ball?"

"Exactly. And I can already see the gears in your minds turning: 'Why is he showing us a tennis ball in an occult course? Is he mad? Should we back away slowly?' Well, perhaps you should, but that's another matter entirely. As it happens," he added, taking off walking again, bouncing the dirty tennis ball in front of him as he went, "this tennis ball quite likely saved a family of four from a horrific fate."

He had them now—right where he wanted them. He didn't smile: that would have been too obvious. But as always when he hit his stride with a new group of students, he felt energy infusing his body.

By the time he finished the story of the ghost dog who alerted his family to the presence of a deranged killer in their home by repeatedly relocating the tennis ball near a locked door leading to a disused attic, every last one of them had his or her attention fixed on him. There was no coughing, no shuffling of papers, no glancing at the wall clock in the back. Their gazes followed him as he prowled the room, up and down the aisles, pausing for dramatic effect at the climax.

As the class hour came to an end, and he worked his way with perfect timing back to the desk in time to take care of administrivia like attendance and class drops, he allowed himself a small smile of satisfaction. Any leftover apprehension he had about his inability to play to an American audience like he did the ones back home drained away.

College kids were college kids, and everybody liked to be scared.

| CHAPTER SEVEN

STONE HADN'T SEEN the other two members of the Occult Studies faculty, Edwina Mortenson and Mackenzie Hubbard, since earlier in the week when he'd briefly met them with Sue Dawes. He didn't hear from them again until his first day on the job; that afternoon he got a call from Mortenson, inviting him to lunch the next day. "We both wanted to meet you in a more informal setting," she said, "and I'm sure you have a lot of questions you'd like to ask."

She'd suggested a restaurant just off University Avenue, and he agreed to meet them there. It would be his first trip downtown on a weekday in his new car, a black four-door Jaguar XJR he'd picked up for quite a reasonable price yesterday afternoon. It was a few years old, but it ran well and looked good. Possibly not the most practical thing, but he couldn't bring himself to drive something boring. Once again, he had to think that the universe was telling him that maybe he was meant to be here after all.

By the time Stone located the restaurant, it was ten past noon. The little café was already packed with students, and downtown workers on their lunch hours. He spotted the pair seated at a back table; they watched him with identical non-expressions as he wended his way through the crowd.

"Sorry I'm late," he said, a little breathless. "Parking's a bit frightful around here." He tossed his overcoat over a nearby chair and dropped down into another across from them. They were both eyeing him as if he'd just blown in from Mars. "Pleasure to see you again. We barely got the chance to chat the other day."

"Dr. Stone," Edwina Mortenson said with a small nod and a tight little smile. She was perhaps sixty, gray-haired and small-eyed, managing to look somehow pinched despite her generous proportions. She wore too much eye shadow, a drapey black blouse shot through with silver threads, and two handfuls of gaudy rings.

Hubbard nodded too. "Good to see you again. So, how are you liking it over here so far?" A few years younger than Mortenson, he slouched in his chair and regarded Stone from beneath his bushy eyebrows and over his neatly trimmed salt-and-pepper moustache.

Stone paused to give the waitress his drink order. "It's been a bit of an adjustment," he admitted. Under cover of perusing the menu, he studied the two of them. They did not resemble each other physically, but their expressions shared a common aspect. Shifting for a moment to magical sight, he examined their auras—his blue-green, hers a sort of pale purplish red—and wasn't surprised to find the jaded, lackluster hues of long-time complacent apathy, tinged with a hint of suspicion and apprehension. *Of course they don't like me. They think I'm going to shake up their comfortable little world.*

And they're probably right.

"I can imagine," Mortenson said, her words dusted with disapproval. "I understand you made the decision quite suddenly to accept the position."

"I did, though they've been trying to lure me in for quite some time. Did you know the original candidate? I was sorry to hear that she'd taken ill so suddenly."

Hubbard shrugged. "I'm sorry too, of course. But just between you and me, she didn't have what it took for the job. I think they were getting a little desperate, to be honest."

"Oh?" Stone raised an eyebrow. His drink arrived and he paused to take a sip.

"Your predecessor left for another position a little over a year ago," Mortenson said. "They've been looking for a replacement ever since, but they've had trouble finding the right person to fill it. Ours isn't a common discipline, after all."

"No doubt," Stone agreed, keeping his voice noncommittal.

"Truth be told, we're kind of a redheaded stepchild around here, as far as most of the administration's concerned," Hubbard said. "We're embarrassing—ghosts and witches don't look too good alongside all the university's world-class programs—but we're also damned popular. Lot of kids think it's an easy A, and there's quite a bit of interest in the occult these days, so we get a lot of tourists, in addition to the ones actually concentrating on the subject."

"Yes…" Hubbard said, with an expression suggesting she'd just bitten a lemon. "Farley in Cultural Anthropology seemed to be of the opinion that you would be good for the department—he felt your research was impressive, and that we could benefit from some…new blood, I believe was what he said. As I'm sure you're aware, he and his enthusiasm are the reason why your employment was fast-tracked. Normally it takes much longer."

Stone didn't answer, except for a brief nod. It couldn't be any more obvious to him that Mortenson, at least, and probably Hubbard as well, didn't share Farley's opinion about his suitability for the department, or the speed at which he was hired.

"We're glad to have you, though," Hubbard said. "Not that Edwina and I weren't doing fine with the department on our own, but I'll be glad to go back to a reasonable schedule. I've got a novel I'm trying to finish up. I was feeling good about where I was with it, but I've barely had time to work on it lately."

"Ah, you're an author, then? What sort of work is it?" Stone didn't recall having seen Hubbard's name in any of the recent literature, but he felt this wasn't the best time to say so.

Hubbard's gaze shifted away. "I'm working on my fourth novel, actually. Horror. Sort of a contemporary take on Lovecraft's Cthulhu Mythos. My beta readers have been quite impressed," he added, almost defensively.

Stone nodded. "Have you sold the others? I'm afraid I don't read much fiction, but I'll make a point to pick them up."

"I—haven't." He picked up his drink. "Not yet. But I'm optimistic. I'm shopping them around to several agents, and I'm expecting to hear back from them any day now."

"Well, then, I wish you the best of luck," Stone said.

"How did your first day go?" Mortenson asked, clearly wanting to move away from Hubbard and his unpublished novels. "Dr. Hubbard and I had meant to get together with you before the quarter started, answer your questions, that kind of thing, but—" She waved her hands in an airy way, as if to say, *what can you do?*

But you'd rather have a chance to watch me flounder about without your expert guidance. Stone nodded. "It went fine, actually. Probably best we didn't try to meet up before that—been terribly busy getting settled in and orientated and whatnot. But everything went well—the students seem interesting, at any rate."

Hubbard snorted. "Bunch of goth kids and hack writers with delusions of grandeur, if you ask me. But they pay the bills, at least until I can get my writing career off the ground."

"Very little *true* interest in the paranormal," Mortenson added. "But most of them do seem fascinated by the vampire lore, so that's something, I suppose."

"Yeah, you love that, don't you?" Hubbard said, rolling his eyes. He glanced sideways at Stone. "Edwina's a bloodsucker nut. Been trying to pitch a course on 'em for years, but the higher-ups won't go for it. Also, she claims she's psychic," he added.

"I *am* psychic," she said with affronted indignation. "So, Dr. Stone, where do you stand on the matter?"

"Er—what matter is that?"

"The *occult*," she said, in the patient tone of someone who was addressing a toddler.

"Erm…I'm in favor of it," he said after a moment with a grin, well aware of the effect he was having. Edwina Mortenson wasn't the first person he'd encountered who'd claimed to be "psychic," or "sensitive," or any of the other new-age terms those who didn't have the Talent used to impress each other. He suspected they would be rather more thick on the ground in California than they'd been in England, so he might as well get used to dealing with them.

Hubbard snickered. "You aren't gonna make any friends that way, Stone. Edwina *believes*. She's convinced there are real vampires and werewolves and wizards out there in the world, hiding away from all us normal types."

"And how do you know there aren't?" she asked, unruffled. Obviously this was a well-worn topic of contention between them. She turned her attention back to Stone. "There are far too many instances of the unexplained in our field of study to believe that there's nothing out there."

Stone continued to look noncommittal, though it was getting more difficult. He shrugged. "Well, I've never seen any of it, but then, I've never seen China either, and I'm fairly sure that exists."

Hubbard let out a bark of laughter, while Mortenson shot Stone a look like she was trying to decide whether he was making fun of her. "In any case," she said with stiff dignity, "welcome to the department, and I do hope you last longer than poor Dr. Conley."

CHAPTER EIGHT

"FUCK OFF!" Althea Avila yelled it as loud as she could, flinging the words back over her shoulder and into the night. Her voice sounded thick, slurred to her ears, which was no surprise given how much she'd had to drink.

"Fuck off yourself, you fuckin' tease!" Ryan yelled back. He stood behind the open driver's door of his old Mustang, as if he were using it as armor between them. A beat of silence, and then: "Hey! C'mon, Althea, don't be an idiot! Get back here! It ain't safe! I'll take you home!"

"Go fuck yourself!" She picked up speed, her knee-high combat boots tromping with satisfying authority through the grass. She didn't run—she didn't think she could keep her balance if she ran—but her fast walk took her quickly into the darkness and away from him.

'Come back to the car'—yeah, right. She'd get right on that, so that fucking pervert Ryan could try to grope her again. They were all the same—you let them buy you a few drinks, dance a couple times, and they thought you owed them whatever they wanted once you left the club.

Fuck that.

Her name wasn't really Althea—it was Melissa. She was twenty-one years old, attended De Anza College, and lived for the weekends when she could go to the clubs, get good and buzzed, and dance the night away to her favorite goth bands. Melissa wasn't a very goth name, though. It made her sound like some goody two-shoes girl who always did what everybody wanted her to. She'd changed it when she turned eighteen—not officially, but Althea was what everybody called her now.

Ryan was a new one. Usually when she went clubbing, she hung out with some girlfriends, a couple of guys she trusted (one was gay, the other was crushing on another chick who didn't know he existed), and a few others from the Stanford crowd. This time, though, the new guy had made quite an impression on her: not only did he have a whole collection of badass piercings and tattoos, but he also guest-DJed and spun some new stuff that she'd made him tell her the names of so she could hunt them up when she got home. They'd drifted off to the bar after his last set, had a few drinks and some conversation, and he'd offered to take her home. She'd told her friends she was going to take him up on his offer, and the two had left together a little after midnight.

If he'd just taken her home as he'd promised, she might have offered him more drinks at her place, agreed to some hot sex, and exchanged phone numbers with him in the morning.

Instead, he'd driven her out to Shoreline Park and tried to rape her.

He wouldn't have called it that, of course—he only thought he was getting his due for all the drinks he'd bought her. He'd pulled the car off the road near a deserted stretch of the park, leaned in, and proceeded to try to kiss her. When she'd shoved him angrily off and told him to go take a cold shower, he'd gotten rough. The only thing that saved her was the fact that he'd had more drinks than she had (if she'd been less drunk, she'd have wondered how he managed to drive as far as he did without getting picked up by the cops). When she shoved open the door and tumbled out of the car, he'd landed face-first in her seat. By the time he scrambled up and got out, she was already almost out of sight.

She kept going, slowing down now as her endurance and adrenaline faded. Behind her, the squeal of tires told her Ryan wasn't coming after her; a quick glance over her shoulder confirmed it. The Mustang's taillights were already receding into the night.

That was about the time she realized that she was alone, it was dark, and she had no way to get home (indeed, she wasn't even completely sure *how* to get home from where she was—she hadn't exactly been watching street signs).

"Ryan, you bastard!" she screamed into the night, and then turned around and headed back toward the parking lot. Maybe there'd be a pay phone there and she could call a cab.

She didn't see them until they were almost upon her. They moved low and fast and silent, hitting her from both sides and the back, taking her down hard. She drew breath to scream, but a hand clamped over her mouth before she could get a sound out. The fetid stench of rotting meat overwhelmed her.

She barely got a chance to struggle before they went about their grisly business, slashing, cutting, pulling her jacket open so they could dig their long fingernails into the tender flesh of her abdomen. She tried to scream again, tried to bite the hand over her mouth, tried to flail her arms or kick her feet, but even if they weren't holding her down, she was already weakening from the fountains of blood spraying from her severed femoral artery.

Her last, inexplicable thought before she died was that she'd never get the chance to hear any of those bands Ryan had given her the names of.

| CHAPTER NINE

As soon as Stone strode into the lecture hall one Tuesday morning a couple of weeks after the quarter had started, he knew something was wrong. A strange quiet hung over the room instead of the usual chatter. He tossed his briefcase and overcoat on the chair, and perched on the edge of the desk. "Morning," he said.

Most of the students greeted him and settled into their seats, but a small group clustered near the back remained where they were, carrying on a low conversation among themselves. They didn't look up.

"You lot back there," Stone called. "Mind taking your seats so we can get started?" When they shuffled and mumbled and made no move to do as he'd requested, he frowned. "Is something wrong?"

They did break their little knot then, all turning toward him. There were five of them, two men and three women, dressed in black, tattooed and pierced. Occult Studies was a popular subject among a subset of the campus's goth population, and each of Stone's classes included at least a couple of them. They tended to band together, sitting in the back of the room and paying close attention to the lectures. Now, though, they all looked troubled.

"Has something happened?" Stone asked, pushing himself off the desk. By now, the rest of the class was watching the goth group as well.

A pale, pixieish young woman with dyed-black hair held up a folded newspaper. "I'm sorry," she said. "We—just found out about—" She shook her head, unable to go on. Instead, she offered him the paper.

He walked forward and took it. It was folded to display an article with the headline: *Body of murdered woman found in Shoreline Park.* He glanced up at them, then back down to scan the rest of the article: Police had found the body of a young woman the previous night. They weren't releasing any details, including the woman's name, but they were asking for anyone who might have seen anything to phone the department.

Stone handed the paper back. "She was someone you knew?"

A young man in a Skinny Puppy T-shirt nodded without looking at him. "Yeah. She wasn't a student here, but we'd see her all the time at the clubs. Her name was Althea."

Stone took a deep breath. "I'm sorry," he said softly.

Tears glittered in the pixieish woman's eyes. "We heard—" she swallowed. "We heard that they thought it was an animal that got her at first, because she'd been—" She bowed her head. The other man put an arm around her.

Stone shook his head. "It's all right," he said. "If you'd rather not be here today—"

"It's okay," said a chubby young woman with short, bright-red hair. "Sorry about disturbing the class. We'll be fine."

Stone eyed them dubiously for a moment, but then nodded, headed back up front, and began the day's lecture. In deference to the five in the back, he toned down his usual dramatic style and instead focused on a more straightforward delivery of the material.

After it was over and everyone had filed out, he headed back to his office. The news of the murder had disturbed him, but only because it had happened to someone at least tangentially connected to him. This early in the quarter he hadn't had a chance to get to know his students very well, but to have something so horrific happen to one of their friends touched a bit closer to home than normal. He wondered how common murders were around here—every impression he'd had thus far was that the area was relatively safe, certainly more so than Oakland or San Francisco further north.

He'd put the whole thing mostly out of his mind until that evening, when he happened to flip on the TV news while poking at some unremarkable sushi he'd picked up on the way home from one of the restaurants in his recommendation pack (he really needed to find himself a housekeeper who could cook soon, he decided). He was barely paying attention to what the talking heads were saying until he caught the words "cannibal killer."

He glanced up, startled, and reached for the remote to turn it up. The reporter was on the scene at the park in Mountain View where the murdered woman's body had been discovered. Police, she said, were still not releasing the woman's identity, but an unnamed source had revealed that the body bore indications of being partially eaten, and that the marks were not indicative of an animal attack. The view switched to a prerecorded press release video from the Mountain View Police Department, where a brisk female officer was assuring the public that they would catch the person responsible soon, and asking anyone who might have seen or heard anything to call the number flashing on the bottom of the screen. She stated that as yet they were not saying whether they believed the killing to be related to a similar murder of a homeless man in late August.

The report finished and the broadcast moved on to the local sports scores. Stone snapped the TV off, thinking over what he'd just heard. *It's probably nothing,* he decided: *most likely some local sicko who'd finally gone over the edge and acted out on his twisted desires.* It was unpleasant, sure, but it happened. In fact, he rather thought the reporter was showing bad taste by dubbing the murderer the "cannibal killer," even if there was apparently another murder with characteristics similar enough that people were asking if it might be the same person.

Whoever it was, Stone was sure the police would catch them soon. It couldn't be easy to hide your traces when you killed people in public and ate them.

Aubrey called the next morning, just to check in and see how Stone was settling in. "Will you be coming home to pick up anything soon?" he asked.

"I should, eventually," he said. "I need to get on with finding where the portal is around here—I know there's one somewhere not too far away, but I haven't had time to check. How are things there?"

"About the same," Aubrey said. "Mr. Desmond called last week—he asked me for your telephone number."

"Did you give it to him?" He hadn't talked to Desmond since the breakup, and didn't particularly want to. He wasn't sure why: it wasn't as if his old master was going to grill him on what had happened with Imogen, or blame him for it. He suspected she'd already explained the situation to him, which was probably why he hadn't tried to contact Stone already.

"I...couldn't think of any reason why not to," Aubrey said, sounding apologetic. "I couldn't very well tell him I didn't have it."

"Don't worry about it. If he calls, I'll talk to him, but I'm not going to seek him out."

"Yes, sir. That's probably best." There was a pause, and then: "How are you getting on over there? Is the position what you expected?"

"Haven't really settled in yet, to be honest. I like the students. The other faculty in the department can't stand me. I suppose I can't blame them, since I'm playing hell with their neat little world. Oh, and there's some sort of cannibalistic killer on the loose."

"In the department?"

Stone chuckled. "That would be entertaining, at least. No, whoever it is, they got a friend of some of my students, so it's a bit closer to home than I'd prefer."

"I'm sorry to hear that. I'd tell you to be careful, but I suspect you probably don't have much to worry about from a rampaging cannibal."

"Yes, I'm far too stringy," Stone agreed. "Anyway, thanks for checking in on me. I'll try to find time to come home soon. If you could have some boxes ready, I'd appreciate it. I can't take much with me through the portal, but I'll want to ship over a few more things I'll be needing."

"Yes, sir." After a moment, he added, "I do hope you'll pop home every now and then. It feels a bit futile, keeping the place up when there's no one to appreciate it."

Stone smiled. He would never tell Aubrey, but it was nice to be missed occasionally. "Just make sure it doesn't fall down 'round my ears next time I do. And if you're planning any wild orgies in the main hall, make sure you've got them sorted before I get there."

"The orgies were completed last week, sir."

"Good man. That's why I keep you around."

❖

For the next couple of weeks, Stone continued settling into his home and his courses, unpacking the various boxes that arrived over time and attempting to turn the rented townhouse into something approximating a comfortable space. His books helped a lot: even though they represented only a tiny fraction of his library at home in England, just having them nearby was soothing. He even got confident enough at driving American-style (did they *ever* signal?) that he took a couple of weekend jaunts up to San Francisco and Berkeley to hunt through dusty used bookstores for more specimens. He still hadn't gotten around to looking for a housekeeper who could cook, though, and knew he'd have to get on with it soon. The dust was accumulating, and he was running out of new nearby takeout places to try.

There were no more reported murders, and gradually the public and the press settled back down to the point where mentions of the Cannibal Killer dropped to an occasional update on page four of a paper or at the end of a news broadcast, stating that police were still searching for the perpetrator but beginning to consider the possibility that he was a transient who'd moved on. There was even talk of allowing children to trick-or-treat on Halloween, with appropriate adult supervision. Stone had heard other professors discussing it in the cafeteria on more than one occasion, combining speculation about the killer with relief that soon they and their childcare providers might be safe in letting the kids out of their sight for more than five minutes at a time.

The one thing that Stone refused to think about, however, was the fact that his birthday was coming up at the end of October. As a rule he didn't celebrate his birthday with any sort of gathering—while he could use his natural charm to feign an interest he didn't feel at faculty cocktail parties and fundraising shindigs, the idea of a party in his own honor to commemorate something he had little to do with seemed rather pointless to him.

Also, this would be his first birthday in the last few years that he hadn't spent with Imogen. Last year, she'd surprised him with a weekend trip to Aberystwyth, where they'd spent the time poking around quaint shops, taking long walks, and sharing champagne and excellent sex at an elegant seaside resort, accompanied by the sound of waves rolling in from the beach.

He didn't tell anyone about his birthday. Aubrey sent him a card and a box full of things from back home: snacks, teas, biscuits, crackers (the kind Brits popped, not the kind Americans ate), a couple black T-shirts from local bands, newspapers and magazines, and a jar of orange marmalade that was more of a joke than anything else, given that he hated the stuff and Aubrey knew it. The box was waiting for him when he arrived home from work; he carried it inside and opened it, and for several minutes just stood there at his breakfast bar staring down into it, broadsided by a sudden wave of homesickness so strong that it physically shook him. He thought he was over that by now.

Happy twenty-ninth birthday, read the note on top of the neatly packed gifts. *I hope you have a wonderful day, and I hope you'll come home to visit soon. Best, Aubrey.*

William Desmond hadn't sent him anything, and Stone hadn't expected him to. His old master shared his opinion about birthday celebrations.

He was stretched out on the sofa in the dark, five Guinnesses into a six-pack and contemplating the last one, when the phone rang. He glanced at the clock: nearly ten. Who would be calling him this late? He thought about not answering, but generally when people called at odd hours it had an equal probability of being important or a wrong number. And besides, the phone was right there, where he'd left it after calling out for pizza three hours earlier. He picked it up. "Yes, hello?"

"Alastair?"

Stone's hand tightened on his Guinness bottle. "Imogen."

Her voice was soft and tentative, like a skittish kitten trying to decide if it was safe to approach a strange human. "I—I hope it's not too late. I thought you might be out. I was just calling to wish you a happy birthday."

He frowned, nudging his foggy brain through the mental calculation. "It's—what—six in the morning there?"

"Almost. I had to get up early." She paused. "How...have you been?"

"Fine," he said, a little too quickly. He could hear the fuzziness in his voice, and reconsidered the last Guinness. "And yourself?"

"All right. Good." Another pause. "Have you been back home at all?"

"No. Aubrey's trying to get me to come for a visit, but I've been quite busy settling in." Idly, he used magic to gather up the untidy spread of pizza crusts, toss them into the box, and close it, then lined up the empty Guinness bottles in front of it. The box from Aubrey sat open on the other side of the table.

The line crackled softly in the silence. "Maybe this wasn't the best idea," she said at last. "I didn't want to upset you. I just didn't want you to think I'd forgotten your birthday."

"I'm not upset," he said, again probably too quickly. "I'm good. And I wouldn't be out. You know I hate parties."

"Did you even tell anyone? About it being your birthday, I mean." Her tone took on a gentle, teasing fondness.

"Of course not." He chuckled. "I've heard about American birthday parties. Last thing I need is old Mortenson from the department trying to slap a party hat on me."

There it was, the little giggle. "I can't picture you in a party hat." Then: "Well…anyway, I hope you had a good day. I should probably get on about…"

"…whatever it is you were going to do," Stone agreed. He knew then that she'd gotten up early specifically to call him, and he thought she probably knew he knew it. "Thanks for calling, Imogen. I appreciate it. Give my best to your father if you see him."

"I will."

He didn't ask about whoever it was she was seeing, even though he was curious. Instead, he broke the connection and tossed the phone back on the table. He thought about getting up to clean up the clutter, but couldn't gather the energy to do it. Imogen's words swirled in his mind, and he knew his chances of getting any sleep tonight hovered somewhere between slim and none despite his exhaustion.

After a moment of deliberation, he levitated the last Guinness over and popped its cap. He was already going to have a hangover in the morning, so what would one more hurt? At least his first class didn't start until eleven.

When he finally did drop off to sleep an hour later, Imogen's face dominated his uneasy dreams.

CHAPTER TEN

THE MEAT FROM THE WOMAN lasted them nearly a month and a half.

Contrary to what some might believe, they didn't hunt for sport. It was too much trouble, for one thing. Despite the thrill that gripped all four of them as they brought their prey down and ate their hot bloody fill, they went out into the night only when their larders were diminished and they were forced to seek fresh meat. To do otherwise would at best risk having to move on again, and at worst, could lead to their discovery. As adapted to hunting human prey as they were with their specialized abilities, they weren't invisible. If someone saw them—especially someone like a cop—they could end up having to deal with situations they weren't prepared for.

Even so, the temptation was sometimes hard to ignore. So much meat, so many warm bodies, steaming organs, blood—more than once, the only reason one of them hadn't succumbed and gone after one of the stupid, blundering cows was because they tried to stay together to prevent just such an incident.

They didn't like the daylight. It wasn't that it burned their skin or represented any threat to their continued existence: it simply made their sensitive eyes hurt. Sunglasses took care of the problem, if they had reason to go out during daytime hours, but they usually didn't.

The four of them shared a derelict two-bedroom apartment that rented by the week in a neighborhood bad even by East Palo Alto standards. Their landlady, a patchy-haired, overweight woman named Belle who spent most of her time stretched out in front of her television set smoking weed and watching soap operas with her scrawny geriatric Chihuahua in her lap, loved them. They were quiet, didn't get into trouble, and didn't ask her for anything. In exchange, she neither asked nor cared about who they were, what they did, or how long they'd been in town. They'd given her fake names that she didn't bother to check, and paid their rent in cash.

They liked it here, they'd discovered. The weather was warm, the scenery was attractive, and the prey was plentiful and trusting. They knew their time here was limited, though: as good as they were at hunting, they were not good at planning. When the hunger struck them, the thought of luring their prey off to a place where they could kill and eat it in peace didn't even enter their minds. Premeditation wasn't something they liked to practice unless forced to. That meant that when they took prey, it was usually someplace where it would be discovered. And that, in turn, meant that they would have to move on before *they* were discovered.

Not for a while, though. They'd remained in their previous location for almost a year before deciding to change their locale. If they were careful, they thought that the rich hunting grounds of the San Francisco Bay Area could sustain them for at least that long.

The next kill would be the key, though. One kill in an area was usually written off as the work of an animal, or a random one-off psychopath. Two, they knew, attracted attention. With each subsequent kill, the chance that they might be caught increased.

They could mitigate the risk somewhat by hunting in remote areas, where animals would ravage the prey before it was discovered—if it were even discovered at all. But that wasn't the way they operated. Risk or no, the adrenaline rush that they all experienced every time they set out to hunt, the constant threat of being discovered, made the meat taste even sweeter.

Freshly killed prey was the best, of course. They could live on stored flesh and did so for most of the time—even they knew that too many indiscriminate killings would not end well for them—but all four of them lived for that time, once every month or so, when they could let their instincts run free and hunt as they were meant to. To track the prey, to bring it down, to taste hot blood and rip still-warm flesh from bone while the last of the body's life force drained away—that was what gave their lives meaning. It was what they were made for.

That was the best part, and very soon they would get to experience it again.

CHAPTER ELEVEN

STONE LIKED TO RUN; it gave his body something to do while he focused on quieting the breakneck speed of his mind. Palo Alto was turning out to be a good area to do it in, too: lots of tree-shaded, meandering streets and lovely parks—not as nice as back home, he decided, but for the foreseeable future this *was* home. He would have to get used to it. And to be fair, the weather was nicer—and a lot more predictable—here.

It was a little more than a week after his birthday. He *had* awakened the next morning with a nagging hangover and a stiff neck from falling asleep in an awkward position on the sofa, but it hadn't taken him long to put the whole thing behind him and get back to business as usual—or as usual as it could be when he was still getting used to all the ways living in America differed from living in Britain.

He was too busy to dwell on Imogen, or even on the fact that he still wasn't convinced he'd made the right decision by taking the Stanford position. His days were filled with classes, office hours, committee meetings, research, and grading the various assignments he'd given his students. He was even contemplating a little extra-credit side trip for his Modern Occult Practices course to some local site that was allegedly haunted, but he hadn't decided on which one yet. Between all that and setting up his magical lab in the basement of the townhouse, he didn't have a lot of time for introspection.

He smiled a little now as he wondered how many other people around here liked to do their running at eleven o'clock at night. It might be odd, but it was cooler and quieter and it wasn't like anything was going to be a threat to him. He didn't know yet if there were muggers around here, but any mundane who tried to mess with him would be in for a surprise. Either there weren't any muggers lurking in the area, or his confidence gave him the air of someone who knew what he was doing, because as yet no one had bothered him on any of his outings.

He'd tried a different direction this time for variety's sake, and by the time he glanced at his watch it was almost 11:30. He was keeping up a steady pace along the edge of a long, narrow park next to a creek; the streetlights illuminated small circles of it, but the rest receded back into shadowy, tree-studded darkness. He paused a moment to orient himself, preparing to turn around and head back toward home, when a movement caught the corner of his eye.

He stopped, still breathing a little hard, and stared into the darkness past the nearest streetlight's glow.

A quick yelp of a scream, cut off abruptly. Male.

Then a shriek: a woman. Also cut off.

Stone's heartbeat picked up. He narrowed his eyes, trying to pierce the darkness in the park's depths, but he saw nothing.

He shifted to magical sight. If anything were there, he'd see the glow of its aura even in total darkness. Without conscious thought he began moving in the direction where he'd heard the voices, his pace quickening with each step. If it was an assault in progress, perhaps he could—

A sound rose from the same direction: a soft sound, halfway between a ripping and a growl. Then a whimper. Stone's magical sight revealed not two figures, but a group of them. At least five.

Two were on the ground, auras radiating flares of terror and pain. The others clustered around one of the downed figures, hunched and intent on something. Their auras glowed odd and reddish against the backdrop of the dim green of the trees, and despite their animal-like movements, they appeared to be human—or at least humanoid.

Stone yelled before he thought: "Hey!" He broke into a run toward the scene. Though he had no idea how he would deal with the situation, he couldn't just do nothing. With any luck his magic was sufficient to cope with the attackers, or at least to frighten them off.

The hunched figures snapped to attention. There were four of them; they appeared to be sniffing the air, their heads moving with an odd, ungainly jerking. Then, almost as one, all four leaped up and took off into the shadows in the opposite direction, abandoning whatever had been the subject of their focus.

For a moment, Stone thought about following—either trying to catch up with them or at least getting within range to throw a spell. But by the time he finished the thought they were already gone. They were fast—certainly faster than he was. Maybe supernaturally fast, and if that were so, he wasn't prepared to take them on right now. Whatever they were, they weren't precisely human. He'd have bet a lot of money on that.

Ahead of him, he heard moaning from the prone form the attackers had been surrounding. Ten feet or so to the left, the other victim stirred, attempting to rise. For a moment Stone was torn on which one to approach first, but the closer one was obviously in greater need. He ran over and dropped down next to the figure, heedless of the wet grass and the bite of gravel on his bare knees.

There wasn't a lot of light, but he could just make out the soft features of a middle-aged, balding man. The man's eyes were clamped shut, his breath rasping and rattling in the back of his throat.

Stone put a hand on his shoulder. "Hold on," he urged. "We'll get you some help."

His gaze moved down the man's body. *Good gods.* The front of his shirt was torn, and his entire torso, from groin to neck, was soaked in blood. Stone couldn't be sure in the dimness, but he thought he saw dark, blood-slicked knots of viscera emerging from a rip in the man's abdomen.

He thought fast. This man wouldn't live long—he knew a bit of healing magic, but he'd never been any good at it and this kind of injury was far too profound to respond to his meager efforts. He glanced around, first to determine that the four shadowy figures weren't returning, and then to pin his gaze on the second figure.

"You!" he called. "Are you hurt?"

"Oh, my God…Douglas!" The figure, upright now but barely, hurried over and collapsed next to the fallen man, clutching at him. "Douglas…oh my God…" She was a woman of about the same age as the man, comfortably overweight, dressed in long skirt and belted tunic. Her voice wavered, bright with panic.

Stone, hating himself for being so abrupt but seeing no other option, gripped her upper arm. "Listen," he said. "He needs help. There's a phone just over there, on the corner. Go and call. I'll see what I can do for him. Unless you've got medical training—?" He could hope, but his brief glance told him this was the sort of woman who attended art gallery openings and genteel brunches, not medical school.

"No…no…Douglas…"

"Go! Please," he added more gently. "You'll help him more by getting someone here fast."

Something in his tone must have gotten to her; she levered herself up and staggered back toward the street and the phone.

Stone turned his attention immediately back to the man. "Douglas. Listen. You've got to hold on. Your wife's gone to get help. But you've got to stay with us, all right?"

The man opened eyes haunted by pain and fear. He flailed one arm as if attempting to reach up toward Stone, but he didn't have the strength to do it. His round moon face was dotted with perspiration. "Please…" he whispered. "Don't…don't go…"

"I'm not going anywhere, I promise." Stone spared a glance toward the woman: she'd reached the phone now and appeared to be fumbling with it. "Come on, Douglas. You can do it."

But it was becoming quickly obvious that Douglas *couldn't* do it. Already his face was going slack, his limply fluttering hand returning to his side. The sharp, sour tang of blood lingered in the air around him.

Stone swallowed. He'd have to try something, even if it had nearly no chance of working. *Nearly none* wasn't *none*, and maybe he could stabilize the man long enough for help to arrive.

He kept one hand on Douglas's shoulder, gripping it in what he hoped was an encouraging manner, and moved the other over the man's heaving abdomen. Harder to do this with so little light, but he couldn't risk a light spell. He would need every shred of concentration he had to even attempt healing.

"Please…" Douglas moaned. "I'm so scared…It hurts…Laura…"

"Hold on…" Stone murmured the words by rote, not even hearing what he was saying. He focused his will on his hand, reaching out to gather magical energy from the air, to hold it and shape it, fighting to remember how he'd been taught so many years ago.

Desmond hadn't been any good at healing magic either: you needed a certain empathic mindset that neither Desmond nor his apprentice possessed in great measure. Stone's introduction to the art had been through a woman of Desmond's acquaintance, and had only lasted a few days; he struggled now to recall the techniques, to reach out to connect with Douglas's flagging life force so he could support it and allow it to build upon his own strength as he fed power into it. Not too much or too fast, or he'd overwhelm the faltering energy like dumping too much water on a fragile seedling.

"Come on, damn you..." he whispered through his teeth. "Fight, Douglas." The effort of will to do this was exhausting, almost as taxing as it would be for him to perform a complex black-magic working.

He soon lost track of time, of how long he stayed like that, crouched over Douglas's dying body, pulling in magical energy and using his will to channel it into the void left by the man's own ebbing aura. *Come on...come on...*

But it was no good. No matter how much power and will he poured into the healing effort, it wasn't enough. With his magical sight focused on Douglas's dimming life force, he couldn't miss it: one moment it was there, flickering and fading like a candle guttering in a windstorm, and the next it was gone. Douglas's living body became nothing more than a couple hundred pounds of inert flesh in the space of an instant.

Stone slumped, barely catching himself in time before he fell face-first into Douglas's ravaged abdomen. He remained there, head bowed, holding himself up on arms shaking from both exhaustion and the cold of the night, until he felt a wavering hand on his shoulder.

It was Douglas's wife; of course it was. Tears streamed down her face. "Is...is he—?" She trailed off; some questions didn't need to be finished.

"I'm sorry..." he whispered without looking up. It wasn't just the fact that he'd been unable to save Douglas that he regretted; it was that he'd sent the man's wife off to call for help, sent her away during her husband's last moments, in the vain and arrogant hope that perhaps he could do something to keep Douglas alive long enough for help to arrive. He should have let her stay and gone for help himself, for all the good he'd done—Douglas would have died either way, but at least his last sight would have been of his wife instead of some stranger.

Her hand was still on his shoulder, warm and trembling. "I...called 911," she said in a small voice. "They'll...they'll be here soon." A pause, and then: "You...don't think they...those...animals...will be back, do you?"

Stone pushed himself up, his arms almost too weary to lift his weight, and knelt next to Douglas's body. He wished he had something cover it with, but he was clad only in shorts and a thin T-shirt for his run. He glanced around again, shifting back to magical sight; other than his own aura and hers and the dim green glow of the trees, no living being stirred in his line of sight. "I don't think so."

She swallowed. "You...tried to help us. You scared them away."

He shook his head.

"You did," she said. "And you tried to help Douglas." Her hand gripped his shoulder.

"I wasn't any help," he said, his tone bleak. "I'm so sorry."

She sank down next to him. "Douglas and I...we were taking a short cut back to our car. We walk...walked...here often." She barely sounded as if she was speaking to Stone; her words tumbled from her, each one twisted and quavering.

He turned his head to look at her then; her face was tear-streaked, her eyes reddened and glittering. "I'm sorry. I wish I could have—"

She patted his arm. "You did what you could," she said. "I—" Her voice hitched; she paused, glanced down at her husband's body, and her face deflated as fresh tears sprung to her eyes. "Oh, God, Douglas…" Her shoulders heaved with her sobs.

Sirens sounded, off in the distance. "They'll be here soon," Stone said. He reached out awkwardly to put his own hand on her arm, as she had done for him. "Are you hurt?" he asked, noticing the dark track of a long scratch on her forearm.

"What?" She looked down. "Oh—no, it's…it's all right. I think I scratched it when I fell." Her gaze cut down toward Douglas's body again, then quickly away.

Stone kept his gentle grip on her arm until the lights of the approaching emergency vehicles drew into view. His mind, however, was far away, focused on the strange auras of the four attackers, and on the news reports about the so-called Cannibal Killer.

CHAPTER TWELVE

LESS THAN HALF AN HOUR LATER, the area was transformed. Several police cars, their red and blue lights whirling, were parked along the edge of the street. A small flock of officers, detectives, and crime-scene photographers had already descended on the park, along with a smaller group of night-owl onlookers attracted by all the lights and action. The police had set up a cordon and were holding the civilians back at the street.

Stone stood off to one side waiting for the detective—one of the first to show up in response to Laura Phelps's call—to get back to him. He'd been told to stay where he was and left under the watchful eye of a young uniformed officer. Stone rubbed his arms, growing increasingly uncomfortable in his light running gear as the night's chill grew.

Laura Phelps herself had been hustled off, and he wasn't even sure she was still on the scene. He wondered if he'd get a chance to speak with her again, or if she'd even want anything further to do with him—with such a stark reminder of her husband's horrific death.

Finally the detective finished talking to the crime-scene people and stumped back over to him. A stocky man in his mid-fifties, with graying brush-cut hair and a perpetual squint, he regarded Stone, notebook open in his hand. "I'm Lieutenant Grider. You the other one who was on the scene?"

Stone nodded. "Alastair Stone. I was out running along the edge of the park, and I spotted something in the trees there."

"You always go running this late, Mr. Stone?"

"Any reason I shouldn't? This isn't normally a dangerous area, is it?"

Grider's eyes narrowed. Obviously he was in no mood to be getting lip from sarcastic Brits at this time of night. He looked Stone up and down as if expecting to spot bloodstains or defensive wounds, and looked a bit grumpy when he didn't. "Okay. Tell me what happened."

Stone took a deep breath, gathering his thoughts and trying not to shiver. It was getting cold, and now that the adrenaline rush was fading, his T-shirt and running shorts were doing nothing against the light, chilly wind blowing through the area. "Just after I spotted movement, I heard two screams: a man and a woman."

Grider jotted that down. "What did you do then?"

"Headed in that direction."

"Just like that?" The detective eyed Stone's outfit. "What did you think you were gonna do? I can't see you hiding a piece in that getup. You some kinda martial arts expert or somethin'?"

"Hardly. I didn't really think about it, to be honest. But if there was an attack, I couldn't very well just ignore it, could I?"

Grider sighed. "That's how civilians get killed." He cocked his head toward the nearby pay phone, the one Laura Phelps had used to summon help. "Ever think of just callin' us?"

"Honestly, no." Between the air's chill and the sheer enormity of what he'd just witnessed, Stone was not currently possessed of an excess of patience. "My first thought was to see if I could help."

"Yeah, okay. Keep going."

Stone told the rest of the story, leaving out only the parts that would require him to admit to magical ability.

Grider stopped him almost immediately. "So how many of these guys did you see crouched over the victim?"

"Four."

"You sure?" He wrote something in his notebook. "You scared off four guys?"

Stone shrugged. "I don't know if I scared them, or perhaps they just didn't want to be discovered or identified."

"So they all just up and took off."

"Yes."

"Which way?"

Stone told him, pointing off toward the far side of the park. When Grider waved him on, he continued, describing the scene after the attackers had left.

Grider took out a cigarette, stuck it between his teeth, and lit it. "I saw the vic, Mr. Stone. Looks like some kind of animal got to him. His wife said he was still alive when she went to call us. Did he talk to you? Tell you anything?"

Stone shook his head. "He was in shock. All he said was that he was afraid, and begged me not to leave."

Grider jotted that down, then fixed his squinty gaze on Stone. "Why'd you send her to call, instead of goin' yourself?"

"I thought they might come back. Also, I thought I might be able to help. I know a bit of first aid." That was a lie, and if Grider called him on it, he'd have a hard time backing it up.

The detective shook his head and glanced over toward where the first responders had erected a small tent over the body to keep the lookie-loos from getting an eyeful. "Guy was way beyond first aid. But from what the lady said, it sounds like maybe you mighta saved her life by turnin' up, so that's somethin' anyway. And her story matches yours, so you ain't a suspect at the moment." He closed the notebook and sighed. "You got some ID on you?"

Stone dug out his wallet and handed over his identification.

Grider studied it, a bit too long for Stone's taste, then frowned. "Haven't been in this country long, have you?"

"No. I started a new position here in September, so I haven't got all my permanent identification sorted yet."

Grider nodded. It was clear he was still trying to find something to pin on Stone, but just as clear that nothing was presenting itself. He handed back the documents. "Okay," he said. "I've got your address and phone number. If I need anything else from you, I'll give you a call. You might have to come down to the station tomorrow and make a statement, or we might have some more questions."

"Of course. Whatever I can do to help."

There was an awkward silence.

"Am I free to go, then, Lieutenant?"

"Yeah. But stay reachable."

Stone barely noticed what his body was doing during the slow jog back to his townhouse. What had those creatures been? Were they connected with the Cannibal Killer? He wished he'd gotten a better look at the attackers, but in any case his knowledge of supernatural beings in this part of the world was woefully lacking. That was something he'd need to do something about quickly, if he intended to stay here. His relatively sudden decision to relocate halfway around the world had meant that he hadn't had time to do his usual exhaustive research before he left. He had a large and impressive magical library back home in England, but the logistics of getting to it quickly were more daunting than he wanted to deal with right now. He knew there was an Overworld portal somewhere in the Bay Area, but he wasn't sure exactly where. Besides, even if he did go home to check his library, he doubted it covered much about supernatural creatures in northern California.

No, he'd need to find someone more local who might be able to help him find the references he needed. Perhaps he could check with Mortenson and Hubbard about any local legends. He thought he might know someone else to ask, but that would have to wait until a more reasonable hour.

By the time he got home, it was nearly two a.m. He let himself in, flung himself down on the living-room sofa, and pulled up a blanket, shivering with both cold and the aftermath of adrenaline.

His mind chewed over the details of what had happened. As much as he tried not to think about them, both Douglas and Laura's faces swirled across his memory: his terrified and agonized, hers grief-stricken and bereft. He'd watched a man die tonight—not just watched, but fought with everything he had to save him, and failed. He knew it wasn't his fault—he doubted that even Desmond's healer colleague would have been able to snatch a man so far gone back from the brink—but it still forged a sort of connection between them, and between himself and Laura, even if she didn't ever want to see him again. He wouldn't blame her if she didn't.

He slept badly, haunted by uneasy nightmares of blood and spilled entrails and the accusing faces of the couple. Finally at four-thirty he gave up trying. He flung off the blanket, got a cup of coffee, and spent the next hour reading in his study. By the time he felt tired enough that he thought he might be able to sleep, it was close to six a.m.

His first class of the day was at ten; he did his best to make himself presentable, but he supposed when you taught Occult Studies, the occasional bout of dark-circled eyes and shadowed stubble just made you look more appropriate to the subject matter. He noticed that many of the students eyed him oddly during the lecture, but none of them said anything until the class was over. He gathered up his papers and prepared to leave, hoping to make a clean break and spend the next hour tossing back weapons-grade coffee in one of the staff lounges, but looked up when a voice said, "Dr. Stone?"

He didn't know her name, but she usually sat two or three rows back near the window. A nondescript young woman with mouse-colored hair and a red Stanford hoodie. "Yes?"

"Is it true?" Her voice was soft, and she glanced over her shoulder toward to door as if fearful of being overheard.

"Is what true?"

"I heard—" She paused, right hand clutching the strap of her backpack. "Was that you? Were you there when they found the…victim? Last night at the park?"

Stone closed his eyes briefly. Where the hell had she heard that? He'd checked the morning paper—it had simply mentioned that "a Stanford professor out running" had been involved. No names.

When he didn't answer right away, she said, "I've got a friend whose family lives in the area near the park. She heard the sirens. A bunch of people went out to see what was going on. She mentioned that a British guy with dark hair was there talking to the cops. Then I saw the paper this morning, and—"

He sighed. "Yes."

Her eyes widened. "Oh, wow. That must have been horrible for you. And after the last one—that's three now, isn't it?"

"I don't suppose it would do any good to ask you not to spread this around, would it?" he asked. He snapped his briefcase shut and started toward the door, hoping she'd get the hint. "Not exactly the sort of notoriety I'm looking for at present."

"Oh..." She didn't look at him. "Well...I did already mention it to a couple of people before I came to class...I'm sorry, Dr. Stone."

"No, it's all right." What else could he say? At any rate, keeping this kind of thing quiet was a vain hope. Somebody was bound to find out, so better that it happened early. "Don't worry about it." He opened the door and motioned her out, then followed her, excusing himself and getting out of there before she could ask any more questions. It didn't matter, though: by the end of the day, he knew he'd be lucky if it was just all over his own department.

CHAPTER THIRTEEN

"I'M TELLIN' YOU, we can't do it again this soon."

His name was Kano—or at least that was what he went by these days. None of the rest of them knew his real name, just as he didn't know theirs. "Real names" represented a part of their lives that none of them wanted to think about anymore. "They're watchin'. We got seen. Now they'll know how many of us there are, and the cops'll be lookin' for us."

"We shoulda killed that fucker," the smallest of them, a wiry woman called Rima with teased hair and hard eyes, said. "The bitch too. We coulda taken 'em, easy. Fuck, we didn't even get anything from the stiff to bring back."

"Nah," said the third, another woman with a larger, taller version of the same lean and nervous figure, who went by Taco. "Kano's right. We gotta be careful."

It was the night following the attack in the park. The four of them sat around the tiny living room of their apartment, smoking, drinking, legs drawn up with skinny twitching arms clutched around them as if they feared their gaunt, spare bodies would fly to pieces if they let go.

"So whadda we do?" the second man asked, stubbing his butt out on the top of an empty beer can. "We gotta get more meat. Ain't no way we'll last another month."

"Dog?" Rima suggested, her lip twisting with distaste around the word.

"No way. I ain't eatin' no fuckin' dog," Taco snapped.

"Maybe we go dig somethin' up, then," the man said.

"Shut up, Grease," Kano said without raising his voice. "Lemme think."

They grumbled, but they shut up. They lit up another round of cigarettes and drank their beer in silence as Kano scrubbed at his mop of wild blond hair and shifted back and forth as if unable to get comfortable on the threadbare sofa.

At last, he said, "We gotta get meat, but they can't find the body this time. And I ain't diggin' up some stiff. We need to go somewhere there's people, but nobody'll find 'em."

"Like where?" Grease asked.

"I gotta think of everything?" Kano flung himself to his feet and began pacing.

"Wait," Rima said after a moment. "I got it."

They all turned toward her. "So?" Kano prompted.

"Homeless guy. Like before," she said. "But we don't kill 'im right away. We knock 'im out and take 'im somewhere."

"Where, though?" Grease asked. "Cops're lookin'. Anybody turns up dead with parts missin', they're gonna know."

"Don't matter," Kano said. "We don't leave the body. We bring it back here. Cut it up, put it in the freezer. Eat it all this time."

Rima grinned, revealing stained teeth. "That way we get the brain."

"Ooh," Taco agreed, head bobbing with enthusiasm. "We never get the brain."

Kano took a long pull from his beer. Finally he nodded. "Okay, makes sense. We'll do that, but only if we gotta. So now we got a plan. We'll do it tomorrow night. But after that we gotta be careful. Can't risk gettin' caught again. Even for the brains."

They all groused about it, but they knew he was right.

Grease, meanwhile, was idly flipping through channels on the apartment's ancient television set. "Hey, look. We got us a *logo*."

It was a local news report, and emblazoned across the bottom of the screen under the professionally somber anchorwoman were the words CANNIBAL KILLER in creepy red letters.

"Turn it up," Kano ordered.

"—after the latest murder attributed to the so-called Cannibal Killer," the anchorwoman was saying. "The victim's wife Laura avoided a similar fate when a Stanford professor out running encountered the scene and the killer was frightened off. We won't be releasing the professor's name since the killer is still at large, but Channel Four has learned that he is cooperating with the police and has given them some useful information. Sally Gonzalez, spokeswoman for the Palo Alto Police Department, has declined further comment citing an ongoing investigation, but she says that there might be a press conference in a day or so. Now over to you, Jerry, with the sports."

The scene switched to the sports scores, and Grease flipped the set off and tossed the remote on the table next to a litter of empty beer bottles. "Professor, huh? That's the guy who fucked us up? We got his scent. Maybe we oughta find out who he is, see if we can track him down."

"Bet he'd taste goooood," Rima agreed, drawing the word out with sensuous relish.

"Will you two fuckin' shut *up*?" Kano slammed his feet down on the coffee table, making the beer bottles jump. "We ain't goin' after no professor. You wanna get caught? Shit, I wonder why I hang with you guys sometimes. Don'tcha got any restraint?"

"Don't like nobody fuckin' up our kills," Grease said sullenly, without looking at Kano. "Feelin' like shit not eatin' for so long."

"Yeah, well, we got a plan. We'll do it tonight. Until then, keep it in your pants, and don't get any ideas about goin' out on your own. We're in this together. That was the agreement. Okay?"

"Yeah, yeah," Grease muttered. Rima and Taco nodded, though they didn't look much happier about it than he did. "But if he fucks with us again, no promises."

"He won't," Kano said. "He's prob'ly scared shitless we'll track him down and eat him. Just let him keep thinkin' that. It's the cops we gotta worry about, not some chickenshit professor."

CHAPTER FOURTEEN

STONE HADN'T INTENDED on attending Douglas's funeral, which was held a week later; not, at least, until his office phone rang the late afternoon a few days after the night of the murder. "Dr. Stone? This is Laura. Laura Phelps."

He stiffened. "Mrs. Phelps?" For a moment his brain refused to serve up the right words: "How are you?" hardly seemed appropriate, nor did "So good to hear from you." Finally, he settled on a gentle, "Is there something I can do for you?"

There was a hesitation on the other end. "I…just wanted to let you know that Douglas's funeral is the day after tomorrow. Ten a.m., at the Methodist Church on Hamilton. It would have been sooner, but the police had to…" Another pause. "I…I'd like you to come, if you would, Dr. Stone."

He wasn't sure he'd heard her correctly. "You—want me to come to the funeral?" The unspoken *why?* was evident in his tone. He wasn't family. This woman barely knew him—why would she want him intruding on her family in their time of grief?

"I…Yes," she said, her voice more steady now, but still soft. "If you wouldn't mind. I know you don't know us, Dr. Stone, but you were there when Douglas… You did what you could, and you scared those horrible people away. I'm sure he would have been grateful for that." The sound of a deep, shuddering breath. "Please come. I'd like to have the chance to talk with you again under…better circumstances."

What else could he say? "I—Of course, Mrs. Phelps. Of course I'll come."

"Laura. Please. And thank you so much."

Stone took the day of the funeral off; the head of Occult Studies' Cultural Anthropology umbrella department, a no-nonsense fiftyish woman named Dr. Beatrice Martinez, didn't say a word about it when she found out why. She'd stopped by Stone's office the previous afternoon to let him know that there were services and programs available for him if he needed someone to talk to about his experience. She'd even brought brochures.

It was an awkward conversation, with Stone quickly getting the impression that Dr. Martinez wasn't the sort who spent a lot of energy seeking help for anything and didn't quite know how to approach the situation. He'd thanked her and told her he was fine (he certainly wasn't planning on unburdening himself to some counselor, though of course he didn't tell her that—he was well acquainted with the political two-step). Obligation discharged, she'd told him to take whatever time he needed, and not to feel compelled to come back until he felt up to it.

He arrived a bit late on purpose—not so much as to be disrespectful, but enough so everyone had already filtered into the chapel and were seated by the time he arrived. That way he wouldn't have to talk to anyone yet.

He slipped inside, accepting a folded program from a solemn, dark-clad young woman standing just outside the door, then shrugged out of his black overcoat and took a seat at the end of the last row of pews near the door. No one turned to look at the latecomer, which was as he'd hoped.

Douglas Phelps, whatever else he might have been, appeared to have been popular; either that, or a lot of people had turned up due to curiosity about his murder. Stone thought it might be the former, though: the crowd that filled almost every seat in the many rows of pews didn't have the look of the professionally curious, with the exception of a couple young men in the opposite rear row who looked like they might be journalists.

The casket (closed, Stone noticed) was at the front, nearly buried beneath a riotous display of floral arrangements and topped with a large framed photograph. Stone studied it, realizing with regret that he'd never had the chance to see Douglas Phelps properly. Between the darkness and the abject terror on the dying man's face, he'd hardly been at his best during the last moments of his life. The photo showed a smiling, cheerful round face with thinning hair, eyes crinkled in mirth, and an easy grin. The face of a man who was happy with his life.

A pang of guilt settled over Stone: if only he'd moved faster after he'd heard the screams, gotten there sooner, he might not be sitting here today. That was absurd, though. Absurd and arrogant.

He sighed, glancing down at the program as the minister led the congregation in prayer. He wasn't a praying man, but he could at least spend the time doing something useful, like learning a bit about the man he'd been unable to save.

Douglas, he found out from the program, had been forty-nine years old, married to his college sweetheart Laura (they were Stanford alums) for twenty-seven years, and had two adult children, a son and a daughter, who lived out of state. He was a successful land developer, active in his church, and coached both boys' baseball and girls' soccer teams when his children had been home. He and his wife shared a passion for art, supporting a prestigious local gallery and a smaller one in San Jose that provided opportunities for low-income artists to display their work.

And none of that mattered a damn bit anymore—none of the plans he and Laura had had for their future mattered—because now he was dead. Killed by unknown attackers while taking a short cut with his wife through what should have been a safe park in an affluent area. Such a senseless loss.

Stone kept his gaze lowered as the minister delivered the eulogy. Then several friends and family members got up to tell stories about the deceased. Nobody mentioned the circumstances of his death. If anyone noticed Stone, they didn't say anything. Perhaps he'd be able to pay his respects and make a quick and graceful exit.

When the service ended, he got up and filed out with the rest of the mourners, moving off to the side of the narthex in an effort to be unobtrusive until he could find an appropriate moment to approach Laura Phelps. The minister had announced that a reception would be held in the community room, which was where everyone seemed to be headed. Stone followed, feeling more out of place by the moment. He didn't belong here, and the sooner he could get out, the better it would be for all concerned.

Laura Phelps didn't show up for another ten minutes; when she did arrive, she was surrounded by a small knot of people. She paused in the doorway a moment until her gaze found Stone, and then she said something to the group and made a beeline directly for him.

"Dr. Stone," she said softly, reaching out her hand. "I'm so glad you came." She looked different, pale, somehow smaller with her subdued makeup. She sounded tired.

Stone took her hand and gave it a gentle squeeze. "You have my deepest condolences, Mrs. Phelps. If there's anything I can do to help you, you've only to ask."

"You're so kind." By now, her entourage had joined them, arraying themselves around her in a protective ring. She nodded toward Stone. "This is Dr. Alastair Stone. Remember I told you? He's—he was there, that night."

Stone had no idea what to say to that, so he remained silent, waiting to see how they would react to the information, and to him. He certainly didn't expect one of them, a young woman who bore a strong resemblance to both Phelpses, to detach herself from the group and fling her arms around him, burying her head in his shoulder.

"Er—" he began, reaching up to pat her back with an awkward hand.

"I'm Sarah," she said into his suit coat. "Thank you so much for what you did…"

For a moment, Stone's reeling brain was convinced she was being sarcastic, but that didn't make any sense. "You're—"

"The Phelps's daughter," she said, still muffled. She pulled back and met his gaze: she was a pretty young woman in her early twenties with brown hair and a wan, tear-streaked face. "Mom told us what you did. How can we thank you?"

Stone blinked. Thank him? For letting her father die? For sending her mother off to make a phone call instead of sharing her husband's last moments? "I—"

A man, a couple years older than Sarah and obviously her brother, stepped forward and put a hand on her shoulder, but he was looking at Stone. "She's right, Dr. Stone. Thank you. If you hadn't been there that night…well, we might be attending our mom's funeral too."

Sarah nodded. "She told us you scared them off when you came by. If you hadn't..." Around her, the other people were all nodding in sympathy.

This was not going at all the way Stone had expected. He thought he'd show up, say a few comforting words to Mrs. Phelps, and endure the stares and murmurings of the family and friends, an interloper in a scene where he had no role. Instead, they were accepting him. Embracing him, even—literally, in Sarah's case.

"I'm so sorry there wasn't more I could do," he said. He knew it sounded trite and lame, but his usual ability to interact with people in a reasonably competent manner had deserted him.

Laura Phelps moved in and put her arms around him. "It's a terrible thing," she said. "A terrible thing that's happened, but the Lord will get us through it." She backed up, hands still on his arms, and took him in. "Thank you for coming today. We all appreciate it."

He didn't remember exactly what he'd said after that point, but it must have been the right thing, because they were still all watching him with sympathy and kindness as he made his exit. He walked as quickly as he could outside and didn't stop until he reached his car and got in.

As he sat there, he realized he still had the funeral program clutched in his left hand. He stared down at Douglas Phelps's kindly, smiling face and a wave of anger gripped him. He didn't know who the attackers were, but he did know they weren't strictly human, that they had some kind of supernatural connection. That had been obvious by the odd tinge in their auras. And they had targeted this innocent man—probably would have devoured him with methodical cruelty if they hadn't been interrupted.

He thought about Grider, the detective responsible for the case. A mundane if Stone had ever seen one—someone who followed the procedure and hunted for suspects in the same way he'd probably done for many years. The same way that had probably found a lot of them over those years. But it wasn't going to work this time. What would happen if Grider or one of the other local cops encountered the creatures? It wouldn't end well, he was certain. And that was assuming the creatures even allowed themselves to be seen again. They'd been spotted this time—would that make them more careful? Would they hunt in more remote areas, where they were unlikely to be disturbed? That made it even less likely that the cops would be able to stop them.

"I'm sorry, Mrs. Phelps," he muttered, jerking the key to bring the Jaguar to life. He couldn't save Douglas Phelps, but he owed it to the man's family to at least try to figure out what the hell had killed him. Once he knew that, he'd decide what—if anything—he could do next.

He had the rest of the day off. Time to visit an old friend.

| CHAPTER FIFTEEN

THE TINY SHOP was located on a side street in downtown Palo Alto, between a noodle house and an insurance office. It didn't look like a shop at all, actually: just a carved, unmarked wooden door that anyone who wasn't looking for it would have passed by without a second glance.

Stone pushed it open and descended a short flight of steps to another door. This one had a small, tasteful metal plate in the middle of it that read:

~ **Huan's Antiquities** ~
By Appointment Only

followed by a series of Chinese characters. He pushed this one open as well and stepped inside. A far-off chime tinkled.

The shop inside didn't look like a shop so much as the aftermath of a particularly discerning tornado. It was small, intimate, and somehow managed not to feel stuffy or cramped, despite the fact that nearly every square foot was filled with shelves crammed so full of eclectic items that they threatened to disgorge them onto the floors of the narrow aisles at any moment.

Stone paused a moment, taking it all in. He couldn't identify a single item on any of the shelves that belonged with any other item near it: old moth-eaten teddy bears shared space with delicate jewelry boxes; dusty antique sporting equipment was draped over a large, modern toolbox; a strange old doll sat on the perch inside an elaborate birdcage, its eerie eyes following Stone as he began moving again, heading up the centermost aisle toward the back. His gaze swept over the shelves and up to the ceiling, where more items hung from hooks. The only thing everything here had in common, he noticed immediately upon switching to magical sight, was that while the items might be priceless antiques, junk, or some of each—none of them were magical.

"Alastair Stone," a pleasant voice said from somewhere Stone couldn't see. "I heard a rumor that you were in the area. I hoped you might come and visit me."

Stone smiled as she stepped out from behind a pile of old books stacked on top of a golf bag: a tiny, slender Asian woman of indeterminate age, dressed in an elegant business suit. Her black hair was pulled back from a high forehead, her dark eyes glittering with merriment. Her smile lit up her face.

Stone made a little bow. "Madame Huan. So good to see you." It had been a couple of years since he had seen her last, back in London during a rare gathering of magical practitioners. He had almost forgotten that one of her shops was based in Palo Alto, though it was only by sheer luck that he had found her here: she spent most of her time traveling the world in search of interesting treasures and raw materials for the magical items she created.

He glanced past her at the beaded curtain through which she had come: his magical sight instantly revealed it to be a powerful ward. As was the case with most shops dealing in magical gear, the good stuff was in the back.

She gestured toward the same curtain. "Please, come back to my sitting room. We'll have some tea and chat. What are you doing in California? On holiday?" Her voice was soft, musical, and held no hint of an accent.

He followed her. As soon as he pushed past the curtain, feeling a vague hum as he crossed the ward, the entire view changed.

Instead of a cluttered junk shop, he was standing in a small, elegantly appointed room with a table, four chairs, and a tasteful assortment of true antiques—many of them magical—as decorations.

"I'm living here now," he said. "I've taken a position teaching Occult Studies at Stanford."

She puttered around and brought a tray over with a teapot, two cups, and a stack of delicate cookies. Her sculpted eyebrow crept upward. "Really? I thought you and Miss Desmond—"

"It—didn't work out," Stone said quickly.

"I'm so sorry," she said, reaching out to pat his hand. Then her tone grew more brisk as she changed the subject: "So you're in the area now. I'm delighted to hear that. Is this a social call, then, or is there something I can do for you?"

"A bit of both," he admitted. "I need to find some information about supernatural threats in this area."

She frowned. "Oh? Have you encountered one?"

He nodded. "A few days ago." He told her about the Phelpses, and the figures he'd seen at the park.

He half-expected her to immediately say, "Oh! I know exactly what that must have been." She didn't, though. Instead, her frown deepened. "How horrible," she said. "I'm afraid I've never heard of anything like that. I've been out of the country until quite recently, though, and haven't been paying much attention to the news since I got back. So if anything new has turned up in the last few months, I might have missed it."

He nodded. "There've been a couple of other murders recently that might or might not be connected. That's part of what I'm trying to figure out."

Madame Huan pondered for a moment. "Well, I can find some books that might be helpful, but I don't know if they'll be of any use in providing information about these…things, whatever they might be."

Stone sighed, nodded. "I appreciate your help, and I'd certainly like to see the books. But whatever they are, I'm sure they'll strike again—and I think they have in the past." He took a sip of his tea. "I don't suppose there's anyone else around here who might have more information?"

She didn't answer right away; in fact, her brow furrowed a little and she didn't meet his gaze.

He leaned forward, waiting. You didn't rush Madame Huan.

Finally, she said, "Well…there might be. But I'm not sure you'd want to get yourself tangled up with him."

"Why not? Who is he?"

She paused again, as if trying to figure out how to answer. "He's—a professional associate of mine, I suppose you might say. He's in the same business, but from a different…perspective."

Ah. Stone was beginning to see now what she was trying not to say. "He's a black mage."

She nodded. "His name is Stefan Kolinsky. He has a shop over in East Palo Alto…he's been here for years, and what he doesn't know about this area isn't worth knowing. He's…a historian, more than anything. He sells items that you probably wouldn't want to buy, but he has an extensive library, along with an information network that can find the answers to just about any question you might have."

Stone's eyes widened. "Well, that sounds brilliant," he said. He himself was a white mage, mostly, though he tended to think of himself as more "pale gray," since his curiosity about anything magical sometimes led him down some dark paths in search of knowledge. The only thing that kept him from slipping further toward the black end of the spectrum was the fact that knowledge was truly all he sought—he had no particular desire to use what he learned to increase his own power, and he was far too self-absorbed most of the time to have any interest in gaining power over others. "Can you tell me where to find him?"

"I can, if that's what you want," she said, still sounding troubled. "I warn you, though: he's an odd sort, and he doesn't do anything for free."

Stone shrugged. "I can pay him. That won't be a—oh," he added as he got a look at her eyes.

"Now you see," she said, nodding. "Do you still want to find him?"

He thought about it, but only for a moment. If there was some dangerous supernatural entity out there killing people and eating them, he needed to find out what it was. "I do," he said. "By the way: there aren't any other mages 'round here who sort out supernatural threats, are there?" he asked, quirking an eyebrow. "I'd hate to step on any toes, being new to the area and all that, but this one's become a bit…personal."

She chuckled, shaking her head. "Same old Alastair I remember. No, I'm afraid you're on your own. But as far as I know, we haven't had a supernatural threat in this area for years, at least not one that was enough of a problem to need…sorting out. Are you sure you didn't bring this one with you?"

"Damn," he said, getting up. "I knew I should have checked those packing boxes before I had them shipped over here."

She laughed, but then sobered. "Be careful, Alastair. This isn't exactly your area, as I recall."

"It became my area when those creatures, whatever they were, attacked those people in front of me," he said grimly.

| CHAPTER SIXTEEN

IT WAS TWO DAYS before Stone heard back from Stefan Kolinsky. Madame Huan had warned him that Kolinsky didn't like telephones, and wasn't sure he even had one. If he did, she didn't know the number. That meant Stone had to choose between showing up unannounced or writing him a letter. He chose the latter and provided few details, merely mentioning that he was new in the area, that Madame Huan had suggested that he might be of assistance with a problem, and that he'd like a consultation if it was convenient.

He sent it off and promptly put it out of his mind, so when a uniformed young man knocked on his door one evening, he had no idea why he was there. "Yes?"

"Dr. Alastair Stone?"

"Yes. What is—"

The young man handed him an old-fashioned, cream-colored envelope. "For you, sir." He bowed and departed before Stone could ask him any further questions.

Stone, intrigued, took the envelope back inside before he opened it. It was made of the sort of heavy stock that you didn't see very often these days aside from wedding invitations, and his name was handwritten on the front in bold strokes as old-fashioned as the envelope. There was no return address, but a wax seal bearing an ornate letter K surrounded by odd symbols held it closed; Stone immediately recognized the symbols as hermetic: a few simple words in an ancient magical language. And then he knew who'd sent it. This Stefan Kolinsky was apparently an even odder duck than Madame Huan had implied.

He broke the seal and opened the envelope. Inside was a single sheet of heavy, deckle-edged paper that matched the envelope. Handwritten in fine black ink in the center of the sheet were tomorrow's date, 4:00 p.m., and an address in East Palo Alto: the same one Madame Huan had given him. Beneath that, also handwritten, it read:

I look forward to making your acquaintance.
S. K.

Stone stared at the paper for a moment. He didn't have any classes tomorrow afternoon; just an office hour that he could easily postpone. He wondered if Kolinsky had somehow discovered that, or if he simply didn't care.

Stone was not yet familiar enough with the geography of the area to know where East Palo Alto was (other than that it was, presumably, east of Palo Alto). He located it on his map and drove there the following afternoon, but before long he had to pull over to make sure he hadn't taken a wrong turn somewhere.

Palo Alto, at least the areas of it he'd visited so far, was an attractive, upscale little town full of quaint restaurants, artsy little businesses, and a combination of professionals, the independently wealthy, and students. He took University, wending his way first past the Downtown businesses and then a collection of upscale homes set back from the street. But when he crossed highway 101, everything changed abruptly.

This place was decidedly more working-class at best, and as he continued following the directions he'd jotted down, the quality of the buildings took a decided downswing. Now, instead of little vegan bistros and hole-in-the-wall bric-a-brac shops, he passed whole blocks of shops with windows covered in bars, battered cars with cracked windshields, and drifts of trash swirling against structures badly in need of renovation. Many of the shops were vacant; among those that weren't, he saw mostly utilitarian businesses like cleaners and fast-food restaurants interspersed with pawn shops, liquor stores, and check-cashing establishments.

Stone frowned, pulling his car into a weed-choked empty parking lot to consult his directions again. He knew little about Stefan Kolinsky, but judging by the quality of the invitation the man had sent him, this hardly seemed the sort of place he would choose to conduct his business.

But no, the street was right. In fact, he was even close to the right block. The address Kolinsky had given him should be just up the street, on the other side. He couldn't see the numbers from here, but the ones on his own side indicated that he wasn't far away.

He got out of the car and glanced around to see if anyone was paying attention to him. No one appeared to be at the moment, so he murmured a spell under his breath and settled one of his favorite enchantments over the car.

He couldn't make it invisible—at least not for more than a couple of minutes, and even then it would drop if he moved away from it—but what he could do was create an illusion that the car blended in with the area where it was parked. Around here, it would look like an old derelict vehicle similar to the others along the street. The best part was, if anyone *was* watching him do it, nothing would change. The illusion wasn't impenetrable, but most mundanes (and many mages) were surprisingly unobservant, especially when they weren't expecting things to be...well...unexpected.

He'd have about an hour before the spell faded, so he got moving, jogging across the street and heading in the direction of Kolinsky's block. He still wasn't convinced he was in the right place, but at least he'd verify it before returning home and writing Kolinsky another letter.

The next block was indeed the correct one, but Stone half-expected that the number he was looking for wouldn't be there. As it happened, he was half-right. The number was there, but it didn't mark any sort of business. Instead, it hung askew on a battered plaque over what looked like an unused doorway set back a couple of feet from building's façade. The door's paint was faded and cracked, and its alcove was choked with trash, empty liquor bottles, and what looked like the remains of a sleeping bag. The smell of urine hung heavy in the air, and Stone had no trouble picturing a sleeping tramp huddled in the doorway.

Stone stood there a moment, pondering. Had Madame Huan given him the wrong address? That seemed unlikely, especially given that his letter had clearly reached Kolinsky. He glanced around again to make sure no one was watching him, then pulled out Kolinsky's reply to make sure he'd read the number right. There it was, matching the number in front of him. What the hell was going on?

He was about to turn away when his gaze fell on the seal, with its collection of odd symbols. They didn't form a spell—at least not one he'd ever seen before. In fact, they seemed to be a nonsense phrase. He glanced at them again, then looked at the door.

A slow smile spread across his face. "Stefan, you sly old dog," he muttered. With one more check for watchers, he faced the doorway, consulted the seal, and spoke the nonsense words in a soft, clear voice.

The air in front of him rippled. When it stilled, a solid wooden door with a hefty metal handle had replaced the former battered and chipped one. Stone pulled it open, knowing it wouldn't be locked. He slipped in and closed it behind him.

He stood on a narrow landing in front of a flight of stairs leading downward. The walls here were badly painted, as shabby and stained as the outside door had been. The stairs were wooden, carpeted in threadbare, fading red. A naked light bulb hung from the ceiling, suspended on an old-style cord. Another door of unadorned wood was at the foot of the stairs.

An odd duck indeed, Stone decided.

The door at the bottom of the stairs was unlocked too. He opened it and walked inside.

At least he'd finally reached a shop. That was something, he supposed, though this didn't look much like any magic shop he'd ever visited before. In fact, it almost looked abandoned. The carpet was as shabby as that on the stairs. Wooden display cases held a few unimpressive items, and a couple of lackluster framed prints—one of a series of dark figures bent over a supine body, and another of a shadowy humanoid figure with a bull's head surrounded by odd sigils in another—hung on walls covered in faded wallpaper. On the far side of the room was another door, narrow and nondescript; it was the sort of door that might lead to a supply closet.

Stone shifted to magical senses, but there was no sign of any magic anywhere in the room. He paused a moment, then crossed to the other door and repeated the words he'd used on the one at street level.

Again, the air shimmered. This time, the small door changed to a rich red velvet curtain hung over a wide, open doorway. *Now we're getting somewhere,* Stone thought, though he wondered how many more magical hoops he was going to have to jump through before he'd reach Kolinsky. The first couple had been intriguing, but the game would get tedious soon if it continued.

He needn't have worried. When he pushed back the velvet curtain and entered the rear of the shop, a lot of things became clearer. Here, the shabby carpet and cheap wooden fixtures gave way to an ornate space that had the aspect of a shop dealing in small and expensive treasures, albeit before the turn of the previous century.

He didn't look around much, though, as his attention was immediately claimed by the man seated at an old-fashioned, roll-top desk in the rear of this new room. The man rose and regarded him silently from beneath heavy, dark brows. He presented quite a contrast to Stone himself: while both were tall, the man was heavier and more powerfully built; his hair, dark like Stone's, was almost unnaturally neat, his severe, old-fashioned black suit perfectly tailored and without a wrinkle or a spot of dust. Stone, in his black Pink Floyd T-shirt, faded jeans, long black overcoat, and hair in untidy spikes from his habit of running his hand through it, felt suddenly underdressed.

"Welcome. I thought I might receive a visit from you at some point, so your letter didn't come as a surprise," the man said. His smile was amused, but not warm: a shark's smile. His age was impossible to determine: he was older than Stone, but aside from that he could have been forty, or seventy, or anywhere in between.

"It's a pleasure to meet you, Mr. Kolinsky," Stone said. He didn't offer his hand; mages rarely initiated casual physical contact with each other; it was considered overly familiar and almost always rebuffed. "I'm Alastair Stone, though I'm sure you already know that. Madame Huan speaks quite highly of you."

Kolinsky chuckled. "Does she? That is a surprise." He moved back toward his chair and settled himself in it with a cat's effortless grace. A casual wave of his hand brought over another chair, high-backed and wooden; it slid to a stop in front of Stone. "Please. Sit down, and tell me what I can do for you."

Stone did sit, but he didn't answer right away. The very question was a test, he knew: the one thing that Madame Huan had made sure to emphasize when they'd spoken was that Stefan Kolinsky never did anything for free. There was always some price, and Stone suspected from the odd gleam in the man's obsidian-chip eyes that Kolinsky's ideas of "payment" might involve things far more—interesting—than mere currency.

"Madame Huan has done more than speak highly of me, I see," Kolinsky said, and this time he seemed genuinely pleased. "I assure you, Dr. Stone: I don't bite. Nor do I require any payment for simple requests. It is only if I decide to honor them that we must discuss…terms."

Stone raised an eyebrow. In spite of everything he knew about this man, he was already starting to like him. "Fair enough, then," he said. "It's my understanding that you are something of an expert regarding the—darker—aspects of magic in this area."

Kolinsky's smile widened. "I…dabble."

"Have you perhaps heard—during your dabblings—of three recent murders in the area? Murders where the victims were partially eaten?"

Kolinsky nodded. "Of course." He tilted his head a bit. "Ah. You would, of course, be the 'Stanford professor' who came across the most recent murder in progress, would you not?"

"I would." Stone saw no point in trying to deny it, and in fact it boded well for Kolinsky's reputation as an information broker. When the other mage merely remained silent and waited, he continued: "I reported what I saw to the police—except that I didn't tell them everything I saw."

"I am not surprised."

"Why do you say that?"

Kolinsky turned to his desk for a moment, and shuffled through a few papers until he found the one he was looking for. He consulted it and then turned back to Stone. "You have not been in the United States very long, Dr. Stone. Your home is in Surrey, England. Until quite recently you were a professor of Occult and Paranormal Studies at Buckingham University. You made the decision to relocate here quite abruptly, yes?"

Stone went still. "You know quite a lot about me, Mr. Kolinsky," he said evenly.

"Of course I do. That is why you consulted me, is it not? Are you surprised that my store of information includes some on you?" He consulted his papers again. "You are the former apprentice of William Desmond, and apparently quite the prodigy. You began your magical apprenticeship at the age of fifteen. Completed it by eighteen, the age at which most apprentices are only beginning their training. Three years is quite remarkable, given Desmond's reputation as an old-school traditionalist. I'm impressed."

Stone acknowledged the words with a slight nod. "If you know as much about the information I'm looking for as you do about me, I'll be impressed as well."

"Ah, you prefer to get to the point. That is refreshing." Kolinsky squared up the small stack of papers and slipped them back into one of the desk's bank of cubbies. "Why do I know that you did not reveal what you saw to the police? I do not know, but I have my suspicions. I would guess that, as a newcomer to this country, you didn't wish to draw undue attention to yourself. The kind of attention you might draw if you admitted that you believed the murderers to be of supernatural origin."

"Murderers?" Stone asked, startled. One thing the police, as far as he knew, had not released to the public was how many murderers there had been. Probably didn't want to start a panic, or wanted to leave some information unrevealed to help weed out crazies with false confessions.

Kolinsky shrugged. "Another guess."

"Oh?"

"Come now, Dr. Stone." His smile took on the edge of mocking. "As I said, I know something of you and your reputation. You might choose to sequester yourself away with your books and your research, but the fact remains that you are one of the most accomplished practitioners of your generation. Are you telling me that you couldn't have dealt effectively with a single attacker—or that you would have chosen to let him or her escape without trying?"

Several seconds passed before Stone responded. "Four," he said at last. "There were four of them. And no, I don't think they were human. Not entirely, anyway." He fixed Kolinsky with a challenging gaze. "Madame Huan was right: you're very good with information. And that's what I've come here to ask you: if you have any idea what they might be."

Kolinsky considered. "Not specifically, no. For the most part, my area of interest is confined to the realm of magic. There are certainly other supernatural phenomena in the world, but if they are not directly related to magic or mages and they do not affect me personally, I don't make the effort to discover details about them. Are you asking me to do so now?"

And here we are at last, Stone didn't miss the slight change in Kolinsky's eyes. "Suppose I were?" he asked, and leaned back in his chair.

"Then the next step would be to agree on terms." Kolinsky's smile widened fractionally.

Stone sighed. "Listen," he said. "I'd appreciate your help. I've heard that you're quite good at this sort of thing, and I've no reason to doubt it. But I also know what you are, and you know what I am. So suppose you tell me what you've got in mind, and then I can decide whether I want to thank you for your time and look elsewhere." He started to rise, continuing to hold Kolinsky's gaze as he did so.

"Sit down, Dr. Stone. Sit down." Kolinsky indicated the chair with a slight head movement. "I assure you: my terms for such a search are quite reasonable, and I doubt you would find them objectionable."

Stone lowered himself back down warily. "Let's hear them, then."

"If I am able to find the information you seek, you will redesign and recast the wards on my shop here. I will provide all the necessary materials, of course."

Stone stared at him, knowing he wasn't succeeding in hiding his surprise. "That's—it?"

Kolinsky nodded. "A trivial, if somewhat taxing, activity for you. Much more difficult for me, as you're well aware."

Stone nodded slowly. He was right: it was the nature of white magic that it was much better suited to permanent or semi-permanent enchantments like wards. Most black mages couldn't cast anything that would last longer than a week or so before it began to decay. Stone, on the other hand, excelled at this sort of protective magic, and he suspected Kolinsky already knew that. "Whoever you've got doing them now did a good job," he said after a moment. "The incantation on the wax seal was a nice touch."

"Thank you." Kolinsky inclined his head. "They were done as part of a bargain I struck with the caster a couple of months back, but…circumstances prevent her from repeating the casting. So your arrival is actually serendipitous, since I find myself in need of such a service. Unfortunately, I have no mages of your persuasion in my debt at this time, so I was beginning to fear I would have to do them myself."

Stone paused again, turning Kolinsky's words over in his mind to make sure there were no hidden traps. "All right," he said. "If you can tell me what these things are, I'll put up wards that will last you six months, minimum."

"Excellent." Kolinsky opened a drawer and pulled out a clean sheet of paper and an exquisite fountain pen. "Tell me what you know of the creatures, and I shall get started on my research first thing tomorrow."

CHAPTER SEVENTEEN

SEVERAL VOICEMAIL MESSAGES awaited Stone when he got back to his office the following morning. This wasn't unusual—most were from students, Mortensen, and Hubbard, but one made him stop and pay closer attention.

The voice was young and male—maybe mid-twenties at most. "Dr. Stone? You don't know me, but my name's Chris Belmont. I'm a freelance journalist, and I'm doing a little piece on the Cannibal Killer for one of the local alternative papers. I'd really like to chat with you for a few minutes, if you have the time. I came by yesterday afternoon, but you weren't there. I got your office hours from your department secretary—I'll try coming by again at one o'clock today. I really hope you'll speak with me. I promise not to take more than a few minutes of your time." He hung up without leaving any contact information.

Stone stared at the phone after he hung it up, trying to decide whether he was impressed by the kid's technique or annoyed at his nerve. The last thing he wanted was to talk to anyone else about the night of Douglas Phelps's death, to go over the same ground again, but failing to show up for his office hour would make it seem like he was hiding from something—not to mention that it wasn't fair to any students who might legitimately come by to meet with him, since he'd blown off the one yesterday.

He took a detour to stop by the department office on his way to his first class. Another of the admin aides, a plump, cheerful woman in her early forties, was sorting through a large pile of papers. "Morning, Laura."

She looked up over the top of her glasses. "Oh, good morning, Dr. Stone. How are you today?" Like most of the faculty and support staff who didn't see him daily, ever since the Phelps incident she had been more careful than usual around him, as if afraid he might suffer a breakdown any moment from the cumulative horror of what he'd experienced.

"Fine, thanks. Did someone named Chris Belmont come by here yesterday looking for me?"

She thought about that. "Oh! Yes. He came in right before I was getting ready to leave, around four-thirty. You missed your office hour. Is everything okay?"

"Everything's fine. Did he say what he wanted?"

"No...just that he was trying to find you and you weren't in your office. I told him to come back today. That's not a problem, is it?" she added with sudden concern.

He waved it off. "No, no, not at all. Just curious. What did he look like?"

"He only stayed for a couple of minutes. Tall, thin, blond, wearing a hoodie...looked like a student, I guess. Sorry I can't be more help, but Dr. Tran came in right about then with this—" she indicated the stacks of papers, "—and the guy left after that."

"All right. Thank you, Laura." He left before she could ask any more questions.

For the rest of the day as he taught his classes, attended meetings, and grabbed a quick lunch at Union Square, his mind kept returning to Chris Belmont and his article. It seemed like a strange time to do a piece on the Cannibal Killer—there had already been extensive coverage both in the papers and on the local television news, including a couple write-ups in the *Stan-*

ford Daily following the death of the students' friend and then again after Stone himself had become involved. Was there anything else to say at this point that hadn't already been said?

The guy did say "alternative press," though, which might mean he had a different angle on the subject. Stone had seen issues of two or three different tabloid-size alt papers left around campus: most of them took a more progressive view than the more traditional ones, their back pages full of ads for dodgy escort services, strip clubs, and marijuana dispensaries.

Ah, well, he decided, it couldn't hurt to talk to the guy. If he got annoying or started asking too many nosy questions, Stone could just tell him he had another appointment and kick him out.

He was five minutes late getting back, held up by a student with a last-minute question. A young man, presumably Chris Belmont (at least he matched Lavonne's description) sat outside his door, long legs pulled up and a battered backpack on the floor next to him. He jumped up as Stone arrived. "Dr. Stone?"

"You must be Mr. Belmont." Stone unlocked his office and waved him in, looking him over as he himself followed, tossed his overcoat across his credenza, and sat down in his desk chair. "Have a seat."

His first impression of Belmont was that he was younger than he'd thought—he had the nervous, twitchy demeanor Stone associated with students, like he wasn't sure what he was doing was the right thing. He had lank blond hair that hung over his eyes, a pale complexion, long gangly limbs, and big hands and feet. As Lavonne had mentioned yesterday, he wore a hooded sweatshirt with a San Jose State University crest, and faded jeans.

"Thank you," Belmont said. He sat down and scrabbled in his backpack, pulling out a yellow legal pad and a ballpoint pen.

"I appreciate you talking to me. I promise I won't take much of your time."

Stone leaned back in his chair and tried not to wrinkle his nose. A slight unpleasant odor wafted from Belmont, like he hadn't showered or washed his clothes recently. That, too, was regrettably common among some subset of the students he taught, both here and in England.

"That's fine," he said. "Let's get on with this, though—I'm afraid I've got another appointment, so I can't chat for long." He glanced up, half-hoping that a student would appear in the doorway, but no such luck. "By the way, which paper did you say you were from?"

"I didn't," Belmont said. "I'm freelance—this is just a project of mine that I'm hoping to sell to one of the alts, like *City Beat* or the *Advance*." He scribbled something down on his pad, then looked back up at Stone. "So," he said, "hope you don't mind me getting right to it, but since you said you didn't have much time—"

"Go ahead."

"Okay." He shifted back in his chair a little and propped the pad in his lap. "Can you tell me about the night you were attacked in the park?"

"First of all, I wasn't attacked. I arrived after the attack had already started."

Belmont nodded, scribbling. "And what happened after that?"

"You can read all about it in the stories that already came out," Stone said, shrugging. "I yelled, and the attacker..." He stopped himself just before he said 'attackers'—the police still hadn't let on that there were more than one—"took off running. I didn't get a good look at him. Can't even be sure it was a man. Not completely."

"That must have been pretty awful," Belmont said. "And Mr. Phelps was still alive when you arrived?"

Stone narrowed his eyes. "I won't be talking about that part, Mr. Belmont. I'm sorry, but I don't think it's exactly proper to be spreading stories about a dead man's last moments just so your little paper can sell more ad space."

Belmont didn't appear offended. "No problem, I'm sorry. So you're saying that the attacker ran away when you yelled? You never got close to him? I heard that the lady—Mrs. Phelps—got pushed down."

"She was on the ground when I got there, yes. The attacker probably shoved her down and went for her husband first since he was the larger target. Who knows, though?"

"Okay." Belmont wrote something down, then looked up again. "So you didn't fight with the guy at all? No heroic rescue? Some of the stories I've been hearing say that you fought him off, made him run away."

Stone chuckled. "Look at me," he said, spreading his arms. "Do I look like the sort who could fight off a crazed cannibal?"

"You never know," Belmont said. "People can do some pretty amazing things when they don't have a choice."

"Well, that may be so, but I didn't do anything amazing. I just showed up at the right time."

"You did try to save Mr. Phelps, though, didn't you?"

Stone sighed. "I tried. Wasn't very successful, was I?"

"From what I heard, there wasn't really much you could do at that point. At least you saved Mrs. Phelps by showing up. That's worth a lot." He wrote something else down. "I don't really have a lot else to ask—I did say I wouldn't take much of your time. Just one more question, if that's okay?"

"Fine." Stone was glad the interview was short and already winding down—he was going to have to air the office out when Belmont left.

Belmont paused, obviously working out the best way to phrase his question. "Some people I talked to…and even some people in the other articles I read about the killer…speculated about it being some kind of supernatural creature. Since the occult's your field, I just wanted to get your take on it. Do you think it's something like that?"

Again, Stone chuckled. "Mr. Belmont, I do teach the occult, but that doesn't mean I believe in ghosts and werewolves and whatnot. I don't know who the killer is—I didn't get any kind of look at him—but my guess is that it's some psychopathic nutter who's broken out of a facility somewhere, or who had a mental breakdown at some point and started hunting humans. I've got no doubt the police will catch him before too much longer."

Belmont wrote that down, nodding, and stood up. "Thank you, Dr. Stone. Once again, I really appreciate your time. I know how busy you are."

"No problem. Give me a call when the article comes out, will you? I'd like to read it."

"*If* it comes out," Belmont said with a sheepish grin. "You can never count on that with freelance stuff."

After he left, Stone gave him a full minute before yanking open the office window. Seriously, how hard was it to take a quick shower in the morning?

CHAPTER EIGHTEEN

ONE MURDER WAS an isolated anomaly. Two were a coincidence. However, the addition of a third murder exhibiting the same pattern as the first two within less than three months elevated the whole thing from the subject of occasional discussion to a conversation topic nearly guaranteed to come up during any meeting of two or more people in the area from Palo Alto to San Jose. It wasn't quite a panic yet, but one or two more murders and it had a good chance of getting there.

They were still calling it the "Cannibal Killer," which told Stone that either the police hadn't gotten anywhere in their investigation, or they were still keeping the fact that there were multiple killers a secret in the hope of weeding out the inevitable cranks who called in to "confess" to the crimes.

In his classes, he could count on finding a group of students huddled together talking about the killings at least once a day. They usually cast furtive glances at him—by now it had spread far beyond his own department that he had been present at the third murder, and prevented a fourth—but it didn't take them long to catch on to the fact that any attempt to discuss the incident with him was met with polite but firm misdirection. Eventually even the most persistent among them gave up.

The local Palo Alto newspaper, the television news broadcasts, and the Stanford paper all ran frequent public-service announcements from the police departments throughout the area. They warned people not to go out alone at night, especially in unpopulated areas, unless absolutely necessary, and to remain vigilant to their surroundings at all times. Stone noticed when he walked back to his office from his classes that he was one of the few who did so alone. Even some of the macho athlete types had taken to traveling in packs. It made sense, given that so far two of the three victims had been male.

Tension ran high by the time Stone got another hand-delivered letter from Kolinsky. It was only a couple of days before the campus closed down for the Thanksgiving holiday, and many of the students were already mentally checking out as they prepared to head home for the week off.

Kolinsky's message arrived one evening as Stone was returning home from work, and suggested they meet for lunch the next day. Stone thought it an odd request, but if Kolinsky had found something, Stone would have met him at the top of the Stanford clock tower.

Kolinsky wasn't there when Stone arrived at the elegant little café on Emerson, just off University, but he arrived a few minutes later. He refused to say anything beyond mild pleasantries until after they had secured a bottle of wine and given the waitress their orders. Stone did a good job hiding his impatience, but only for so long.

"So," he said, watching Kolinsky swirl the wine in his glass. "Have you got something for me?"

"Yes and no."

"What's that mean?" He glanced around to make sure no one was watching them, but the place was so busy at lunchtime that the general murmur of conversation blended with their own. "Do you know what they are, or not?"

"No. Not precisely. But I do have some information for you." He raised his hand as Stone started to speak. "You have no obligation as yet. I am still pursuing some leads. But I wanted to pass along what I've found in case it might assist your own research."

"All right, then: let's hear it."

"First, the police have no leads. They are still convinced they are seeking mundane killers, of course, but they have had no success in tracing any DNA evidence found at the scenes of the crimes."

Stone frowned. "That seems odd. The victims were eaten. That implies quite a lot of saliva, doesn't it?"

"Presumably, yes. But all of their DNA tests have come back inconclusive."

"What do you mean by 'inconclusive'? They can't find any matches?"

"They can't isolate any usable samples."

Stone didn't bother to ask how Kolinsky knew this. It didn't matter. Either the man was lying to him, or he had ways of getting the information. For now, Stone went with the latter. "Does that suggest anything to you?"

"Only that you are almost certainly correct that the killers are some sort of supernatural beings, and not mundane humans."

"I already knew that," Stone said impatiently. "So what sorts of supernatural beings around here kill people and eat them?"

"That is the difficult question. As far as I know, there aren't any such creatures native to this area. The murders have only started in the last two to three months, suggesting that something has recently arrived in the area."

"Or been summoned to it," Stone added.

"Or that." Kolinsky swirled his wineglass again, took a sip, and nodded appreciatively. "An excellent vintage."

Stone, whose tastes ran more to Guinness than white wine, nodded. "Anything else?"

"Not at present. But as I said, I do have some discreet inquiries out. I expect I will hear more within the week. Check back with me after the holiday weekend."

"Well, it's something, I suppose." He glanced up. "What about things that *aren't* native to this area? If something's arrived recently, it must have come from somewhere."

Kolinsky shrugged. "Any number of creatures hunt human prey, but most of them are quite rare, and generally keep to areas of low population. As I mentioned at our first meeting, my fields of interest generally focus on magic and its practice and practitioners, so I haven't done an exhaustive study on cannibalistic supernatural creatures. I will, of course, pass on anything I find as soon as possible." He raised an eyebrow and took another sip of wine. "I have ulterior motives: my wards are beginning to lose potency."

They didn't discuss the Cannibal Killer over the remainder of lunch. Stone picked up the check and Kolinsky didn't object.

On his way back to Stanford, his mind turned over possibilities, and by the time he reached his office, Stone had come to a couple of conclusions. The first was that he would finally need to get on about finding the local teleportation portal. If the creatures didn't originate in the area, there was a chance he might find something in his extensive magical library back home to give him a clue. He did owe Aubrey a visit, and the Thanksgiving holiday would be an ideal time to plan one.

He just hoped the Cannibal Killer wouldn't strike again while he was gone.

CHAPTER NINETEEN

WHEN STONE FOUND OUT where the portal was located, he decided that someone must be having a good joke.

He drove down to Sunnyvale, a pleasant bedroom community about twenty miles south of Palo Alto, that weekend. He was getting better at navigating American roads by now: he no longer engaged the windshield wipers instead of the turn signal, and he'd only made one potentially disastrous left turn recently when he'd allowed his mind to wander during one of his favorite Pink Floyd songs on the radio (the oncoming driver had waved what he thought was an admonitory finger at him—only later did he remember that the middle digit in America didn't mean the same thing as it did in Britain).

He found the place with little trouble and pulled the car into a space in the small car park (*parking lot*—he was still working on the local terminology) behind it. He hadn't called ahead.

Apparently it wasn't a joke: the place really was called *A Passage to India*. It was a small, well-kept Indian restaurant in the middle of a block full of trendy cafés, pubs, and nightclubs. Stone had deliberately chosen to arrive as they were opening at eleven a.m., both because he didn't want to deal with a potential lunch rush and because, with the eight-hour time difference between California and England, he didn't want to arrive home in the middle of the night.

As he'd hoped, the restaurant was empty except for a tall, somewhat horse-faced woman sitting at one of the rearmost tables. She appeared to be marking up a copy of the menu, but she looked up when Stone entered. "Welcome," she said. "Please, sit anywhere you like."

Stone's eyes widened. Her accent was British: the Leeds area, if he wasn't mistaken. "Thank you," he said. "Nice to hear a voice from home."

The woman smiled; her oversized teeth contributed to her equine appearance, but her eyes sparkled with good humor. "Indeed it is," she said. "How did you hear about us?"

"Well, that's the thing." Stone didn't sit down. "I'm not actually here for lunch. I'm more interested in…travel." He studied her face as he said it, to see if there was any reaction. He couldn't tell if she was a mage: it wasn't possible for them to recognize each other, even using magical sight, unless they had recently done something magical that left an auric residue. He wondered how he'd explain his odd remarks if his intel had been incorrect and this *wasn't* the location of the portal.

"Ah," she said, getting up. "You'll want to talk to David about that. If you'll wait here, I'll get him for you."

She disappeared through a beaded curtain in the rear of the restaurant. Stone barely had time to examine the impressive mural of Ganesh on the wall before the curtain rustled again. The woman came back through, followed by a balding man who was both shorter and wider than she was.

"Hello!" he called. "Marta tells me you're a fellow countryman." His accent was British too, though further south than the woman's. "I'm David Halloran. This is my partner, Marta Bellwood."

"Alastair Stone," Stone said. "Pleasure."

"Indeed it is!" He waved at the curtain they'd come through. "I understand you need to take a trip. You must be new around here, or else you don't travel much. I'd have remembered a fellow Englishman coming 'round."

"Fairly new, yes. Been here a couple of months now. I'm teaching up at Stanford."

"Really? Wouldn't have expected that. At any rate, you picked a good time to come down. Place will be packed in an hour. If you'll just come with me, I'll show you our...facilities."

He led Stone through the beaded curtain and down a hallway past a kitchen from which enticing aromas emanated. Stone noticed Marta didn't follow them. "So, are both of you—"

"Oh, no. Just me. But Marta's used to the whole routine by now, so if I'm not here, you can feel secure in dealing with her." David glanced around to make sure no one was watching, then made a small gesture and a door appeared in what had formerly been a blank wall. He opened it and waved Stone in.

"This is a bit odd," Stone said as they descended a short staircase that ended at another door. "I don't think I've ever seen a portal in a restaurant before."

"This place used to be a mundane magic shop—you know, the top-hat-and-rabbit variety—many years ago," David said. "After the owner died, Marta and I took it over, but since the shop was doing poorly we decided to refit the place and re-open it as a restaurant."

"And this is the only portal in the area?"

"It is. They keep talking about building another one up in the City, but you know how that goes."

Stone did. Permanent teleportation portals were prohibitively expensive to build, even if you could find someone with the expertise to do it. Generally new ones were only built when a large group of mages in a geographical area could get together and sort out the cost and the logistics of doing so. And since getting mages to agree on *anything* was only slightly easier than Middle East peace talks, Stone understood why it had never happened.

"So, where are you going? London?" David made a complicated gesture at the door and it swung open. Behind it was a small room, occupied only by the swirling, multi-hued form of the teleportation portal. Roughly seven feet in diameter and circular, it hung in the middle of the room with no frame or other structure supporting it. Its colors shifted through the spectrum, vivid and alive with energy.

Despite its ethereal beauty, Stone barely glanced at it. He'd seen and traveled through enough portals in his magical career that they no longer held any special allure for him. "Close. I've got a private portal back home. Need to pick up a few things."

David whistled. "Really? A private portal? Nice. Not many of those around these days."

"It's been in the family a long time. Most people don't know about it, since the one in London is so close, but..." He shrugged. "What can I say? It saves me the train ride."

"Well, you're welcome to use this one whenever you like. If you travel often, we'll see about getting you a key to the place so you can get to it when we're closed."

"Brilliant, thanks," Stone said, nodding. "Just let me know what I need to do to chip in for upkeep and whatnot. I expect I'll be popping home whenever I can get away. Which I doubt will be as often as I like."

"Oh, we can deal with that some other time," David said cheerfully. "I'll leave you to it, then—sounds like you know what you're doing. Just be sure to lock up if you come back when the place is closed. Alarm code is 7337."

It took Stone only a few moments to calibrate the portal to point at its counterpart back home. He took a few deep breaths to center himself, and then stepped inside.

| CHAPTER TWENTY

ONE OF THE THINGS that mages didn't usually talk about was that nobody liked the Overworld. It was a necessary evil, a convenient way for them to make journeys of great distances in a short time, but Stone had never met anyone who referred to the trip as "fun" or "pleasurable."

He paused a moment to get his bearings after stepping through. Around him, hazy fog swirled in what looked like a tunnel made of ragged gray cotton. A pathway stretched out in front of him with no landmarks or light, but yet the way forward wasn't dark, either. Far in the distance, black *things* moved this way and that like patrolling fish.

Nobody knew what these things were, but everybody who traveled the Overworld knew they were dangerous. A lot of mages refused to even use the portals, not trusting themselves to maintain the calm required to avoid attracting the things' notice. It was one of the first lessons new apprentices were taught, before they were allowed anywhere near a portal: never enter one when angry, disturbed, drunk, or otherwise not mentally composed. Attempts to study the Overworld and why any sort of excessive emotion drew the things like a beacon had been unsuccessful; a few mages had tried, but they'd either never returned or been driven insane.

Still, if you could keep your wits about you and move at a steady pace, the Overworld was safe enough and it was undoubtedly worth the effort, especially when you had to get somewhere in a hurry. After one near-disastrous trip during his apprenticeship, Stone had learned many years ago to control his emotions sufficiently that the Overworld's denizens didn't find him tasty. By now, using the portals to travel halfway around the world fazed him no more than boarding a commuter train into London.

He walked briskly forward, his gaze and his attention focused fully on the far-off dark area that represented the other end of his journey. His feet made no sound on ground that was solid but springy, as if he were crossing a firm mattress, or a forest floor covered in a thick carpet of moist, dead leaves. His mind was calm; the creatures swirled around in the fog but continued on their own inexplicable errands and didn't approach him. When he felt himself tensing (it was almost inevitable—the place was damned unsettling even if you'd been through it as many times as Stone had), he quieted his mind by repeating complex magical formulae under his breath as he kept walking. His voice came out inflectionless, dead, without any hint of nuance or reverberation.

The trip took about five minutes total. Even the longest of Overworld journeys, from one side of the Earth to the other, never lasted longer than ten minutes, which was good because spending much more time than that there was enough to drive even the sanest mage to take unwise chances. Back at A Passage to India, Stone had set the portal so it pointed at his own private one back home—it was sort of like routing one of those old-fashioned air-powered message tube systems you'd see occasionally in very old buildings. Once you set the destination, there was no way to get lost. You simply entered at one end and walked until you came out the other end. No thought or navigation required. If you entered a portal without calibrating it, you ended up wherever the last traveller had pointed it. Stone himself had never done this, but he'd once heard a story of a young mage fresh out of his apprenticeship who had entered a portal in Boston expecting to come out in the Bodleian Library in Oxford, and instead had found himself in the basement of a disreputable little shop somewhere in Moscow.

The exit loomed large now, a roughly circular space made of darker clouds than the rest of the Overworld. When he crossed it, he felt a brief rippling sensation, somewhat like stepping through a curtain charged with a faint electrical current, and then he was on the other side.

He emerged in darkness, and immediately summoned a light spell around his hand. The spell illuminated a small room with rough walls made of gray stone blocks, a heavy wooden table and chair near one of the walls, and a small bookcase with a few tomes stacked haphazardly on its shelves. On the far wall was a wooden door clad with stout iron bands.

Stone didn't pause; all of this was as familiar to him as anything else at his home. He crossed to the door, opened it with a simple spell, and pulled on a rope that lowered a set of wooden stairs leading to a rectangular hole in the ceiling roughly seven feet long by three feet wide.

At the top of the ladder he used magic to shove aside a heavy stone cover, then climbed up and out and replaced the cover behind him. It was probably a good thing that most people didn't know about his family's old private portal, because even mages who were old hands at traveling in this manner might find emerging from a crypt into a mausoleum a little creepy. Stone himself thought it was amusing, and that it would make a great site for some kind of vampire-related prank if he ever felt compelled to come up with one. The portal, built in his grandfather's day, had been put here to hide it from prying eyes, and it had worked: so far nobody had ever located it. But even he had to admit that the whole thing was a bit over the top.

After another spell to unlock the outer door, he stood in the middle of a small cemetery. Stone shone his magical light around, taking in the thirty-odd headstones that were slowly being reclaimed by overgrown vegetation. Behind him, the mausoleum loomed tall and ominous, the only structure of its kind in the area. A low rock wall provided a boundary, and a dirt path, only slightly less overgrown, led up in the direction of a massive old house across a field to the south.

It was in that direction that Stone headed, making a mental note to ask Aubrey to hire someone to cut down the weeds in the cemetery. The caretaker himself would insist that he was up to the task, but there was only so much time in the day and Aubrey wasn't getting any younger.

Stone had called ahead to tell Aubrey he was coming, so the perimeter lights were blazing around the front part of the house. He stopped a moment to take it in. It hadn't quite sunk in how much he'd missed the place until he came back. As crumbling and in need of repair as it was, it had been his home for almost the entirety of his life, and his own property since his father's death. He wished that it was possible to reveal his magical abilities so he could commute to Stanford from here, but given the British and American governments' shared love of pointless bureaucracy, even the passport issue would probably prove so frustrating that it would outweigh any benefits. And that was even leaving out the whole "magic" thing. No, he'd just have to settle for popping home now and then, and not letting himself be seen in England by anybody but Aubrey and other mages.

"Dr. Stone, is that you?"

Stone snapped out of his thoughts to see that the front door had opened and Aubrey was hurrying down the steps in his direction.

"Sorry I'm so late," he called back. "Had to sort out the local portal, and they didn't open until eleven."

Aubrey hustled him inside and insisted on fixing him a cup of tea and a ham and Branston pickle sandwich, even after he insisted he wasn't hungry. "Aubrey, really, I'm fine. You've probably got more important things to do than look after me this time of night. I'll be fine."

"Nonsense, sir. It's no trouble at all. You're staying for the week, then, I hope?"

He hadn't specified it on the phone because he wasn't sure of his plans, but it wasn't like he had anything to do—or anyone to do it with—back in Palo Alto. "Yes, yes, I'm staying. But I'm serious—don't put yourself out on my account. I need to hunt up some books, so I'll be down in the library for a good part of the day tomorrow. Aside from that, I don't plan on doing much of anything. Might go into London for a bit to chat with Eddie Monkton tomorrow or Wednesday." Eddie was an old colleague who looked after an unofficial library full of magical tomes and academic papers. If Stone couldn't find what he was looking for in his own library, that would be his next stop.

"Well, it's good to see you, sir. I thought I'd see to picking up what we'd need for a proper American Thanksgiving dinner tomorrow, unless you've other plans. I was just going to head up to the pub if you weren't coming, but it will be good to cook for someone again. If there are any other friends you'd like to invite, just tell me who and I'll see to that as well."

Stone didn't even bother trying to talk him out of it. Aubrey had been an honorary part of his family since before Stone was born, acting as caretaker for the rambling old structure as far back as his father's day. His fondest desire in life was to make himself useful. Stone had to admit that a home-cooked American-style Thanksgiving dinner would be infinitely preferable to another night of takeaway in his study back in California. "Just let me know if there's anything I can do to help."

"That's...quite all right, sir. I'll manage."

Stone chuckled. "Go ahead and say it: 'stay away from my kitchen, since we both know you'll burn the water or cut your hand off or something.'"

"I didn't say that, sir." His tone, however, suggested that they both knew he didn't have to. He paused a moment. "Oh, there's one other thing," he said. "William Desmond called again yesterday. He asked if you'd be home this week, and mentioned that he'd like to see you if you have time."

Stone poked at his sandwich, suddenly even less hungry than he'd been. He knew it would happen eventually; there was only so long he could avoid Desmond. He just hoped the man only wanted to catch up about magic, and not about Imogen. It had taken him several days after her call last month before he could get her out of his mind again, and reopening old wounds wasn't on his to-do list for the holiday.

His library, he discovered the next day when he roused himself from bed far earlier than he preferred and headed down to the basement, was woefully silent regarding supernatural threats native to the western United States.

It wasn't a big surprise. The collection was impressive by any standards, dating back through several generations of mages and including everything from ancient tomes to rare volumes that, should he ever decide to put them on the market and find the right buyer, could probably net him enough funds to completely renovate the house.

Not that he ever would, of course. Like most mages of his particular school of the Art, Stone regarded knowledge as the most valuable thing he could possess, far more than money or other material goods. He suspected it was the reason why he'd felt an immediate kinship with Stefan Kolinsky, despite their diametrically opposed personal philosophies on magic's practice.

As impressive as the library was, though, its contents concentrated largely on magical esoterica, rituals, formulae, and other practical aspects. There were some history books, of course, along with biographies of famous practitioners and a few thick tomes covering magical phenomena through the ages, but most of the latter focused on Europe. There was simply too much to be learned about the study and practice of the Art for any mortal mage to master it all in even the extended lifespans they usually enjoyed, so Stone had chosen to specialize in practical magic in the classical European hermetic paradigm. That left big gaps in his knowledge, and unfortunately for him at the moment, supernatural creatures were one of those gaps.

He spent nearly three hours hunting for anything that might be useful, but by almost eleven a.m. he had to admit with reluctance that he wasn't going to find what he was looking for. He levitated himself back to the floor from a promising stack of books balanced precariously on a shelf fifteen feet up, ran his hand through his hair, and murmured the spells to return the others to their proper places without conscious thought.

By the time he headed back to his upstairs bedroom suite, showered, and dressed in fresh clothes, it was nearly noon. He set off in search of Aubrey, wondering if there were any leftovers he could raid.

The old caretaker was in the kitchen, putting away the dishes from the previous night and wiping down the countertops. "Ah, sir," he said. He looked apologetic. "I'm afraid Mr. Desmond called again. He's invited you to dinner tonight at his home."

Stone paused in the act of digging in the refrigerator and sighed. "All right," he said, resigned. He found the other half of last night's sandwich and a Guinness, and carried them to the kitchen table. "Thank you, Aubrey. I suppose I might as well get it over with, then. I'll call him today. I need to go talk to Eddie anyway, so I'll be in London."

Aubrey put away his rag and eyed Stone for a moment as if trying to decide whether to say something. Finally, he said, "Are you...all right, sir?"

Stone put down the sandwich. "Of course I am. Why wouldn't I be?"

"No reason. You just seem—a bit obsessed."

"That's hardly unusual, is it?"

"No...but I just haven't seen you quite so preoccupied lately. Is it Miss Desmond?"

"No. Yes...I don't know. Perhaps a bit, but it's really more that I'm trying to track down some information I need, and I'm not finding it. Remember I mentioned the cannibal killer?"

"You said that one of your students' friends was a victim, if I recall correctly."

Stone nodded. "It's gotten worse, though." Sandwich forgotten, he caught Aubrey up on the situation as it stood today, including his presence at both Douglas Phelps's last moments and his funeral.

Aubrey's eyes widened. "That's horrible," he said. He paused, and when he spoke again, his tone was careful. "But, sir...it sounds like there was nothing more you could have done. You saved that woman's life. I hardly think it's down to you to catch the killers. That's the police's job, isn't it?"

"Aubrey, I don't know what these things are, but they're not human. Not completely. Do you honestly think the police will have a prayer of finding them if they don't want to be found?

They've already killed at least three people—and those are just the ones that have turned up."

"But—"

"But nothing." Stone shoved the plate containing the rest of the sandwich away. "Even if the police do manage to corner them in the act, I don't know what they're capable of. They might have run away because they recognized I was a mage. If that's so, then the police will be walking into a deathtrap. At least if I can get some sort of idea of what they are, I might be able to—"

"To what, sir?" Aubrey asked quietly. "Are you planning to go to the police and tell them how you know that the creatures aren't human? Do you think they'll believe you? And what if they do? Won't that cause all sorts of problems for you?"

Stone lowered his head, scrubbing at his hair with both hands until it stood up. "I don't know, Aubrey. I don't know. I just feel like I have to do *something*. Otherwise aren't I partially responsible if anyone else gets killed?"

He flung himself up from the table before Aubrey could answer. "Ah, bugger, I don't know. I just want to find out what I'm dealing with. Once I know that, I'll go from there. Don't wait up for me—if I know old Desmond, he'll keep me there half the night. I might just stay over in London and come back in the morning."

CHAPTER TWENTY-ONE

STONE SLOUCHED INTO ONE CORNER of the backseat of a black cab and tried to convince himself that his steadily growing headache was merely psychosomatic.

It was almost seven o'clock. The cab crawled through the traffic-choked streets of London; all around, dazzling headlights flared bright flashes into the oily puddles on the streets. A morose, sleety rain fell, as it had been doing for most of the day.

He'd spent the better part of the afternoon with Eddie Monkton at the unremarkable brick terraced house near Hackney that hid one of the finest and most comprehensive repositories of magical scholarship in Europe. Between the two of them they'd come up with nothing useful.

That wasn't entirely true, actually: they'd come up with quite a lot of things that were potentially useful. Almost too many, in fact, though none of them matched up closely enough with what Stone knew to be the facts to give him any real confidence that he had his answer.

"Sorry, mate," Eddie, a slim, cheerful man with a thick Cockney accent that tended to make people underestimate his keen intelligence, had told him when he'd finally been forced to give up or risk arriving late to his dinner appointment with Desmond. "'Fraid we're a bit light on North American supernatural beasties 'round these parts."

Stone nodded, stowing his notebook away in the pocket of his overcoat. "Thanks, Eddie. I appreciate the help, and in any case it was good to see you. It's been too long."

"Ring me next time you're in town and we'll have a pint. I'll keep looking, and send along anything else I find."

Now in the cab and getting close to Desmond's Regent's Park home, a bottle of vintage Chateau Mouton-Rothschild on the seat next to him, Stone was momentarily amused by the thought of what might happen if the cab were in an accident and the emergency personnel got a look inside his notebook. *Cannibalistic creatures of NW USA*, the heading read in his nearly illegible scrawl. What followed was a list several items long, some crossed out and others with question marks next to them:

- ~~*Wendigo*~~

- *Werewolf (?)*

- *Skinwalker (?)*

- *Ghoul (?)*

- ~~*Cannibal Dwarf*~~ *(?!)*

That last one had convinced Stone that he was grasping at straws and that it was time to pack it in. Sure, they were a legitimate—albeit obscure—Native American legend and therefore as potentially valid as any of the others, but firstly the creatures he'd seen had been far too large to classify as any sort of dwarf, and secondly, the Native tribes from which the legends originated didn't come from anywhere near northern California. Even if the dwarves existed, he doubted they'd had a sudden desire to pick up stakes and relocate West.

The others were a bit more promising, particularly ghouls and skinwalkers, but neither fit the profile of what Stone had seen the night of Douglas Phelps's death. Skinwalkers were exceedingly rare—there had been no documented sightings of even one in at least a hundred years, let alone four of them—and every case he and Eddie could discover indicated that they always worked alone.

Ghouls, by contrast, were known to hunt in packs, but they almost never went after living prey. Instead, they staked out remote cemeteries and culled the meat they needed from freshly buried corpses. Once again there hadn't been any documented cases, but there *had* been enough mysterious grave robberies and possible sightings over the years in less-populated areas that they represented the most plausible possibility among known supernatural creatures. Stone made a mental note to check with Kolinsky when he got back to the States, and to do more research into ghouls' nature and reasons why they might start hunting live prey.

The cab pulled off the road and double-parked in front of an elegant four-story building on Hanover Terrace. Stone got out, paid the driver, and deployed his black umbrella as the cab rumbled back off into the stream of traffic. For a moment he just stood there on the sidewalk in front of the building, taking deep breaths and straightening the lines of his overcoat and suit. Normally he wouldn't have dressed up quite so much, but in light of recent events he'd decided that there was likely to be enough tension as it was without contributing to it.

The door was answered promptly by a livery-clad servant—Desmond always had tended toward the old-fashioned. "Evening, sir. He's expecting you," the man said as he stepped aside to let Stone in.

Stone crossed the familiar lobby toward elegant stairway without really seeing it; he'd been here scores of times over the past fifteen years, and had even lived here for a while during the early part of his apprenticeship. The building was old, immaculately kept, and home to only three other residents aside from Desmond, who had the top two floors to himself and quite probably owned the entire place through some byzantine series of holding companies.

Stone didn't know exactly how wealthy Desmond was, but like himself, his master came from a very old British magical family. There weren't many of those left anymore; despite the fact that the Talent was passed along gender lines (female mages passed it to daughters, male mages to sons), it couldn't be counted on to pass reliably and often didn't. Sometimes it disappeared entirely, and at that point the family became just another mundane clan with gradually receding memories of what they once were. Stone himself was somewhat of an oddity, the fifth in an unbroken male line of mages. That didn't happen often. Desmond had never discussed his own history, but Stone suspected his master's line went back even further than his own did.

He mounted the stairs to the third floor, where an open chamber carpeted in plush red was dominated to the left and right by magnificent oil paintings and on the opposite wall by an ornate wooden door. Stone's ring was answered in less than a minute by a somber man clad in an old-fashioned suit. "Dr. Stone. Good evening. May I take your coat?"

"Hello, Kerrick. Good to see you." He shrugged out of his overcoat, handed it over along with his umbrella and the bottle of wine, and followed the other man down a hallway into a large room. He barely registered it: nothing had changed in all the years he'd been coming here, and he doubted it ever would. Same simple but opulent furnishings of heavy, dark wood; same antique globe showing various magically interesting spots around the world; same carefully assembled skeleton of a panther-like creature not known to mundane science; same thick drapes and candle-filled chandeliers, no doubt lit by magic since they were too high up for it to be practical to light them any other way. Stepping into this place was like stepping back in time a hundred years.

William Desmond turned as Stone came in. "Alastair. I'm so glad you could make it." He indicated one of the sofas. "Please, sit down. Dinner will be served shortly. Would you like something to drink?" His voice was a rich baritone, welcoming but measured.

"No. Thank you. And thank you for the invitation." Stone settled himself at one end of the sofa, but didn't allow himself to get too comfortable.

The first time people met Desmond in person, they tended to think he was abnormally tall. In reality, he was a little under six feet, but he had a master thespian's ability to dominate any room he occupied. He had broad shoulders, a narrow waist, and steel-gray hair elegantly swept back from a high forehead. His eyes were a piercing pale blue, missing nothing beneath strong brows.

He was almost certainly one of the most powerful mages currently alive on the planet. In all the time the two of them had associated, from his apprenticeship through their shared magical research, Stone had never once seen him smile.

"You're well, I trust?" Desmond asked. He had crossed the room and was pouring himself something from a decanter on a tray. "And you're sure you won't have a drink?"

Stone shook his head. "I'm fine."

"Settling in over there in America?"

Stone couldn't quite work out the odd tone in his voice. "For the most part. It's been an adjustment, but I do like the students."

"And how are they adjusting to you?" Desmond brought his drink back over and sat down opposite Stone. "I'd imagine you're quite different from what they're accustomed to."

Stone chuckled. "The students like me just fine. Can't say the same for the faculty, though."

"I assume that they don't possess the Talent."

"No. Though one of them does claim to be psychic."

Desmond sighed, his disapproval clear. "I've heard that about Americans. It seems you can't turn around over there without encountering someone who claims to have mystical abilities."

They chatted for a few minutes without saying much. Stone inquired about how Desmond's magical research was going and sat back to let him hold forth; he did this on purpose because it was the easiest way to keep Desmond from asking too many questions about his own activities, and more importantly, about his reasons for leaving the UK so abruptly. Stone was quite certain Desmond knew what those reasons were, but that didn't mean he wanted them brought up as the subject for mealtime discussion.

After about twenty minutes, Kerrick appeared in the doorway. "Gentlemen, dinner is served."

"Excellent. Thank you, Kerrick." Desmond rose with surprising grace for a man his age. He paused a moment, waiting for the servant to leave, then started out of the room toward the dining room, motioning for Stone to follow. When they reached the end of another hall lined with elaborately carved marble urns, he paused in the doorway.

"Alastair, I apologize for not telling you, and I hope you won't mind, but we've another guest for dinner tonight. I tried to reach you earlier today, but you were unavailable."

"Oh? Why should I mind?" Another dinner guest wouldn't necessarily be a bad thing: the more people to spread the conversation among, the less likely that Desmond would bring up anything Stone would prefer not to talk about.

"Yes. She arrived late this afternoon, and I could hardly send her away."

Stone froze. "She?" He glanced into the dimly lit dining room and spotted a slim, shadowy figure seated on the other side of the table.

No. He can't. He wouldn't...

"Alastair. Hello."

CHAPTER TWENTY-TWO

SHE HALF-ROSE IN HER SEAT when Stone appeared. In her cream-colored sweater and fashionable dusty-blue scarf, she looked very young and quite apologetic.

"I'm so sorry for crashing your and Dad's dinner party. I was in town and popped in on a whim. I had no idea Dad had…plans." She hovered there, half-sitting, half-standing, her hands gripping the edge of the table. "I could go if you like. I know this is a bit…awkward."

"Imogen." Stone realized he was standing dead still. He forced himself to relax, and even managed to call up a smile. "No, of course you won't leave. It's good to see you." He cut his gaze sideways to Desmond next to him, but the older man's expression was unreadable as always. If he'd planned this, he was hiding it well.

"Well, then, it's settled," Desmond said, taking his seat at the head of the table and waving Stone toward one across from Imogen. The table was formally set with fine china, silver, and crystal. Stone took rather more time than he could have shaking out his heavy cloth napkin as a pair of servants came in bearing trays, bottles of wine, and carafes of ice water.

Desmond waited until they departed before speaking. "How is Aubrey?"

"He's well," Stone said. "Bit lonely, I think, rambling around the place on his own."

"I suppose he might be," Desmond agreed. "First time you've been away so long since University, isn't it?"

Imogen shifted in her seat and became very interested in her soup.

Desmond either wasn't getting the hint, or he was and didn't care. His hawklike gaze came up and fixed on his daughter. "You haven't told me why you haven't brought—what was his name again?"

"Robert," she said under her breath.

Stone looked back and forth between them, surprised to see Imogen's brown eyes flashing.

"Robert," Desmond repeated, nodding. "Why haven't you ever brought him around with you?"

"He's off on business," she said without looking up. Stone didn't miss the irritation in her tone. "He'll be back tomorrow."

"I see," Desmond said. "Alastair, I don't mind admitting I've missed you around here. Been getting nowhere with that transformation formula we were working on before you left. I've got Hornsby picking up the slack, but he's rubbish. Sloppy training, no discipline." He took a long drink from his wineglass. "Discipline's dying these days. Nobody has the will to learn magic properly anymore, let alone teach it." With sudden sharpness, his head jerked up. "Have you any plans to take on an apprentice?"

Stone shook his head. "Not...presently, no." He hadn't touched his soup yet.

"You're more than due for it, you know. What are you now, almost thirty?" When Stone didn't answer, he continued, "Long past time, especially given how young you were when you started. Haven't they got anyone with proper Talent over there in America?"

"I haven't looked," Stone said. "I've been busy settling in at Stanford. It's quite a bit larger than the program at Buckingham."

Desmond snorted. "Don't know why you bother teaching mundanes anyway. Always wondered that. You've got such potential, Alastair. Finest apprentice I ever had, and yet you spend your time convincing mundanes that everything we do is some sort of charade."

It was an old argument, and had about the same chance of getting anywhere tonight as it had all the other times Desmond had brought it up. Stone's shoulders ached with knotted tension, and any appetite had long since deserted him. "With all due respect, I don't think that's something we need to be discussing right now. For one thing, I'm sure it's quite boring for Imogen, listening to us go on."

She shot Stone a look that was almost as hard to read as her father's, but she did look like she'd rather be just about anywhere else but here.

"Yes, I suppose you're right," Desmond conceded, a bit grudgingly. "I apologize, Imogen."

The rest of the meal passed with somewhat less overt stress, but by the time they had retired back to the big sitting room, all settled in their chairs and sipping an excellent after-dinner liqueur, Stone's back and neck had both joined his shoulders in tightening up, and the nascent headache he'd had in the cab had blossomed into a full-blown throbbing distraction.

Under cover of contemplating a second glass of liqueur, he studied Desmond and Imogen. They were currently engaged in what the casual observer would take to be a genteel discussion involving Imogen's plans for the Christmas holiday (Desmond wanted her to come home *sans* Robert, while she made it clear that the two of them had already arranged to spend the holiday at his family's home in Devon).

Stone knew better, though: he had enough experience with both Desmond and Imogen that he could see the potential incipient flare-up coming a mile away.

Imogen apparently did too, because she glared at her father and shook her head. "I'm not talking about this right now," she said. "We can discuss it later. It's terribly rude to discuss family matters in front of Alastair."

Never mind that up until a few months ago, the plan had been for Stone to become part of the family. Never mind that he'd spent more time in Desmond's company over the past several years than she had.

Inexplicably, her words stung him. "You know," he said, "I should be going anyway. Promised Aubrey I'd help him with clearing the gutters tomorrow, since he's getting a bit unsteady on the ladder." He moved to stand. "Thank you so much for a lovely dinner. It was delicious, and it was good to see you both. We'll have to do it again some time." *Some time in the next decade would be about right.*

To his credit, Desmond didn't try to stop him. "Thank you for coming. I was hoping to get a chance to consult with you on that transformation, but I know how busy you are and I need to drum it into Hornsby's head in any case. The boy will never amount to anything if he doesn't push himself harder." He rose gracefully from his chair and set his glass on the table. "I'll have Kerrick get your coat and I'll see you out."

"Let me," Imogen said, also rising. "I'd like a moment with Alastair before he goes, if it's all right with you."

It clearly wasn't, but Desmond was far too good a host to show it. He sat back down and reclaimed his glass. "Be well, then, Alastair."

Imogen was silent until they got to the ground floor, drifting along beside him as if deep in thought. He shrugged into his overcoat and paused in the lobby, waiting for her to speak.

"I'm so sorry," she said, reaching out to touch his arm in a tentative, birdlike gesture. "I swear to you, I didn't know you were coming. He didn't tell me. He didn't even know *I* was coming until this afternoon."

He nodded. She could never lie to him; he didn't even have to look at her aura to see that she was telling the truth. "It sounds like your father isn't fond of Robert," he said in a neutral tone.

She searched his face for a moment, as if trying to find hidden motives in his words. "He isn't," she said at last, dropping her gaze. "It's nothing against Robert, mind you. It's just that he's not…well, you."

Stone raised an eyebrow. "I never got the impression your father thought of me as anything beyond a protégé." Despite his and Imogen's half-spoken plans, he'd never brought up the subject directly with Desmond. He certainly wasn't the old-fashioned sort who would consider asking for Imogen's hand in marriage, even though Desmond probably would have approved of the gesture. Desmond knew about them, of course—it had been hard not to, there for a while—and made it clear that he not only approved, but actively supported the liaison, but they hadn't discussed any of their plans with him. They were adults, which in Stone's mind meant that the whole thing wasn't anyone's business but theirs, at least not until they'd made it official. It appeared he had avoided that potentially landmine-fraught discussion, if nothing else.

She offered a faint smile. "I told you before—you were the son he never had. He's tremendously proud of you. He's just not very good at showing it. As I'm sure you well know."

"Hadn't noticed," he said. "So…you and Robert—have you made anything official yet?" It wasn't any of his business, of course, but after the evening's fiasco he felt that she had no right to protest.

"Not yet," she said, shaking her head. She rubbed at the bridge of her nose. "He's so busy with the restaurant—he's trying to open another one in the West End, so he's been busy quite a bit lately. " She paused, and didn't meet his gaze. "What about you? Have you…met anyone, over there in America?"

"No. Been…a bit busy myself, with this and that." He remembered then that he'd planned to ask Desmond what he knew about cannibalistic entities, but between his growing headache and Imogen's unexpected arrival, it had slipped his mind. Too late now—he was hardly prepared to go back up there after making his exit.

Her eyes glittered in the chandelier's flickering glow. "I hope you do. I really do. You deserve someone you can share your world with." She hugged him, then stood on tiptoes and brushed a gentle kiss on his cheek. "You deserve to be happy, Alastair. I think maybe you won't let yourself believe that, but you do."

She turned to go then, retracing her steps to the stairway without looking back. He watched her, keeping her slim figure in sight until she disappeared into the shadows of the third floor. Then he pulled up the collar of his coat, hefted his umbrella, and headed back out into the rainy night.

More than ever he wished he hadn't promised Aubrey he'd be home for their little mock-Thanksgiving dinner on Thursday. Right now, all he wanted to do was step into the London portal and head back to Palo Alto.

CHAPTER TWENTY-THREE

STONE RETURNED TO PALO ALTO on Sunday afternoon to find that the Cannibal Killers had claimed another victim while he was gone.

He carried only one smallish box and his overnight bag with him through the portal, not wanting to risk anything else if things in the Overworld should take a bad turn; the rest, consisting of four boxes of books and an athletic bag full of magical paraphernalia, he'd packed up and left with Aubrey to ship when the post office opened on Monday. Nobody had bothered his car at A Passage to India, which was a good thing given that it hadn't occurred to him until three days into his visit that he probably should have taken a cab down instead of driving.

"I kept an eye on it for you," David Halloran said when he mentioned it on his way out. "It's usually pretty safe 'round here, though."

He'd spotted the headline on the front page of the *San Jose Mercury News* as he headed toward the parking lot:

Cannibal Killer Suspected in Recent East SJ Murder

He fumbled in his pocket for change, bought a copy, and read the article on his way back to the car. The victim, an as-yet-unidentified male transient in his mid-twenties, had been discovered in a vacant lot east of Highway 101 the Friday after Thanksgiving by some children chasing a stray dog. The article didn't go into detail about the body's condition, but reading between the lines it was easy to discern that, like the others, it had been partially eaten.

That made four now, or at least four that had been found, and Stone wasn't a damned bit closer to figuring out what was killing them. He tossed the paper on the passenger seat and headed back to his townhouse.

When he got there, he found three messages on his machine: one from Edwina Mortenson, who had some questions about his plans for the final exam for his Modern Occult Practices course; the second was a salesman who wanted to talk to him about contracting services. He deleted the salesman and hit the button to play the third and final message.

"Dr. Stone? This is Laura Phelps." Her voice sounded thin and sad, though she was obviously trying to hide it. "I hope you had a good Thanksgiving. I was wondering if you might want to…have a cup of coffee sometime. It's hard to explain, but…I feel a connection with you, since you were the last one to see Douglas alive. It's fine if you don't want to—I'm sure you're busy, and probably want to forget about it, I understand. But…anyway, I'll leave you my number just in case."

Stone stared at the phone. He had to play the message over again so he could jot down the number.

He met her at a little coffee shop on Castro Street in Mountain View the following afternoon. It was the week before finals; with the students all heads-down into their cram sessions, he didn't see the point in assigning them too much extra work. He gave them back their most recent essays and hung around in his office for the better part of the morning in case anyone had questions, but when only two students showed up before noon, he felt safe in ducking out for a couple of hours.

The first thing he thought when he saw her was that she was either ill or her grief was hitting her much harder than he'd feared. She sat at a small table, her fingers wrapped around a steaming mug. She looked pale and tired, her makeup neat but minimal, her faded jeans and oversized sweatshirt—possibly her husband's—obviously chosen for comfort rather than fashion. Even Stone, who barely knew her, could tell that they were far from her usual style.

"Hello, Mrs. Phelps," he said softly.

She looked up, startled, from where she'd been staring at a folded newspaper. "Dr. Stone! Oh, I'm sorry. I got here a little early, and I guess the time got away from me. I'm so glad you came."

Stone took the seat across from her, setting down his own mug. He studied her for a moment, frowning. "Are you well?"

She smiled faintly. "I don't know. How well can I be, really? But I suppose I haven't been feeling my best lately, aside from…the obvious."

"Are your children still in town? Have you anyone to look after you?"

"You're sweet to care," she said, eyes glittering. "But don't you worry. Sarah and Cory have gone back East for now, back to work. They're coming for Christmas, but until then I've got plenty of friends who make sure I don't get to spend too much time alone."

Stone nodded. He believed her: he'd seen the number of people, everyone from teenagers to those old enough to be the Phelps's parents, who'd shown up at Douglas's funeral. The couple clearly had strong roots in the area, and a lot of people who gave a damn about what happened to them. To her, now.

He started to say something, but she spoke at the same time. "Did you have a good Thanksgiving?"

"I suppose I did." He caught himself before he mentioned his trip home; normal people didn't just take jaunts halfway around the world for four-day weekends. "Got caught up on some work at home, mostly."

She nodded, twisting her napkin in long, pale fingers. "I heard...they found another victim."

"I saw the paper today," he said, keeping his voice neutral.

"I hope the police catch them soon. It would be nice to have...closure, I guess."

"It would, yes." He couldn't shake the feeling that she was dancing around something, but as yet couldn't pin it down.

"I've been thinking a lot about what happened. Having nightmares about it, even. My friends are suggesting that I should see a therapist to help me work through it."

"That might be a good idea," he said.

She drew a long breath and raised her gaze to meet his. "You might think I'm going crazy for saying this, Dr. Stone, but..." When he didn't jump in, she looked away again. "Those...whoever it was who killed Douglas. Did you think they were...strange?"

Stone went still, pausing in the act of raising his coffee cup. "Strange?"

"Odd. Not quite...right." She shook her head, frustrated, and dropped the napkin. "I'm not explaining it very well, am I? Maybe because I'm not sure how I *can* explain it."

"It was a horrible thing. You were under a lot of stress that night. I'm sure everything looked strange."

"Yes, but..." She let out a long sigh. "Maybe it's just after I found out what you do...what you teach...it started to color my thoughts. But when I let myself really think about what happened, it seemed like they were...I don't know...moving differently. More like animals than people. Did you see it?"

Stone didn't answer right away. When he did, it was with care. "Did you mention this to the police at all?"

"No, no. I'm sure they'll just look at me like some sort of crazy woman, traumatized by what I think I saw. And maybe I am. I don't know. I didn't get a good look at them, after all—they shoved me down and went for Douglas." Tears sprang to the corners of her eyes; she snatched up the napkin with a convulsive jerk and dabbed at them.

Stone was silent, unsure of what to say that wouldn't sound trite.

She sniffled. "I'm sorry. I still do that sometimes. A lot, actually."

"Of course you do," he murmured. "You're grieving. I wish there was something I could say to help you."

"You're helping me just being here." She ducked her gaze like a little girl. "You don't think it sounds odd that I feel like you're the only one I can discuss this with, without having to explain myself?"

"Not at all. I understand. If talking gives you comfort, please don't hesitate to call me whenever you like."

She laughed, just a little. "Don't worry—I won't be bothering you constantly. But I might just take you up on that, every now and then." She reached across the table and touched his arm; her sleeve pulled up a bit, revealing the scratch she'd gotten from being pushed down by the attackers. It was healing now, pink and puckering against the paleness of her skin. "Thank you. I want you to know I appreciate your time. I'm sure you must be busy."

"Never too busy," he assured her. The least he could do after failing to save her husband was to be available if she needed someone to talk to.

CHAPTER TWENTY-FOUR

THE NEXT WEEK PASSED in a flurry of activity. Unlike on Monday, Stone didn't get any respite from students dropping by his office for the remainder of Dead Week; when he wasn't lecturing (which essentially amounted to entertaining his students with various stories of the paranormal and, in one class, actually showing them a horror movie), he was in his office answering their questions, explaining to them why he couldn't offer them any extra-credit projects at this late date to help bring their flagging test scores up to an acceptable average, or putting the finishing touches on his final exams. When he wasn't doing any of these things, he was cloistered away in some meeting with Mortenson and Hubbard or one of the committees he'd been roped into joining by virtue of the fact that he was the newest faculty member and hadn't made sufficient protest. By the time he got home, usually accompanied by something from one of the nearby takeout restaurants when he remembered to eat, he was so tired that all he wanted to do was pass out on his couch.

He couldn't do that, though. Every time he was tempted to, he remembered Laura Phelps's tired, sad face across the table at the coffee shop, and his resolve to get to the bottom of the Cannibal Killers returned. He dragged himself upstairs to his study and continued poring through the books he'd brought home, looking for anything he could find on ghouls, skinwalkers, and other cannibalistic creatures. It proved to be fascinating reading—he'd never devoted much time to learning about supernatural creatures because the theory and practice of magic itself had provided more than enough material to keep him busy for as long as he was willing to spend—but it wasn't giving him the answers he sought. He tried not to get discouraged, but he couldn't shake the thought that he was failing Mrs. Phelps, failing Douglas...hell, even failing that unnamed transient man who might not have had to die if Stone could have put things together faster.

Kolinsky sent him another hand-delivered letter three days into Dead Week, but he couldn't get away long enough to go talk to him until Friday evening. They met at a genteel little bar in Los Altos over a bottle of wine that Kolinsky recommended and Stone paid for.

"I still don't know what the murderers are," Kolinsky said without preamble once they were seated. "But they are not unique."

"What do you mean, not unique? You're saying there are more of them than this lot?"

"Not around here, that I could find," Kolinsky said. He lifted a fine leather briefcase from the floor, pulled a file folder from it, and spread a few photocopies across the table. "The police probably already have this information, though I haven't seen it in the news media yet. Similar killings have occurred in other parts of the country, over the last few years."

Stone leaned in to get a look in the dim light. Each page included a neat note in the upper corner identifying the date and the newspaper from which it had been copied. "Detroit...Atlanta...St. Louis..."

Kolinsky nodded. "In every case, the killers murdered four or five people over as many months, then disappeared without a trace."

Stone frowned. "If I didn't know better, I'd wonder if we weren't dealing with a werewolf infestation."

"Werewolves are rare—rarer still in this country. And aside from that, only a few of the killings coincide with periods of a full moon." He pulled out another paper. This one wasn't a newspaper story; instead, it looked like some sort of official document. "This is the only police report I've been able to obtain so far describing the killings without any redactions. It seems that they are keeping some facts about the murders from the general public."

"Such as?"

In answer, Kolinsky merely handed over the sheet.

Stone scanned it. After several seconds, he stared at Kolinsky, stunned. "They're not just eating them. They're slicing bits off for takeaway."

"Yes."

Stone leaned back in his chair, letting his breath out. "So we're definitely not talking about some kind of animal here. These things use knives. They're intelligent." He paused, trying to remember anything about the sort of cannibalistic creature who might do such a thing. After several moments, he shook his head in frustration. "I don't know. This isn't my speciality even back home. I'm a researcher, not a monster hunter. Dangerous supernatural creatures that are intelligent are so rare that I've only ever even heard of documented cases of two or three. And those were in Europe. Is it different around here?"

Kolinsky shook his head. "No. I have not heard of any in this area since I arrived here more than twenty years ago. A few spirit manifestations, summonings gone awry, that sort of thing, but never anything corporeal. And from everything I understand to be true about them, they don't hunt in urban areas."

Stone tossed the police report back on the desk. "So what the hell do you think they are?" he said a little too loudly, then lowered his voice when a couple other diners glanced at him in disapproval. "I have some ideas, but I want to hear yours first. What sorts of things are intelligent and eat humans?"

"Hard to say." Kolinsky shrugged. "Wendigo—but not around here. They certainly wouldn't be able to hide in an area such as this, and in any case they're solitary hunters. You saw these creatures—you said they were roughly humanoid in size and shape?"

"Mostly, yes. I didn't get a good look at them, but they didn't strike me as particularly large. The only unusual things about them were their heightened senses and the way they ran—hunched over, but not on all fours like an animal."

"Hmm…" Kolinsky leaned back in his chair and stared up at the ceiling for several seconds. "The only other thing that comes to mind is ghouls, but I've never heard of any in this area."

"That was my guess," Stone said. "I did some research back home where I've got access to better resources, and they're the only thing I could come up with that seems even remotely close to fitting what's going on here."

"Yes, I came to the same conclusion. It's possible, but it doesn't fit completely. Ghouls are feral creatures, little more than clever animals. They're generally found near graveyards, and almost never in heavily populated areas. I can't see them hunting among large groups of people, and as far as I know they don't use tools. They dig up bodies, eat their fill, and move on. And more importantly for our hypothesis, I've never heard of them seeking out live victims. They only require meat from human beings to sustain them; it isn't necessary for the meat to be fresh. It is much easier for them to obtain it by digging up graves than it is by committing murder."

"They do hunt in packs, though, don't they?" Stone asked, still considering. Then he sighed. "No, you're probably right. They're rare as it is, and they don't fit the *modus operandi.*"

"Yes, they are indeed rare," Kolinsky said. "I could find no reports of any confirmed ghoul activity in the United States in the last twenty years. They tend to confine themselves to small colonies in remote areas to avoid detection, and for all their unpleasant habits, they're clearly quite discreet."

"So suppose you're right," Stone said. "How do you detect them?"

"You mentioned that you noticed an oddness in the killers' auras when you encountered them. Do you think you could recognize it should you encounter it again?"

Stone thought about it. "Not sure," he said at last. "Possibly. But I didn't see it for long, and I was a bit preoccupied at the time. And besides, I can hardly go driving around with my head hanging out the window, trying to spot it." He shook his head. "There's got to be another answer. I'd say I was wrong and these were just a gang of psychopaths, except for the oddness in their auras. Definitely not your garden-variety humans. Whatever they were, they had some connection to the supernatural." His gaze sharpened as a new thought occurred to him. "Could they be humans who've undergone some kind of magical transformation? That sounds like the sort of thing your lot would be up to—is there anyone around here you might suspect?"

Something in Stone's expression must have changed, because Kolinsky's right eyebrow crept up. "I assure you, Dr. Stone, if it were the case, I am not your mad scientist. I have no use for a pack of cannibalistic minions." His eyes glittered. "And even if I were, do you expect that I would tell you?"

A momentary chill settled over Stone, but he shook his head. "Hardly seems your style. But if you happen to hear anything—" He waved vaguely over his shoulder. "Those wards aren't going to last forever. Although…" he added, "if you'd care to alter our deal a bit, I'd be willing to sort them out for you now, as an act of good faith—assuming that if you don't come up with any better answers in a reasonable amount of time, you'll let me take advantage of your information-finding services free of charge at some future date."

Kolinsky regathered his papers, put them in perfect order, and put them away. "Define 'reasonable.'"

"Let's call it a month. I'm already concerned that they're going to strike again before that and kill someone else, but I understand these things take time. What do you say?"

"You have a deal, Dr. Stone."

"Right, then. I'll come 'round tomorrow, so I'll have time to rest on Sunday before finals week starts. Unless these things get me before then."

CHAPTER TWENTY-FIVE

STONE DIDN'T HAVE A LOT OF TIME to pursue his investigation during finals week: between administering exams, grading them, and trying to get as much of a jump on his various administrative tasks as he could, he had even less time left for other activities than he had during Dead Week. This fact frustrated him, but it couldn't be helped. Time travel was well outside the available skill set for even the most advanced of mages, much as many of them regretted this fact.

He spent most of his time while the students were actually taking their exams sitting at the front of the classroom with a notepad and a stack of books, going over the same pages multiple times in the hope that he'd missed something. He'd dropped by the Stanford library during one of his breaks and checked out several more volumes on the subject of urban and folk legends, thinking he might have missed something by limiting himself to established supernatural threats. As a mage, he knew that a surprising number of the old stories most mundanes considered to be tantalizing but harmless fodder for campfire tales actually had some basis in fact. Usually that basis ran fairly far afield from what was actually going on, but if your average citizen had any idea of the things that really *did* go bump in the night, he'd probably run away in terror.

Still, Stone couldn't help but feel disgusted that he was getting nowhere. He'd upgraded Kolinsky's wards as he'd promised, but so far the man hadn't come up with any new information. Stone had even, one evening after getting off work at nearly eight o'clock, made a pilgrimage to the park where Douglas Phelps had died, and, while pretending to walk nonchalantly past the place where the killing had occurred, took some readings of the area's magical aura in the hope that, if he should spot any traces of the creatures again, he'd recognize them. It would have been easy to find the location even if he didn't know exactly where it was: someone had erected a white cross on the site, and it was surrounded by the brittle, strewn remains of flowers and a few other small objects of the type that popped up with what seemed to be almost spontaneous persistence around the sites of murders and traffic fatalities.

It had only been a month or so since the killing had occurred, which meant the magical energy was still relatively strong around the site. Magic always left traces, but usually with things like spells, the remnants faded quickly. Death, however, as well as prolonged strong emotion, lingered much longer. In some cases, such as concentration camps or hospitals, the area's aura could be permanently changed.

The energy was still there, Stone found, but it didn't help much. The residue from the creatures' auras flickered around the edges, but the sheer wall of negative energy that Phelps's terror and pain had generated overwhelmed it. It was like trying to taste a few drops of fruit juice in a gallon of water: it was there, but so diluted as to be almost useless.

There's another lead gone, he thought, glancing around as he headed back to his car. He didn't expect that anyone would jump him—certainly not that the creatures would return to the scene of one of their past murders and attempt another one—

but nothing about this whole business was making sense. Best not to take anything for granted.

If only he could talk to Grider, or one of the other cops assigned to the case, and see if they'd found out anything. It was entirely possible that they'd discovered some scrap of evidence or information that would be useless to their mundane methods, but invaluable to his magical ones. If they had, it was probably sitting in some evidence locker somewhere, or written up in a report the public would never see.

It didn't matter, though—Grider hadn't been exactly forthcoming with information at the scene of Phelps's murder, and Stone hardly thought he'd be willing to share any of his information with some smartass civilian, even one who had been there when things had gone down.

Stone had gotten into his car and switched on the ignition when a thought came to him along with the strains of Pink Floyd drifting from the Jaguar's speakers: maybe Grider *would* talk to him. He'd just have to position things correctly. After all, the detective wasn't the only one with potentially helpful information about the case. Maybe if he offered a little *quid pro quo*, even a hopeless mundane like Grider might be willing to make a concession or two.

That didn't mean he'd be easy to get through to, but it did mean that perhaps, if Stone was lucky enough and Grider was desperate enough, it might give Stone a bit of leverage he wouldn't otherwise have. It was worth a try, and at least this way he wouldn't feel quite so guilty if the cops managed to blunder into the killers and ended up getting themselves torn to pieces.

| CHAPTER TWENTY-SIX

STONE PULLED HIS CAR into a spot a block from the coffee shop and shut off the ignition, but he didn't get out. Instead, he gripped the steering wheel and took a few calming breaths. Outside, early-evening Christmas shoppers drifted down a tinsel-and-light-bedecked University Avenue, chatting, window shopping, oblivious. He often marveled at how most people could go through life without managing to notice so much of what was going on around them.

It was a little after seven. He envisioned Grider seated at a tiny table, glancing at the window, glancing at his watch, probably wondering if Stone was going to show. The cop seemed the punctual type.

Was he going to show? Why had he proposed this meeting in the first place? He must have been mad. As soon as he got out of the car and entered the shop, a lot of things could change fast. He'd planned what he intended to say, but conversations could spiral out of control before you knew it.

And Grider was a detective: that meant he was trained to interrogate suspects. Trained to notice minute changes in expression, tone of voice, breathing rate. If Stone went in there, how long would it take before Grider figured out that he wasn't telling the whole story? It didn't take the ability to read auras to tell when someone was hiding something.

His mind's eye flashed back to Douglas Phelps in the park: the blood, the torn body, the terrified expression. The man had a wife. A family who'd loved him. He had not only been murdered—he'd been partially eaten. Once again rage welled up as he thought about it. "Partially eaten" wasn't the kind of phrase that anyone should have to hear in reference to their loved one, at least not in a civilized world.

These things, whatever they were, had already struck numerous times, and they would strike again. Stone was sure of it. Neither Kolinsky's research nor his own was coming up with definitive answers fast enough. And the police would get nowhere on their own. If he could give Grider some leads without revealing anything about his own abilities, maybe the detective would give him something he could use without even realizing it. It was a chess game—but Stone had no idea who between them was the better player.

A dangerous gamble, but as the weeks passed and the Cannibal Killers remained at large, a necessary one.

Stone flung the car door open, got out in a single, almost savage motion, and slammed it shut behind him.

Grider was waiting for him. Dressed in a windbreaker and Dockers, the cop slouched into the corner of a booth against the far wall, his eyes scanning the front part of the shop. Stone saw him tense as he came in. He got a cup of coffee and took it over to the table.

"Was thinking you might not show," Grider said, taking a pointed glance at his watch as Stone sat down.

"I'm a bit surprised you agreed to the meeting."

Grider grunted. "So'm I, actually. This is fuckin' crazy, if you'll excuse my French. I got murders to solve. I don't have time to talk to crazies."

Stone didn't take offense. When you were in his line of work, you got that a lot. "So why did you, then?"

"Hell, I dunno." He contemplated his coffee with morose frustration. "Maybe I don't get calls often from crazies with doctorates."

Stone watched him silently for a moment over his own coffee. Then he asked, "Still no leads on the murders?"

Grider's gaze came up. "If I had any, I wouldn't be here." His eyes were brown, small and shrewd and hooded. "Tell you what: why don't we cut the preliminaries? You got somethin' to tell me, let's hear it. I got about a hundred things to do."

"Fair enough." Stone decided he liked Grider. One of the things that irritated him about most Americans was how they were so obsessed with making each other feel better. They were so careful not to cause offense with their words that they often ended up saying nothing at all. A little old-fashioned directness was refreshing. "I discovered something."

"Yeah? What?" Grider's eyes narrowed. He pulled out a black leather-covered notebook and flipped it open.

"Something you might already know about, but I'll tell you just in case. And there was something at the scene that I saw and didn't tell you about, too."

"Why didn't you say anything at the time?"

"I didn't think you'd believe me, honestly. I was a bit flustered by the whole thing. But now I've had some time to think about it, I decided I'd best pass it on to you in any case." Stone deliberately made his usual brisk tones sound uncertain.

"Okay, let's hear it. Then I'll decide what to do about it."

Stone stared down into his cup, letting the pause stretch out. "First, these things have attacked before, in other places."

Grider stiffened, and he leaned forward. "How did you know that?"

"I did some research. Hear me out, Lieutenant. That's not all I have to tell you."

"Where have they attacked before?" Grider's expression was blank, but Stone didn't need magical sight to see that the cop knew at least something about the other attacks, but was trying to act like he didn't.

"Detroit, Atlanta, and St. Louis, that I found. I'm not certain those are the only instances."

"Holy Christ." Grider dropped his hand to the table and picked up his cup again. "What the hell are you doing, Stone? Did you decide to play Junior Detective or something?"

"I thought you already knew about it," Stone said.

"I did know about it. What, you think I'm not doin' my job? We already knew about the connection, but it wasn't exactly easy to track down. The press kept 'em quiet to avoid a panic. How the hell did some Brit fresh off the boat find—"

"Is that important? I just wanted to make sure you knew. What I don't know is whether the others were able to find any useful evidence. Footprints, DNA traces—"

"That's none of your business," Grider said, and paused to jot something down in his notebook, then flipped back a few pages. "You said you saw four of these guys."

Stone nodded.

"And you're sure they were all involved. Some kind of…cannibal gang."

"They were all clustered around Mr. Phelps. They ran when they heard me approaching."

"I know I already asked you this at the time, but did anything come back to you about what they looked like? Could you identify any of them if you saw them again?"

Grider had indeed asked him these same questions at the scene. He wondered if the detective was trying to trip him up, trick him into revealing something he hadn't mentioned before. "No. I was too far away to see any features, and the area was shadowed."

Grider shook his head, looking disgusted. "I should haul your ass in for this, Stone, just because. Last thing I need is some wannabe Sherlock Holmes poking his nose into my investigation."

Stone's heart beat a little faster. He covered it with a light tone: "Well, if you intend to do that, at least wait until I've given you the rest of my information."

"Oh, great. You got more. You sure you didn't take fuckin' home movies at the scene?"

Stone regarded Grider silently over his cup. "Do you want to hear what I've got to say or not, Lieutenant? If you plan to arrest me, I'd like to make a few calls first."

Grider dropped his gaze, frustration still evident on his face. He waved a vague hand. "Yeah, fine. What else?"

"I suspect you won't believe this, but I think...the killers might not have been precisely human."

Grider stared at him long and hard, then let out a loud sigh. "I shoulda known," he said, shaking his head. "Of all the witnesses I gotta deal with, I get Professor Nutball."

Stone shrugged. "I said you wouldn't believe me. But I know what I saw. It's the truth that I didn't see specific features, but I did see them run away. And whatever they were, they didn't move like anything human."

Grider didn't speak for several seconds. "And how exactly do you define 'didn't move like anything human'? Were they on two legs? Four? Eight?"

"Two. They were definitely humanoid. That much I'm sure of."

"Humanoid. What are you, Mr. Spock or somethin'?" He glanced around past Stone, toward the street. "You got Captain Kirk and Scotty waitin' outside to beam you up when you're done?"

Stone ignored him. "They moved quickly, far faster than a normal human. They ran in a crouch, like an animal would. That's why I didn't get a good look at them. I suspect their senses are heightened to the point where it wouldn't be easy to get close to them without alerting them." He looked hard at Grider. "*Have* you found any DNA evidence, Lieutenant? I don't know much about your line of work, but it's my understanding that saliva contains quite a lot of it. And I'd imagine it's difficult to eat someone without leaving saliva behind."

Suddenly, Grider looked tired. "What are you tryin' to tell me, Stone? That they're—what—werewolves or something? I know you teach that spooky bullshit up at Stanford, but in my mind that just makes you an educated crackpot instead of the garden variety. You know what the difference is? You use bigger words, and you smell better."

He leaned back in his chair and sighed again. "I don't have time for this. How do I even know if you're telling the truth about any of this stuff?"

"I'm telling you the truth about everything I saw. I assume you corroborated my story with Mrs. Phelps's?"

Grider mopped at his forehead with his napkin. "She didn't tell us much. After she got pushed down, she pretty much checked out. Full-blown panic. She said there was more than one of them, but that's all. She wasn't even sure how many, exactly. She sure as hell didn't say their eyes were glowing red or they had fangs or anything."

"I didn't say anything about there being some sort of occult connection. Just because I teach it doesn't mean I believe in it." Stone shifted in his chair and took another long drink from his coffee cup. "As I said, I just got a bit flustered that night, with everything that happened. I haven't been in the country for long, and I'll admit to being a bit nervous about how I might be treated by the police." He shrugged. "If I'm guilty of anything, it's paying too much attention to sensationalistic media. But since there's been another murder after Mr. Phelps's, I felt that I should tell you what I saw, even if you don't believe it. I hope you'll keep that in mind before you decide to arrest me for obstructing justice."

Grider waved him off. "I'm not gonna arrest you. Even if I wanted to, I don't have time to deal with the paperwork. I know you're not the murderer, since you weren't even in the country when the first one happened. That's all I care about." He glanced up, meeting Stone's gaze. "Anything else? Spooks floating around the crime scene? A getaway car disguised as a hearse?"

"You aren't going to bother me with that sort of thing, Lieutenant. Believe me, I've heard them all." Stone lowered his voice and leaned forward. "But whether you believe in it or not, there are dangerous things out there. I'm not saying they're supernatural, but I'm also not having you on: they're fast, and they're dangerous." He stood. "Is there anything else you need from me tonight?"

"Nah. I can't guarantee you won't get a call from somebody else in the department about your little investigation, especially if there's another murder or it turns out you somehow got access to something you shouldn't have." His expression was almost grudging. "But hey, thanks for the tips."

Stone set his cup down and nodded. "There's just one other thing, Lieutenant."

Grider glared. "Somethin' *else* you didn't tell me?"

"No. I've told you everything." He paused a moment. This wasn't going to be easy. His meeting with Grider had gone a long way toward reinforcing what he remembered: the man was so mundane that he wouldn't acknowledge a supernatural threat if it ran up behind him and yelled *Boo!* He sat back down. "I...wanted to ask you a question."

"What?" There was an edge of impatience in the cop's tone. He drained the last of his coffee mug and set it down hard on the table. "Stone, I got things to do, I told you that. If we're done here—"

"It will just take a moment. I know this is an unusual request, but given that you're at an impasse in your investigation—I have a…friend who's got a talent for getting impressions from physical objects."

"What the hell do you mean, 'impressions'?" Grider let go of the tenseness that was about to propel him up out of his chair and settled back, resigned. Then his eyes narrowed. "You're talkin' about more of this psychic horseshit, aren't you?"

Stone nodded. "It's not horseshit, Lieutenant. I'm well aware that police departments sometimes employ psychics to help them locate missing people. I'm merely asking you if you would consider it in this case. My…friend is very good at this sort of thing, but he needs something to work with."

Grider didn't answer right away. He bowed his head, rubbing at the top of his nose with both hands like he was trying to massage away a headache. "We ain't got a missing person, Stone. We got four dead people. And we know where they all are."

Damn, how did mundanes ever get anything done? Stone let a harder edge creep into his tone. "Listen, Lieutenant. I know you don't like me, and you don't respect what I do. That's fine. I don't give a damn what you think of me. But your job is to solve these murders, catch these people, or creatures, or whatever they are, before they kill anyone else. And I'm offering to help you, in a way that won't require anything from you except to share something that's doing you no good."

"What makes you think I even got any evidence this friend of yours could use?" Grider asked. "They didn't exactly drop their wallets at the scene."

"You already said you didn't get any DNA evidence. That implies that you had something to try getting it from."

Grider stood in a sudden motion. "Stone, I'm goin' now. I gotta think about this. You're askin' me to hand off evidence to some cockamamie psychic friend of yours, just on your word. It don't work like that. Ever heard of the chain of custody? That means if I let anything out of my control, even if your wacko friend *does* get something, we can't use it. I don't suppose this *friend* would be willing to come into the station and do his little parlor tricks in a controlled environment, right?"

The slight emphasis he put on the word told Stone everything he needed to know. Grider was sharper than he looked. "No," he said. "I doubt that he would." He too rose. "Just let me say this, Lieutenant: if I'm wrong about what I'm suggesting, then you haven't lost anything. The evidence is useless to you. If my *friend*—" he put the same subtle emphasis on the word that Grider had, to show him that he got it, "—can't get anything from it, then you're no worse off than you were when you started. But if he can…if I *am* right…would you rather have these things off the street, or would you rather have more people die while you work to tie everything up in a neat little procedural bow?"

Grider zipped up his windbreaker with a decisive motion. "We're done, Stone. Thanks for the info. If I need you—or your friend—for anything else, I'll give you a call."

Stone didn't try to stop him as he left the shop. He waited, standing there until his heart rate slowed back down to normal and Grider was out of sight, before heading back to his car.

He shouldn't be surprised; not really. He didn't know why he'd even expected that the encounter might go any differently than it had. Grider was all about procedure—he'd probably been on the force for at least twenty years, and he was old enough that he was probably looking at retirement in the next few years.

Rocking the boat this late in his career wasn't something he'd be inclined to do—especially when the rocking involved changing worldviews that had probably been part of his personality since before he became a cop.

Still, though, none of that was helping Stone. He got back into the Jaguar, slammed the door shut, and gripped the steering wheel until his knuckles whitened.

He was out of options. Kolinsky hadn't come up with anything new. His visit to the scene of Phelps's death hadn't turned up anything but vague and useless flashes, buried under a mountain of terror and pain.

Suddenly he was tired, more tired than he'd been in weeks.

| CHAPTER TWENTY-SEVEN

AUBREY CALLED THE SATURDAY MORNING after the quarter ended, asking if Stone was planning to come home for Christmas, and if so, when.

"I don't know yet," he said, phone stuck between his ear and his shoulder as he put together a quick breakfast of orange juice and the remains of a burrito he'd found in the back of the fridge. He hadn't had much chance to get any exercise over the last few days, so he'd planned a good long run up at the campus before he settled in to start marking final exams and preparing grades. "Got a lot to do yet before I can go anywhere—you know how it is. Just because the students are done doesn't mean I am."

"Yes, sir. Let me know, though. Even if you can only make it for a day or two—unless you've got plans, of course."

Stone didn't know if he had plans or not. He'd hit a dead end on the Cannibal Killer investigation, but he couldn't bring himself to just give up on it. He mentally amended his plan for the day—instead of driving up to Stanford, he'd take the car downtown and park it somewhere, go for his run, and then pick up a Christmas gift for Aubrey, so he could get it in the mail in time to make it to England if he ended up not going in person.

He could already see this whole bi-continental thing was going to be inconvenient at times, and for once regretted how easy it was to move back and forth using the portals, which meant he didn't even have travel difficulties as an excuse for staying away. "I'll keep you updated, Aubrey. But I'll be honest with you—I don't really fancy being ambushed by Desmond again." He'd told Aubrey about Imogen's presence at the dinner party the day after he returned.

"If you come, sir, I'll lie to him if he calls."

"Good man." Stone grinned.

He got a later start than he'd hoped, so it was almost eleven before he headed out. His original amended plan had been to just start his run at the townhouse, since it was close enough to Downtown that it wouldn't be too far to go. The weather was brisk but not too cold, the sky a brilliant chilly blue. Just about ideal conditions, but if he was going to try to find something for Aubrey, probably at one of the shops on University, he didn't want to end up having to carry it home. Instead, he drove the few blocks to Downtown, cruised around for fifteen minutes until he found a parking spot (seriously, parking in downtown Palo Alto on a weekend this close to Christmas rivaled London for sheer futility), and then set off on a circuit of some of the rambling, tree-lined streets in the area. He liked to change up the routes of his runs for variety's sake, and though he preferred parks, open-space preserves, and the various paths around Stanford, this wasn't a bad choice for a change of scenery.

It felt good to get out again, to put the stresses of the last couple of weeks out of his mind for a while and let it just meander over whatever happened to occur to it. He passed numerous people, some out shopping, some just out for a walk on a cold sunny day, some pushing baby strollers or being dragged along by dogs. He wasn't quite ready to admit it to himself yet, but he did like Palo Alto more than he'd expected to. Not as much as back home, of course—he doubted he ever would. The vast, rolling, tree-covered hills, low rock walls, meandering lanes, and peaceful livestock pastures that surrounded his home back in Holmbury were as much a part of him as the bustle of the London streets, and none of that would ever change. But this was a pleasant enough place, full of unique little shops and intelligent people and attractive scenery, that it would suffice quite nicely as a second home. He even caught himself beginning to consider what he'd do next year, if he ended up signing on for the long haul at Stanford. This year was in many ways probationary on both his part and the University's: since they hadn't had time to do their usual lengthy interview process with him, they had to decide whether his performance was up to the standards they required, while in the meantime he had to decide whether teaching here full-time was sufficiently attractive to convince him to make his relocation permanent.

He had no doubt about the former: already the head of the Cultural Anthropology department had confirmed that his students were crazy about him, and even an informal poll of Mortenson and Hubbard had led to their grudging admittance that he was doing a fine job. So it would be all down to him, in a few months, to decide whether he wanted to come back next year, to accept the tenure-track position he knew they planned to offer him, and to shift his primary residence from England to California.

A big decision, but fortunately one he didn't have to make for a while. For now, he could focus on the rest of the year, and continue trying to figure out where the mysterious Cannibal Killers were hiding—if they were even in the area anymore. If they were running true to form (assuming that they were the same ones who had been active in the other cities), they were about due to pull up stakes and leave for someplace else. That didn't make Stone feel any better, though—just because they weren't plaguing the Bay Area anymore didn't mean they wouldn't prove equally dangerous wherever they ended up moving to. Possibly more so, since the likelihood of there being any mages in the new location to figure out that something supernatural was afoot was fairly low. Stone didn't know how many mages there were in the United States, but if the number in England was any kind of indication, he doubted there were more than a few hundred. And of those, only a few dozen were likely to be more than minor talents, with the training and the power to deal effectively with a threat of this nature. So that meant that all signs pointed to the fact that, if he wanted to have any chance of ferreting out the killers before they moved on, he'd have to get on with it soon.

No pressure.

He hadn't been paying much attention to where he was going, altering his course based on signal lights and whether he could cross a street without having to stop for traffic. When he finally glanced up at a street sign, he realized he'd made it several blocks southeast of the core Downtown area, in another tree-lined, mostly residential neighborhood he'd never been in before. He stopped for a moment, puffing just a little, and took stock. It was nearly noon already; he should probably head back so he could pick up Aubrey's gift and get started on his exam grading.

Across the street from where he stood was an odd little market, barely larger than a single-family home. He stopped a moment to verify that it was, in fact, a business. It didn't look like a convenience store; in fact its somewhat rundown, old-fashioned appearance gave him the impression that it had been there, in the middle of a neighborhood otherwise full of small, older homes, for many years. *Odd,* he thought; he'd seen plenty of equally strangely-placed little businesses back home in England, but this was the first one in the US. But since it was here, he decided that he could do with a bottle of water before he started back.

He was preparing to cross the street when movement caught the corner of his eye near the little market's door. He stopped, mostly hidden behind a parked car, and took a look.

Someone was coming out of the shop, which certainly wasn't unusual. What *was* unusual, he realized a second later, was that it was Laura Phelps. She shoved her way outside, carrying her purse in one hand and a lime green tote-style shopping bag in the other. She hadn't noticed Stone yet; in fact, she seemed a bit furtive, glancing left and right almost as if fearful that someone would spot her. Then she made a right turn and headed purposefully down the street, back toward Downtown.

Stone jogged across the street toward her, ignoring traffic, ignoring the horn blaring at him from an angry Mercedes driver forced to slam on his brakes. "Mrs. Phelps!" he called.

She stopped. For a moment she didn't turn, but just stood there like she was unsure of where she was. Then she faced him and smiled. "Dr. Stone! What a nice surprise to see you. How are you?"

He hadn't seen her since they'd met for coffee; the intervening time had not been kind to her. She'd lost weight, her skin was an unhealthy blotched pale, and the gray at the roots of her honey-blonde hair suggested that she hadn't visited a salon in recent memory. She was dressed a little better than the last time he'd seen her, but her weight loss made her clothes hang on her like those of a little girl who'd raided her mother's closet.

"Haven't seen you in a while," he said. "I've been thinking about you. Thought of calling you once or twice, but I didn't want to intrude."

"It wouldn't be an intrusion," she said, clutching her shopping bag closer to her. "Please don't ever think that. It's just that I—just haven't really felt like talking to anyone lately. Haven't been feeling well. I'm sure it's just that I'm having a hard time coping with everything that's happened."

"I'm so sorry," he said. He nodded back toward the tiny market. "Odd little place...do you shop there often?"

She shook her head. "Oh, no," she said. "I was just in the area and I decided I needed a couple of things, so I picked them up. I'm parked down the street a bit," she added, indicating the direction with a nod of her head.

Stone studied her for a moment, shifting to magical sight. Her aura, normally a strong clear gold, was dappled with dark spots. That wasn't unusual: one of the things that could temporarily change a person's aura was prolonged negative emotion such as grief, despair, or anger. Mrs. Phelps had certainly had enough of those—probably all three of them—in the last few weeks to do a number on even the strongest of auras. But still, it worried him: another common cause of auric disruption was illness.

"Mrs. Phelps," he said carefully, "Please don't be offended, but I'm concerned about you. Have you seen a doctor recently?"

She nodded, with a faraway smile. "I have. And he's told me I need to take better care of myself. I assure you, though, there's nothing wrong with me that a few good nights' sleep and remembering to eat won't help." Her hand tightened on the strap of her bag. "It really is nice to see you, Dr. Stone, but I'm afraid I need to go now. I'm meeting someone, and if I don't leave soon I'll be late."

"Of course," he said. He didn't believe a word of it, but he couldn't very well accuse her of lying right there in the middle of the street. "You don't mind if I give you a call sometime, do you?"

"No, that would be nice," she said. "I'd like that." She raised her hand in farewell, the one that wasn't holding the shopping bag. "Take care, Dr. Stone. You really are sweet for worrying about me."

And then she was gone, moving quickly off down the street as if she didn't want to give him time to reply.

He stood there watching her go, frowning. He shifted back to magical sight and continued to study her aura, watching the little red flares and dark patches bobbing around in the gold like some kind of otherworldly lava lamp. Despite what she'd said about being fine, Stone knew otherwise. Something was wrong with her—maybe something she didn't even know about herself.

He sighed, once again frustrated at being unable to do anything useful. It was entirely possible that Mrs. Phelps's symptoms could be caused by her profound grief. This wasn't, after all, a simple case of a middle-aged woman losing her husband to an illness, or even to a traumatic injury like an auto accident or industrial mishap. Being present while cannibals did their best to eat someone dear to you naturally took things up to a higher plane of horror. Who could even tell how someone might react to such a thing? Stone doubted that much precedent existed in the psychiatric literature.

By now, Mrs. Phelps had disappeared around a corner, leaving him standing there staring down an empty sidewalk. When a boy on a bicycle whizzed by from behind and nearly hit him, he decided to resume his original plan: pick up a bottle of water, head back toward Downtown and try to find a gift for Aubrey, then return home, probably grabbing some takeout along the way. He pushed open the door to the tiny market and stepped inside, accompanied by the clanky tinkle of a brass cowbell attached to the inner handle.

It was like stepping back in time. Stone paused in the doorway a moment, orienting himself. The shop seemed even tinier than it had from the street, dingy and cramped, its three narrow aisles formed by old-fashioned, shoulder-height wooden shelving units stacked with dusty cans and boxes. There were a few modern touches: a series of coolers along the back wall full of beer, soft drinks, and water, an electric lottery ad, a couple of neon beer signs. But everything else, from the stock on the shelves to the small rack of magazines and comic books off to the left of a pegboard full of toys from twenty years ago, looked untouched, somehow faded, like they didn't quite belong in this reality.

"May I help you?"

Stone jerked himself back to the here and now and oriented on the voice: off to his right, behind a small counter, was a man. He was perhaps sixty, short and stooped and pale, in a simple white shirt with the sleeves rolled up and a white bib apron. He peered at Stone through wire-rimmed glasses.

"Er—" Stone said. "Sorry. I was just thirsty, and I saw your little shop."

The man nodded slowly, then indicated the cooler cases with a jerk of his head. "Is there anything else?" His voice was creaky, as if he didn't use it often.

"No. Thank you." Stone went to the back of the store, feeling like he almost had to turn sideways to make it down the aisle without getting dust on himself, even though he was far from wide. He cast surreptitious glances at the products as he passed them; after only a handful of months in the United States he hadn't acclimated himself very well yet to American consumer goods, but he'd have readily bet that those he was seeing here were not the sort of things he'd find at one of the huge, brightly-lit supermarkets that seemed to exist on every streetcorner. He wondered if anyone ever bought anything here other than drinks and lottery tickets.

Mindful of the old man's gaze on him, he selected a bottle of water and carried it back toward the counter, shifting to magical sight as he did.

Even the place's aura was strange. Not hostile or malevolent, just...strange. The store held an aspect of anticipation, almost as if it were waiting for something to happen, but also of something very old, very settled. Stone had seen auras similar to this second part back in England: old shops, pubs, places where people gathered for a shared purpose. He re-evaluated his opinion of the store: perhaps it did have a regular customer base, but just not right at the moment.

He put the bottle down on the counter, dug out his wallet, and handed the man a five-dollar bill. While he waited for his change he looked past the man at the items behind the counter. There wasn't much: a rack of cigarettes, a large chest freezer with a folded newspaper and a stack of what looked like invoices on top of it, and the lottery-ticket machine.

Behind Stone, the bell clanked again. He turned a little in time to see another man entering the shop. This one was maybe in his thirties, his thin, wiry body gangly like a teenager's, and he wore faded jeans and a baseball-style jacket with a San Francisco Giants logo on the back. He glanced at the counter, nodded to the proprietor, and drifted off down the aisle toward the drink cases.

The proprietor cleared his throat, then slid three dollar bills and a small pile of change across the counter at Stone, watching him all the while over the tops of his glasses.

"Thank you," he said. "Come again." His creaky voice was pleasant, but it was clear even without any sort of magical-sight cheating that he didn't really mean it.

"Cheers," Stone said, and made his escape. Suddenly, the place was making him edgy—not like he was in any kind of danger, but like he'd just walked into the kind of pub where everybody had known each other for twenty years and he wasn't one of the regulars.

Back outside, a chill breeze sliced at him. He zipped up his light jacket, took one last glance through the door (the young newcomer had carried a six-pack of beer up to the counter and was conversing with the proprietor) and then headed off. He hoped he would be able to find something for Aubrey without too much hunting.

| CHAPTER TWENTY-EIGHT

B

Y THE TIME STONE GOT BACK to his townhouse it was close to two o'clock, and he'd made a vow to himself that any shopping he did in the future would either be taken care of during off hours or, even better, via mail order. The Downtown shops had been packed with Christmas shoppers to the point where Stone had on at least four separate occasions contemplated abandoning his search until a later time. Only his guilt about the fact that he likely wouldn't be going home for Christmas kept him focused on his mission instead of on satisfying fantasies about letting loose with some devastating but nonlethal magic to get all these people *the hell out of his way.*

He pulled the Jaguar into the little one-car garage and headed out to the mailbox, juggling two shopping bags and another from a take-out falafel joint in one hand. He'd gotten Aubrey two gifts: a handsome, hand-knitted wool scarf (he'd noticed while at home that the caretaker's old one was fraying, and if left to his own devices Aubrey tended to use things until they disintegrated rather than go shopping—he was one of the few people who hated the process more than Stone did) and a vintage copy of an obscure Agatha Christie mystery novel from what had already become one of his favorite shops: an upscale used and collectible bookstore tucked away on a little side street not far from University. He'd even, in a brief fit of holiday cheer upon discovering that the bookstore wasn't packed with people, lingered there to buy gifts for Edwina Mortenson and MacKenzie Hubbard: a rare collection of writings by Edgar Cayce for the former, and a fifty-year-old collection of H. P. Lovecraft stories for the latter.

He almost didn't look at the mail when he got back inside. Tossing the stack on the breakfast bar along with the shopping bags, he was about to see if he had any Guinness left when one of the envelopes caught his eye among the bills, correspondence from the University, and advertising circulars.

It was a simple, white business envelope, sealed but with no return address or stamp. Instead, the word *Stone* was scrawled on the front in a hurried hand.

Stone frowned. It didn't look like Kolinsky's handwriting, and in any case the black mage wouldn't send anything in a basic white business envelope—especially not one with the brownish ghost of a coffee stain adorning its lower right corner. He popped the top off the Guinness, took a long drink, then slit open the envelope.

Inside were two folded pieces of plain white copier paper. When he carefully unfolded them, a tiny baggie containing an object wrapped in a piece of tissue dropped out onto the counter. Stone ignored it for the moment, focusing on the inner of the two larger sheets, which had only a brief typed message:

```
Stone—
Something for your friend.
I can't believe I'm doing this.
```

There was no signature, but the note did include a local phone number.

For a moment, Stone just stared down at it, not quite believing he was seeing it. Then, hands shaking just a bit, he carefully opened the baggie and undid the little tissue-wrapped package.

He almost didn't see what was inside, almost dropped it because it was so small. He held his breath so as not to accidentally blow it away, then contemplated the tiny object.

No explanation was included. Stone was sure that if this had in fact come from Grider, the detective was breaking any number of rules by doing this, so he was taking as many precautions as possible not to have it pinned on him should Stone prove to be the nutter that he suspected he was. But there was no question about it was: the tip of a fingernail, barely an eighth of an inch wide and half that tall, ragged on the bottom as if it had been torn off—and it had an even tinier dark, dried bloodstain on it.

Stone swallowed, still not daring to breathe near it. He hurried over and dug a magnifying glass out of one of the kitchen drawers, turned on the overhead light, and bent down to peer through the glass at it. It looked like someone had sliced it in half, right in the middle of the bloodstain. Like maybe Grider had kept half for himself and sent the other half to Stone. Stone pictured the detective seated at his desk when no one else was around, possibly late the previous night, carefully preparing his little missive and then driving by Stone's home to drop it off in a wild hope that the crazy occult professor might be able to use it to help find the animals killing the people of his city. He imagined how hard it must have been for Grider to do it, and wondered how many times he'd almost aborted the plan before finally slipping the envelope into the mailbox.

His respect for Grider shifted upward several notches as a tingle of anticipation grew at the back of his neck.

He could grade the exams tomorrow. He gathered up the folded package and the Guinness and headed for his basement.

❖

Stone was glad he'd spent the time to get his magical laboratory sorted out in the few months since he'd moved into the townhouse. It hadn't gone as quickly as he'd wanted it to; it also wasn't as thorough as he wanted it to be, given that he hadn't decided yet whether he'd be staying past the end of the year.

He couldn't ask anyone else to help him—paying a husky football player or two to haul heavy furniture around was one thing, but directing the same students to set up sturdy tables and shelves in a room full of creepy old books and a large ritual circle inscribed on the floor with latex house paint was another matter entirely. And he couldn't very well ask the only other two mages he knew in the area: Madame Huan was a bit old to be toting furniture around, and while the thought of Stefan Kolinsky doing anything more physical than walking from his car to a fine restaurant was amusing, it was hardly helpful. That meant a whole lot of delicate levitation spells to lower the various components of a properly stocked magical lab down the wooden staircase, since Stone was hardly a strapping example of physical prowess himself.

Still, he was grateful that the place even *had* a basement: as he'd come to find out when he'd specified his requirements for a rental, most houses in California didn't come equipped with any sort of underground space. This was due to the earthquakes the area was known for; while they weren't exactly common, they occurred frequently enough that getting a new single-family dwelling code-certified for a basement was difficult at best and prohibitively expensive at worst. He'd been quite lucky to find this place, an anomaly even in the older neighborhood where it was located, and the basement's existence had convinced him to agree to pay more than he'd planned for the privilege.

He hurried down the stairs, put the little package containing the fingernail on one of the tables after sweeping several pages of scribbled magical formulae aside, and then moved with assurance among the shelves as he gathered the books and materials he would need.

Tracking spells—using a physical object associated with a person as a symbolic link to trace that person to a location—weren't something Stone had a lot of practical experience with, but he'd excelled at them during his apprenticeship. If the fingernail did in fact come from one of the Cannibal Killers—or even better, if the blood did—then it should be a relatively simple matter to establish an association between it and its owner. He could then follow that link, or direct someone else to, and theoretically find the quarry at the other end.

Of course, a lot of variables were involved: *was* this in fact a piece of one of the cannibals? He didn't think Grider would be sloppy enough to send him the piece of fingernail without being sure it hadn't belonged to Douglas Phelps (in which case the ritual wouldn't work: you couldn't trace a dead person). Was whatever kind of supernatural creature the cannibals were specimens of even trackable via this type of ritual? It was designed to work on humans: if they weren't human, then there was no way to know whether it would find them. And finally, was the sample still fresh enough to be viable as a tether object?

Stone wasn't too worried about this last one: with the level of psychic energy that a murder generated, he was fairly sure the sample, tiny as it was, would remain potent for a long time. Certainly longer than a few weeks, even without any sort of magical preservation.

He had gathered up what he'd need and had just gotten up to begin customizing the circle for the specific type of ritual he planned to do when a thought occurred to him and made him sit back down.

Assuming that the ritual led him to the Cannibal Killers—or at least the one who'd unwittingly contributed to the sample—what then? What was he going to do if he found them? He glanced up at the clock on the wall: it was a little after two-thirty in the afternoon. The setup for the ritual would take at least an hour; he could probably do it more quickly, but since he had only the single sample and it was unlikely he could get another one if he botched the tracking, he wanted to make sure everything was checked and double-checked before he began.

The ritual itself wouldn't take long—maybe fifteen minutes to half an hour, assuming the creatures were trackable in the first place. But that that point, he'd get a link—sort of an astral breadcrumb trail—that would lead him to where they were located. That assumed they didn't move, too. It was possible to build an additional component into a ritual that would allow continued tracking if the subject didn't stay in one place, but it made things a lot more difficult and required a better sample than the one Stone had.

So the bottom line was, he'd get one shot at this: one shot to track them to wherever they were, and once he had the data it would have to be done quickly before the link faded. His mind flicked back to the night of the attack on the Phelpses—to how fast the killers had moved, how inhumanly. They no doubt had some sort of claws they could use to rip flesh with, and since he had a piece of fingernail, that probably meant the claws were somehow retractable or otherwise under the control of the creatures.

He had to do it. The alternative was to call up Grider and have him present during the ritual so they could move fast if Stone got anything, and that wasn't going to happen. As much as Stone wanted to see these killers captured or killed, he wasn't ready to risk anyone else finding out about his magical abilities. No, he'd have to do the ritual and, if he found anything, just hope Grider was at the other end of the phone number in the note.

If he wasn't, Stone would have to think about how far he'd be willing to go to see an end to this.

He spent a little over an hour customizing the circle. The one painted on the floor was generic, the sort of circle used as a starting point for the vast majority of rituals. If Stone had any ability in the kitchen at all, he might liken it to baking a cake: most of them required the same basic-level ingredients, and it was the custom touches that differentiated them. He didn't, though, so he had to settle for embellishing the standard circle with a series of customizations using different-colored chalk, candles in holders, and sticks of incense in small braziers (he'd pulled the battery out of the basement smoke alarm shortly after he finished creating the lab).

Every few minutes he'd step out of the circle to consult a book he had open on the table, comparing his with the one pictured in its pages. Yes, he was being overly cautious, but the consequences of failure were too high to rely solely on his usual level of confidence in his own abilities.

When the circle was finished, he slowly paced around it three times while carrying the book, examining it for any defects. He was stalling, he knew, but the clock didn't begin ticking until he actually started the ritual. Until then, he had time to stall.

It was a bit after four o'clock now. There were no windows in the lab, but Stone knew the sun was already beginning its descent. By the time he finished, it would be fully dark. And he still had no idea what sort of place the cannibals might be holed up in, or even if they were all together. Aside from the fact that there were four of them, he knew essentially nothing about them.

"Enough," he said aloud. He unfolded his map of the area and settled it just off to one side of the center of the circle with three different-colored pens next to it. He retrieved the little package containing the fingernail from the table, slipped out of his Doc Martens, and stepped in stocking feet into the middle of the circle.

He'd left enough space to sit comfortably, so he folded his long legs into a modified Lotus position that had proven not to stiffen him up too badly in the past. He glanced around the perimeter of the circle, lighting each of the candles and the incense sticks with tiny infusions of magic, and willed power into the construct. The circle closed with a satisfying magical thrum, like a small, well-behaved machine.

He took several deep, centering breaths, feeling his body relax as his mind entered the focused, meditative state that was most conducive to working magic. It was another thing young mages learned early in their training, and a common cause for the failure of apprenticeships: if you couldn't master your own mind, you had little hope of mastering the forces of reality that you'd have to manipulate to do more than rudimentary spellcasting or rituals.

The world of the lab, with its bare concrete walls and wooden staircase, fell away. In its place were the ordered, starkly elegant lines of the forces that held the universe together. The lines that mundanes might sense, but would never see. They shimmered and danced all around Stone, each one a masterpiece of mathematical perfection, each one with its own distinct and immutable purpose. When the universe was in harmony, all of these lines interacted with each other to form a thing of such unimaginable beauty that apprentices often lost focus during their first few rituals due to the sheer distraction of just *staring* at it. It was like a magical high, and, as Stone himself had discovered during a few experiments in his University days, a much more spectacular and meaningful experience than any pharmaceutical version could hope to match.

Slowly, carefully, he opened the paper packet, removed the tiny fingernail fragment, and placed it in a shallow bowl on a stand in front of him. He didn't hesitate now: he knew what he was doing and how to do it, so all that was left was the final step: feeding power into the tether item, and then concentrating as the magical concept colloquially expressed as "as above, so below" became reality and led him to the original source.

If it worked.

For a moment, he feared it wouldn't. The process was usually straightforward: once the power touched the object, a connection was made between it and whatever was connected with it, and that connection became visible among all the other lines and forces. It was a simple matter then to follow the connection to its other end, and then mark its location or follow its trail.

In this case, though, something seemed to be resisting his efforts. Instead of snapping an instant connection between the small and the large, the energy surged and roiled as if trying to find something but failing. It didn't feel like active resistance, of the sort he might get if he were trying to track another mage; instead, he got the impression that it the energy was simply not certain how to lock in on its target.

Stone added more power, careful not to overwhelm the tiny bond: if he did, the fingernail would be destroyed prematurely, and the line joining the two ends would collapse before he had a chance to track it.

And there it was!

"Yes…" he murmured. "I've got you now…"

Inside the bowl, the tiniest of *whuff*s accompanied the tiniest of flaring flames, and the fingernail fragment disappeared. For good or ill, this was all he was going to get.

Carefully holding on to the connection, he twisted so he was facing the map. This was the tricky part: trying to sync the real world up with the magical world so he could identify the location the connection was showing him. He concentrated hard for several moments, then picked up a red marker and made a dot on the map where the wavering line of energy pointed. He couldn't see the exact location through all the glowing lines of magic, but he could tell it wasn't too far from where he was now. It was still on the map, which meant it had to be somewhere in the Bay Area.

He let the connection go, allowing his body to slump as the tension left his shoulders. Even in the meditative state, magic was tiring work. He allowed himself less than a minute to sit there, breathing hard, sweat trickling down his back and soaking into his T-shirt, and then he got up, grabbed the map, and spread it out on the nearby table. Where would the dot be? Somewhere out in one of the undeveloped areas? Up in San Francisco, where it would be easy for even a cannibal to lose himself in the crowds?

The red dot he'd made was right in the middle of East Palo Alto.

| CHAPTER TWENTY-NINE

STONE PULLED THE JAGUAR into the parking lot of a 7-Eleven and consulted his map again.

He'd left the townhouse half an hour ago, taking with him the marked-up map, a copy of the local Thomas Guide, and a separate piece of paper on which he'd copied down the phone number from Grider's note.

He was second-guessing himself again. He knew it as he sat there in the parking lot and waited for a trio of young men in oversized football jerseys and backward-facing baseball caps to slouch by and pile into a clapped-out Chevy sedan. He knew it, but he couldn't help it.

His first shocked thought when he'd seen the location of the red mark on the map was that Stefan Kolinsky *was* somehow involved. He didn't know anybody else connected with East Palo Alto, and the location seemed a bit too much of a coincidence to be a coincidence. But after a moment's consideration and a little more study of the map, he realized he was jumping to absurd conclusions. In the first place, Kolinsky was potent enough magically that he could hide from a tracking spell with ridiculous ease. Hell, Stone himself could do it, and Kolinsky had to have many years' experience on him. Second, the dot was nowhere near the location of Kolinsky's disreputable little shop. Stone still had no idea why the elegant, old-fashioned mage would want to have his business premises in such a sketchy neighborhood, but even he couldn't make himself believe that the man would choose to maintain his home there as well.

Unfortunately for Stone, none of this helped him very much. Eliminating Kolinsky from the suspect pool was all well and good, but the area indicated by the red dot, he'd discovered when he'd cross-referenced it against the more granular maps from the Thomas Guide, encompassed a residential area consisting largely of high-density apartment buildings and multiplexes. Which meant that while the spell had worked—it had latched on to something and shown him where its counterpart currently was—it hadn't given him enough specific information that he could call up Grider and send him on his way. What was he supposed to say? "Yes, hello, Lieutenant, this is Stone. I've tracked your suspects to a several-block radius in Eas Palo Alto. Yes, those are all apartment buildings, so you're looking at sorting through several hundred people. Glad to be of assistance!"

Maybe not.

Like it or not, he'd need to get more involved in this hunt than he wanted to. He didn't have the thread anymore—he'd had to let it go when he'd set out in the car, or he'd probably have run into a parked car before he reached the end of his own street—but the ritual had given him a stronger sense of the elusive aura he'd noticed at the scene of Douglas Phelps's murder. He thought the odds were reasonably good that if he went to the area the dot marked and cruised around a bit, he might be able to narrow things down sufficiently that a call to Grider might actually give the man something he could use.

He tossed the maps back in the passenger seat after double-checking the route to the location, then started off again. He was glad that he had his mind firmly around driving on the wrong side of the road by now; the traffic was not only heavy, but more than once a car darted out in front of him or cut him off, forcing him to slam on the brakes.

From the sidewalks in the commercial districts and near larger apartment buildings, knots of young men lounged against walls and on street corners, some of them eyeing the Jaguar as it rolled by. Probably hadn't been the best idea to bring it here—too conspicuous alongside the majority of older cars and motorcycles on the road—but it couldn't be helped at this point.

He was approaching the area the red dot indicated now, and slowed down so he could make occasional shifts to magical sight for a few seconds as he drove. The dot was small, but the map he'd used had covered a lot of territory, which meant that when he compared it to the Thomas Guide map it ended up covering three large blocks and possibly more. This wasn't going to be easy.

Stone noted that the area was derelict even by the standards he was expecting. The blocks consisted of old three-story apartment buildings interspersed with rock-strewn vacant lots, dirt parking lots, and streets lined with cars. Some of the vehicles didn't look like they'd moved from their spots in the current year, and when the streetlights worked (odds were about fifty-fifty) he could see where the lower windows of the apartment buildings were covered with stout bars and, in some cases, plywood sheets. Bright sprays of graffiti decorated the buildings, the fences, and even some of the vehicles.

He'd driven past about three-quarters of the area he'd defined when the feeling began growing stronger. He shifted to magical sight again and sensed the traces, tantalizingly nearby, but too diffuse to track effectively. He was close.

Ahead of him, a man and a woman darted across the street, got into a massive, battered Cadillac coupe parked half a block away, and pulled out. Stone took advantage of the rare empty space, gunning the Jaguar forward and pulling in just ahead of a

Mustang about to make a U-turn into it from the other side. The driver flipped Stone off and yelled something as he continued past.

Stone waited to make sure he was gone and that no one else was paying attention before muttering the spell he'd used when visiting Kolinsky in his shop. At least now the car would blend in, for an hour or so anyway. If he was still here in an hour, he was doing something wrong.

He got out, pulled his black wool overcoat tighter around him, and set off at a brisk walk down the street toward the apartment buildings. He wasn't too concerned about anyone bothering him: there weren't that many people around right now, and if they did hassle him, he was almost certainly capable of dealing with them long enough to make his escape. He didn't *want* to have to do that, though, so he kept his head down and concentrated on walking like he belonged there.

All around him, the tantalizing, mingled odors of several different ethnicities' cooking wafted from various windows: he thought he could pick out Chinese, Mexican, and the savory, meaty smell of spiced beef roasting on a grill. It was still early for dinner, but his stomach rumbled nonetheless.

It was fully dark by now, even though it was only a bit after five o'clock. A steady stream of cars rolled by, blasting out strains of rap, rock, and what sounded like Mexican polka music. The occupants seemed to be ignoring Stone, though, which was a relief. In fact, the only people who paid him attention were a couple of slouched teenagers on a street corner who nodded a greeting, and a young mother and father pushing a baby in a stroller. Stone revised his opinion of the area: poor, but not necessarily threatening. He chided himself for believing the accounts he'd read about how dangerous American cities could be.

Except for the psychotic cannibals, of course. They were still pretty dangerous.

He turned to watch the couple with the baby go by, with uneasy thoughts of what might happen if one of the cannibals got hungry and nipped out for a light snack one evening. He had to find them. Grider had taken a big chance sending him that sample, and he wasn't going to let it go to waste.

He continued walking, shifting back and forth from natural to magical sight and noting the locations of the functional public telephones in case he had to call Grider in a hurry. There were two of them; he'd seen two more while walking around the three large blocks, but their receiver cords dangled loose like shredded metal snakes.

As luck in such things often worked, he didn't get any definitive information until he'd made almost the full circuit of the large blocks, and was coming back around toward where he'd left his car. Approaching a cluster of ramshackle two- and three-story buildings a little more than a block away from his starting point, he caught a faint image of the same unsettled, bizarre aura he'd noticed clinging to Douglas Phelps. He stopped, glanced around to make sure no one was paying attention to him, then shifted over fully and examined the buildings.

Whatever it was, it was definitely coming from one of them. There were three in total, arranged around a central courtyard awash with trash and pockmarked with rocks and scrubby dead weeds. A child's broken Big Wheel lay upside down just off the central walkway.

Stone's heartbeat quickened. He couldn't get anything more without moving closer—he thought for perhaps five seconds about doing just that, trying to get something better to give Grider, but quickly dismissed the idea. He wasn't a cop, he wasn't trained for dealing with these kinds of situations, and his combat magic was woefully out of practice. At best, he might be able to take down one of them before the rest either took off or went after him. Better to let the professionals handle it. He doubted the creatures were bulletproof.

"What'cha lookin' at, man?"

Stone stiffened, snapping back to normal sight to see two young men watching him from the sidewalk. Both wore baseball caps, oversized black Raiders jackets, and baggy jeans. Willing himself to stay calm—they probably meant no harm, and if they did, he could deal with them—he shrugged. "Nothing, really. Just taking a walk."

"You ain't from around here," the smaller of the two observed.

"No. I was visiting a friend."

They exchanged glances, obviously not believing that somebody like him would have a friend around here. "You got a smoke?" the larger one asked.

"Sorry." He didn't have time for this; he needed to get back to the phone and call Grider. "Fresh out."

While they considered that, he took a moment to examine them with magical sight. It would be quite embarrassing if it ended up that he was standing on the street chatting with two of the killers without realizing it. But no, their auras were strong and fully human—one blue, one greenish-gold—the few dark spots on each probably representing their less than healthy lifestyle habits.

Finally they shrugged. "Yeah, whatever," the larger one said. Someone called to them from across the street and he added, "See ya, man," and the two of them took off at a jog in the direction of the call.

Stone let his breath out. Best to get out of here before he attracted any more attention.

The nearest phone was, thankfully, one of the working models. He dug out Grider's number and punched it in, tapping his foot and looking around with impatience as if expecting all four of the killers to be bearing down on him at any moment.

The phone rang. And rang. "Come on, Grider, you bastard," he muttered. Ten rings. Fifteen. Twenty. Had the guy given Stone his phone number and then decided to go out drinking or something?

"Grider."

Stone had been about to hang up and reconsider his decision not to investigate the buildings himself; the voice startled him and he bobbled the receiver. "Grider. Stone here."

Pause. "What do you want?"

The voice was gruff, but Stone didn't miss the anticipation behind it. "My friend might have some information for you."

Another pause. "You're shittin' me."

"Hardly. Do you want it or not?"

"Where are you? Is that rap I hear in the background?"

Stone lowered his voice. "I'm at a pay phone in East Palo Alto." He gave the location and glanced back over toward the three buildings, but so far he hadn't seen anyone go in or come out—at least from the front.

"What the *hell* are you doin' there?" Grider let out a loud blast of air, his voice rising in volume. "Stone, *please* tell me that you didn't actually *go* where you got this psychic brainwave. You can't be that big an idiot."

"I've not gone near the place," Stone said, keeping his tone even. "I'm not a fool. But I didn't get enough from the sample to be able to make a definitive call. I didn't think you'd fancy being sent to check out several city blocks' worth of apartments."

The line crackled and buzzed as Grider's silence stretched out. "Okay. Fine. I still think this whole thing's full of shit. But assuming it isn't—tell me where I'm lookin'."

Stone did, describing the three buildings in question as well as he could—both their location on the street (he couldn't give

Grider an actual street address since he didn't see any numbers)—and a description of them and the cars currently parked near them. "I think it might be on the ground floor, but I can't be sure. You don't exactly get specifics with this sort of thing."

Another pause, probably for Grider to write all of that down. "Okay. Okay. You did your bit. I dunno if it's gonna do a damn bit of good, but I'll check it out. Just get your ass outta there. *Now.* Got it? I see you anywhere nearby when I get there, I'm haulin' you in."

"Understood. I'm leaving now. But I'm telling you: don't come alone. If I'm right and they are here, you don't want to face them without backup. Believe me on that, if nothing else. And keep me out of it. You got an anonymous tip, that's all."

"Not a problem. You think I'm gonna admit to this? Go home, Stone." Grider hung up.

Stone paused for a moment, took one more glance at the buildings, and then did as he was told.

As he pulled the Jaguar out of the parking space, he hoped the whole thing hadn't been a false positive—or worse, that it wasn't, and Grider didn't take it sufficiently seriously. The detective could be frustrating in his mundanity, but he was still the most refreshingly no-bullshit person Stone had yet met in California. He didn't want the man's death on his conscience.

CHAPTER THIRTY

WHEN HE GOT HOME half an hour later after a quick stop at a Chinese takeout place, Stone forced himself to go to his study and start grading the final exams and papers for his courses.

The alternatives were equally undesirable: spend the rest of the evening camped out in front of the television news waiting for any reports of what might have happened, or go out somewhere and get good and drunk. The problem with the former was that it was entirely possible that nothing *would* happen, and he'd end up wasting the evening; the problem with latter was that he didn't usually get drunk alone unless he was in the middle of one of his black moods and he didn't have anybody else to drink with. He added finding some pub-hopping companions to his mental list of things to do (it was right below "get a housekeeper who can cook") and then, carton of General Tso's chicken and bottle of Guinness in hand, headed upstairs.

His concentration was shot, but he'd expected that. Every few minutes he'd glance at the phone as if expecting it to ring, but it didn't. He started on the easiest stack of papers: he could grade the finals from his Intro to the Occult course in his sleep, which was essentially what he was doing.

When the phone finally did ring, it startled him; he'd given up a while ago thinking that it would, and applied himself fully to the next batch of essays. He glanced at the clock: a little after eight, and almost three hours since he'd left the apartments. He let it ring a couple more times, then picked it up. "Stone here."

"Stone." Grider's voice sounded ponderous, weary.

A shiver ran up Stone's spine. "What happened? Was my friend right?"

"Yeah. We gotta talk."

"Did you get them?"

"No."

"Then how do you—?"

"Listen. I can get away for a little while. Looks like I'll be pullin' an all-nighter, but I ain't had dinner yet. You know a bar called the Fifth Quarter, on El Camino?"

"No, but I can find it."

"Meet me there in half an hour. I'll fill you in. I owe you that much."

"Lieutenant…" Stone didn't want to ask, but he had to. "No one was killed, were they? None of your people?"

"No. Just show up, I'll tell you."

Grider was already there when Stone arrived. He was in the back room, in a scarred wooden booth all the way in the far corner. Stone had deliberately left the radio in the car off, but the room's numerous TVs—presumably normally tuned to sports given the bar's name—were now all showing news reports. The crawl across the bottom of the closest one read *RAID IN EAST PALO ALTO*, and another said *NEW LEADS ON CANNIBAL KILLER FOLLOWING POLICE RAID*.

"Siddown," Grider said, waving Stone to a seat across from him.

Stone sat. A waitress came by and dropped off a soft drink in front of Grider; Stone ordered the same.

"I got some wings comin' if you want any," Grider said, taking a long pull from the soda. "Damn, I wish this was a beer. Or a shot o' whiskey."

Stone studied him for a moment. The cop looked tired; a dusting of graying stubble sprinkled his jowls. "So...?"

He sighed. "So. First off, you were right. That's where they were." His eyes narrowed. "You *sure* you didn't get close? Didn't try to get a quick peek in on 'em or anything?"

What was he implying? "I give you my word, Lieutenant: I never got closer than the pave—er, sidewalk out front. I told you, I wasn't even sure which building it was, just that it was probably one of that group. Putting aside the fact that I didn't want to cause any suspicion if they were there, I also didn't want to risk having them decide I looked tasty."

Grider nodded, holding his gaze for a few more seconds before focusing on his drink again. "Okay, so I took a couple patrol units over there with me, with a few more on standby if things panned out. Told 'em it was an anonymous tip, like you said."

"And they weren't there?"

"We spread out and surrounded the buildings you told us about—there were five of us, so we were able to cover decently. That's when somebody smelled smoke."

Stone stiffened. "Smoke?" He glanced up at the TV screen: the picture was grainy and too far away to make out details.

"Yeah." Grider pulled a large white handkerchief out of his pocket and swiped it across his forehead. "Hey, at least it helped us find the right place fast. But by the time we converged on it, it was already lit up."

"What happened then?"

"Called in the fire boys and more backup. Place burned pretty good before they put it out, and messed up the one above it and the two on either side, too."

"What started the fire?"

"Don't know yet. The forensics guys are still out there picking through the scene—we probably won't know for sure for a while, unless somebody was real sloppy."

Stone nodded. "So I'm still not following—if they weren't there and your evidence was destroyed, how do you know you had the right place?"

"Because all our evidence *wasn't* destroyed." Grider took another pull at his soda, his mouth twisting in distaste. "Damn, that diet stuff's vile. Anyway, they got the fire out before it destroyed the whole place. And I'll give you three guesses what we found in the freezer."

"Meat," Stone said in a monotone.

"Yeah. Neat little packages, all wrapped up in butcher paper. They'd left the fridge and the freezer open, but I guess it was still protected enough that the fire just singed it. Only a few, and we ain't had time to check 'em yet, but I'll bet my retirement fund that we're gonna find it's part of their takeout stash. We also found some burned bones. Again, haven't checked 'em, but…"

Stone nodded, the enormity of all this sinking in. He'd been right about the location—that part didn't surprise him, since the tracking spell had never failed him if it managed to get a bead on its quarry—but the Cannibal Killers had somehow gotten wind that something was up and made their escape before the police arrived. He let his mind travel back over the time when he'd been there: *had* it been possible that one of them had seen him? Had they gotten a look at him during Douglas Phelps's murder, and remembered?

He sighed. "I'm sorry, Lieutenant."

"Hey, don't be." He paused a moment as the waitress returned and set a basket of wings soaked in barbecue sauce in the middle of the table. "I didn't believe you—part of me still doesn't want to—but you came through. Maybe we didn't catch 'em, but they're on the run now. And I didn't tell ya the best part."

"There's a best part?" Stone leaned back, trying not to wrinkle his nose at the wings' tangy, cloying aroma.

"'Scuse me—starving. Feel free," he added, already gnawing his way through the first wing. He picked it clean and wiped his hands on a napkin before continuing. "I talked to the landlady. She was in the next building over. She gave us some good intel."

Stone raised an eyebrow. Maybe this wasn't as bad as he'd feared. "Are you allowed to tell me what it is?"

"Yeah, I can tell you. It wasn't as much as I hoped, though. She's a pothead, hardly ever leaves the apartment 'cept to go buy weed. She said they always paid on time, in cash, dropped through the slot on her door. So she ain't seen 'em since they moved in."

"Did she give you names? descriptions?"

"Yeah. Names were fake, of course. Expected that. Descriptions were vague. Two male, two female, all kinda sick-lookin'—pale, y'know. Meth-addict types. One guy and one girl're white, and she thinks the other two might be Hispanic. She didn't remember anything like hair color or identifying marks. She did say they didn't look freaky, though, except maybe like they might be stoners too. No fangs or claws or anything."

Stone pondered that. "You're going to have a difficult time keeping the fact that there are four of them secret now."

"Yeah, I know. We'll just have to act like it's a new development we just found out about. I'd be surprised if that chick isn't already yappin' to the news media, tryin' to work this into some kinda deal. You know: 'I Was the Cannibal Killers' Landlady,' or some shit."

"No doubt." Vulture-like press was as much a fixture on his side of the world as it was here. After a pause, Stone sighed again. "Well. Do you think they'll stick around at this point, or move on?"

"Who can tell? They've moved on before, and bein' made might spook 'em enough that they won't be my problem anymore. But that just makes 'em somebody else's problem, y'know?"

Stone nodded, then something occurred to him. "Unless they took some of their stored meat with them, they might need to hunt again soon."

Grider gave him an odd look. "Stone, I can't help thinkin' you know more about this than you're tellin'. Whaddya mean, 'need' to hunt'?"

"I don't know anything about it, Lieutenant. I have a few theories, but they're all firmly in the realm of the supernatural, which means you likely won't believe them. I know how hard it was for you to believe the psychic information. Probably best if you just continue on the assumption that these killers are dangerous, probably faster and more powerful than a standard human, and deserving of as much caution as you can manage."

"Yeah." Grider finished his drink and began gnawing at another wing. After a moment, he looked at Stone again. "Why am I thinkin' all of a sudden that whatever you did to find that place, it didn't have fuck-all to do with bein' psychic?"

Stone shrugged, getting up. "Think what you like, Lieutenant. As for me, unless you need me for anything else, I've got a lot of papers to grade. And I'm sure you've got quite a bit to do before you can go home tonight."

"Who says I'm goin' home?" Grider asked sourly.

CHAPTER THIRTY-ONE

"F UCK, FUCK, *FUCK!*"

"I *told* ya we shoulda hunted down that fuckin' professor, Kano! Didn't I tell ya?"

The four of them were currently holed up in an abandoned warehouse a few blocks from their former apartment building. They weren't using any light, fearful they might be spotted by someone passing by, but the alterations to their natural vision from their condition meant that they didn't need to. They saw things better in nearly no light than they did in broad daylight.

"We gotta kill 'im," Grease said. He was crouched in a corner, learning against a rusting wall of corrugated metal, gnawing on a bone from the last of the homeless man they'd killed. "We gotta. It's personal now. I want to rip his guts open and suck his skull dry." He bared his teeth, his normally retracted fangs poking out in anticipation.

"Shut *up*," Kano growled. He paced the area, fists clenched and teeth gritted. "We got a lot more to think about than that right now."

"We gotta leave," Taco said. "It's time to move on. That was too close."

Rima nodded. "If Taco hadn't smelled the professor guy checkin' out the apartment…" She shuddered, pushing herself off the wall where she'd been leaning. "The cops showed up so fast—he musta told 'em."

"Place burned," Grease said. "They ain't gonna find shit."

"Don't be so sure," Kano said. "We didn't have time to do a good job on it."

"It don't matter," Taco said. "If the cops are on to us—they prob'ly talked to that cow of a landlady. She prob'ly told 'em what we look like."

"Names won't get 'em nowhere," Grease said. "And she was so stoned I bet she didn't even remember what we looked like. Ain't seen her since we moved in, yeah?"

"Long as she got her money, she didn't give a shit," Taco agreed.

Kano sighed. He threw himself back down to the floor and snatched another piece of meat from the small pile between them. They hadn't been able to bring everything—it would have looked too conspicuous—but they'd taken enough to last them a few days, along with their knives. "I dunno. I kinda wanna go after the professor too. Nobody ever fucked us up like that before, and he shouldn't get away with it."

"So why not?" Grease asked, looking hopeful. "We do it, chop him up and take him along with us, and head off somewhere else."

"Maybe we will," Kano said. "Maybe we will. We all got his scent. We can find him. But not quite yet. We gotta lay low for a couple days. Cops'll be crawlin' all over the place lookin' for us. We gotta dig in and hide. We can stay here, I think."

They'd broken into the warehouse, a derelict and seemingly abandoned structure bordering a large vacant lot in an industrial part of town. "Long as we keep quiet, we should be okay for a day or two. Cops can't look everywhere at once. Anybody gets nosey—we get food for a few more days."

"And another brain," Rima said, licking her lips.

"Then we kill the prof?" Taco asked.

"Yeah. We gotta track him down, but that shouldn't be hard. Follow him till he's somewhere quiet. Kill him, then go."

Grease lounged back against the wall. "Where you wanna go? Nowhere with snow. I hate fuckin' snow."

"Mexico's nice and hot," Taco said. "It'd be easy. Nobody ever sneaks across the border *that* way."

"Maybe," Kano said. "For now, we sit tight, keep quiet, and wait. Once the heat's off, then we move." He smiled an unwholesome smile. "I wonder if professor brains taste better than homeless-guy brains."

CHAPTER THIRTY-TWO

ABSENT ANY DEFINABLE NEXT STEPS for tracking the Cannibal Killers, Stone forced himself to concentrate on finishing up grading the rest of his exams.

On Monday, he spent half a day in his office taking care of some last-minute work, dropped off the gift books for Mortenson and Hubbard (they weren't in their offices, which made the whole process easier), submitted the final grades to the department, and left after grabbing a cup of coffee and an energy bar at one of the few open cafes. The campus, normally bustling with students and faculty, wasn't quite deserted on the first day of the holiday break, but it was certainly emptier.

Grider hadn't called him back yet, and he didn't think calling the detective to see how things were going would be his best idea. He supposed he'd hear it on the news if they caught the killers, but two days after the raid, the media frenzy surrounding what had occurred at the East Palo Alto apartment building had begun to die down a bit. At least nobody from the press had been sniffing around him, which meant they hadn't made the connection between him and the tip on the killers' location. That was *one* thing that had gone right, anyway.

Stone thought the odds were good that the four killers had fled the area now that they'd been discovered, but there was no way to be sure. He didn't have another sample to do a ritual with, and he figured the reason Grider hadn't offered him one was either because he didn't have it, or, more likely, because now that the department had a definitive line of investigation, the evidence was watched a lot more closely than it had been before. Either way, there wasn't a damned thing Stone could do without something to work with.

He didn't want to go back to the townhouse after leaving campus—he'd been spending entirely too much time shut up in his study or his magical lab lately, and the clutter had gotten so annoying that he'd finally taken a couple of hours on Sunday and cleaned up the worst of it himself.

Madame Huan, he'd learned to his disappointment when he tried phoning her a few days ago, had already left on another of her extended trips overseas in search of raw materials for her magical items. So he drove over to Kolinsky's on the off chance he might find the black mage there.

Kolinsky, as it happened, was at the shop. Stone got through the wards with no difficulty (he hadn't duplicated the Latin nonsense-word trick, opting instead for something more straightforward but significantly more potent), descended the stairs, and knocked on the inner door. "Mr. Kolinsky? Are you there?"

The door swung open. Kolinsky was at his usual spot at his desk on the other side of the room, going through a stack of yellowing papers and comparing them to some small, unidentifiable objects in an old box. "Ah," he said, taking a loupe from his left eye and swinging his chair around. "Dr. Stone. I thought I might see you. I heard about the police raid on Saturday night. Did you have anything to do with that?"

"I did. Would have been nice if the police had caught them, but at least it seems they're on the run now. I wonder if they haven't left the area, but I can't do anything else to try to track them down now." He frowned. "I still haven't any idea what they are, though. It still seems like ghouls are the best bet, but ghouls don't rent apartments and wrap their supper in tidy little packages in the freezer. At least none I've ever found reference to."

"Nor I," Kolinsky agreed. "So what will you do now?"

Stone sighed. "I haven't got a bloody clue. I should just call it a day and head back home for the holiday break, but I don't feel comfortable doing that until I know those things aren't still lurking about somewhere. But the only way I'll know that for sure is if they kill someone again."

"I wish I could be of more assistance," Kolinsky said. "I fear that your first experience with my particular specialty hasn't been as impressive as you hoped."

"Well, you got your wards out of the deal, anyway," Stone said, shrugging. "I'll probably hit you up for some other bits of information in time, but right now I'm just sick of the whole situation. I want them to catch these animals and be done with it."

He didn't see much point in lingering at Kolinsky's shop—he'd half-hoped the man would have some piece of information to spur his investigation in a new direction—so he bid him farewell and went home. He still needed to wrap up the package for Aubrey and post it, which he thought he should probably do before people got off work and resumed their pre-Christmas shopping frenzy.

When he got home, the light was blinking on his answering machine. He hit the button, wondering if Grider had turned something up.

"Dr. Stone?" Aubrey's voice came from the tiny speaker. "I hope you're doing well. Just checking in with you to see if you're planning to come home for Christmas, and if so, when I might expect you. Please call—I expect I'll be up late reading tonight."

Stone gripped the edge of the counter and bowed his head. He knew he was going to have to make this call soon, but he hadn't wanted it to be today. Ah, well—best to get it over with. He picked up the phone and punched in the number.

It was answered on the second ring. "Dr. Stone?"

Stone raised an eyebrow. "How did you know?"

The old man's voice was laced with amusement. "It *is* after nine, sir. Not many others call so late. Especially when I haven't just left them a message less than half an hour ago."

Stone chuckled. "Touché." He paused, trying to figure out the best way to say it, and finally went for the direct approach: "You asked me about Christmas. I'm afraid it's looking like I won't make it back—or if I do, it will just be for the day."

"I see." Aubrey's voice was flat, but Stone knew him well enough to hear the disappointment.

"I'm sorry, but it can't be helped. I'll tell you the whole sordid story if you have the time."

"Of course, sir."

He carried the phone into the living room, dropped down on the couch, and caught Aubrey up on the latest developments in the Cannibal Killer case.

The old man listened without comment until he finished. "That's...dreadful," he said at last. "It's a shame that you were able to get so close, but they escaped. But, sir..." His voice took on a careful edge. "Do you...well, do you think it's wise to involve yourself in this? What if these creatures come after you?"

"If they do, at least I'll know where they are," Stone said with a confidence he didn't entirely feel. "And I'll deal with them. Somehow. I'm not exactly defenseless, Aubrey."

"No, sir. But you did say they were fast and dangerous. If they all attacked you at once—"

"They aren't going to attack me, Aubrey. They don't even know who I am. Besides, I'm fairly sure they're gone by now anyway. Once Grider's people turfed them out of their little nest, what's the point of staying in the area? They've moved around before."

"You're probably right," Aubrey agreed. "But please, be careful."

"I will. And I'll try to get home for a couple of days at Christmas if I can. But I want to be sure they're gone before I leave."

CHAPTER THIRTY-THREE

By late Wednesday afternoon, Stone was already bored. He wished he hadn't gotten through all the grading so quickly—at least it would have given him something useful to do.

He'd already taken another pass at cleaning the townhouse, wrapped up Aubrey's gift and sent it off, and reorganized his magical lab even though it didn't need it. He went through the syllabi for his upcoming courses to make sure they were all in order, revisited the idea of planning a field trip (not the Winchester Mystery House—even though he was fascinated by it and made a mental note to visit it at some point soon, he was fairly sure most of the students had already seen it), and even briefly considered giving Mortenson or Hubbard a call to see if they wanted to get a cup of coffee. That thought didn't last long, though—he decided that if he was that bored, maybe he *should* just head back home and let the Cannibal Killers sort themselves out without him.

There still hadn't been any updates on the case, at least not in the papers or on the local news. The official police line was that the killers had probably moved on, but that people should still remain vigilant and avoid going anywhere alone after dark.

He sighed, tossing the newspaper back down on the breakfast bar. Maybe he'd go out to a club tonight. Back home, he often went into London to seek out small, obscure clubs featuring up-and-coming local bands, but he hadn't done it yet here. Mostly it had been because he was too busy with work, but part of it was because he didn't want to go alone. Imogen, when she hadn't been busy with her own activities, had loved going to clubs with him—her taste in music was considerably more on the pop side than his, but they'd both enjoyed making a new find they could both agree on. Going alone seemed...wrong somehow. Sort of desperate.

Still, he thought as he opened the paper back up to the entertainment section, he'd have to get over that eventually. Maybe he'd even meet someone new. He wasn't sure he was ready for that either, but he couldn't mope about Imogen forever. That stage of his life was over: might as well get fully used to it.

He found a couple of likely places: one on Castro Street in Mountain View, and another on Murphy in Sunnyvale, not too far from A Passage to India. He jotted down the addresses to check on his map, but that still gave him several hours to kill in the meantime. He considered his options, and his mind returned again to the odd meeting with Laura Phelps. He'd been meaning to give her a call and see if she was feeling any better—this seemed like as good a time as any to do it.

The phone rang several times before it was picked up. "Hello?"

"Mrs. Phelps? Alastair Stone. Just calling to see how you're doing."

There was a pause. "I'm...all right. Still missing Douglas, but...getting a little better. It was good to see you the other day. I hope you're well." Another pause. "Have you been following the news? It sounds like the police might have some leads on..." She let that trail off.

"I have," he said. "It's good news—I think they'll catch them soon."

"I do hope so. It's so hard…thinking they're still out there somewhere."

Stone frowned. Her voice still had that tired, beaten edge to it. He supposed it wasn't surprising, given that it had only been a bit over a month since the murder. "Are your family there yet?"

"Not yet. They can't get off work until late next week. You know how it is—young people, jobs that aren't flexible about time off…"

She sounded so sad and lost that he spoke before he thought about it: "Mrs. Phelps—would you like to have dinner with me? I've got some plans for later on tonight, but if you're not busy, perhaps we could just chat for a bit. I hate to think of you being alone so much."

"Oh, I'm not alone," she said, chuckling. "I've got friends who come by to visit—just not so often right now, since everyone's caught up in holiday plans. But yes, I think I'd like that. You've been so kind to me, and I appreciate it."

"You're being kind to me as well. I'm alone today too, so some company would be welcome. Shall I pick you up at seven?"

"That would be great. Thank you, Dr. Stone."

He took her to an artsy little place he'd discovered recently, a few blocks off University. The dinner crowd was brisk but not overly stifling, the walls covered with local artwork he thought she might appreciate.

"It *is* good to get out every now and then," she admitted as she sat down. She wore a simple long-sleeved tunic and peasant skirt, her hair tied back and still graying at the roots. Her perfume was strong, and smelled of roses. She still looked pale and tired, with deep circles under her eyes.

"How are you getting on?" Stone asked.

"Oh, all right," she said. "There's a lot to do—insurance, dealing with Douglas's affairs and his personal items that I don't want to keep…that kind of stuff. But it keeps me busy. And like I said, my friends come by often."

For a while they just chatted about innocuous topics as their appetizers and drinks arrived. Stone didn't want to bring up anything that might upset her, so he kept the conversation light, and mostly focused on her. He asked her about her children, about her and Douglas's patronage of the arts, about her experiences at Stanford. All the while he watched her closely for signs that he was upsetting her with his questions, but he got no impression that he was. She seemed relieved to talk about something that wasn't related to the murder or the murderers.

During a brief lull in the conversation, she smiled at him. "We're talking a lot about me, Dr. Stone. What about you?"

He chuckled. "Not much to tell, really."

"Oh, you're too modest. I'll bet you have all kinds of interesting stories to share."

You'd win that bet, he thought wryly. *Too bad I can't tell you many of them.*

"For example," she added, "What part of England are you from, originally?"

"I doubt you'd have heard of it," he said. "It's a little village called Holmbury St. Mary, in Surrey."

"I've heard of Surrey," she said. "Partial credit?"

"Absolutely."

"What brought you over here to America? It seems so…exotic to me to move halfway around the world for a job. I'm not sure I could do it."

He paused, considering how he wanted to respond. "There was a bit more to it than that," he said.

"If you'd rather not say—"

Oddly, even though he didn't normally even want to think about the situation with Imogen, telling Laura didn't seem so difficult. Maybe it was her motherly demeanor, or the fact that she seemed so lost without her own love. "I...had a bit of relationship trouble. We'd known each other for years—she's the daughter of one of my mentors. I thought we'd be married, but...it turned out she had other plans. When the job offer came up over here, I decided if I was going to change my life, I might as well do the thing properly."

"Oh..." she said kindly. "I'm so sorry. That must have been difficult for you."

In perspective, compared to what she'd gone through, it hardly seemed so. "These things happen," he said. "I'm all right with it now. And I've found that I do like it here. I might even stay."

"Was there a chance that you might not?"

"The position's initially just for the year, but I already know they want to keep me. Unless I completely bollix things up before the end of the academic year, I expect they'll bring me on permanently."

Her smile was gentle, maternal. "And there's no chance of going back home and convincing her to change her mind?"

"No. I'm not even sure I want that, to be honest. There were...other issues that would have made things difficult for us, if we'd married. It was probably for the best, all things considered."

"You don't believe that," she said. "Do you?"

He shrugged and picked up his wineglass so he didn't have to look at her. "I don't know. But it doesn't matter, really, anyway, does it? It won't change."

"Okay, I'll stop bringing it up, then," she said, reaching across the table to pat his arm. She glanced at her watch. "You mentioned you had something else going on tonight. I'm not keeping you from anything, am I?"

He shook his head. "Oh, no, not at all. I just thought I might check out a club tonight. Listen to some local bands. They don't even get started until after ten o'clock or so. So you needn't worry I'm planning to duck out early on you."

Her expression went odd for a moment, then she smiled. "A club, hmm? Douglas and I used to go to jazz clubs sometimes. There's a great one down in San Jose—little hole-in-the-wall place on Stevens Creek. Which one were you going to, if you don't mind my asking? What kind of music do you like?"

"I was deciding between two, but I think I might start out at Busby's on Castro in Mountain View. I'm a bit more rock than jazz, I'm afraid," he added with a rueful grin. "If that doesn't pan out, there's another one in Sunnyvale called the Darkwave. Heard of it?"

"Neither one," she said. "But then, new ones are always popping up. I'm sure you'll have a great time. Are you..." she hesitated, searching his face for a moment before she continued "...maybe looking to meet someone new?"

He shrugged. "Not in the plan, but if it should happen...who knows?"

"Well, have fun in any case," she said. She pushed back from the table and stood. "If you'll excuse me, I need to find the little girls' room."

"Just back there," he told her, pointing to a hallway leading toward the back of the restaurant.

While he waited for her to return, Stone thought about Imogen—specifically about the answer he'd given Laura Phelps when she'd asked if he intended trying to win her back. Not that it mattered—she'd made her decision, and he had to respect it.

She was with Robert now. Stone had known her long enough and cared enough for her that he genuinely hoped she'd find happiness with him.

Relationships between mages and mundanes were rare, especially when the mundane was aware of the mage's activities. Stone had met other mages who'd successfully hidden their magic from their spouses and partners, but aside from David Halloran and Marta Bellwood down at A Passage to India, he'd never encountered a successful partnership where the mundane was in on the secret. Even if the nonmagical person *had* grown up surrounded by it like Imogen had, the power issues, insecurities, and resentments almost invariably arose at some point in the relationship. Stone had known from the time he was a child that he had magical talent, so he'd never had to deal with the idea that someone close to him would be able to read his emotional state, physically overpower him, or even kill him with a thought. It was a sobering thing to think about, but it wasn't like it hadn't happened to others. No, it was probably for the best the way it was.

Laura returned, dropping back down into her chair with an apologetic smile. "Sorry," she said. "It was a bit crowded in there."

They finished up soon after and Stone drove Laura back to her home, a modest two-story on the edge of Palo Alto. "Thank you again," she told him. "You'll have to come by sometime and let me fix you a home-cooked dinner."

"I might take you up on that," he said. "Speaking of that—you don't happen to know anyone who's looking for a housekeeper job, do you? I need to find someone to come in a few times a week and tidy up. Bonus if she can cook."

"I might," she said. "Let me check with a couple of friends and I'll get back to you." She paused a moment after pulling her key from her purse. "Be careful, Dr. Stone. Those creatures are still out there somewhere, and…"

He patted her arm and nodded. "Don't you worry. I think they're gone, but even if they're not, I don't plan on going anywhere deserted any time soon."

| CHAPTER THIRTY-FOUR

IT WAS AFTER TEN when Stone arrived at Busby's. He could tell the place was packed even as he drove by: the pounding beat of rock music filled the street through the open door, and clusters of people spilled out onto the sidewalk, drinking, smoking, calling cheerfully to each other. He didn't get a good look as he drove by, but the crowd seemed to consist mostly of students, celebrating their freedom from classes and studies until after the first of the year.

Did he really want to do this? He was already beginning to reconsider. He did need a break from evenings at home, but he spent enough of his time with students when he was teaching them. And besides, he was more interested in actually hearing the bands than in being surrounded by a bunch of intoxicated kids looking to get into each other's pants. *Kids,* he thought, amused. They weren't that much younger than he was—less than a decade. He hadn't exactly been a choirboy at that age himself.

What finally decided it for him was that he couldn't find a parking space anywhere near the club. Between Busby's and the other bars, clubs, and restaurants on Castro, he'd be lucky if he could park closer than two or three blocks away. Not a big deal, but when combined with everything else, it was making the whole idea a lot less appealing.

Besides, there was still the other place, the one in Sunnyvale. What was it called? Darkwave or something like that. Sounded a little more goth than he'd normally choose, but at least the parking was better. If nothing else, he'd noticed when he'd gone down to use the portal at A Passage To India that there was a large shopping mall a block south with a sizeable outdoor parking lot.

The area around Darkwave wasn't any less populated than that around Busby's. Most of the little bistros in the area were still open, with people strolling up and down the street, bar-hopping and pausing to window-shop.

The club itself was bigger than Busby's, with its name spelled out in eerie purple neon above double doors manned by a pair of black-clad security types. Once again there was no parking nearby, but this time that didn't deter Stone: he simply shifted to Plan B and headed for the mall's parking lot. Since the mall itself was closed by this point, he quickly found a spot only a few rows over, under a bright sodium-vapor light that cast everything in a weird yellow glow. He shrugged into his black overcoat (which would fit right in at this place, he thought with amusement), locked the car, and headed back toward Murphy Street.

In retrospect, he decided an hour and a half later, he probably should have left earlier. He'd given it his best shot, hanging out near the bar with a glass of Guinness, people-watching and trying to get into the spirit of the place, but for whatever reason it wasn't working. Maybe it was the music, a pounding, discordant mishmash designed primarily to pump the crowd up and get them moving on the dance floor. It was working well, but Stone hadn't come here to dance. He'd allowed a pretty girl in a leather jacket and ripped fishnets to lure him out once, but since the dance consisted more of flailing around without seeming to care about who you slammed into (and who slammed into you), he ended up thanking her and cutting it short.

Maybe it was the fact that he couldn't get his mind off Laura Phelps, which, in turn, meant he couldn't get his mind off the Cannibal Killers. He wondered if they would continue hanging over his head, dominating his thoughts for the indefinite future even when there was no evidence that they were still in the area.

Regardless of the reason, however, he finally had to admit that he wasn't in the mood for crowds, or music, or even being out tonight. It had been some time since he'd experienced one of his sporadic dark moods—in fact, the last time had been just following Imogen's bombshell announcement before he'd left home—but he couldn't deny that this had all the earmarks of another one coming on. The best thing he could do for himself right now was get out of here, drive home, and go to bed. Sometimes, if he didn't succumb to the temptations of trying to drown the whole thing in alcohol, a good night's sleep could head it off before it got a good hold on him. But staying here now, in a place where he didn't fit in and was reminded of that fact with every thumping beat of the music, would do nothing but make it worse.

He glanced at his watch: twelve thirty. If he left now, he could be home by a little after one, and there was no reason he couldn't sleep half the day away tomorrow. No obligations, no requirements, nothing hanging over his head. It sounded good. *Gods, I'm getting old,* he thought, half in frustration, half in amusement. *Not even thirty and already choosing bed over clubbing.*

The cold, bracing air outside revived him a bit; he hadn't realized how stuffy it had been in there until he was away from it. Most of the strolling couples were gone now—aside from little groups on the sidewalk in front of the club smoking and chatting, the street was mostly empty of pedestrians. He didn't pass anyone as he headed back up Murphy and across to the lot where he'd left the Jaguar. It was there, right where he'd left it, though only a few cars remained in the lot. He set off toward it, hands in his pockets and humming one of the songs from the club under his breath.

He smelled them before he saw them: a sour, rotten, spoiled-meat stench. He got his magical shield up a bare instant before something slammed hard into him from behind, knocking him off his feet.

He went down awkwardly in a wild flailing of arms and legs, and then they were all on him. He didn't have time to think—he didn't have time to do anything but put every ounce of his concentration into keeping his shield up. If he let it drop, he was dead.

Two of them were in his face: a male and a female, all stringy hair and gaping fanged mouths and eyes glowing with a mad light. Their skinny arms clutched and scrabbled at him, trying to get purchase on the shield with fingers tipped in wickedly sharp claws. Two others lunged in from both sides, piling on to keep him down.

Stone struggled to get his breathing under control, mind spinning to come up with something, *anything*, he could do to get out of this. A glance told him that help wasn't likely to show up before his shield failed: by now, most of the parking lot was empty.

The shield did nothing to stop the fetid odor rolling off them in waves. The creatures hissed and growled, sounding more like animals than anything even remotely human. Stone had never seen a ghoul in person—even the pictures in books hadn't been that detailed—but even though he'd never heard of them attacking living prey, he had no doubt now that ghouls were exactly what he was facing. He tried to shove them off so he could get back up, but their combined weight was too heavy for him to budge, even with adrenaline coursing through his body. Sweat dripped down his forehead and stung his eyes. *Damn it, concentrate!*

He gathered magical energy from the air—it was harder because he knew his life depended on sending enough of it to the shield that it didn't slip—formed the pattern in his mind, and released it with a roar. It was an indirect spell, not designed to injure but just to send them reeling so he could get up and put some distance between them. The spell lashed out in all directions, shoving the writhing bodies backward.

Back—but not far enough.

The spell barely moved the furious things a few feet from him.

What the hell—?

It had been a long time since Stone had been in any sort of magical combat, but he knew his own power. That spell should have sent all four of them halfway across the parking lot! Why hadn't it—?

They were already coming back in. Stone staggered backward, using the momentary break to reinforce his shield, trying to get one of the few cars in the lot between him and the ghouls before they were on him again. It would be easy enough to escape them if he could only get far enough back that he could drop the shield for a moment: a simple levitation spell would get him high enough above them that they couldn't reach him—unless, of course, ghouls could jump. He didn't know. And even then it would be risky: his levitation spell was versatile, but it wouldn't get him anywhere fast.

He didn't make it to the car. "Get him!" one of them yelled—a tall, skinny scarecrow of a man with wild blond hair and a Lynyrd Skynyrd T-shirt—and they all lunged toward him as one.

Stone barely registered the fact that they spoke English—barely made the connection that they must be able to function in society if they'd rented an apartment without arousing suspicion. They moved fast—just as he'd suspected, faster than any normal human should be able to. He'd only made it about half the distance to the parked car before they were on him again, intent on using their combined weight to bowl him over a second time.

"Gonna rip yer fuckin' guts out!" one of the women yelled, her grin revealing sharp canines and releasing another blast of breath straight from a freshly opened grave.

"Yer brains're gonna taste *good*," the other man agreed. His voice was guttural, growling, feral.

Stone lashed out again just before they hit him. This time, he didn't waste effort on shoving them away. His endurance was good from all the running he did, but anybody who told you that physical combat didn't drain your reserves fast was either lying or hadn't been in a fight before. Already he was panting, his heart pounded, sweat ran down his back.

The spell he flung at them was one of this favorites, and one he rarely got occasion to use: focused eldritch lightning illuminated the dark parking lot, crackling eerie light and shadow on the ghouls' ugly faces as it flew from his fingers and limned their skinny bodies.

They shrieked, falling back a few steps, and the smell of charred flesh mingled with the miasma surrounding them. Stone was grateful he'd taken the time to charge up a couple of his magical focus items, or that spell would probably have brought him to his knees. Even so, his head lit up with pain and he tasted blood tricking down his upper lip. He hadn't held anything back, but he wouldn't be able to throw around too many more like that, even with the items' help.

"Get him, damn it! Now, while he's weak!" the blond one yelled. His bare arms were singed with black spots where the lightning had hit him, but as Stone watched in horror, they were already beginning to heal, to knit up and slough off the burned skin. Next to him, the others were doing the same thing.

Bloody hell, they were healing faster than he could hurt them!

Things were not looking good for the home side.

Stone continued backpedaling, keeping the nearest car in the periphery of his awareness. He was closer to it now; if he could just get to it, he might be able to use it as a barrier long enough to—

They lunged forward, cat-fast and predator-deadly, their rotting-corpse stench hovering around them in an almost visible cloud. They slammed into Stone's shield again, and this time its normally clear boundary flared a dark pink as it absorbed the brunt of their attack. Magical feedback traced his neural pathways with bright, sharp pain. He felt himself falling backward, felt the shield hit the car behind him and then his head hit the shield with a thud. Bright lights flashed in front of his eyes, and for a second, blackness began to grip him—

No no can't black out if I do I'm dead

And then, suddenly, the world was bathed in light far brighter than the ones in Stone's head. Dazzled, he squeezed his eyes shut, keeping his focus firmly on the shield, trying to gather the energy for another spell.

Tires squealed. Shrieks, a series of sickening crunches, and then something else—something big—hit the shield. More pain thundered through Stone as the barrier, stressed beyond its endurance, flared and died.

For a second, Stone could do nothing more than just stand there, swaying, and wait to feel the long, filthy claws tearing into his tender flesh. He opened his eyes expecting to see the ghouls there in his face...

...and stared.

A car—something big, several years old, and American—idled barely three feet in front of him, its headlights hurting his eyes, its big engine rumbling. In front of him, the four ghouls were heaped over each other, their limbs bent at odd angles, blood pooling beneath them, moaning.

"Come on!" yelled a voice. The car's driver door was open and a figure stood there, half-in and half-out. "They won't stay down long. Get in!"

Stone had no idea who the figure was, but at this point, he didn't care. Whoever it was, he had a working vehicle and the means to get him the hell away from the ghouls. In his current state, that was good enough.

He sidestepped the pile of fallen ghouls (already their limbs were starting to knit themselves back into their normal configurations), flung open the door, and almost fell into the passenger seat. As soon as he was in, the man gunned the engine and took off.

"Did they hurt you?" the man demanded, his tone urgent. "Did they scratch you?"

"I—I don't think so," Stone rubbed at the back of his head, trying to work his way past the cotton-wool fuzziness and throbbing pain from the combination of the magic he'd been tossing around and the hit he'd taken when he'd fallen. His shield was softer than the car, or the concrete, but that didn't mean the knock hadn't hurt like hell. Already they'd cleared the parking lot and were heading off in the direction of the freeway. He glanced over to see who his rescuer was.

And froze.

The man driving the big car was Chris Belmont, the young reporter who'd interviewed him in his office a few weeks ago.

CHAPTER THIRTY-FIVE

FOR A WHILE Stone was unable to think of anything coherent to say. He continued staring at Belmont as the reporter drove through the nearly deserted Sunnyvale streets and merged onto El Camino Real.

The young man was dressed much as he'd been when he'd come to Stone's office: jeans, hooded sweatshirt, athletic shoes. The interior of the car smelled like gym clothes that had festered unwashed in a sweltering locker, but he ignored that.

"What—" he began at last. "What are you doing here? What the hell is going on?"

"Are you sure you're all right?" Belmont asked, glancing over. "No cuts or scratches?"

"No. I hit my head, but I don't think it's anything serious."

"Your nose is bleeding."

"That's nothing," he said. He pulled out a handkerchief from the inner pocket of his overcoat and mopped at it; the trickle was already stopping. "Didn't come from the—from them." He narrowed his eyes. "Why do you keep asking me that? You know more about these creatures than you're letting on, don't you?"

Belmont was silent, returning his attention to the road.

"You do, don't you?" Stone pressed. "You're not a reporter at all."

"No, I am a reporter," Belmont said. "But yeah, I know more about them than I let on. I've been following them for a while now."

"Following them?" Stone rubbed at his head again, wishing he had some ibuprofen or something to take the edge off the pain. "Why?"

"That's kind of a long story, and not one I want to tell right now."

"Where are we going, anyway?" Stone glanced out the window: they'd reached the edge of Mountain View now, still on El Camino. Stone had learned a while back that this road was the main non-freeway artery that tied big chunks of the Bay Area together; if they continued in the direction they were traveling, they'd reach Palo Alto in a few minutes.

"Just driving around for a bit. Then we'll turn around and I'll take you back so you can get your car."

"You think that's wise? Someone must have called the police by now."

"They won't find anything. You saw how those things regenerated. They're already long gone, and their blood will degrade before the cops can get any kind of samples."

"Hold on." Stone twisted in his seat for a better look at Belmont. "You sound like some sort of expert on these things. If that's so, we need to compare notes."

Belmont chuckled. "Maybe we do. But I don't think I'm the only one here with secrets, am I, Dr. Stone?"

Stone wondered how much Belmont had seen of the magic he'd been throwing around, but right now that wasn't even in the top ten on the list of things he had to be concerned about. "You'd win that bet," he said, nodding. "Perhaps we should go somewhere and have a chat."

"Soon," he said. "Some of what I want to talk about, I can't just tell you. I have to check with my—superiors first."

"Superiors? You mean whatever organization you work for?"

"Sort of. Listen, Dr. Stone—you were holding your own pretty damn well against those things when I came by. That right there tells me you're not just a college professor. But I also know if I *hadn't* come by, you'd probably be dead now. So you owe me not asking questions I can't answer yet. We will talk—I want to know about you, and you want to know about me. But not tonight. Tonight, I'm gonna take you back to your car, stick around until you get away okay, and then I'll be in touch again tomorrow. Okay?"

What could he say? Belmont was right about his chances if he hadn't intervened: his shield had been seconds away from going down, and once it had, he didn't think he'd have been able to take them out long enough to get away from them. "I guess it'll have to be," he said. "I don't like it, though. How do I know you'll call me?"

Belmont grinned. "You don't. You'll just have to take my word for it. But believe me—I have my reasons for wanting to know what's going on with you, too. Like I said, I just have to talk to some people first." He was already flipping a U-turn at the Grant Road intersection. "If I were you, though—just a piece of advice—I'd stay home tonight."

"You think they'll come after me?" The thought scared Stone more than he wanted to admit. He replayed the scene in his mind's eye: the swift, inhuman movements, the skinny, clawed hands, the gaping mouths. No matter how well versed in magic he was, no matter how powerful, the thought of something hunting him that wanted to *eat* him hit him in a visceral, primal way. He wasn't even an enemy to them—he was prey, pure and simple.

He was food.

"Probably not tonight," Belmont said. "I don't know if they even know where you live. But they have ways to track people, once they're familiar with them. That's probably how they found you at the club. Just stay inside, keep your doors locked, and you should be fine. You've got protection on your house, right?"

Stone nodded, let his breath out slowly and pushed both hands through his hair. "All right," he said at last. "I'll do as you say. But if you don't call me tomorrow—"

"I *will*."

They drove the rest of the way back to the parking lot in silence. Stone half-expected to see the area surrounded by police cars with whirling lights, but it was deserted except for a young couple walking back to their car. He gave them a quick once-over with magical sight to determine that they weren't ghouls in disguise, then let himself relax a little. That only lasted a few seconds, though, as he put together what that meant. "They're gone already."

"Yeah." Belmont drove the big car over to where the fight had occurred, coming to a stop in front of a dark-colored puddle. His headlights illuminated it, revealing it to be black, not red. Anyone who didn't know what it was would take it for a puddle of leaked oil.

Stone stared at it. "They bled red," he said. "I saw them."

"Yeah. But I told you, their blood degrades fast. The good news is, it'll probably take them the rest of the night to heal those injuries. I hit 'em pretty hard with the car. Which means you probably don't need to worry about them coming after you tonight. I'd still stay inside, though."

"What about you?" Stone asked. "If they can track me, they can track you."

He didn't answer that. "Which one is your car?" He started the car moving again.

Stone pointed out the Jaguar; Belmont drove over and pulled up next to it. "Until tomorrow, then."

Stone got out of the car. Belmont didn't move until he'd had the chance to walk all the way around the Jaguar and verify the tires were all inflated, and then get in and start it up. It purred to life: either the ghouls hadn't known which car was his or, after the fight hadn't gone the way they'd expected, they hadn't paused to perform any acts of vehicular sabotage before escaping the area to lick their wounds.

Maybe literally, Stone thought with some distaste. He lowered the driver's side window and leaned out. "I just realized I hadn't thanked you."

In answer, Belmont merely waved out his own window.

The reporter didn't move until Stone had made it out of the parking lot. A glance in his rearview mirror revealed Belmont's car rolling off in the opposite direction, then disappearing around a corner.

Stone's hands shook on his steering wheel. He wanted nothing more than to drive to the nearest bar, order several of something sinfully alcoholic, and drink until he couldn't see straight. Anything to forget about the fact that some creature straight out of a nightmare—hell, a whole *pack* of them—wanted to turn him into tomorrow night's dinner.

He didn't do that, though. Instead, he got back to the freeway and drove to Palo Alto without ever exceeding the speed limit. When he reached the townhouse, he checked his wards, double-checked that every door and window was locked, and then performed a thorough search of the inside of the house using both magical and mundane senses. Only then, satisfied that the creatures hadn't somehow discovered where he lived and infiltrated his home, did he allow himself to relax.

Just a little.

Certainly not enough to sleep for the remainder of the night.

CHAPTER THIRTY-SIX

BY NOON THE FOLLOWING DAY, Stone looked terrible, felt worse, and had convinced himself that Belmont wasn't going to call.

It wasn't that he hadn't *tried* to sleep. Around four a.m., he'd even gone up to his bedroom, lay down, and tried a few meditation techniques that normally put him out in minutes. This time, though, even after downing three ibuprofen tablets to take the worst of the edge off the throbbing in the back of his head, the techniques had done little more than distract him for a few seconds until he heard—or thought he heard—some new imagined noise in the dark.

He was acting like a fool. He knew this. He was hiding like some callow apprentice, like a child afraid that the bogeyman under the bed was going to hunt him down and drag him into its dark, bone-strewn cave. He knew all of this objectively, but it still didn't stop him from jumping at shadows and stiffening at every noise. It wasn't as if the bogeyman in this case wasn't frighteningly real. It was more like that old saying: "It's not paranoia if they really *are* out to get you."

He'd thought about calling someone, but who would he call? Belmont had already made it clear he wasn't going to say anything else tonight, and he'd never given Stone a number anyway. He wasn't listed in the phone book, either. Kolinsky didn't have a phone—or at least hadn't revealed the number if he did have one. Madame Huan was off in China somewhere hunting down magical components. He even thought about calling Desmond to see if his old master knew anything about these strange new ghouls, but decided it would require too much explanation that he didn't feel like offering right now.

That left only Grider...if he could get through to the number the detective had given him at this late hour. Stone did plan to call him, but not until after he'd talked to Belmont. Asking him for help would be pointless and, as with Desmond, would require too much explanation.

In the end, he simply wandered the house until dawn, occasionally pausing in his office to try to read, or in his living room to stare at something mindless on the television without paying any real attention to it. When the sun came up he made another halfhearted effort to sleep, tossing and turning until he finally gave up in disgust. Finally, he went down into his lab and spent the remainder of the morning powering up a couple of magical items that wouldn't tire him out too much more. If he planned to go after the ghouls at some point, he'd need all the punch he could lay his hands on—best to get started.

The phone rang at a little after noon, and Stone made no attempt to stall. He bounded across the room and snatched it up before the second ring died out. "Yes?"

"Dr. Stone." There was none of the former amused tone in Belmont's voice. "Glad to hear you're all right. You took my advice, I see."

"Let's get to it, Belmont. I haven't had a good night. Did you talk to these...superiors?" He was surprised at how ragged his own voice sounded.

"I did. And they've agreed to talk with you. They feel it's time. They were very curious about what I told them about you."

Stone took a slow deep breath. This whole situation had the danger of spiraling out of control fast: how many of these "superiors" were there, and how many people was he going to have to reveal his magical abilities to in order to find out what they knew about the ghouls? "All right, and—?"

"And...I'd like to invite you to dinner this evening. Is seven o'clock all right?"

Stone glanced at the clock on the wall: it was only 12:15. "Dinner? Belmont, I really don't fancy waiting that—"

"I'm sorry, Dr. Stone. That's the best I can do. But I promise you—if you come, you'll get the answers to all your questions. And I hope you'll give us some to ours. Believe me, it's better this way."

What could he say? It wasn't as if he could force Belmont to meet with him any sooner. "Fine, then," he said, resigned. "Tonight at seven. Where?"

"There's a restaurant in Los Gatos, on Santa Cruz Avenue." He gave him the address. "There's no sign out front, but you can't miss it—it's a big Victorian house set back from the street. Just tell the maître d' you're my guest."

"All right. I don't like it, but it's your show. I'll see you tonight."

Stone didn't leave the house for the remainder of the day. Now that the sun was up and people were out and about, he was less concerned about the ghouls staging a frontal assault on the townhouse, so he spent the afternoon catching up with a few things he hadn't wanted to risk doing last night.

He finished up a bit of leftover takeout he found in his refrigerator, then took a long, hot shower (he'd taken one last night when he got home but visions of the ghouls catching him naked in his bathroom limited it to five fast minutes). He went outside and walked the perimeter of the townhouse's lot, adding a few updated touches on the wards so they would violently repel anything living that wasn't either himself or a mundane human or animal. He tidied the townhouse a bit, and powered up another magical item—this time a pendant like a tiny feline skull—early enough in the day that he could recover from the energy drain that doing so always took out of him. It was the tradeoff white mages had to deal with: unlike black mages, they couldn't (or more precisely, *wouldn't)* pull energy from other people to power their spells, but channeling their own power into the focus items they used still meant that the power was expended and had to be regained.

He deliberately didn't speculate about what Belmont and his "superiors" might be up to. It would be pointless: they could be anything from a group of investigative reporters to some kind of paranormal monster-hunting firm to a secret government organization tasked with dealing with supernatural threats. Stone had never heard of any such things in England, but the USA, he was finding, was a very different place in many ways.

Better to just wait and see, he decided.

That, and hope he wasn't walking into a trap tonight.

He arrived at the restaurant at ten after seven. He'd intended to get there a bit early, but he'd never been to Los Gatos and hadn't reckoned with the holiday traffic. The night was cold and intermittently rainy, with thick black clouds obscuring any vestige of the moon.

The town, he discovered, was an upscale little village about twenty-five miles south of Palo Alto, tucked away in the shadow of mountains off Highway 17 on the way to Santa Cruz. Santa Cruz Avenue was one of the town's main drags, lined on both sides with all manner of artsy little shops, eateries, and bars. It reminded Stone a bit of University Avenue, but more tightly packed. This close to Christmas on a weeknight it was jam-packed with meandering cars and groups of happy shoppers flitting from shop to shop in search of that perfect last-minute gift.

Stone finally found a parking spot in a lot just off Santa Cruz. He shrugged his black wool overcoat on over his dark suit (he didn't know what sort of restaurant it was and decided it was better in this case to be overdressed than underdressed) and set off.

It wasn't raining hard enough to use his umbrella—he'd noticed that Americans, especially the men, didn't carry them as often as Brits did, and even when they *did* carry them it had to be practically a deluge before they'd actually *use* them—but he brought it along anyway. It was a sturdy thing and if nothing else, if the ghouls attacked him again he could use it as a weapon.

Belmont hadn't been kidding that he couldn't miss the place: he drifted along with the jostling crowds until he reached the address, then stepped just out of the stream to get a good look at it.

It was a beautiful old Victorian, two stories tall, far too large to have started life as a residence unless its owner had been very wealthy. A low wrought-iron fence with a gate bounded it from the sidewalk, the house itself set back from the street by a grassy front yard with a meandering brick walkway leading to a short flight of steps. The place even had a turret on the second floor. As Belmont had said, no sign indicated its name or the fact that it was a place of business, but a cheerful glow shone from inside, and bright perimeter lights illuminated the grassy area out front.

In a shoddier state of repair (*like my place back home,* Stone thought wryly) the restaurant could have looked like a haunted house, but as it was, it appeared inviting and as cozy as a place that big could manage.

Hoping he wasn't making a big mistake, Stone shoved open the gate and entered the yard. Halfway up the brick walkway, he paused to switch to magical sight, checking for hidden threats in the yard and around the front part of the house. He was relieved to find none; in fact, the house's aura seemed inviting: a place where people felt comfortable and at home.

Encouraged, he crossed the rest of the yard, mounted the steps, and tried the door.

It swung open easily. Just inside was a small parlor decorated with period-appropriate prints and bric-a-brac on shelves, along with a loveseat upholstered in red velvet. To his right was a sweeping staircase leading up to the second floor; to the left, an open archway had a velvet rope stretched across it. A sign hanging from the rope read *Dining Room Closed.* He looked around for any sign of the maître d' that Belmont had mentioned.

In only a few seconds, barely enough time for Stone to take in the small lobby's décor, a man hurried in. Tall, thin, and elderly, he had pale skin and wispy white hair that clung gamely to a spotted, mostly-bald pate. "Good evening, sir," he said. "I'm terribly sorry, but the restaurant is closed tonight for a private affair. Might I suggest—"

"I'm Alastair Stone," Stone said. "I'm a guest of Mr. Belmont. Sorry I'm a bit late—the holiday parking's a bear."

"Ah!" The old man's demeanor changed instantly. He smiled, revealing a mouthful of crooked teeth. "Of course, Dr. Stone. Forgive me. Mr. Belmont mentioned you'd be coming. Please, come with me. May I take your coat and umbrella?"

Stone handed them over and followed. The man led him up the staircase and through a doorway into a large, open room.

Stone paused for a moment, taking the place in. The décor was similar to the room below: pastoral prints on the walls, flocked wallpaper, old-fashioned light fixtures made to resemble gas lamps. A series of tables dotted the room, each one set up for four to six people. Each table was covered by a white linen cloth and set with fine china, silver, and glassware. Its formal, old-world elegance reminded Stone of Desmond's place in London.

Most of the tables were occupied. A quick count told Stone that there were perhaps thirty to forty people in the dining room, about equally split between men and women and ranging in age from early twenties up to a couple who looked to be in their seventies or even eighties. Oddly, there were no dividers, tall potted plants, or any of the other devices restaurants employed to maintain an illusion of privacy among the tables.

"Please," the maître d' said gently, "Follow me."

Stone did so, and the man led him to a table at the front of the room, facing a bay window that afforded a beautiful view of the shoppers and cars bustling by on the street below. He got only a glance at this, though: most of his attention was focused on Belmont, who was already seated at the table.

The reporter stood as Stone and the maître d' approached. "Thank you, Joseph," he said, smiling. As the old man bowed and moved off, Belmont waved Stone to a seat. "Dr. Stone. You made it. I'm glad." He wasn't dressed in his usual hoodie and jeans today; instead, he wore slacks and a dark green sweater over a white, collared shirt, and had combed his floppy blond hair into a semblance of order.

Stone sat down in the indicated spot. There was one other person at the table: an Asian man in his fifties wearing a sport coat over a blue turtleneck sweater. "Dr. Stone," Belmont said,

"This is Dr. Orville Lu. Orville, this is Dr. Alastair Stone. Remember, I told you about him?"

Orville Lu smiled. "Oh, yes. Welcome. Dr. Stone. It's a pleasure."

"Indeed," Stone said, nodding. Neither he nor Lu offered to shake hands. He turned back to Belmont. "What's going on?" he asked under his breath. "There've got to be at least thirty people here. Do they all know about this?"

"Patience," Belmont said. "I said everything would be clear soon, and it will. And yes, they all know about this. But they don't all know about you, except that you're a friend and that you were invited tonight."

Another man, almost as old as Joseph the maître d, came over with a bottle of wine, filling glasses. "Dinner will be served as soon as everyone arrives," he informed the table before drifting off to the next one.

"Who else are we expecting?" Stone asked, nodding toward the empty seat. He let his gaze travel over the rest of the group: the light was too dim to see well, but he thought he recognized a man seated two tables over. He couldn't place where he'd seen him, though. He also noticed that several of the guests were casting surreptitious glances in his direction, clearly trying not to be obvious about it. A couple of them looked apprehensive.

"Not many more," Belmont said. "Shouldn't be long. This time of year it's always hard to find parking around here, as you probably found out."

"Why are they looking at me like that?" He indicated a couple of the most recent people who'd glanced his way. "Like I'm making them nervous?"

"You are," Lu said. "We're all a bit nervous, to be honest. We're not a group that's comfortable having outsiders know about us."

"No, I suppose not," Stone agreed. If they were some sort of covert supernatural-threat-hunting group, much of their advantage would come from anonymity. It didn't even strike him as odd that such a group would include elderly members: some of the most potent mages he'd met in his lifetime had been of advanced age. He wondered if there were any other mages in attendance tonight.

"Ah, here we are," Belmont said, smiling. "Welcome. I hope you found the place all right." He rose, addressing someone behind Stone.

"Oh, yes. Thank you, Christopher."

Stone stiffened and spun in his chair. The voice sounded familiar, but it couldn't be—

He didn't even try to hide his wide-eyed shock. "Mrs...Phelps?"

Laura Phelps gave him a faint, kindly smile. "Hello, Dr. Stone. I didn't expect to see you again so soon, but it's always a pleasure." She wore an outfit similar to the one she'd worn last night (had it really only been last night? It seemed a lifetime ago now): tunic and flowing peasant skirt, both of which hung loosely on her slimmer frame.

Thoroughly confused but nonetheless recalling by rote the manners driven into him during years of boarding-school attendance, Stone stood and pulled Mrs. Phelps's chair out for her. "It's—good to see you too. Surprising, but good. You're part of this group as well?"

"A new member," she said, nodding. "I'm still learning about it."

Apparently she was the last one they were waiting for, because as soon as she was seated, a door opened in the back of the room and three waiters came out bearing plates of salad. They circulated among the tables distributing them, then made their unobtrusive exit.

"So," Stone said. "I don't mean to seem impatient, but when do I find out why you've invited me here?"

"After dinner," Belmont said. "We'll finish up, socialize a bit, and then there'll be a presentation."

Stone forced down a cynical chuckle: it didn't help to be picturing this lot with laser pointers and pie-chart slides. "Fine," he said. "I've waited this long...I can wait a bit longer, I suppose. So, Mrs. Phelps: how long have you been included in this?"

"Since...shortly after Douglas was killed," she said. "Christopher here came by to interview me, we got to talking, and...it just sort of happened."

"I see." So she'd known the truth for weeks now, and hadn't told him anything about it. Inexplicably he was annoyed, but he supposed that, from her standpoint at least, there wasn't any reason to tell him anything. As far as she knew, he was just a college professor who'd showed up at the right time to prevent her own murder.

He picked at his salad, sipped wine, and continued casting glances around the room when he could get away with it. His magical sight revealed nothing more than the same feeling of belonging and "home" as he'd gotten outside; several of the guests' auras looked a bit unusual, but nothing so far out of the ordinary that it pinged any warning bells in Stone's mind. He did notice that Laura Phelps's own aura had settled down somewhat from the last time he'd checked: the gold was a bit more muted, but the roiling black spots indicating emotional distress or illness were smaller and more faded. She was finally beginning to cope with her husband's death, he thought. That could be nothing but good for her.

The waiters came by and picked up the salad plates. While Stone and the others waited for the entree, Belmont entertained them with anecdotes about stories he'd written. Orville Lu, who turned out to be a physician at an East San Jose emergency room, shared some accounts of his own experiences. Stone, for his part, mostly stayed quiet and listened. There was still something nagging at him about the man two tables over, but his stubborn brain refused to serve up the connection. He was about to ask Belmont about it when the doors to the back room opened again and the waiters returned, this time pushing elegant carts stacked with covered plates.

It took a while for a waiter to reach Stone's table, since it was farthest from the kitchen. The food smelled wonderful, especially given the less-than-appetizing takeout leftovers he'd had for lunch. The waiter served Stone first, setting a fine china plate in front of him and removing the cover to reveal a simple but beautifully arranged meal of chicken breast, wild rice, and a medley of vegetables. As he waited for the waiter to finish with the others, he thought it odd that Mrs. Phelps hadn't been served first, but decided it had to be because he was a guest. He also thought it a bit strange that no one had been consulted about their meal choice. Even at affairs he'd attended where the menu was limited, there was always at least a choice between a meat dish and a vegetarian one. He certainly had no complaint—everything looked good to him—but it was unusual for everyone to be served exactly the same thing. He glanced idly across the table at Belmont's plate, then away, and then quickly back again.

Belmont didn't have exactly same meal he did. The rice and the vegetables were the same, but Belmont didn't have chicken. In its place were a couple slices of light-colored meat—perhaps pork, or white-meat turkey.

He frowned a little, flicking his gaze left to Laura Phelps's plate, and then right to Orville Lu's.

Both of them had the same slices of meat as Belmont did. Neither had chicken.

Trying not to be obvious about it, he glanced sideways toward the closest neighboring table. Six people occupied it, and all of those he could see had the slices. No chicken. They chatted with each other, smiling, forking food into their mouths with gusto.

He looked back at Belmont. The reporter was watching him intently, an odd thoughtful expression on his face. So was Lu.

Laura Phelps's face showed concern, and a little sadness.

Slowly, very slowly, a crawling chill began at the base of Stone's spine and worked its way upward to settle at the back of his neck, raising the hairs there. With deliberate calm he set his fork back down next to his plate. He hadn't touched his food yet.

A gentle hand covered his. "You've figured it out, haven't you?" Laura Phelps asked softly. "I'm sorry. I know it's not easy for anyone, at first."

CHAPTER THIRTY-SEVEN

For a moment, Stone couldn't move. He couldn't think straight. He stared at Belmont, gripping the arms of his chair, eyes wide, breath coming in short sharp bursts. "You..." he began. It came out as a rasp.

And then the momentary paralysis broke. He almost leaped to his feet—almost flung down his chair and took off for the exit before any of them knew what was happening. That was what his instincts were telling him to do: get the hell out of here now while only the people at his own table knew he was on to them, while he still had the advantage. If he could get outside, lose himself in the crowds, they wouldn't be able to catch him.

But he didn't do that.

He didn't do that because he saw the expressions in Belmont's eyes, in Lu's, in Mrs. Phelps's. There was no predatory gleam, no hungry glare, no sign that they were preparing to fall upon him and rip him to pieces. Instead, they all looked sad, resigned, calm.

Sane.

As sane as a pack of cannibals could look, anyway.

"I'm sorry, Dr. Stone," Belmont said. "I know it's a shock. You caught on faster than I expected—I should have guessed you would. But I couldn't just tell you. You had to see for yourself."

Stone paused before speaking to make sure he had his voice under control. "What...the hell..." he began.

In the rest of the room, the word appeared to be getting around that the cat was out of the bag. From every other table, people were glancing in Stone's direction, then quickly looking away. They looked for all the world like a bunch of curious coworkers who'd just found out that one of their own was expecting a baby, or had been caught cheating.

"You're cannibals," Stone said in a monotone. It didn't sound so much like an accusation as a simple statement of fact.

"Yes," Belmont said.

"You're ghouls."

Belmont shook his head. "Not the way you think."

This was unreal. "What do you mean, 'not the way I think?'" Stone demanded, his voice pitching a bit higher, taking on a harsh edge. "You either eat human flesh or you don't!"

"We do eat human flesh," Orville Lu said. "But we don't kill anyone to get it."

Stone could barely believe he was sitting here calmly having this conversation. "You don't. So—what, then? You dig up graves? Raid funeral homes? Sneak bits out of hospitals?" Then he remembered what Lu did for a living. "Oh, dear gods..." he muttered. "You do."

"Dr. Stone." Belmont's voice was calm and even. "Please. Let us explain. And I hope you'll forgive us, but we do need to eat. Getting what we need in a way that doesn't harm anyone isn't always easy to do, so it would be disrespectful to let it go to waste."

Disrespectful. They were worried about disrespecting the human beings whose flesh they were eating. Stone closed his eyes a moment, feeling suddenly lightheaded. "By...all means," he said, waving vaguely in Belmont's direction. "I hope you'll forgive *me,* but I won't be joining you." As it was, his interior workings were currently engaged in an unpleasant argument with what he'd already eaten; though normally he was not at all squeamish, the thought of eating anything else he'd been served here—even the chicken—struck him as a very bad idea.

"I promise you, nothing you've been served has been in contact with—anything of ours," Lu said.

"Just the same, I'm not hungry anymore," Stone said, pushing his plate aside. He glared at them. "You'd better start talking. I don't know why you're even telling me any of this at all—I don't know if you're in league with those things that have been killing people, but—"

"Dr. Stone, how could you even *think* that?" Laura Phelps demanded. Her voice shook, and tears glimmered in the corners of her eyes. "Do you think I would cooperate with the animals that killed Douglas?"

"I don't know why you're cooperating with *this* lot," Stone said. "Were you a…cannibal…all along? When I met you?"

She shook her head. "No. That's when it happened. That night."

Stone was about to ask her to explain, but then memories flooded back to him. "That's why you were so concerned about whether I'd been scratched, wasn't it?" he asked Belmont.

The reporter nodded. "Yeah. That's how it spreads. It's usually not an issue. Almost nobody runs into those things and survives, so it usually doesn't matter."

"So that scratch on your arm—" Stone said, turning back to Mrs. Phelps.

"Yes. Christopher came to see me a couple of days after the attack. He told me he was a reporter. I almost threw him out for being so rude, but then he asked me about the cut on my arm, and told me what would happen to me if I didn't let him help me."

"What *would* happen to you?" He paused a moment. "Wait. You'd turn into one of those other things?"

"No," Lu said. "Worse. She would have turned into a fully feral ghoul."

Stone's brain reeled from all this new information. He held up a hand. "Hold on, hold on. You're telling me there are three different types of ghoul?" Up until recently, he hadn't even been aware that *one* type existed in the real world. Now there were three?

"Feral, semi-feral, and non-feral," Belmont said. "The third type—that's us—is very rare. The second type is almost nonexistent. In fact, we think the four we've met might be the only ones of their kind."

There were so many things Stone wanted to ask, to know, but most of them weren't important now. He looked around the room; almost all of the others had gone back to eating, but still sent occasional glances his way. "You say you're rare. You don't look rare to me. There's got to be—what—thirty of you in here? How many more are there?"

"Thirty-four in here. And no others that we're aware of," Lu said. "There are only a few pockets of us in the country. We don't reproduce, so when we die out, we're gone. Laura here is the first addition to our colony in over five years."

"So you lot are the entire non-feral ghoul population in this part of the country?" Stone realized how insane those words sounded, but he plowed on nonetheless. "And none of you kill people? How do you manage that?"

"We have a system in place," Lu said. "Our kind can pass as normal humans, so all of us have jobs. Most try to get jobs in places where they have access to flesh without harming people to get it."

"EMTs, workers in hospitals and funeral homes, abortion clinic workers…" Belmont said. "Anywhere we can get hold of it without harming a living human."

Stone's dinner threatened another return appearance. He swallowed hard and was fairly sure he'd gone as pale as most of the ghouls. When he spoke, his voice shook a bit with mixed revulsion and anger. "So you just…take it? Nip off with an amputated leg here, a gallbladder there…aborted fetuses? And you don't think there's anything *wrong* with this?"

"Right or wrong is irrelevant in this case, Dr. Stone," Lu said gently. "We need flesh to survive. We didn't choose our condition, but now we have to live with it. And the only way we can do that without killing—without becoming feral ourselves—is to do what we do. It's distasteful, yes. But what else would you have us do? You can't blame us for wanting to live."

Stone didn't have an answer for that. His mind was still struggling to wrap itself around the enormity of what he'd just been told. "How do you…distribute it?" he asked. "Surely not all of you have jobs where you've access to what you need."

"We have locations where we can go," Belmont said. "Central repositories. We only have to eat human flesh once a month or so. The rest of the time, we eat normal food like everyone else."

Suddenly, Stone remembered where he'd seen the old man two tables over. He pointed. "The little shop in Palo Alto," he said, looking at Mrs. Phelps for confirmation.

She nodded. "That was my first time going there. You just tell the man a special word, and he gives you a package from the freezer behind the counter. I was scared to death you'd figure out what I had in my shopping bag." Tears still shone in her eyes. "It's horrible, Dr. Stone. When Christopher told me, I thought hard about just killing myself rather than becoming…what I am."

"What changed your mind?" Stone asked. His tone was numb, not accusing but simply asking.

"A couple of things," she said. She twisted her cloth napkin in her hands and didn't meet his gaze. "The first one is that if I died, I'd want to join Douglas in Heaven. But our church teaches that if you commit suicide, your soul will go to hell."

Stone wondered how God felt about flesh-eating ghouls, but didn't ask. "And the other?"

Belmont answered: "We're pretty hard to kill, Dr. Stone. As you saw last night."

Tears streamed down Mrs. Phelps's face now. "I tried," she said in a small, shaky voice. "A couple of nights after Christopher told me, the whole thing just got to be too much for me. I slit my wrists. They healed up in a few seconds." She dabbed at her eyes with her napkin.

Stone bowed his head. "So what do you want from me?" he asked at last. "What the hell can you possibly want from me?"

"We want the same thing you want: to find those four creatures and take care of them before they kill anybody else," Belmont said.

"Take…care of them. You mean destroy them."

"Yes."

"Why? Aren't they sort of—I don't know—your brothers, or something?"

"No," Belmont said, the single word full of anger. "They're threatening everything we have here. They kill people, and do it in messy ways that attract a lot of attention. We've managed to stay completely under society's radar for a lot of years by being quiet, keeping to ourselves, and minding our own business."

"But if the police start looking for flesh-eaters," Lu added, "they might start looking more closely at some of our activities. We've been able to hide them because no one expects body parts to go missing. But now…"

Stone thought about Grider, and what he would do if he found out about this group. "So you want to kill them. And you want me to help."

"I saw what you can do last night," Belmont said. "I don't understand it, and I'm not asking you to explain it to me. But I saw it. We're not the only ones who don't fit the standard human template."

Stone didn't try to deny it, but he shook his head. "You're right—I do have some abilities that normal people don't have. But you saw what a bloody lot of good they did against those ghouls. If you hadn't come 'round, bits of me would be passing through their digestive systems right about now."

"We can help each other," Belmont said. "The others—" Here he indicated the rest of the table occupants "—don't know anything about your…abilities, and we won't tell them. But we know things about feral ghouls that you don't know, and you can do things we can't. Between us, we might be able to hunt them down and take them out when they aren't expecting it."

"You're placing a lot of trust in me," Stone said, scrubbing at his hair with both hands. "What makes you think I won't go straight to the police and tell them about the lot of you? Even if you tell them about me, given the current wave of murders, I'd say they'd be more likely to believe the existence of ghouls than mages."

"You could do that," Belmont said. "If you get up and leave here, none of us will stop you. But if we don't do something about the ferals, they won't quit. They might leave here…but they might not. Especially since it seems like you've pissed them off, Dr. Stone. Trust me on this: that's not a good place to be."

They had a point, Stone had to concede. He remembered how he'd been last night: for all his power and his knowledge and his training, jumping at shadows and afraid to sleep for fear of being attacked in his home by a pack of savages. He didn't want to live that way. He'd either have to go on the offensive or quit his job at Stanford and return to England, and he wasn't ready to go back yet. It felt like admitting defeat.

He sighed, looking around the table first at Orville Lu, then at Belmont, then finally at Laura Phelps. They all looked so normal. So innocuous, like a group of Rotarians or book-club members getting together for a dinner meeting.

He was a mage: he dealt with all sorts of odd beings, spirits, and entities in the practice of his Art. Was this really any different? Human flesh, as long as no one was killed specifically to get it, was just meat, right? Any inherent value it had was only because other humans *gave* it that value. And these beings weren't human. Not precisely, anyway.

He was rationalizing. He knew it. He could get up and walk out right now, and if they were telling the truth, they wouldn't stop him. But they were right: the four killers wouldn't stop what they were doing because he was too disgusted by his potential allies' dietary habits to work with them.

"Fine," he said at last. "I'll help you, if I can. But we'll have to talk later. I need to get away from here now. I can't sit here and watch you eat." He stood.

"I understand," Belmont said, and Lu and Mrs. Phelps both nodded.

"One more question before I go, if I may," Stone said.

"Of course."

He indicated the dining room. "Why this? Why do you all get together and break out the good china for your little cannibal-fest?"

"We don't do it often," Lu said. "Maybe twice a year. One of our group owns the restaurant. As for why we do it—it's simple." His voice was gentle. "We do it to remind ourselves that despite our condition, we're still civilized beings. That we're still…human."

| CHAPTER THIRTY-EIGHT

STONE STOPPED ON THE WAY HOME from the restaurant and picked up a bottle of single-malt Scotch. He chose a well-lit shop where he could park near the door, and scanned the area thoroughly on the way both in and out.

He was disgusted at himself—this kind of apprehension wasn't at all like him—but he did it anyway. He didn't know how those ghouls had tracked him before, so he didn't know how to take any precautions against it beyond hypervigilance and the tweaks he'd done to the wards around his house. He wished he'd thought to ask Belmont and Lu about ways to protect oneself from semi-feral ghouls before he'd left, but it was too late now.

He barely paid attention to the route as he drove the rest of the way home. His mind refused to quiet, bombarding him with questions, thoughts, and observations for which he had very little satisfactory response. He doubted he'd get much sleep tonight, either; that was part of the reason he'd bought the scotch.

He'd just agreed to help a pack of cannibals. Never mind that they were *good* cannibals, and they were trying to rid the world of *bad* cannibals: was there really a difference? The only thing that separated them was that the former group got their human flesh without killing anyone specifically to get it, while the latter group hunted it down like prey. Philosophically, did it matter? They both ate people—a taboo so deeply ingrained in the human race that most people wouldn't even eat human meat to save their own lives. Just because they dressed it up with linen tablecloths and fine china and civilized talk, did that make it any better?

He thought about Belmont—the reporter had come to him to make sure that he hadn't been bitten or scratched in the encounter in the park. He didn't have to do that; he'd done it because he, and presumably the rest of his tribe, didn't want to see anyone else suffer their fate. They not only weren't trying to grow their number, they were actively working not to. He thought about Orville Lu: an emergency-room physician. A man who by definition had taken helping people to be his purpose in life. He wondered if Lu had been a doctor before he became a ghoul, or whether he'd chosen the job to give him easy access to the food he required. He wondered if the doctor were ever tempted to be a little less than thorough in when faced with a grievously wounded patient, in the hope of supplementing the group's larder.

He thought about Laura Phelps, a simple, upper-middle-class suburban wife with two grown children and a husband she'd loved, whose life had been irrevocably transformed by one chance decision: to take a shortcut through a park one night after attending a show. Was she evil or wrong or condemned based on events she had no control over? He'd spoken to her at least twice after she'd already become something not quite human. Had she been any different? He hadn't noticed, other than to attribute her melancholy and her diminished appearance to grief over the loss of her husband.

He sighed as he hit the button to open his garage door. None of these questions had answers, because this was probably a situation that no one else had ever had to deal with. He knew his abilities would be useful—possibly pivotal—in the hunt for and disposal of the rogue ghouls. He also knew that, if Belmont had been telling the truth, his group had knowledge about ghoul nature that Stone would find invaluable, if for no other reason than to help him figure out ways to avoid the killers. As many times as he turned it over in his mind, he couldn't come up with a viable course of action that didn't involve casting his lot in with Belmont's group. After the killers were dealt with, he could re-evaluate his options. But until then, *better the devil you know* seemed to be the operative phrase.

He checked the wards when he got inside: nothing had triggered them, so either the ghouls hadn't figured out where he lived yet, hadn't healed up sufficiently from Belmont's vehicular assault to feel like hunting, or they'd simply decided he wasn't worth the effort. He couldn't afford to believe that latter one was true, though: even if they were nothing more than predators who weren't inclined to harbor grudges, he still needed to behave as if they did. The last thing he needed was to lose focus and have them jump out of the shadows at him again, since he probably wouldn't be lucky enough to be rescued by Belmont a second time.

How had Belmont known he was there, anyway? It seemed quite a coincidence that the reporter would turn up in the exact place he was at exactly the right time. If Stone didn't know better, he'd swear Belmont knew he was there, and had been watching the parking lot just in case Stone got attacked. But how could Belmont know where he was? He hadn't told anyone—

But he had.

His mind went back to the night he'd had dinner with Laura Phelps. She'd asked him where he'd be that night, and then shortly afterward had excused herself to use the restroom. The phones were down the same hallway—it would have been easy for her to make a quick call.

So this colony of civilized ghouls was looking out for him, apparently.

Even by his standards, life was getting very, very strange.

He tossed his coat over one of the stools at the breakfast bar and was about to head upstairs to his study when he spotted the red light flashing on his answering machine. He paused, deciding if he wanted to answer it, but finally thought he'd better. Perhaps Belmont was calling to give him more information about where to meet up tomorrow. He hit the button and leaned against the counter, listening.

The voice was not Belmont's, but it was every bit as familiar.

Much more familiar, in fact.

"Alastair? Are you home? If you are, please pick up. I really need to talk to you. I'm in Palo Alto, at the Hyatt. Room 1407. Please call me when you get in."

Stone stared at the machine, stunned. "Imogen…" he whispered.

She was here?

What the hell was going on?

As he picked up the phone to call her back, he wondered how many other ways his life was going to spiral out of his control tonight.

CHAPTER THIRTY-NINE

THE HOTEL WAS ONLY a few minutes' drive from his townhouse. She wouldn't tell him anything on the phone, but she begged him to come over. Even over the line, he could hear her voice shaking. He promised he'd be there in a few minutes and headed back out, grabbing his overcoat, not even taking the time to change out of the suit he'd worn to dinner. Whatever was wrong with her, it had to be bad if she'd flown all the way over here from England without telling him she was coming.

She answered the door on the first knock. His first impression was that she looked very young, even more so than usual. Her eyes were sunken in deep hollows and glittered with tears, her cheeks blotchy as if she'd been crying recently. She wore jeans, a soft white sweater, and white socks with no shoes.

"Hi," she said. Her smile was wistful, sad, a little lost. She looked him up and down. "You didn't have to dress up..."

"Hi," he said. "This was...a surprise."

"Tell me about it," she said with a shaky chuckle. "Thanks for coming. Please, come on in."

He did, and closed the door behind him. "Imogen—what are you doing here? Did you fly all the way over here just to see me?"

"Do you want something to drink?" she asked, puttering around at the room's mini-bar.

"I want to know what's going on," he said. "Are you all right? Has something happened?" He took off his overcoat and tossed it over the back of a nearby chair.

"You could say that," she said. She picked up her own drink, something amber in a tall glass, and dropped into another chair with a sigh.

Stone didn't sit down. "Your father—?"

She shrugged; the ice cubes in her glass rattled. "Dad's off somewhere in France visiting a colleague. When I told him I wasn't coming home for Christmas, he said he didn't fancy hanging about in that big old place by himself. He left last week."

"Imogen..." Stone began pacing the small confines of the room. "Why are you here? Why did you come all the way over here without even calling ahead? I could easily have already gone home for the holidays."

"I called Aubrey," she said. "He said you hadn't left, and probably wouldn't be going home until Christmas Day, if then."

Nice of him to let me know, Stone thought a little sourly, but he had to forgive the old man: it wasn't as if Aubrey—or anyone else sane—would assume that someone would catch a plane halfway around the world on a whim. "So you came here instead."

She nodded. "I had a lot of airline miles saved up. It just seemed like—the right thing to do at the time. Sort of...impulsive, like when you decided to take the position here."

"But what about Robert?" he asked. "I thought you and he had plans with his family for the holiday."

"So did I," she said, her tone taking on an edge of bitterness as tears glimmered once again in the corners of her eyes.

"Wait..." The pieces were beginning to fall together now. "Something's happened between you and Robert. Is that what you're not telling me?"

She stared down into her drink and nodded. "It isn't that I'm not telling you. It's that—it's hard to tell you. I'm afraid you'll say 'I told you so,' just like Dad probably would if I told him. And you'd have every right to."

He studied her for a moment, her curtain of shimmering brown hair that hung down low over her eyes, her slim fingers clutched around her glass. Part of him—a small part—wanted to say exactly that. Wanted to rub it in, that she'd left him for another man, a mundane, who apparently hadn't lived up to her expectations.

But as he watched her sitting there, miserable and dejected in her chair, the primary thing he felt was sadness—not just for her own loss, but for what might have been between them if none of this had happened. He dragged the room's other chair over across from her and sat down in it. "Imogen, I'm so sorry. I really am."

She made a soft little half-laugh, half-snort. "You know, I actually believe you."

"Do you...want to tell me what happened?" He kept his voice low, gentle, non-judgmental.

"There's not much to tell," she said with a shrug. "Remember when you were visiting Dad, I mentioned that Robert was away a lot because he was looking to buy another restaurant?"

"I remember something like that, yes." He remembered it with perfect clarity.

"Well...he was away for a few days. I didn't expect him back until late last night. On Wednesday night, I realized I'd left a jacket at his flat so I went to pick it up. I had a key." She downed a healthy portion of her drink and set the glass down on the table. "When I got inside, I heard voices. At first I was afraid—I thought someone had broken in. But then I recognized Robert's voice, and…a woman's."

Stone reached out and put a hand over hers. "What did you do?"

She let out a brittle laugh. "I was a little out of my mind, I guess. When I flung open the bedroom door and found them…in the act, I yelled a few choice things at Robert that Dad would probably be quite shocked that I knew."

"Good for you," Stone murmured with a chuckle.

"I think the woman—whoever she was—thought I was some sort of mad thing. She gathered up her clothes and got out of there fast. Robert tried to explain everything, of course—that it was all a misunderstanding, that I was taking the whole thing the wrong way. He must think I'm very naïve. So," she said more briskly, "that was the end of that, wasn't it?"

"I'm still not sure why you decided to come here, though," Stone said. "That's quite a long trip. Why didn't you just call me if you wanted to talk?"

She spread her hands. "I don't know, really. Like I said, it was an impulse. I couldn't tell Dad, even if he was home. Not just because of the 'I told you so' thing, either."

"Oh?"

"Come on," she said, chuckling. "Think of Dad. He never liked Robert anyway, even when I fancied him. Can you imagine what he might do if he found out he'd cheated on me?"

Stone winced. "They'd never find the body, would they?"

"Or else he'd end up a frog or something. I mean, *I* wanted to chuck him off the nearest tall building, but it's not like I'd actually *do* it."

"I see your point," Stone admitted.

"So…that left tracking down one of my girlfriends from University or my workmates and crying into my drink while they patted me on the back and told me what a cad Robert was, or…"

"Or flying across the ocean to unload the whole thing on me." He kept his voice light so it didn't sound like an accusation.

She blinked tears away. "I know. It's horrible, isn't it? I realized that about halfway across. I've left you for him and now I'm coming to you for comfort after he cheats on me? I wouldn't be surprised if you told me to go to hell, now I'm here. I'm sort of surprised you actually came at all."

"Well," he reminded her, "you wouldn't tell me what was going on until I got here. Probably wise of you, all things considered."

"So now you know," she said, raising her head a little. "I'll understand if you want to go, but…I really would like it if you'd stay. At least for a little while."

Stone didn't answer right away. His mind was going off on several different tangents, and it took him a few moments to sort them all out and figure out which of them he wanted to pursue. There were valid reasons for simply getting up, bidding her goodbye, good luck, and have a nice life—no one would blame him for it. She had, after all, dumped him, and now she'd come halfway around the world trying to get him to commiserate with her over the fact that the man she'd dumped him for hadn't been faithful. He had every right to be angry and hurt, to want to punish her as she'd punished him. Part of him was, and did.

But as he looked at her sitting there, waiting patiently with glittering, hopeful eyes for his answer, he found that he didn't truly want any of those things. Did he still love her? He didn't know. But he did still care for her—at least enough that he didn't want to cause her any more pain. "I'll stay for a bit," he said at last. "We can catch up on old times without your father hovering about like a vast bat."

That made her laugh, and she finally brought her head up and looked at him directly. "You look good in a suit," she said. "Let me get you a drink, all right? If I don't have what you want, we can call room service."

He got up from the chair. "I'll do it. I'm sure I can find something. I'm not exactly picky."

"Except about beer," she said.

The mini-bar was well stocked with tiny representatives of various types of liquor. Hardly the full-sized bottle of The Macallan he'd picked up on the way home, but it would do for now, especially since he didn't want to get pulled over for DUI when he returned to the townhouse. He dumped some ice in a glass, emptied the little bottle over it, and took an experimental sip before turning back to where he'd left Imogen.

Only she wasn't there anymore. She was standing directly behind him, a little to his right, regarding him with an odd expression. "You really do look good in a suit," she said softly. "You should wear one more often." She reached out a hand and ran her fingers over a fold of his sleeve. "I didn't take you away from anything, did I? I didn't even ask if you were...seeing someone."

"I'm not," he said. He didn't move away from her touch. "I was out having dinner with some...friends."

"So you're settling in here, then, are you?" Again, there was a strange undertone to her voice, wistful and a bit sad. "There's no chance you'll be coming home after the year's over?"

"Haven't decided yet. I suppose it will depend on a lot of things, but it's not something I'm ready to make up my mind about. Not until closer to when I have to, at any rate."

Her hand moved up his sleeve until it was on his upper arm; she gave it a gentle squeeze. "Why don't you take your jacket off?" she asked. "And this." With her other hand, she toyed with the knot of his tie. "I know how you hate ties. You'll be much more comfortable with it off, won't you?"

Stone swallowed, forcing his breathing to remain calm and steady. The back of his neck was warming, a little tingle running through his body. "I—" he began, surprised at how ragged his voice sounded. "We—shouldn't…"

"Why not?" She continued to work on his tie until she had it loose enough to pull over his head. She tossed it aside. "Hmm? Why shouldn't we?" She took hold of his lapels and began sliding his jacket off his shoulders, slowly and deliberately. "Would you be surprised if I said I wanted you, Alastair? Right now. No strings. No expectations."

"Imogen—" Stone took a step back, but only a small one.

"I never stopped loving you. I told you that. It was just…the magic. The idea of being an afterthought in your life…" She slid his jacket the rest of the way off and tossed it next to the tie.

"You weren't an afterthought…" Almost without conscious volition, his own hands took her shoulders in a firm but gentle grip.

"Do you still love me too, Alastair?" she whispered. Her fingers worked on the buttons of his shirt, slipping inside to caress his chest, her gaze never leaving his face.

He still didn't know, wasn't sure…but at this moment the possibility seemed more likely than it had a few minutes ago. She was a bundle of contradictions, always had been: small and slim, she might seem at first to those who didn't know her to be elfin, almost childlike, in need of protection—but Stone knew better. She was the daughter of William Desmond, the sort of man whose overpowering personality would, if you let it, roll over you like one of those monster trucks the Americans seemed to be so fond of. To survive that kind of upbringing—or that kind of apprenticeship—you had to be made of strong stuff.

Imogen might not have magical talent, but under her pixieish exterior was a core of solid steel.

He pulled her to him, bowing his head and drawing her into a kiss. The anger, the hurt, the sense of betrayal all melted away as his body responded to her touch. It might not last—he had no illusions about that—but right now he didn't care. She wanted him. He wanted her. How much more complicated did it need to be?

They moved as one with urgency and the deftness of practiced ease, casting off bits of clothing, caressing, kissing, reacquainting with each other's bodies as if there had been no absence. Stone stroked the warm, soft skin of her back, breathing in her mingled scents of alcohol, light perfume, that lavender shampoo she liked, and memories flooded back of other times, other places. His grip on her tightened, and hers matched it, her nails scraping over his back in a way that sent electric tingles up and down his body.

"Are you sure?" he asked.

Her only answer was to dig her fingers in harder, pulling him down into a more insistent kiss.

Afterward they lay together, entwined, her bare leg draped over his, her head snugged into his shoulder, her hand idly tracing the contours of his chest as he stroked her back with the kind of light touch he might use on a baby animal. She chuckled, her face half-buried.

"So gentle now…" she said. "I'm glad you weren't before. Oh, Alastair…if it'll make you feel any better, you're much better in bed than Robert was."

"You say that *now*," he murmured with a lazy smile. "You probably told him the same thing, didn't you?"

"What, that you were better?" She laughed. "No, silly. I have *some* tact."

He kissed her shoulder. It felt so good to just lie here with her, to laugh, to not think about ghouls, or murders, or even what he'd have to finish up preparing for the beginning of the next quarter. None of it mattered right now. "At least you had someone to compare me to."

She raised her head a little. "You mean you didn't—there wasn't—anyone else?"

"No. Not since you and I got together, anyway. And not since I got over here."

"No *wonder* you were so…motivated," she said. Her eyes sparkled. "I suppose I should be grateful for that, at least." But then she frowned. "Still…I never thought you'd…that you wouldn't meet someone else."

He shrugged. "Been busy. Job, and magic, and…other things. It just hasn't been a priority. Especially since I'm not sure yet I'll be staying."

"When do you have to decide?"

"By the end of the academic year, I suppose. They've already let me know that the position's mine, if I want it. Associate professor to start out, tenure track, the whole bit. I could make full professor before I'm forty."

"Quite the rock star, you," she teased. She shifted position, snuggling in closer and sending a most pleasant sensation through his body.

"Mmm…"

"It would be a lot to give up. But don't you miss home?"

"I do," he said. "I like it here—it's fine, in its way. But—"

"But it's not home."

And it's overrun with ghouls, he thought, but just made a noncommittal noise that turned into a groan of pleasure as she wriggled in even closer. "You'd best stop that," he said in a mock warning tone, "unless you want to have another go."

"Took you long enough to catch my hints."

"I'm slow, but I get there eventually," he said, rolling over toward her and leaning in for another kiss.

| CHAPTER FORTY

THE SUN STREAMING IN through the window woke Stone with a start the next morning. He sat up abruptly, disoriented. "What time is it?"

Imogen still lay next to him, propped up on her side. "It's all right," she assured him. "Everything's fine. You looked so tired I let you sleep."

"What time is it?"

"Almost eleven."

"Bloody hell." He wasn't normally an early riser, but he never slept that late. He remembered drifting off shortly after midnight, Imogen's head still on his shoulder as she breathed softly in sleep. He dropped back to the pillows now, his blood going cold as he thought about what could have happened.

He hadn't taken any precautions against the ghouls tracking him here. He hadn't scanned for them, put up even temporary alarm wards—he hadn't even done anything about concealing his car, which was parked right out in front of the hotel. If they'd found him here—if they'd attacked while he'd been in bed with Imogen—there was no way he could have protected either of them. Images rose unbidden in his mind, of bloody claws ripping at Imogen's flesh, yellowed fangs gnawing on her bones—

Stop it, damn you. That isn't helping.

"Are you all right?" She was watching him with concern. "You looked—angry, all of a sudden."

"Just at myself," he said.

Her face fell. "You mean you—" She gestured, encompassing them and the bed, her meaning clear.

He pulled her into a hug. "Oh, no, no. Not that. Just—remembering some things I should have done."

"Don't worry," she said with a sly smile. "I'm on the pill."

For a moment he stared at her blankly, then he chuckled and sighed. "You are something else, Imogen. But that's not it either. I need to be getting back home. How long are you staying?"

"My return ticket's for Monday morning," she said. "I suppose I should see to arranging another day or two here at the hotel."

"Don't be daft," he said. "Of course you'll stay with me. I've got a guest room, as long as you don't mind my pathetic attempts at housekeeping and my empty refrigerator." He sat up on the edge of the bed. "Do you want the shower first, or shall I?"

"I hear they're having a drought here," she said. "Suppose we conserve water and share?"

Stone wasn't sure whether bringing Imogen home with him was the best idea, but she was probably safer at the townhouse than she'd be anywhere else, especially if the ghouls somehow found out she was connected with him. That hardly seemed likely, though—they might have advanced tracking abilities, but they weren't superhuman. And for all he knew, they weren't even looking for him anymore. He'd have to ask Belmont more about them when they met up again.

"This is nice," Imogen said when they were inside. "And your housekeeping's not nearly as bad as you led me to believe."

"I've had some time to kill," he said. "I need to find a housekeeper, though. I keep getting sidetracked and forgetting to do it, but it's becoming a priority."

"Still existing on takeaway every night?" she teased, opening his refrigerator to peer inside. "Ah. Not even that. Just the inevitable supply of Guinness. Are you *ever* going to learn to cook? I can't imagine how you stay so thin eating like that."

"Oh, give it a rest," he said, but the amusement was evident in his voice. "Come on. I'll show you around the place."

She followed him as he pointed out the living room and dining room (bypassing the door to the basement lab), then took her upstairs. "Here's the guest room," he said, dropping her two suitcases on the bed. "A bit tidier than the rest of the place since I never use it, but mind the dust."

"Oh, I do hate dust," she said with a mischievous smile. "Are you sure I can't just sleep with you?"

"I'll…take that under advisement," he said, looking so serious that she had to laugh. He completed the tour by showing her the study and the master bedroom. When he finished, he said, "So—what do you think of the place?"

"Well…" she said slowly. "It's a lot smaller than your place back home, but I like it. It's…you."

"What, small and untidy?"

"And dusty," she agreed with a grin. "So—you're on break, then? Do you have time to show me around? I've only ever been to New York City in America—this is quite different."

"I can," he said. "But not today. Unfortunately, I do have some things I need to take care of. I'm waiting for a call."

"Mmm," she said. "That's too bad. But I understand. You didn't exactly expect me to come swooping in and disrupting your life. I'll find something to do for the day. Maybe I'll even find a market and see if I can cook you dinner."

"You don't cook any better than I do," he reminded her. Then his expression grew serious. "Listen, Imogen, I have to tell you something. I probably should have told you before I brought you here."

"Well, if you're hiding another woman, you're doing a good job of it."

"It's not that," he said. He took her into the living room and waved her toward a chair. "I know you don't like to think about—well, magic—but there's a bit of a…situation going on with me right now."

"Situation?"

"I've run afoul of some rather nasty sorts. I'm not sure if they're looking for me anymore, but they're not the kind of people you want to run into."

Her eyes widened. "What do you—?"

"Here's the thing," he said. "I've tinkered with the wards on the house—nothing that's not a mundane human or animal should be able to get past them, apart from me, of course. So if I end up having to go out for a bit today, I need you to stay inside. Can you do that for me?"

She leaned forward. "Who are these people? Are they mages? And what do you mean, 'run afoul of them'?"

He thought about not telling her, or giving her an incomplete story that would scare her enough to stay inside without frightening her unnecessarily. But this was Imogen—Desmond's daughter. She'd grown up surrounded by magic. It was only fair to let her know what she was getting herself into if she stayed with him. "They're not mages. They're supernatural creatures called ghouls. And they've been killing people around here for the past several months."

"And you've pissed them off?" She stared at him, wide-eyed. "How did you manage that?"

"Long story." He sighed and shook his head. "I probably shouldn't have brought you here. It was a bad idea. Why don't you let me find you a nice hotel, and—"

"I'm here now," she said. "And if these things are as nasty as you say they are, if they're still after you, they'll see you with me anyway, right?"

"If they are," he said reluctantly.

"So it's better I'm here behind your wards, then, isn't it?"

"It is if you stay in," he said.

"I will. If it's just for the day, anyway. Will you be gone long?"

"I don't know. I doubt it. Two or three hours, maybe. I've...met some other people who know about the ghouls. The plan was to compare notes about how to track them down before they find us."

She frowned. "Track them down? Alastair, you're a professor, not some kind of superhero. Don't the police do that sort of thing around here?"

"They would if they had an idea what they were looking for, or how to deal with it if they did. These things would rip normal policemen to shreds."

"But they won't do that to you?"

"Not if we find them before they find us." He wished he were as confident of that as he was trying to sound. "Anyway, I told them I'd help, but I feel guilty asking you to stay here by yourself. I'd bring you along, except they're a secretive lot and I doubt they'd appreciate surprise plus-ones."

"Don't worry," she assured him. "I'll be fine. I'll poke around in your books or watch a movie on your telly or something. Just promise me we can go out and do something tonight when you get back."

"Of course," he said. "I appreciate your understanding about this."

"Well, like I said, I *did* impose on you. It's only fair." She gave him an odd smile. "Thank you, Alastair."

He frowned. "For what?"

"Just…being you. Even if this all just turns out to be a fun weekend together and doesn't lead anywhere…you really did make me feel better when I was a mess. And you didn't have to. You had every right to toss me out on my ear."

"That's me," he said. "Picking up strays again. I—"

The phone rang.

"Sorry," he said. "I have to get this."

It was Chris Belmont. "I guess you got home all right. Any sign of the ferals?"

"Not yet. Any chance they've written me off as a bad job?"

"Who knows? Like I said last night, these are the first of their type any of us have seen. Can you meet with us today? Just a few of us—the ones who can help, and want to."

"For a bit, yes. Can't stay too long, though. I've got a…guest, and I'm not comfortable leaving her alone here for too long."

"You know, the sooner we take care of this—" Belmont began.

Stone cut him off. "I know. I know. But this can't be helped. I'll meet you today, and we'll see where it goes."

"Okay." He didn't sound happy about it. "The meet's in San Jose, at Dr. Lu's place." He gave him an address. "Can you be there in an hour?"

Stone glanced over at Imogen, who was watching him. "Best to get it over with, I suppose. I'll be there."

He hung up the phone and slumped a little.

"You have to go." She got up and came over, settling herself down next to him with her head on his shoulder. "You go do what you have to do. When you come back, you pick a nice restaurant and I'll take *you* out to dinner."

"Mmm," he said. "Sounds lovely. I warn you, though—I'm not a cheap date."

She turned his head with her hand on his chin, and leaned in to kiss him. "Won't put out for any old hamburger or pizza, hmm?"

"Of course I will," he said. "Do you think I'm an idiot?" He gently extricated himself from her grip and got up before things got out of hand. "I'll be back in two or three hours. Remember—stay inside."

"I love it when you're forceful," she teased.

CHAPTER FORTY-ONE

ORVILLE LU'S HOUSE was a large, two-story Spanish-style place in an upper-middle-class South San Jose neighborhood. By the time Stone arrived, there were already several cars parked in the vicinity, including two in the driveway.

Lu answered Stone's knock quickly, as if he'd been waiting. "Dr. Stone. Thank you for coming. The others are all here."

He led Stone down a tiled hallway into a living room furnished in expensive but comfortable-looking style. Stone paused in the doorway, taking a mental roll of the attendees.

There were six of them in all: in addition to Lu and Chris Belmont, there were two other men and two women, none of whom Stone recognized. Except for Lu, all of them were at the younger range of the group Stone had seen at the restaurant. Laura Phelps was not present.

"Please sit down," Lu said, waving Stone toward a chair. He didn't introduce the others. "We have refreshments if you're interested."

Stone sat, trying not to think too hard about the absurdity of sharing 'refreshments' with a group of cannibals. The offerings looked innocuous enough, though: a pitcher of lemonade and a plate of sugar cookies.

"So," he said. "You want me to help you. I said I'd do what I can, but as I told Mr. Belmont, I can't stay long today, so best if we get on with the bit you need me for. I've also got more questions."

"Of course," Lu said. He nodded toward Belmont. "Chris, why don't you start?"

Belmont leaned forward in his chair. "Okay. So what do you know about ghouls in general, Dr. Stone?"

"I only know about the ferals, and even then not much. They raid fresh graves and don't generally hunt live prey, correct?"

"Yeah. They're still pretty rare, but they're around. They keep to themselves, away from populated areas, and don't usually become a big problem unless someone blunders into them when they're hungry. But these guys—the semi-ferals—are something new. They're smart. They can pass as human beings. Drive cars. Maybe even have jobs. And worst of all, they seem to have a much more developed version of our sensing abilities."

"Explain," Stone said. "I assume they track by scent, yes?"

"Right. And they're damn good at it. We have the ability to an extent, but because of what we are, it's a lot less keen."

"What *are* you, exactly?" Stone asked. "That was one of my big questions."

"We're ghouls who don't kill people," Lu said. "We've found each other from all over the western U.S.—our commonality is that when we were infected, someone helped us through the process so we didn't have to go hunt down prey."

"Wait a moment," Stone said, holding up a hand. "You mean that's all it takes to make a 'safe' ghoul? You've no desire to kill anyone? Even if you're ravenous with hunger?"

"We don't test that," Belmont said. "That's why we've got our network. There's always food available, to anyone who needs it. Maybe not much sometimes, but we don't need much. Most of the time we just eat regular food."

Stone pondered that a moment. "So...that explains you lot. That's what you did with Mrs. Phelps when she got scratched—helped her through the transition. But what I don't understand yet is how those four ended up the way they did. You said last night that if you hadn't convinced Mrs. Phelps to let you help her, she'd become a full feral, right?"

"Yes," one of the two women said. "That's the way it usually works."

"So how are those four different, then?"

"We're not sure," Belmont said. "That's one of the things I've been investigating. The best I can guess with the info I've been able to find is that they were interrupted in the middle of the process of 'civilizing' them. Maybe they were attacked by ferals and another of the civilized groups managed to find them and help them, but something went wrong. I don't know."

"So your group isn't in contact with the other civilized groups? How many of them are there, by the way? Are there little ghoul dinner parties going on all over the country?"

Belmont narrowed his eyes. "No, Dr. Stone. We're not in contact with them. It's safer that way. Most of us know one or two in other groups. I don't think anyone knows how many total there are, but I do think we're one of the largest and most established."

"So nobody thought to mention that four escapees from cannibal charm school were running around loose?"

Belmont's expression darkened further, so Lu quickly stepped in. "You have to understand, Dr. Stone: these four, as far as anyone knows, are utterly unique. They're in a 'between' state—not fully feral, but not fully civilized. I don't think anyone expected what happened. The group they were with probably just thought they'd gone feral and would find a place to hide themselves like the others do."

"Fine," Stone said. "So where I do I come in? What do you want me to do?"

"You found them once," Belmont said. "We want you to find them again, so we can get a group together and take them down for good."

"You can't find them yourself?"

"No. Like I said, we don't have their tracking capabilities. They can follow scents better than any dog. We're better than a normal human, but not anywhere near that good."

Stone sighed, spreading his hands. "Well, then, you're out of luck. I can find them, yes, but not without something to track by. My methods require a personal item, a bit of the body like hair or nails or blood—that sort of thing. I used up my only sample when I did my last tracking."

"Damn," Belmont said, gripping the arms of his chair in frustration. "Then we're screwed. I wish I'd known you needed something like that before—I could have picked it up in the parking lot before we left."

"Yes, that would have—wait!" Stone held up a quick hand. "Wait a moment. Belmont—is your car here?"

"Well…yeah. Of course. But—"

"Please tell me you didn't wash it since that night."

"I didn't, but—"

Stone leaped up out of his chair. "Come on, then." He hurried back out of the house, leaving the others to trail in his wake. Belmont had hit the group of ghouls hard with his car; Stone didn't allow himself to hope that there might be a bit of one or more of them wedged into the grille or under the bumper, especially after the previous night's rain, but the possibility certainly existed.

Belmont's battered old car was parked in the driveway. Stone crouched down in front of it, examining it. The car wasn't even close to new, and had one of those grilles with a lot of nooks and crannies just right for catching bugs and bits of road debris. "Let's hope they caught a bit of you..." he muttered to himself as Belmont, Lu, and one of the women came up behind him.

For a moment, he thought he was out of luck. Magical sight wouldn't help him here, since any tissue or bits he found would no longer contain any life force to hold an aura. He crouched down lower, peering methodically into the grille's various holes, starting at the left side and working toward the right.

The front end showed clear evidence that Belmont had hit something: he concentrated most of his effort in that area. He was acutely aware of the gazes of the three ghouls on him as he worked; it made him a little nervous, even though he knew (*did he know?*) that they weren't eyeing him like a tasty ambulatory steak.

And there it was! Wedged into the bottom of the grille on the driver's side was a piece of torn denim about the size of a dime, stained with some of the blackish substance that ghouls' blood degraded to.

"Aha!" he said. "Here we go. Someone get me a container of some kind, with a lid. And tweezers, if you've got them."

He heard footsteps receding; a couple minutes later Lu came into view off to his side. He offered Stone a small Tupperware container, the kind you put sandwiches in, and a pair of tweezers. Stone took them without taking his eyes off the sample, afraid if he lost track of it he wouldn't be able to find it again. He opened the container and with a careful, steady hand he plucked the tiny remnant free, dropped it in, and put the cover back on.

"There," he said. "That should do it. Let me see if I can find any more of these, in case something goes wrong."

He didn't, though. If any other "souvenirs" had remained embedded in the car's front end, the wind or rain had dislodged them. "Damn," he said, getting back up. "Just the one shot, then."

He followed them back inside where the others waited. "So how long will it take you to do this?" Belmont asked. "Can you do it here?"

"No. You're not set up for it here—I need to go back to my place. And before that, I'll need to pick up some materials. Figure from the time I leave here, two or three hours minimum."

"And then you'll know where they are?" one of the other men asked.

"Yes. Unfortunately, there's not enough of a sample to do the more complex ritual that would let me track them if they move, though. It'll be like the other night—I can find where they are, but we'll have to move fast once we have the answer."

"Let's go, then," Belmont said, starting to rise.

Stone held up a hand. "Wait a moment. We've got time—the clock doesn't start until I actually do the ritual. I have another question or two first. And besides, I can't have you lot all trooping into my home. As I told you, I have a guest. I doubt she'd understand." He pointed at Belmont. "You can come with me. The others can wait somewhere nearby. When we have an answer, we'll go from there."

None of them looked happy about that, but they grudgingly agreed.

"What about your questions?" Lu asked. "I'd like to begin as soon as we can."

"Well, that's the thing," Stone said. "Before I find these creatures, I want to know what you're planning to do with them. I saw how hard they are to kill. I don't fancy the idea of ending up as either lunch or a cannibal myself because they overpower us. How do you kill them? Do any of the standard supernatural weapons work? Silver? Cold iron? Wood?"

"You cut their heads off," Belmont said. "That's really about the only way to do it. Or else completely burn their bodies to ash. Anything else, they'll come back from."

"Why didn't you just do that when you hit them?" Stone asked. "That would have taken care of the problem, wouldn't it?"

"They were dazed," Belmont said. "Not out. And do you know how hard it is to cut off a human's head in a hurry? I didn't exactly show up with a chainsaw."

"But you will this time, right?" Stone asked.

"We'll be ready for them this time," Lu said. His face was set in a mask of anger and resolve. "Believe me, Dr. Stone, we want them gone as much as you do. As we mentioned at the dinner, they threaten our whole way of life."

"Yeah," Belmont said, looking much the same. "Besides that, they're killing people. It needs to stop, and nobody else even knows what they are, let alone has the ability to stop them. If they try, we'll either end up with more dead people or more ghouls, neither of which we want."

"Right then," Stone said. He got up. "I'll go pick up the materials I need, and be back at my place in an hour and a half or so. Mr. Belmont, you'll have to wait outside until I get there—you won't be able to cross my wards."

"That's fine," he said. "I'll pick up a couple of things for you on the way. He pointed at the larger of the two male ghouls. "Connell there is a security guard, so he has access to armor. I know you have that shield thing, but if it goes down you'll want some protection. We'll run by his place and pick up the stuff, then I'll continue on to yours."

Stone was about to protest, but armor wasn't a half-bad idea. "Fine. Just wait in your car until I arrive." He gave Belmont the address, then turned to Lu. "Dr. Lu, may I use your phone?"

"Of course." Lu led him out to the kitchen, then left to give him privacy.

Stone stood there for a moment, looking around a kitchen that, with its bright colors, upscale stainless-steel appliances, and pile of bills on the counter, was altogether too normal looking to be owned by a ghoul (*does he cook human flesh in here?* he couldn't help wondering) and thinking about what he'd just agreed to do.

He still didn't like it—all of this action-hero stuff was foreign to his usual more scholarly style, and the thought of getting into another fight with the four killers scared him more than he wanted to admit. He knew he could just locate them and then send Belmont and his crew after them—but he also knew his magic could make the difference between success and failure. Not many of Belmont's group looked like they were skilled at combat and strategy—this would be a hard fight all around. They'd need all the help they could get.

He thought of Douglas Phelps again, of his terrified expression, his shaking voice pleading for help, of his two grown children and his grief-stricken wife who'd been pulled into this whole mess far more than she'd ever bargained for. None of them had asked for any of this. He snatched up the phone and punched in his own home number.

It rang several times, and Stone stiffened as his machine picked it up. Was Imogen there? Had the killers somehow figured out how to get past the wards? His mind spun horrific images of them inside the house, crouched over her body, bloody claws tearing at—

The machine beeped and he spoke in a rush: "Imogen, it's me. Are you there?"

The line picked up almost instantly. "Alastair. Hello." She sounded a little breathless, but otherwise normal. "Sorry I didn't answer—I figured I should just let it go to the machine. Is everything all right? Are you coming back soon?"

"Not long now. Listen, Imogen—there's a bit of a change of plan. I need to take care of something today. I don't know how long it will take, but there's no way around it."

There was a long pause. "So we won't be able to do something tonight, then?"

"We might—I don't know yet. I'm just telling you there's a chance we'll have to wait until tomorrow. I'm sorry."

Another pause. When she spoke again, she sounded disappointed. "It's all right," she said. "I understand."

He knew she didn't and ached at her tone, but the faster he got this done, the faster he could get back to spending time with her before she had to return home on Monday. "Thank you. I hope I can finish it up and we can make a late dinner, if you still want to. Also, there's someone coming by. He might get there before I do, so don't be alarmed if you see him. He's thin, blond, early twenties. He'll be outside in his car."

"You want me to invite him in if I see him?"

"No—he won't be able to pass the wards. He's—not quite human. I just didn't want you to be worried if you saw him."

"All right."

"Good. I'll be home soon." Impulsively, he added, "Imogen? Tell you what. To make up for this—if I can get this handled, I'll come back home for the rest of the holiday. You can come down and stay at my place. I'm sure Aubrey will be happy to see you."

"You're serious."

"Completely."

"Well, then. I suppose I can put up with being left on my own for one day." She chuckled. "And I promise to keep you busy, and try not to scandalize poor Aubrey too much."

"It's a plan, then. See you soon."

He hung up the phone and walked slowly back out to the front room where the others were waiting. He had no idea where that had come from—he certainly hadn't intended to make such an offer. But now that it was out there and he couldn't take it back, he realized he didn't want to.

He still didn't know if this would lead to anything permanent—or even if he wanted it to. But it was certainly on the table now.

All he had to do was take care of the ghouls first.

It took Stone longer than he expected to gather the materials he'd need for the ritual. Normally he would just go to Madame Huan's shop to buy the few things he didn't have on hand in his lab, but since her shop was closed while she was away, he drove over to East Palo Alto to see if Kolinsky's place was open. When he found a note on the door (written in Latin and hidden behind the wards so only those who knew how to get in would see it) stating that Kolinsky had been called away and would be back in an hour or so, he had to improvise.

Fortunately, none of the items needed to cast a circle were inherently magical—circles were nothing more than a way for a mage to focus his will on what he was doing, so all the power came from his own abilities. Still, Stone was acutely aware that he'd only have one shot at this ritual, so he wanted to ensure that he did everything within his power to get it right.

By the time he arrived in Palo Alto and rolled up in front of his townhouse, it was after four o'clock and the sky was already growing dim. He spotted Belmont's car parked out front; Belmont himself sat slouched in the driver's seat, looking bored until he spotted Stone and opened his door.

Stone pulled into the garage and got out, waving Belmont back. "Careful," he called. "Stay back and let me adjust the wards, or you'll get a nasty shock."

"Nice trick."

"Haven't had a chance to test it yet, but let's not test it on you." Stone checked the wards to make sure nothing had disturbed them, then quickly paced around the front part of the yard, pausing twice to mutter incantations under his breath and make brief adjustments to their energy patterns to admit Belmont. He didn't alter them enough to allow all of Belmont's group in—trust was one thing, but giving unknown cannibals access to one's home was something else entirely. "Where are the others waiting?"

"There's a restaurant not far from here. I've got the number. They're just hanging out in the back and ordering drinks until they hear from us."

Stone nodded, finishing up with the wards and heading for the garage. "Come on, then. Let's get this taken care of."

He knew something was wrong as soon as he entered the house. "Imogen?" he called, surprised that she hadn't come to meet him when she'd heard them talking outside. "Are you here?"

"Problem?" Belmont asked.

"She might be asleep," Stone muttered, more to himself than to Belmont. "Hold on. I'll find her and introduce you, and then we can get started." Without waiting for an answer, he vaulted up the stairs two at a time. "Imogen? Where are you?"

He shoved open the door to his bedroom. It was empty. So was the guest room, her two suitcases still on the bed where he'd tossed them when they'd arrived this morning. She wasn't in the study or either of the upstairs bathrooms. "Imogen?" He called more loudly now, forcing himself to remain calm. There had to be an explanation. She had to be here somewhere. He hurried back down the stairs and paused to try the door to the basement lab. It was locked tight. "Belmont, did you see anyone down here?"

Belmont was in the living room, looking out into the townhouse's minuscule backyard. "Nobody. You sure your friend didn't just step out or something?"

"I told her to stay put," Stone said. "That it might be dangerous to leave the house until I got back." His heart pounded harder now, and an uncomfortable sensation crawled up his spine and made him shiver. "Imogen! If you're hiding, this isn't funny!"

"Dr. Stone?" Belmont had crossed the room back toward the front of the house. His voice sounded odd.

"What?" Stone whirled, half-expecting to see Imogen standing there next to him.

Instead, Belmont pointed wordlessly at the front door.

At first, Stone didn't see what he was pointing at, but as he got closer it became obvious:

The door was open.

Not open very far—just enough that it hadn't latched, as if perhaps the occupant had stepped outside for a moment to get the mail or check out something in the yard.

Oh, bloody hell...

The crawling sensation up Stone's spine increased, and a chill of terror settled over him. He wheeled back around on Belmont again. "How long have you been here?" he demanded, more loudly than he'd intended.

"Out front? About...half an hour, maybe."

"And you didn't see her? Didn't see anyone?" Stone flung the door open the rest of the way, flicked on the perimeter lights, and stalked out into the small front yard.

Belmont shook his head. "I didn't see anybody, except a few cars driving by and a kid walking his dog about fifteen minutes ago. Nobody near the house."

"And you didn't see that the door was open?"

Belmont glared at him. "Come on, man. The whole thing was in shadow. How was I gonna see that from the street?"

Stone knew he was right, but that didn't make him any less impatient for answers. Where *was* she? Had she ignored his request to stay inside and gone off for a walk? Gotten tired of being alone and decided to call a taxi and go back to the hotel?

That didn't make sense, though. First, her suitcases were still here. Second, she wouldn't have gone without leaving him a note. And third and most telling, she'd never go off and leave the front door unlocked and unlatched. She could be a bit flighty sometimes, but she took security seriously.

Stone stopped in the middle of the yard and tried to slow his mind down. *Think, man.* This wasn't the time to let his emotions get the better of him. He turned around and started back toward the house.

He almost didn't see it, because it had rolled off the edge of the walk that led to the front door, but as he drew closer a flash of white caught his eye. He hurried over, and snatched it up. It was a fist-sized rock with a piece of white paper affixed around it with a plastic zip tie. His heart thudded harder. "Belmont!"

Belmont came running from where he'd been examining the left side of the yard. "What? Did you find something?"

Stone was already detaching the paper from the rock with shaking hands, making himself slow down so he didn't tear it. He fumbled it open and together he and Belmont read the few words scrawled on it in black ink:

Stone

We have the bitch. Shes alive for now. Dont call cops. Go to the phone on the corner of Vernon and Hiway 9 in Santa Cruz at 7:30 tonite. Come alone. You bring anybody else well eat her and send you the bones.

PS: We might eat her anyways. She looks delishus. Dont be late.

CHAPTER FORTY-TWO

STONE DIDN'T REALIZE HE'D SAGGED until Belmont caught him. He righted himself with difficulty and staggered back inside the house, closing the door behind Belmont, then dropped down onto the bottom of the stairs. His hands clutched spasmodically at the note, his thoughts a solid wall of interference inside his head, preventing anything coherent except a horrific slideshow of what the ghouls might be even now doing to Imogen. "No..." he moaned. "How the *hell* did they—"

Belmont crouched in front of him. "Dr. Stone."

Stone ignored him, staring down at the note again. "They've got her...They've got her and they're going to kill her..." Why did he even get involved in any of this in the first place? What the hell was he thinking? And bringing Imogen here? He should have gotten her an early ticket and sent her back home, away from all this danger. It was his fault that she—

"*Stone.*" Belmont's voice was more forceful now. He grabbed Stone's shoulder and shook him. "Listen to me."

Stone didn't want to listen to him. He didn't want to listen to anyone. He just wanted to leap up, track down every last one of those cannibal bastards and unleash hell upon them. If white magic didn't have the punch to get the job done, then he'd use black magic. What did its long-term effect on him matter, if he let them kill Imogen?

Belmont slapped him, a sharp blow across his cheek.

He reeled back on the stairs, catching himself with one arm before he fell over backward. Without thinking, he glared and raised his other hand—lightning crackled around it.

"Stop it *now!*" Belmont ordered, shoving his hand away. "Stone, you have to *think*. Don't go all panicky on me. If we're gonna deal with this and get her back, we have to be smarter than they are."

For a moment, Stone almost hit him with the spell anyway. But he didn't. Instead, he sagged again, bowing his head into hands that still clutched the note, scrubbing at his hair. "You're right. You're right." He brought his gaze up to meet Belmont's and he held out the note. "You know these things better than I do. Do you think they'll—"

"I think they want you," Belmont said. "They want to lure you into a trap so they can grab you."

"And eat me as well."

"Yeah."

"At which point they won't have any reason to keep Imogen alive, so—"

Belmont sighed. "Yeah."

Stone raised his head and looked at his watch. "It's four-thirty now. Do you know where this phone is they want me to go to? Is it far?"

"It's in Santa Cruz," Belmont said. "This close to Christmas, traffic will be light, without a lot of the work commuters. But it's still about fifty miles from here. It'll probably take you an hour to get there. I'd give it a little extra time—sometimes there are accidents on 17."

An hour? "No...that will barely leave me enough time to do the ritual to find them. I've only got a bit more than an hour before I have to leave."

"You can't do it that fast?"

"I—I don't know. The circle's still up, so it's possible, but just barely. And that's only if I can clear my mind enough to do it. So many variables. If I get it wrong—"

"Okay, okay…" Belmont paced in front of the stairs. "What if you—"

There was a knock on the door.

Stone jerked his head up, exchanging shocked glances with Belmont. Who could be showing up now? He jumped up before Belmont could stop him and flung the door open.

Lieutenant Grider stood there on the porch, dressed in his familiar windbreaker and rumpled shirt. "Afternoon. I was in the area, so I thought I'd just drop by to check if you—" He paused as he got a good look at Stone. "Holy shit, Stone. What's the matter with you? You look like somebody just punched you in the gut."

Stone deflated, taking an involuntary step backward. Grider was the last person he wanted to see right now. For a second, he thought about just slamming the door in the detective's face, but all that would do was convince Grider all the more that something was up. "Lieutenant. Not a good time right now. What do you want?"

Grider's squinty gaze shifted from Stone to Belmont behind him, and then down to the piece of paper Stone still clutched in his hand. "What's going on?" His voice was laced with suspicion.

"What makes you think something's going on?" Stone struggled to keep his tone normal, but he knew he wasn't succeeding. Off to his left, Belmont hovered and remained silent.

"Look. I'm not some rookie. I been doin' this a long time, and I've caught guys red-handed who were better at denyin' shit than you are right now. So spill."

Stone closed his eyes. He could lie—tell Grider that it was something personal and none of his business—but he doubted the man would believe him. Normally he was a good liar, but this wasn't a normal situation. "I can't do this, Lieutenant. Yes, something's going on. But I can't tell you what it is. I can't risk it. I'm sorry."

"It's about the Cannibal Killers, isn't it? You been freelancin' again." Before Stone could stop him, he stepped inside the house.

Stone didn't deny it. He couldn't. His mind was in chaos right now, his body barely managing to remain still when all he wanted to do was *act*.

Grider reached out his hand. He didn't snatch the paper away from Stone—his intentions were obvious, and Stone could have pulled it back.

He didn't. He simply stood there, waiting, as Grider's eyes flitted back and forth over the crudely-written words. "Holy Christ," he whispered, shaking his head. He looked back up at Stone and held up the paper. "Who is—?"

"Her name is Imogen." Stone's tone was dead. "She was visiting me from back home. She's…a good friend." Sudden anger rose in him. "Listen to me, Lieutenant. You are *not* involving the police in this. I don't give a damn whether you believe me about these things being supernatural, but if you bring in a lot of bumbling mundane cops, Imogen's going to end up dead." He narrowed his eyes. "And if that happens, Lieutenant, it won't go well for anyone involved."

"That a threat, Stone?"

"It's a promise, Lieutenant."

They glared at each other for a few seconds like a couple of rams getting ready to knock heads, until Belmont broke the silence: "Guys, this isn't helping. Come on. Time's wasting. We need a plan."

"Who the hell are you?" Grider demanded.

"This is Mr. Belmont," Stone said. "He's a friend. He's...familiar with the situation, and helping me deal with it."

Grider swiped at his brush-cut hair. "Fuck," he said. "More civilians." He glanced at his watch. "Not much time to make a plan. You got one? Please tell me you're not plannin' to just show up at that phone like a lamb headin' to slaughter."

Stone didn't answer that right away. To Belmont, he said, "You'd best call the others and tell them there's been a...change of plan. Don't give them any details about the location. Just tell them to stand by."

Belmont nodded and headed toward the kitchen.

"Others?" Grider demanded. "What others? How many people you got involved in this mess?"

"They're friends of Belmont's," Stone said. "And to answer your question: No, I wasn't planning on just showing up. I've got a few tricks they don't know about. But I need to find them first, and I'm not sure I've got time to do that."

Grider looked like he was about to ask a question, then he stopped. "Wait. Find them—you mean like you found 'em before? With your psychic shit or whatever it was?"

"Yes."

"Because that worked so well last time."

"Actually, it did," Stone said. "I just didn't have all the details before."

"And you do now."

"No, but I have more than I did before. That's part of why I'm telling you to keep your policemen out of this. If you involve them, not only Imogen will end up dead. They will too. These things are more than a match for them."

"C'mon, Stone. My guys are trained. They have guns and armor. You're tellin' me these things are bulletproof?"

"I'm telling you they regenerate—they heal up damage fast." Stone didn't have any more time to be coy about the nature of the ghouls. It would take too long to explain things to Grider if he had to examine everything he said. At this moment, he didn't care what the detective found out, as long as he got out of his way.

Grider glared. "How the hell do you know that?"

"They attacked me a couple of nights ago. They'd have killed me if Mr. Belmont hadn't showed up in his car and gotten me out of there."

"Wait—what? You got *attacked*? Where? And you didn't report it?"

Stone's anger rose again. "Lieutenant, *enough*. I told you—I haven't time to give you the whole story. Every minute I waste explaining things to you is a minute closer to those animals killing Imogen. Now get out of my way and let me do what I need to do."

Grider didn't move. He stood there, still glaring at Stone, but something in his expression changed. His eyes narrowed until they were barely visible slits. He looked like he was wrestling with a tough problem.

"Okay," he said at last. "I don't get what's goin' on with you, Stone, but I think it's more than you're lettin' on. I won't bring the department in on this until after you've had your shot—on one condition."

Stone had already turned away from him and started down the hall after Belmont. "And what's that?"

"You let me help. Not anybody else from the department. Just me."

Stone stopped and turned back. "Out of the question." He sighed, shaking his head. "Lieutenant, these things have killed enough people already. If you get involved, the odds are good they'll kill you too. I won't have any more deaths on my conscience."

"It ain't your call. If you don't let me help, as soon as I'm away from here I'm gonna call in the department. This isn't just about you and your girlfriend, Stone. These things are killin' people—they need to be stopped. And besides, I've got resources you don't have. I can make things happen that you can't."

"I could stop you, you know," Stone said evenly. "I could prevent you from leaving this house, and you'd never be found."

"Maybe, maybe not. But you wouldn't."

"What makes you think so?"

"Because I'm good at readin' people, and you're not like that." He lowered his voice. "Listen. I know this is dangerous. I know I might get killed. I don't care. All I want to do is get these things off the street so they don't hurt anybody else. I ain't gonna see retirement anyway, so at least I'll go out with a bang."

Stone frowned. "You aren't—?"

He leaned in closer. "Big C." He tapped his head. "Brain tumor. Slow growin', but someplace they can't get at. Had a checkup a few months back. Headaches I couldn't shake, nausea…figured the doc'd give me somethin' and that'd be it, but it didn't work out that way. I got another couple years, max. Maybe six months useful." His expression hardened. "And if you tell anybody I told you that, I'll run your ass in."

Stone was about to answer when Belmont came back in. "They're standing by," he said. "Said the restaurant won't kick 'em out as long as they keep buying drinks." He looked back and forth between Stone and Grider, obviously realizing he'd interrupted something. "So…we got a plan?"

"We find out where they are, and we go in," Stone said. "I don't think they'll expect us to figure out where their base is this fast. I don't think they ever worked out how I tracked them to their place in East Palo Alto."

"You sure you can do it?" Belmont asked. "You said it might take too long." He looked at the clock on the wall. "Already almost five. That doesn't give you very long if it'll take us an hour to get there."

Stone was all too aware of that. The tracking ritual was one of his strongest spells, but the tiny bit of bloodstained denim wouldn't make as good a tether as the fingernail had, especially since the blood had already degraded. He suspected the only reason he'd gotten the results he had before was because of the nail itself, not the blood. There was a chance he wouldn't get anything at all from this sample. If he were only more familiar with them, he could—

He almost smacked himself in the head. Idiot! This whole situation had thrown him off his game, but he'd have to think a lot more clearly than that if he was going to get to Imogen before they killed her. "I don't need to track them!"

"Huh?" Grider asked, confused.

"They've got Imogen! I'll track *her*. If she really is with them, it will lead us right to them. And if she's not, then we'll just find her, get her back, and then go on from there." He was already heading toward the door to the lab.

"Makes sense," Belmont said, following. "You must have something of hers you can use to—"

"I don't need anything of hers," Stone said. "Though I'll grab something anyway—not taking chances. And it won't take an hour, either. I just need to tweak the circle and I can do it in fifteen minutes."

"What the hell is he talking about?" Grider asked Belmont. "What's this 'circle' thing?"

"No time," Stone said, changing direction to run upstairs. "Belmont—just entertain the lieutenant, will you? And don't interrupt me while I'm downstairs. I need to get this done."

CHAPTER FORTY-THREE

"IF YOU DON'T SIT STILL, we'll kill you right now."

Kano sat in the back seat of the windowless van, glaring at the figure next to him. He couldn't see her face because of the pillowcase they'd thrown over her head, but despite the fact that her hands were tied together in front of her with a plastic zip-tie and her ankles were duct-taped, she flung herself around in her seat with mad ferocity.

"Want me to smack 'er?" Rima was back there with them, on the other side. Taco was driving, and Grease sat twisted around in the front seat, watching the action.

"Nah," Kano said. "She ain't goin' nowhere." He gripped the figure's shoulder. "I'm not kiddin', though, bitch. You don't knock it off, it'll be easier for us just to kill ya."

The figure stopped struggling. A moan escaped from the pillowcase.

"That's better," Kano said, removing his hand and patting her.

"I still can't fuckin' believe how easy that was," Rima said.

Neither could Kano. When they'd pulled up in front of Stone's place in the stolen van, they could all smell her in there. Disappointed that Stone himself wasn't home, they quickly hatched a new plan to grab the woman inside if they could get to her. The problem was, they couldn't get past some kind of barrier around the house. None of them understood what it was, but they could all sense it, and knew instinctively that trying to get past it, or even getting near it, would be a bad idea. Wasn't going to happen.

Kano and Taco had been outside the van debating how to proceed when the door to the townhouse had opened and a small, slim woman had emerged. "Hello!" she'd called, looking at Kano. "You must be the one Alastair said would be coming by."

Kano, thinking faster than usual, had called, "Yeah. That's me. How you doin'?"

"Would you like to wait for him? He should be home in an hour or so."

"Uh…yeah. That'd be great. But we have some things we need to bring in for him. If you give us a hand we can do it in one trip."

"All right, then." For a moment, she looked nervous, glancing back and forth as if expecting she might see someone else. When she didn't—the street was currently deserted—she pulled the door almost shut and hurried down the walk toward the van. "What have you brought?"

"Some—uh—boxes of books he wanted," Kano said, taking a chance that since Stone was a professor, books were something someone might bring him.

"Ah!" She seemed to take that explanation without question, continuing to approach the van.

As the woman got closer, Taco took hold of the van's sliding side door and began to open it. "We'll each take a box," she said. "You can take the light one."

The bitch was quick—Kano had to give her that. When she got ten feet or so from the van, her eyes narrowed in suspicion. "Wait a moment," she said. "You won't be able to come in. Alastair said you couldn't get past the wards."

The smell of her sudden rising fear was so strong that Kano probably noticed it before she consciously did herself. Moving with supernatural speed, he and Taco leaped forward and grabbed her before she could bolt back toward the house, clamping a hand over her mouth so she couldn't scream, and hustled her into the van. Once she was in, Kano slammed the door shut as Grease and Rima moved into action with the duct tape, zip ties, and pillowcase. They'd been prepared to grab Stone, but whoever this woman was, she obviously meant something to him. They could use that—and maybe get two for the price of one if they played their cards right.

Taco jumped into the driver's seat and was about to head off when Kano said, "Hang on a minute. Gotta leave a note." He fumbled in the glove compartment and found a grubby piece of paper and a pen. He thought a moment, then scrawled a note as the others made noises of impatience.

"There," he said. "We gotta make one stop on the way back to get a phone number." He jumped out, found a rock, zip-tied the note to it, then tossed it up the walk toward the front of the house. Unlike them, it passed through the wards with ease. He got back in and slammed the door shut. "He finds it, he'll come. If not, then we just eat the bitch. Win-win."

At first, the others hadn't been keen on relocating their base somewhere so far away, but they were getting tired of constantly having to move around. The warehouse in East Palo Alto had proven to be less abandoned than they'd thought. Twice they'd had close calls as people had entered it—the first time a small group of homeless people, the second time a pair of gangbangers. It hadn't been easy for the ghouls to resist the temptation to attack them and feast like kings, but they'd managed it long enough to hotwire a car the following night and get the hell out of there.

For the next few days, they'd moved around from abandoned building to abandoned building, but with the cops on constant alert and at least basic versions of their descriptions circulating, they knew if they remained in the area it would be only a matter of time before someone spotted them and called it in. They had to get away for a while.

They'd picked the Santa Cruz mountains because the area was remote enough that nobody was likely to bother them, but close enough to a large food supply that they wouldn't have any trouble finding victims when they needed to hunt again. Rima, the only one of the group who had any prior familiarity with the area, had suggested it as somewhere they could regroup, get away from the cops, and decide their next moves. That had been yesterday, and once they made the decision it had been easy to drive around up in the hills until they found a remote house, killed the occupants, and took over the place.

It was dark by the time they arrived back at the place they'd chosen. After deciding to grab Stone, they'd ditched their stolen car and replaced it with a white, windowless work van that hadn't looked like it got used much. With any luck, nobody would notice it missing until they abandoned it somewhere far away.

Taco pulled up next to the front door and the others hustled the woman out, half-shoving, half-carrying her into the house. Once they were all inside and the door was shut, Kano pulled the pillowcase off her head. "You're a pretty little bitch, aren't you? Stone's got good taste." He reached out and ran a yellowed fingernail along her chin.

She jerked her head back, glaring with flashing brown eyes. She writhed in Rima and Grease's grip, making angry moaning noises behind the tape over her mouth.

"Got some spirit, too. I like food with spirit." He patted the top of her head. "Maybe we'll eat Stone in front of her…or her in front of him. We'll see."

The woman's muffled moans grew louder, but stopped abruptly when they dragged her into the living room. Her gaze fell on a bloody dead body laid out on the floor near a hallway. Kano grinned. "Yeah, you're gonna wanna shut up," he said. "Unless you wanna end up like him sooner'n expected." To the others, he said, "C'mon. Let's get her settled in so she can't get loose. We gotta go get ready to call Stone. Ain't got much time."

"Where we gonna stash 'er?" Taco asked. "We didn't exactly plan for holdin' nobody."

"There's a walk-in closet in the back bedroom," Grease said. "Found it this morning. No windows or nothin'. Nobody'll hear her. Just toss 'er in there and wedge the door shut. Leave 'er tied up. She ain't strong enough to get loose anyway."

Nobody had any better ideas, so they wrestled her down the hall to the bedroom. Kano flipped on the light switch inside the closet; all he saw were clothes and shoes neatly arranged on shelves and racks. "Yeah, okay," he said. "Drop 'er there and let's go."

"We gonna leave anybody here with 'er?" Rima asked. "You know, t'make sure she don't get away?"

"She ain't gettin' away," Kano said. "She's scared shitless, and you really think she's gonna break outta there?" He wedged a chair firmly under the closet's doorknob. "'Sides, I ain't leavin' any o' you fuckers behind t'get tempted. We gotta keep her alive 'til we got Stone."

The others muttered angrily, but none of them protested. As Kano suspected, none of them trusted any of the rest of them to be left alone with such a tempting meal. A fresh kill would be more satisfying than the one already rotting on the floor. And he was right: between the locked door, zip tie, and duct tape, this little slip of a girl wasn't going anywhere.

Grease grinned as they all trooped out of the bedroom and back down the hall. "I'm gonna like this," he said. "Eatin' 'em one piece at a time an' makin' 'em watch. It's like dinner and a show. Pretty fuckin' fancy."

"You think he'll come after her?" Taco asked. "Maybe he ain't got the balls to risk it."

"He'll come," Kano said. "If he doesn't, we'll send 'im the bitch's head."

"After we eat the brains," Rima said.

"Well, yeah, of course. Not like she'll need 'em anymore."

CHAPTER FORTY-FOUR

DOWNSTAIRS IN HIS MAGICAL LAB, Stone sat in the middle of the circle he'd just finished adjusting, closed his eyes, and took several slow deep breaths, employing the meditation technique he normally used to clear his mind before beginning a ritual.

It wasn't working.

His mind refused to settle down, refused to stop sending him nightmarish pictures of Imogen in the hands of the ghouls. His heart continued pounding too hard, too fast. Every nerve in his body jangled, pulled taut like a guitar that had been strung too tightly. He felt as if he would fly apart any second.

It was 5:15.

He couldn't afford to lose control like this. Imogen's life depended on his ability to pull himself together and do what he had to do.

Was she still alive? Had they lied to him to get him to come running after her? He knew they wouldn't release her—there was no logical reason why they would. They wanted him dead. If he ran into their trap with his eyes open and they slaughtered him, there was no reason why they would let her go. She'd just become another meal for them.

Damn it. Stop! You were trained better than this. Use your brain and get on with it.

He placed the map off to his right side and Imogen's hairbrush in his lap, then took more deep breaths, closing his eyes. This spell would be easy. If she was still alive, it would find her. That was the way tracking spells worked: the closer you were connected to the target, the easier it was to find her. Blood relationships worked best: parent and child, siblings, grandparents. After that, the best possible connection was a romantic relationship, especially one that included a sexual component. Even better if the relationship involved actual love.

He thought back to the previous night. Well, they had the sexual part covered in any case. The love—he wasn't sure. He hoped it would be enough.

He closed his hand over the hairbrush in his lap, took one more centering breath, and began the ritual.

When he ran up the stairs from the lab and slammed the door shut behind him twenty minutes later, he found Grider and Belmont pacing the living room, the former peering at the books on his shelves and the latter looking out the window into the darkness.

"I've got it!" he called, waving the map. "She's alive! And I know where she is."

Both of them hurried over. "Where?" Belmont demanded.

Stone swept papers and books to the side on the coffee table and slapped the map down. He'd gotten a few better ones since the last time he'd tried to track the ghouls, and this one covered Santa Cruz and its surrounding areas. He stabbed a finger down on a spot some ten miles northwest of the town itself. The map showed that the area was heavily forested, with only a single winding road snaking up toward and past the point he'd indicated.

"She's there." He looked up at Grider and Belmont. "Do you know the area?"

"That's pretty remote," Grider said. "Santa Cruz Mountains, up past Felton—not many people up that far. Mostly hippies, and people who want to get away from it all."

"How long to get there?"

He shrugged. "We can probably still do it in an hour. There won't be any traffic on that road, but you can't drive as fast unless you got a car that can fly."

"How close can you pinpoint the location?" Belmont asked.

"I can find it," Stone said. "We get close, I'll be able to home in on it. That's the beauty of tracking someone you have an actual connection to. Much easier to follow the trace."

"Let's go, then." Belmont hopped up. "You want me to drive?"

"I'll drive," Grider said firmly. "They might recognize Stone's car if they left anyone behind to guard the girl. And if that piece of junk out front is yours, I don't trust it not to break down before we get there."

"I need to make a stop first," Stone said.

"What?" Grider and Belmont both stared at him like he'd grown a third arm. "I thought we were in a hurry."

"It's necessary. We'll need all the help we can get. You two go to the restaurant where the others are waiting. I'll be along in plenty of time. I need to have a quick chat with someone who doesn't have a phone."

They didn't look like they thought much of the idea, but time was ticking so they grudgingly agreed. Belmont gave Stone the name and address of the restaurant and the phone number to reach them at, then he and Grider departed in Grider's car, leaving Stone alone in the townhouse.

No time to waste. He'd already gathered up the power objects he'd infused while he was downstairs; he wore the ring and the pendant, and the third, a crystal wrapped in wire, was in his pocket. He locked up the house and drove as fast as he could get away with to Kolinsky's shop, taking side streets to avoid the Friday-night traffic on University Avenue. He glanced at the dashboard clock as he drove: 5:45. He'd be cutting it short, but he needed to talk to Kolinsky.

The black mage was seated, as usual, at his roll-top desk when Stone pounded down the stairs into the back of the shop. He swung his chair around calmly, appearing unaffected by Stone's obvious agitation, and pulled off a pair of old-fashioned reading glasses.

"Dr. Stone. You were here earlier today. I am sorry I had to step out and missed your visit."

"I need your help," Stone said, still puffing. He didn't even bother to play the game of pretending it didn't mean anything to him; as good an actor as he was normally, there was no way he could pull it off now, and he knew it.

Kolinsky raised an eyebrow. "What can I do for you?"

"I don't have much time. Do you have anything that's effective against ghouls? Advice, items, whatever? If you've got anything that interferes with magical regeneration, I'll take it."

"Dr. Stone," Kolinsky said, expressionless. "First of all, you are of course aware that any methods I might suggest, you would undoubtedly find…distasteful."

"I don't give a damn what they are," Stone snapped. "It doesn't matter. As long as I don't have to kill anyone other than the ghouls, I'll take them." He shoved his hand through his hair and glanced at his watch again. "I don't have time to waste, Kolinsky. Just tell me what you've got and what you want for it."

"Regeneration," Kolinsky said, almost to himself. "Yes…interfering with that is probably your best option." He jotted down a quick note with an elegant fountain pen. "Regeneration…Ah. Yes. I might have something you would find useful. As I said, though, it makes use of a powerful black magic technique, so I suspect it will not perform as well for you."

"Will it work?" It took an effort of will for Stone not to rock back and forth from foot to foot in his impatience.

"It will, yes." He turned in his chair a bit more and raised his hand. A drawer in a tall cabinet slid open and a wooden box about the size of a shoebox floated out and settled itself on his desk. He opened it and withdrew a long knife with a matte-black blade and a handle wrapped in dark red leather. He slipped it into a sheath of the same red leather and offered it to Stone hilt-first.

Stone withdrew it from the sheath and examined it with magical sight. Its aura, an unsettled, roiling amalgamation of purple, red, and black, gave no indication of its function. It felt odd in his hand, as if it were shifting around in an effort to get comfortable. The blade was etched with sigils that he couldn't read, but that made him uneasy to look at.

"What's it do?" he asked. "I assume I have to do more than stab them with it."

"It's meant to be used by a black mage," Kolinsky said. "It will negate regeneration, yes, among other things, but in doing so, it draws its energy from the life force of the wielder. As you can see, that would not be a problem for a black mage. But for you—"

Stone drew a slow deep breath and let it out. Kolinsky was, of course, talking about the difference in the way that black and white magical techniques were powered. Black mages siphoned off life energy from other people and used that to supply their power—depending on the morality of the particular mage, that could include anything from making the victim tired to killing him and reducing him to ashes. White mages generated power within themselves, or employed infused items such as the ones Stone had prepared. "So you're saying that if I push this thing too hard, it could kill me."

Kolinsky nodded gravely. "Yes. I suggest you have a care with it, and don't use it unless you have to, or for too long."

Stone looked down at the knife, then back at Kolinsky. He thought about Imogen, and what the ghouls could even now be doing to her. He sensed—vaguely—that she was still alive, but how long would that last? He shoved the knife back into the sheath. "What do I owe you?"

"We will settle up when you return," Kolinsky said calmly. "I still owe you for the remainder of the wards you built. Bring it back to me in acceptable condition and we shall call it a...rental."

Stone nodded and looked at his watch again. "Anything else? Anything you might have found out that might help me?"

"I am afraid that is all I can offer you at the moment. Though at a more convenient time, I should be very interested in hearing what *you* have discovered."

"If I live through this," Stone muttered. "Thank you, Mr. Kolinsky."

"Good luck, Dr. Stone."

"I suspect I'll need it."

CHAPTER FORTY-FIVE

IT WAS 6:20 when Stone got to the restaurant. Belmont was out in the parking lot, scanning the street and pacing in agitation. He hurried over as Stone drove up. "Come *on*," he said. "It'll be close as it is. Grider's already worked out the best route, and all the armor and stuff's in the trunks."

Without waiting for an answer, he ran back inside to collect the others. Less than two minutes later, they were on the road.

"What's that thing?" Grider asked, glancing over at Stone in the shotgun seat. The mage was turning the knife over in his hands, inspecting it more carefully than he'd been able to do back at the shop. Belmont was in the back seat, and the remainder of his group followed in another car.

"Something to help me against the ghouls," Stone said.

"Ghouls? So they got a name now? Why didn't you tell me this before?"

"Would it have helped you?"

Grider let out a loud sigh. "Stone, it's gonna take us some time to get there. Start talkin'. I wanna know what I'm getting into."

Stone figured there wasn't any harm in telling him at least some of the story, especially since the cop was taking a big risk in helping them at all. If nothing else, it would be a way to keep his mind busy so he didn't think about what might be happening to Imogen. Choosing his words with care, he gave Grider an abbreviated description of the ghouls and what he knew of their abilities. He said nothing about Belmont or any of the other non-feral ghouls, nor did he speak directly of his own magical powers.

Grider listened without interrupting until Stone had finished. "How the hell do you know all this stuff?" he asked. "Did you know it when you came to talk to me?"

"Not definitively. I wasn't sure until the night they attacked me."

"And what about him?" Grider jerked his head toward the back seat. "Where's he figure in all this?"

"I'm a reporter," Belmont said. "I specialize in…weird stories. I heard about this one a while back and started digging into it."

"You ain't writin' a story about this," the cop growled. "Got it? This whole situation's makin' me itchy as it is—you know how many regs I'm breakin', doin' this?"

"Don't worry, Lieutenant," Belmont said. "It's way past that now. We need to deal with these things. They're too dangerous to leave alive."

Grider grunted. "Yeah, about that. I don't like it. I'm supposed to arrest people. Run 'em in, lock 'em up, let the legal system sort 'em out. I don't kill people unless there's no other option."

"These aren't people," Stone said. "They might look and sound like humans, but they're not. Not anymore. They'll be nearly impossible to kill unless we hit them hard before they figure out we're on to them. And if we *don't* kill them, they'll get away and this will start all over again."

"He's right," Belmont said. "Taking them prisoner's not really an option."

Grider was silent for a long time. They were on Highway 85 now, heading south. "Damn good thing it's so close to Christmas," he muttered. "Lotta people on vacation already. Roads'd be a nightmare otherwise."

Stone wasn't fooled by the change of subject. "Lieutenant?" he asked softly. If he couldn't make Grider understand that nothing short of killing the ghouls would work in this case, it would put the entire operation—and Imogen's life—in danger.

"Look," Grider said, slamming his hand down on the steering wheel. "This isn't easy for me, okay? I'm still not convinced I believe any of it. I still think these guys are just a pack of psychos." Stone started to say something, but he waved him off. "But," he said with emphasis, "I've seen enough to know that maybe I might be wrong. Maybe there *is* stuff out there I don't understand. Just don't expect me to be happy about it."

"I don't expect you to be happy about it," Stone said. He set the knife aside and spread the map out over his lap. "All I expect is that you'll either help us or stay out of the way."

Everyone subsided into silence as Grider continued driving. Stone stared down at the map in his lap, but he couldn't see it very well in the darkness and didn't want to cast a light spell or turn on the dome lights. He didn't need to see it yet—not until they got closer.

He was taking a big chance doing this. There were a lot of variables in play, and he had no way to know which way things would go. The ghouls could call the phone where they'd told him to go from the location where they were holding Imogen. They could go somewhere else to call, leaving her with a guard or locked up somewhere. They could even conceivably be planning to attack him when he got to the phone itself. He had no idea how populated the area near it was, but he doubted they'd take the chance of attacking him in public.

Essentially, he wasn't sure of anything except that Imogen was still alive last time he checked, and that the ghouls wanted him dead. If they *were* calling from where they were holding Imogen and he and the others didn't make it there in time, then they'd miss the phone call. He wondered how soon they'd kill Imogen if that happened. Did they want him badly enough that they were willing to wait in case he got caught in traffic?

He didn't know, and that was what was bothering him.

He glanced out: they'd left 85 and were now on a smaller freeway with two lanes each way and thick forest on both sides. Traffic on their side was heavier than on the other; they still moved forward at a decent pace, but not fast enough for Stone. It was 6:52, according to the dash clock. "Is this likely to get any worse?"

"Nah, this is good," Grider said. "Like I said, you lucked out that this is the holiday season. Commute over 17's usually a mess. Just keep your fingers crossed that everybody drives nice and nobody has an accident."

Stone hadn't thought of that. An accident now, anywhere ahead of them, would probably doom Imogen: the center was a concrete divider and the shoulders weren't wide, so getting past an obstruction would be nearly impossible. "Thanks for that," he muttered.

There was something else he hadn't thought about too: How had the ghouls grabbed Imogen in the first place? The time between his call to her and when Belmont arrived was only a couple of hours. Like his own group, the ghouls would need at least an hour to get back to the Santa Cruz area. That didn't leave much of a window for them to snatch her, and it was broad daylight at the time. Had the wards somehow failed? Had the ghouls figured out a way to get past them? They were designed to repel, but if the ghouls could endure the pain of contacting them, perhaps they'd been able to shove through by main force and regenerate on the other side. Still, that would have been pretty damned obvious in an upscale neighborhood in the middle of the afternoon. Someone would have noticed. Hell, *he* would have noticed: he'd checked them, and there'd been no sign that anyone had tried to breach them.

The only other possibility—and an uncomfortably likely one—was that Imogen had somehow disregarded his request and left the house on her own.

If she'd done that, had she simply gotten bored and decided to take a walk, or had the ghouls come up with a way to lure her out? Stone closed his eyes, frustrated. Imogen was smart, and wouldn't be easily fooled. The ghouls would have needed a damn good story to convince her to leave the safety of the house.

There was no way to know the answers to any of these questions. Stone didn't even know for certain that the ghouls had taken her at all, though the fact that his ritual had pinpointed her up a winding road in the Santa Cruz mountains meant the odds were good that they had. His best hope was that the ghouls had either left her locked up somewhere while they went to deal with him, or else left one of their number behind to guard her. If either of those happened, Stone and the others could get her out with relative ease. However, if they had to face all four ghouls at once while struggling to keep Imogen safe long enough to get her away from them, things could go pear-shaped in any number of ways.

They continued driving. Although traffic still ran smoothly and there were no noticeable slowdowns, the drive seemed interminable to Stone. No one spoke; Stone wasn't even sure if the rest of Belmont's group were still following them. It was full dark now, so only the dazzle of headlights was visible behind them.

"Here's our turnoff," Grider said, pointing ahead at a sign that read *Mt. Hermon Road*.

Stone risked a small light spell, shielding it with his hand, and held it over the map. "Roads get a lot twistier after this."

"Yeah, but there shouldn't be much traffic, and I've been drivin' these roads for twenty years." Grider swung the car off at the exit. "We'll go through Scotts Valley and Felton, then it's all uphill, twisty, and a metric assload of trees from there."

"Are you still sensing her?" Belmont asked.

Stone nodded. "It's not strong, but I'm not surprised. It does degrade over time unless I do the ritual again. I can find the place, though."

"Houses up there are spread out a lot," Grider said. "People like their privacy. At least it won't be like those apartment buildings in EPA."

Stone glanced at his watch. It was 7:15. "Cutting it close."

"Best I can do," Grider said. "Just hold on and keep it together."

Stone grew increasingly restless as they drive past one small town and then another shortly afterward. As soon as it exited the second town, the road narrowed and began to climb. Grider drove as fast as he could safely get away with, but the twists and turns kept their speed down to under thirty. Periodically, sheer drop-offs loomed to one side, sometimes without any sort of barrier to keep the car from sailing over the edge if Grider lost control. Stone gripped the armrests, gritted his teeth, and tried not to look at the time.

There was little traffic on the road once they left Felton, so they could now verify that the car containing the rest of their group had caught up to them and was following closely as they ascended. The trees grew thick along both sides of the road, their branches forming dappled canopies over their heads. Occasionally, a small animal skittered across from one side to the other; twice the headlights picked out the shining eyes of deer lurking just off the road. "Hope those things stay put," Grider muttered.

More time passed, and eventually even Stone's willpower couldn't keep his eyes off the clock. It was 7:35. "We're late," he said in a monotone.

"Almost there," Grider said. "You gettin' anything?"

Stone concentrated, looking down at the map. "We're close. Just go slowly, and stop when I tell you."

Grider slowed the big car down to a crawl, creeping along, peering out the windshield into the night. The only illumination came from their own headlights, and those of the car behind them. It looked like there was nothing ahead of them but more trees on both sides.

"We'll have to be careful until we know whether they're here," Belmont said. "They'll know your scent, Stone, and mine. If they notice us coming—"

"Chance we'll have to take," Stone said. "If they're here, we'll have to hit hard and fast, and—stop!" He sat up straighter in his seat and pointed off to the left side of the road. It was hard to see, concealed by overhanging trees, but a mailbox almost fully hidden behind a thick trunk announced the presence of a house. "It's there, I think."

"We're not goin' down there," Grider said. "I'll pull forward a bit and we'll gear up and go back on foot. If they *are* there, let's not gift-wrap ourselves for 'em by goin' in the front entrance. You gettin' anything from your girlfriend?"

Stone didn't bother to correct him about the relationship. Instead, he focused again, and tensed. He no longer felt the familiar connection. "Nothing."

"Shit," Grider snapped. "Does that mean—"

Breathe. Don't lose it now. "I don't know," he said dully. "It might just mean that they have her in a basement or something, or it might just be wearing off. It doesn't last forever. I'm going to believe that until I see otherwise."

Grider pulled the car off the road about a hundred yards up and stopped, the tires crunching on the gravel of the shoulder. There wasn't much of one here; he had to park with his driver's side wheels on the pavement. After a moment, the other car came to a stop behind them. All four doors opened and Belmont's ghoul crew piled out.

Grider was already opening the trunk of his car. "Let's make this quick," he said under his breath. "If what you say's true and they can smell us from a long way off, we're gonna lose the element of surprise fast." He pulled out three Maglite-style flashlights and offered two of them to Stone and Belmont. "I hope your guys brought your own gear," he said. "I didn't know I was doin' this, so all I got's what's in the car."

The ghouls were already clustered around the trunk of their own car, pulling out various items and handing them around. Belmont came back with an armload of something black, which he offered to Stone. "Put this on," he said. "It'll only protect your torso, but at least they'll have a harder time ripping your guts out. Be careful, though. You too, Grider. Don't get scratched."

Grider was pulling his own light body armor out of his trunk. He shrugged out of his windbreaker, revealing an automatic pistol in a sidearm holster. He took that off too, put on the armor, and then replaced the holster over it. Finally, he removed a pump-action shotgun and two boxes of shells, and stuck the latter in his jacket pockets.

Stone, who'd never worn body armor before, had trouble getting into the bulky vest. Between Grider and Belmont they got him strapped in, and he pulled his black overcoat on over it. It was a little snug, but he wanted the extra protection of the coat's thick wool shell.

"Any of you guys got guns?" Grider asked as the other ghouls approached.

Lu shook his head. He held a samurai-style sword; the others had machetes, baseball bats, and crowbars. "If you're going to shoot them, aim for the head," Lu told Grider. "This is no time to be squeamish. Remember, they aren't human. Not anymore. It's not murder to kill them."

Stone watched him soberly. Lu was a doctor—a healer—but now his face was set hard and his eyes were resolute. Someone was going to die tonight—it would either be the Cannibal Killers or them. And if they died, Imogen was dead too. The fact that he couldn't sense her anymore clawed at him, ramping up his impatience.

"Let's do this," he said.

CHAPTER FORTY-SIX

"WHY THE *FUCK* AIN'T HE ANSWERIN'? Does he *want* us to eat the bitch?"

Kano stood next to the pay phone two miles down the hill from the house they'd commandeered, listening to it ring. His skinny fingers gripped the receiver so hard that if he'd been stronger, he'd have broken it. The phone had been ringing steadily for two minutes with no pickup on the other end. Aside from them, the area was dark and deserted.

"Ring some more. Maybe he got stuck in traffic." Taco stood next to him, shifting from foot to foot and glancing around in apprehension, as if expecting someone to attack them. Grease and Rima waited in the idling van. "Told ya we shouldn'ta gone so far away."

"You wanna get caught?" Kano shook the receiver. "Damn it, answer the phone, motherfucker!"

"You don't think he figured out where we are, do you?" Taco took another nervous look around. "You think he can find us?"

"How the hell can he find us? He's a freak, but he ain't *that* good. I—" The line clicked, and he held up a swift hand to silence what Taco was about to say.

"Hello?" The voice was female, and sounded like a teenager.

Kano mouthed "*Fuck!*" and shook his head violently at Taco.

"Is somebody there?" the voice asked. "Who are you looking for?"

Kano almost slammed the receiver back in the cradle, but instead he drew a deep breath and forced his voice to sound calm and pleasant. "Uh, hi. We're tryin' to reach somebody. Guy named Stone. Is he there?"

"Sorry," said the voice. "Nobody here but me and my friend. We were riding by on our bikes and heard the phone ring." In the background, there was a giggle.

"You sure there's nobody else there?"

A pause. When the voice spoke again, it sounded nervous. "Uh, listen, we gotta go. 'Bye." The line went dead.

Kano swore again and hung up with a loud bang. "Fucker chickened out."

"Then we eat the bitch," Taco said, shrugging. "Either way we get to eat. His loss."

"We're still gonna find him." Kano stumped back over toward the van and climbed into the driver's seat. "He ain't gettin' off that easy. Just like we said in the note—we eat the bitch and send 'im the bones. Then we hunt 'im down. Maybe we hold 'im somewhere and cut pieces off while he's still alive."

"I ain't never et nobody in front of 'imself before." Grease grinned in a most unwholesome way. "I like it."

"Me too," Kano said. He pulled the van back out, made a U-turn, and headed back up the hill. "Maybe we test it out on the bitch first. And we still got them old hippies to finish up too."

"Faster," Rima said. "I'm gettin' hungry again already just thinkin' about it."

| CHAPTER FORTY-SEVEN

STONE SCRAMBLED DOWN THE HILLSIDE, trying not to trip over any roots or lose his footing on the leaf-strewn ground. Despite the fact that approaching the house by the dirt road leading down toward it would be foolish, he regretted their decision to go in by descending the steep hillside that dropped off from the road above. Any element of surprise they would get by creeping through the trees would be negated if any of them lost footing and tumbled arse-over-teakettle down toward the house.

Aside from the faint light of the moon and the very occasional headlights of a car going by, it was utterly dark. No perimeter lights illuminated the shadowy bulk of the house, nor was there any light coming from the inside. All Stone could see from his current position was that the steeply sloping dirt road opened out into a large cleared area, with two separate buildings of approximately equal size at its east and south sides.

"Two houses?" he whispered to Grider.

"I think one of 'em's some kinda garage or workshop," Grider whispered back. The detective was puffing a little and making a lot of noise; obviously he wasn't used to this kind of exertion anymore.

Belmont touched Stone's arm; the mage slowed down and waited for Grider to get a little ahead of him. "It's quiet,"

Belmont said. "I smell them, but it's not strong. I'm not sure they're here."

"Can ghouls see in the dark?"

"Yeah. Them probably better than us. But this close I should be getting a stronger scent."

Stone would have to take his word for it: all he could smell was the heavy, woodsy aromas of pine needles and decomposing leaves. As his eyes adjusted to the dim light, he saw that the southernmost of the two buildings was a rambling, single-story house, while the other one was boxier and taller with four large doors in the front: Grider was probably right that it was a garage, perhaps with storage space above it. He saw no cars parked anywhere outside; the only vehicle was some sort of small four-wheeled ATV off to the side of the garage building. A large covered woodpile sat on the near side of the house next to some sort of wheeled machine Stone couldn't identify.

Belmont and a couple of the other ghouls had reached the house. They crouched low so as not to be visible from the windows, and waited for the others to catch up.

"What now?" Lu whispered.

"We go in," Stone said. "Find Imogen, and get her out."

"Hold on." Grider held up a hand. "If they're in there—"

"They're not in there," Belmont and one of the other ghouls said at the same time.

Grider's eyes narrowed. "And how the hell do you know that?"

"Don't ask questions like that, Lieutenant," Stone said. To Belmont, he said, "Anyone else in there?"

There was a long pause as Belmont sniffed the air. Then he stiffened.

"What?" Stone demanded.

"Someone's dead in there." The ghoul's voice was hollow.

"What?" Stone came up out of his crouch as terror gripped him. "Are you sure?"

"Yeah." The other ghouls were nodding.

"Well, let's get in there. Maybe you're wrong!" Stone started forward, but Grider grabbed his arm. "Let go of me," he growled.

Instead, Grider tightened his grip. "Stone, keep it the fuck together. I know this might be bad, but don't get us all killed."

For a second—just a second—Stone thought about sending the detective flying, as images of what he might find inside took over his mind again. Then he sighed and slumped. "You're right. I'm sorry."

As Grider let loose of Stone's arm, Belmont was giving orders. "Zeke, Hannah, you stay out here in case they come back. If you smell 'em coming, send up an alarm."

The two ghouls nodded and took off back into the night.

The rest of the group, with Belmont in front, Stone in the middle, and the remaining ghouls and Grider bringing up the rear, crept along the wall toward the steps leading to the front door. Grider had his shotgun at the ready; those who had flashlights held them, but didn't turn them on yet.

Belmont tried the door. It was unlocked. "That's not good…" he muttered.

"Hippies up here leave their doors unlocked all the time," Grider whispered back. "Get inside."

Belmont shoved the door open and hurried into the house. Stone followed, tense, gripping Kolinsky's knife and prepared to put up a magical shield instantly if anything ambushed them.

Nothing did. The house was quiet and dark. They stood in a small entry area, with open doorways to the left and in front of them.

"They're not here," Belmont said again.

"Damn, I smell it now," Grider said.

So did Stone, now that he was inside. It wasn't strong, but it was unmistakable: the coppery tang of blood mixed with something even less pleasant, mingled with the stronger aromas of bread and flowers. "Where?" he asked Belmont.

In answer, Belmont headed through the doorway to the left. "I think there might be two of them."

"Two bodies?"

"Yeah." He flipped a light switch.

For a moment, Stone could do nothing but stare. Behind him, Grider breathed, "Fuck…"

The room beyond the doorway was a small dining area, and beyond that was a kitchen. On the floor halfway between the two, a body lay spread out, its arms flung forward as if the victim had made a desperate run for freedom and not gotten very far. The body had been gutted; a spray of blood covered the otherwise pristine white tile floor and dried on the floral paper of the nearby walls.

Stone took a step forward. He didn't want to get a better look at the body, but he had to. He had to know.

When he drew up next to Belmont, he nearly sagged in relief. "It's not Imogen." The body was female, but the graying hair and larger frame revealed it to be a much older woman. Clearly the ghouls had feasted upon her and hadn't bothered to clean up—could that mean that they weren't worried about their food supply for the foreseeable future? Stone felt a pang of guilt at his relief—just because the victim hadn't been Imogen didn't mean that this woman wasn't worthy of the same anger at her senseless death—but he didn't have time for compassion right now.

"I'm gonna have to call this in," Grider said.

"Not yet," Stone said. "Come on—Belmont, you said there were two bodies."

"Found the other one," came a call from a short distance away. Stone, Grider, and Belmont hurried back out and through the other opening.

Lu and the other ghouls had turned on the light in here as well: this room was an open living room with sofa, chairs, and coffee table. The far wall was dominated by a brick fireplace and a long, floor-to-ceiling picture window. A sliding door opened onto what looked like a deck.

Stone barely glanced at all of this, though. His attention was drawn instead to the right side of the room, where a hallway led off to where presumably the bedrooms were located. On the floor directly in front of the hallway was another body.

"Damn," Grider said. "Looks like they took out the owners."

This body was male, looked to be about the same age as the woman in the kitchen, and was similarly mutilated. He lay face down in a large, spreading puddle of blood, drying but still clearly tacky, soaking into the cracks in the wooden floor. Bloody footprints led down the hall toward the rooms in the back of the house.

"Well, they're not hungry, at least," Stone said without a trace of humor. "But where the hell is Imogen?" He rounded on Belmont. "No more bodies?"

"Can't tell for sure," he said, waving toward the man. "This one and the other one are pretty strong. But I don't think so."

Stone hurried off down the hall. "Imogen!" he called. "Are you here? Imogen!" As he progressed, he flung open doors, shining his flashlight inside. Grider and Belmont followed behind him, the detective with his shotgun in one hand and his flashlight in the other.

The first three doors, two on the left and one on the right, were a bedroom, an office, and a bathroom. All were quiet and empty. Where could she be? Had the ghouls killed her and stashed her body somewhere? Was she held prisoner in the garage? Had they somehow taken her with them, even though he'd sensed her presence here before the tracking spell faded?

Almost without paying attention, Stone grabbed the knob of the final door and tried to shove it open as he had the others.

It was locked.

"Grider!" he called. "Can you get this open?"

"Yeah. Stand back."

Stone and Belmont took a couple steps back, and Grider kicked in the door. He swept the flashlight and the shotgun barrel around, scanning the room.

"Anything?" Stone called.

"Nobody here. C'mon in."

Stone turned on the overhead light. This was obviously the master bedroom: a large bed covered with a patchwork quilt dominated the wall under the window. The rest of the furniture was of heavy wood. The only thing odd about it was that a chair was wedged under the knob of a door on the room's near side. Stone tensed. Was this where they'd locked Imogen in?

Before Grider or Belmont could stop him, he crossed the room and yanked the chair out, flinging it aside. "Imogen? Are you in there?" He listened a moment; when there was no answer, he pulled the door open.

Inside, it was dark. Belmont and Grider crowded up behind Stone as he located the light switch and flipped it on. What he saw made him pump his fist. "Good old Imogen! I knew she wouldn't just sit here and take it!"

The room was a large walk-in closet, with racks of clothes on either side, and shoes neatly arranged on shelves below them. In the center was an open area, and it was this Stone was looking at.

On the floor were two pieces of torn duct tape and the remains of a plastic zip tie.

Grider pushed past and picked up the zip tie. "Looks like it got chewed through or somethin'. But where'd she—"

In answer, Belmont nodded toward the ceiling.

It took Stone a couple of seconds to spot what he was indicating and put together what it was: a piece of rope with a knot on the end of it hanging down, about six inches long. Someone, probably the lady of the house, had attached a blue silk flower to the end of it and wrapped it in blue ribbon. Stone grasped it and pulled, and a wooden stairway much like the one in the portal room at his home in England lowered.

He wanted to cheer. Imogen may not have magical talent, but she had a brain every bit as sharp as his own, and she hadn't let herself panic. "Come on," he said. "Let's see where she's gotten to." Without waiting for a reply, he stuffed the knife in his belt, mounted the stairway, and climbed.

"How the hell did they miss this?" Grider growled, following behind him.

"In a hurry, maybe," Belmont said. "And probably figured she'd stay tied up. Go check it out—I'll tell the others where we're going and catch up."

Stone got to the top of the ladder and poked his head in through the hole in the ceiling, shining the flashlight around to make sure nothing was about to jump him. He was looking at an attic, packed with dusty boxes and building materials. The ceiling was low enough that he couldn't stand up straight; he crawled up out of the hole to give Grider room, crouching to look around.

The attic space appeared to take up the whole of the upper part of the house. "Imogen!" Stone called. "Are you up here? Are you hiding? It's safe to come out now. They're gone."

No answer.

"Look!" Grider called. He too had climbed free of the hole and had gone off in the opposite direction from Stone.

Stone hurried over as quickly as he could manage while hunched over. It didn't take spotting the footprints in the dust on the floor to see what Grider had found: the detective was shining his light in the direction of the wall that made up the far end of the house. As Stone drew closer, a cold breeze crept across the floor and chilled his legs.

An open hole, perhaps eighteen inches square, stood open to the outside. Grider was hunkered down, examining it. "Looks like it was a vent of some kind. Kicked out." He indicated the edges with his flashlight beam as Belmont came up behind them. "Could she get out of there?"

Stone nodded. "She's small and thin. Easily." He poked his head out and looked down; a metal grate lay on the ground below the hole. "Not much of a drop, either." He grinned. "They underestimated her. A lot of people do that. They left her without a guard, and I think she got away from them." He pulled back from the hole with a chuckle. "And they don't even know it yet."

"So where'd she go?"

Stone was about to answer when a panicked cry split the silence from somewhere outside the house.

| CHAPTER FORTY-EIGHT

"Damn!" Belmont snapped. "They're back already!" He gripped Stone's arm with one hand and Grider's with the other. "Be *careful*. Don't let them near you. Don't go off on your own."

"Don't worry," Stone said, and yanked his arm free. "No intention of getting scratched. Come on." He shoved past Belmont and ran in a half-crouch toward the stairs, which had returned to their closed position as soon as they no longer bore weight.

Fear gripped him as he reached the bottom, but he shoved it down. He didn't have time to be afraid now. Imogen was still out there somewhere, and the ghouls would be looking for her as soon as they realized she was gone. He broke into a run down the hall, ignoring the visions of the dead couple on the floor, of the glowing red eyes and yellowing nails and wide straining mouths. This time, they didn't have him by surprise.

The other ghouls except Lu had already headed outside by the time Stone reached the entryway. He pulled the knife from the sheath in his belt and gripped it.

"Be careful," Lu said. He appeared to be looking for something; after a moment he found it and flicked on several light switches. Perimeter lights outside the house sprang to life, flooding the open dirt parking area in front of the house with illumination.

Grider crossed the front room and took cover, crouching low and shotgun ready, peering out a large bay window into the cleared area in front of the house. "Where the hell are they?"

Stone wasn't sure either. He slipped out through the front door and ducked behind a chair on the porch. The perimeter lights were useless: the ghouls must still be out among the trees somewhere. He switched to magical sight and was rewarded with a quick glow of an aura darting across the road leading down toward them. "I see one!" he called. "Right side of the road, moving fast." He glanced right and caught sight of one of Belmont's crew heading toward the dark bulk of the garage. Two others pulled back, scanning the trees from near the house.

"Don't get too separated!" Belmont called. He was on the other side of the porch, looking out over the scene. "I think they got Zeke already!"

Stone stayed in magical sight—these things moved fast and they were good at concealing themselves, but they couldn't hide their auras from him. When a fast-moving glow popped up again where he thought the previous ghoul might be, he gathered magical energy from one of his power objects and flung it in the direction of the glow. He didn't know if he hit it.

Where was Imogen? Had she run away? Had the ghouls caught her as she tried to escape on foot? As far as he knew, she had little or no experience in the woods, and of course she'd have no idea where she was; if she'd tried to get back to the road the odds were fifty-fifty that she'd either gotten away or chosen the same direction the ghouls were heading back from, in which case they'd have spotted her.

He couldn't worry about that now, though. Imogen was either safe or she wasn't, but he wouldn't help her by fragmenting his concentration and getting himself killed. He crouched lower behind the chair and looked for another shot.

Behind him, the sound of glass shattering, then Grider's loud shriek of "Holy fuck!"

Stone spun and poked his head back in through the open door in time to see one of the semi-ferals hit by a blast from Grider's shotgun. The ghoul screamed and staggered back, then lunged forward. Grider, clearly not wanting to chance getting in range of the flailing claws, backpedaled, whipped the stock of his shotgun backward, and shattered the bay window, then dived out through it onto the porch in a hail of glass shards. He rolled up, his arms protecting his face.

Stone only got to see this for a second, though, because the ghoul Grider had hit was nowhere near dead despite being peppered with a face- and torsoful of shot. He shrieked and waved his arms, blood blossoming from dozens of tiny wounds, but already his body was regenerating the damage. Stone flung a concussion blast at him, blowing him backward and out through the hole he'd made in the sliding glass door at the back of the house.

He was about to follow it up with another spell when someone yelled, "Back!" Whoever it was grabbed him from behind and yanked him backward. His heart pounding, he struggled to redirect the spell and extricate himself from the attacker's grip when he realized it was Belmont. "Let me go!" he snapped.

"Don't get close to them, damn you." Belmont let him go, but his expression was grim. "They can take a lot more than you think and still keep coming! They—Stone! Watch out!"

Belmont shoved Stone backward again, backpedaling himself, as a fast-moving ghoul came barreling out of the trees to their left, heading straight for them. Belmont raised his sword and Stone staggered toward the house, preparing another spell.

The ghoul didn't make it to them. Another form, moving almost as fast as it was, hurtled on a collision course with the attacking ghoul. The two of them went down and rolled, screaming and flailing.

Stone took a second to recover his breath and take stock of the situation as he could see it. The two flailing ghouls, one on their side, one not, seemed occupied with each other at the moment. One of Belmont's crew was probably dead. Grider was on the porch, still recovering from his trip through the plate-glass window, but he was upright with his shotgun ready. Stone couldn't see any others out in the cleared space in front of the house.

He glanced over toward the garage and his breath caught in his throat. "Belmont!"

The big garage had four doors: three roll-ups each large enough to admit a single vehicle, and, closest to the house, a normal human-sized door. This latter door was open. One of the enemy ghouls darted across the garage's front and ducked in through the opening, while another one followed more cautiously.

Behind Stone, Grider's shotgun roared again, but the ghoul ducked and the shot missed. Stone was about to fling a spell in the ghoul's direction when once again Grider's voice pierced the night: "Holy shit, who the hell is that?" an instant before the roar of an engine grew louder and drowned him out.

Suddenly more light blazed in front of the house. Stone spun again in time to see a large vehicle—a van or truck—entering the scene at a high rate of speed, headlights blazing, rear end fishtailing back and forth.

It was heading straight for him, Belmont, and the two ghouls still struggling off to their left.

Before he could move, before he could dive out of the way, the van slammed on its brakes and veered away from them, its tires crunching and squealing in the gravel. Tires still screaming protest, the van's front end slammed into the second of the two roll-up garage doors—straight into the ghoul that had been sneaking across toward the far door. Her own agonized screams rose over the sound of protesting metal as the roll-up door gave way and buckled backward, pinning her between it and the front of the van. One of the headlights hadn't broken in the collision, and it picked out the ghoul's bloody, broken form, struggling to free herself.

"Who *was* that?" Belmont demanded.

Stone wasn't listening. His eyes widened as a small figure staggered free of the van and, swaying, tottered around behind it and into view.

Imogen?

No...

She was alive! Relief flooded him—but only for a moment. Why was she here? Whose van was that? Why had she returned?

She gripped the back side of the van, peering around. "Alastair?"

Oh, bloody hell.

She didn't seem to have spotted him, but her voice would attract every semi-feral ghoul in the place. He had to get her out of here. He made a fast decision: if he could get her up on the roof of the two-story garage, even the athletic ghouls would have a hard time getting to her. He could go up there with her and pick them off before they got close.

He gathered energy...

Something slammed into him from behind, knocking him forward, tearing the back of his coat with a loud ripping sound and disrupting his concentration. At the same time, Belmont caught hold of his arm and yanked him sideways. The end result was that the ghoul from the house, apparently recovered now, sailed past him and rolled up, clutching a large chunk of Stone's coat.

"Did he get you?" Belmont demanded, wheeling around to face the ghoul.

"No." Stone could barely get the word out; his heart pounded, his breath rasping in his throat. If Belmont hadn't pulled him free—

But where was Imogen?

He flung himself out of Belmont's grip in time to see Imogen's slim form staggering in through the door on the near side of the garage.

Right into where at least one ghoul lurked.

"Imogen!" Before Belmont could react and grab him again, Stone pulled up his shield and levitated himself as fast as he could manage toward the garage.

"Stone! Wait!"

Stone didn't stop. Behind him, Grider's shotgun roared again—a quick glance over his shoulder revealed the ghoul on the ground, facing in Stone's direction. He must have tried to follow, but Grider shot him again. Belmont was running toward the garage, and off in the distance, another of his crew had joined the one trying to fight off the semi-feral.

Stone couldn't do anything about that now, though. Imogen was in the garage, and he didn't know who else was in there with her. The other ghoul, a female, still screamed as she continued trying to rip herself free of the van and the garage door; her body twisted into bloody, painful contortions, ripping wounds open and regenerating them almost instantly.

There were four of them. As far as Stone knew, they were all still alive, and anything but decapitation or burning would only inconvenience them.

Inside the garage, the growling shriek of a chainsaw fired up.

"Imogen!" Stone dropped the levitation spell and ran in through the open door. No lights were on inside; the only illumination came through the mangled garage door from the outside perimeter lights.

Stone shifted to magical sight and fumbled for a switch, all the time mindful that one of the ghouls might be hiding, preparing to leap out at him. The chainsaw's whine drowned out the other sounds, and two pungent odors mingled in the air: rot and gasoline. "Imogen!" he called again. He found the switch and flipped it on.

Above him, banks of harsh fluorescents buzzed and sputtered to life. He ducked to the side behind some machinery, taking in the scene in one fast glance.

Near the back wall, one of Belmont's crew brandished the chainsaw at his attacker. The ghoul, a male, danced just out of its reach, swinging a metal pole.

"Alastair!"

Stone jerked his head to the side. Where was she? For a moment panic gripped him as he couldn't find her, but then she rose up behind the trapped female ghoul near the van. She held the long handle of an axe, which she swung in a wild arc in the general direction of the ghoul's head. The shot missed its mark, but the axe blade buried itself in the ghoul's shoulder. The ghoul shrieked, increasing its efforts to get free, ripping the axe from Imogen's grasp.

"Imogen!" Stone yelled. "Get back! Don't let it touch you!" He started in her direction, but the garage was packed with machinery so he couldn't run.

Imogen, eyes alight with terror, backpedaled out of the ghoul's range, ducking behind a worktable. Behind her, the other two roll-up doors were still closed.

Stone, heart pounding, skirted the trapped ghoul and picked his way around more worktables, metal drums, and piles of scrap wood and metal. If he could just get to Imogen, he could blow one of the closed doors open and get them out that way, but he had to reach her first. If that ghoul got loose and went after her—

To his right, a scream of pain. He didn't want to waste time looking, but he risked a quick glance in time to see the chainsaw clatter to the ground with one end of its chain, broken and flapping, wrapped around the other ghoul's metal pole. Belmont's ghoul clutched his spurting arm, which the broken chain had nearly severed. The other ghoul, his back to Stone, moved in for the kill.

Stone acted on instinct: if he'd been thinking straight he might not have done what he did next. Imogen's cries ringing in his ears, he gathered magical energy and flung a spell at the advancing ghoul. He couldn't risk fire or lightning in here, not with the strong gasoline spell permeating the air, so he settled for a concussion blast. It hit the ghoul in the ribs, blowing him backward past Belmont's ghoul and into the wall. Judging by his scream of pain and the way his body doubled over sideways, it had been a solid hit that would have killed a mundane, but Stone couldn't wait to see the results.

"Go!" Belmont's ghoul yelled. "Get her out!"

Stone didn't wait. He didn't know if the ghoul would regenerate the damage, but his primary concern now was Imogen. He hurried the rest of the way across the garage to where she was crouched behind the worktable, keeping a wary eye on the trapped ghoul. She'd picked up a hammer from the table and held it in a shaking hand.

Stone crouched next to her. "Come on," he said, panting. "Let's get you out of here." He pointed his hand at the garage door directly in front of him, two over from where the ghoul was pinned, and tried to shove it upward.

It didn't budge. Probably locked, and he didn't have time to figure out how to unlock it.

Okay, bigger magic, then. This was going to hurt, even with his focus items, but it was still faster and safer than trying to pass two hostile ghouls on the way back to the door. He glanced over and saw Belmont coming in, looking around, taking in the scene. Then he was all focus again, pulling in magical energy, shaping it, drawing additional power from his ring.

"Stone! Look out!"

Stone didn't hesitate. He flung himself sideways, and that probably saved his life. Still, pain lit up his calf as something struck it, and he pitched forward to slam into the garage door. He fell hard, rolling over and trying to leap back to his feet. His leg was on fire with pain, and a glance down showed blood rapidly staining his pantleg. Damn! He'd been focusing so hard on taking down the garage door that he hadn't put his shield back up!

What the hell had hit him?

And then he saw it as Imogen yelled something inarticulate that was half-scream, half-roar of rage, and flung her hammer. The trapped ghoul was still trapped, still writhing, opening up new wounds and healing them with obscene speed, but she must have gotten hold of something and threw it at Stone. This time, Imogen's aim was true: the hammer smashed into the ghoul's head. The ghoul screamed in rage, lunging toward Imogen, nearly ripping her torso apart trying to free herself.

"No!" Stone yelled. Eyes blazing, teeth bared, he redirected the magical energy he'd gathered to take down the door and hurled it at the ghoul.

The blast hit her hard, and would have knocked her back if she hadn't been firmly wedged between the front end of the van, the ruined garage door, and a bolted-down, solid metal worktable. As it was, a horrific wet ripping sound rent the air as the ghoul's abdominal area twisted and split. Her scream rose higher into a shriek.

And she still wasn't dead.

She writhed there, blood gushing from what would have been mortal wounds in a normal human, clawing at the car, at her own abdomen, at the van, while her burning, inhuman eyes focused on Stone.

And then Belmont was there, behind her. "Go!" he yelled. He held a handsaw he'd picked up from somewhere, and as Stone watched in fascinated horror, he swung it at the ghoul woman's neck.

It wasn't a neat job. Her head didn't come free in one smooth motion as it would have if he'd been using a sharpened sword. Instead, her shriek was abruptly cut off as her windpipe was severed, and more blood (how did she even *have* so much blood?) spouted and plumed, bathing Belmont in red gore.

And *still* she wasn't dead.

Her body twitched and bucked, holding on to life with supernatural persistence. One flailing arm slammed hard into Belmont. He dropped the saw and it clattered down.

Stone had almost turned away, back to Imogen, when the blade hit the ghoul's neck, but he paused to watch for another second or two when she refused to stop moving. It was good that he had. Almost too quickly to follow, the saw blade hit the concrete floor and sparked, igniting the source of the gasoline smell—a pool of it that had spilled when Imogen's careening van had slammed into the garage and taken out a pair of metal drums just inside.

The ghoul woman, her lower body already soaked in it from her efforts to wrest herself free from the van, went up like a torch. Flames licked around her, leaping out to ignite the rest of the gasoline, creeping toward the wooden worktables and piles of scrap wood on the floor. Her agonized shrieks grew louder as whatever magic kept her alive tried to reunite her half-severed head with her neck. Somehow, she found strength that had eluded her before, just enough to budge the van the inch or two she needed to get free. And then she was gone, running screaming through the night as the flames rose to engulf her.

"She's headed toward the house!" Stone yelled. He was barely standing now, his lower leg soaked with blood. "Come on—we have to get out of here before the whole place goes up! Imogen! Go!"

"Get out!" Belmont yelled. "I'll help him!" And then he was gone toward the back of the garage where his friend still struggled with the remaining ghoul.

Imogen paused, turning back to Stone, eyes huge with terror and shock that grew more intense when she saw the blood. "Alastair!"

"Go!" he barked, struggling to stay upright as his vision grew swimmy. "Get out! Now! I'll follow!"

She took one last desperate look at him, but obeyed. The fire hadn't quite reached the edge of the van yet, so she ducked low and slipped out through the hole into the night. "Come on!" she yelled back through.

"Keep going!" Stone ordered, and she disappeared again. Belmont and the ghoul were still struggling on the other side of the garage, but he knew in his current condition he only had maybe one more spell in him before he collapsed. He made the decision fast, gathered his will, and staggered out through the same hole Imogen had. The fire was close: he felt its heat reaching for him as he made it through and hit the ground rolling.

Outside, he blinked through the grayness and the smoke, trying to make out what was going on, what had happened out there since he'd entered the garage. Where were the others? Where was Imogen? Had she gotten clear of the buildings?

He spotted two things at once: the first was that the female ghoul from the garage, lit up now like some kind of ambulatory bonfire, had made it to the house and finally collapsed in a crackling, jerking heap at the top of the stairs to the front door. Already, the deck and parts of the house were catching fire.

The second was Imogen, running out into the open area away from the fire. Relief washed over him—she was going to get away! Even if he didn't survive this, she had a shot at escaping. Where were the other ghouls? He shifted to magical sight, trying to pick them out, but he couldn't—

And then he saw it: the hellish red aura of one of the semiferals, moving with unholy speed across the clearing from the other side—

—on a collision course with Imogen.

And she didn't see him.

"Imogen!" he tried to yell, but she couldn't possibly hear him from this far away. And there was no way he'd be able to run to them before the ghoul reached her. Hell, he couldn't run at all.

His hand touched the knife in its sheath at his belt—the one he'd gotten from Kolinsky. He couldn't fling it at the ghoul, not even with magic. To function, it had to be up close and personal.

Once again, he didn't think, but merely acted. Summoning up every shred of power he had left in himself and his focus objects, driving down the grayness encroaching with increasing persistence on his brain, he formed it into a force that lifted him off the ground and flung him toward the ghoul. He gripped the knife in front of him, pointed like some kind of mad projectile. He'd only have one shot at this. If he missed, Imogen would be dead, and probably so would he.

Behind him, someone yelled, but he ignored them.

He was moving so fast he could barely see where he was going now; every bit of his will was focused on the ghoul's ugly red aura.

At the last second, Imogen realized what was going on and threw herself sideways.

The ghoul spun in toward her, yelling obscenities into the night. It raised its arms, its long fingers and wickedly sharp nails pointed at her as she tried to scrabble away—

But now its back was to Stone.

His knife hit it high in the center of its back, plunging into its flesh as if it were made of butter instead of flesh and bone.

If its screams had been loud before, they were nearly deafening now, and they had a different quality—now, they were the sound of an animal in mortal agony.

As if knowing that something was terribly wrong, it bucked and reeled, trying to reach its hands around to get a grip on Stone, but what small attacks it could manage from its position bounced off his coat and the body armor beneath it. But it didn't seem to be weakening. Even with the knife sunk into its back, it still struggled to pull itself forward, to slice at Stone, at Imogen, at whatever it could reach. Once again, obscenities mingled with its screams of pain.

Stone gripped the knife with both hands, certain that if he let go, all would be lost. It wouldn't be enough to simply stab it. That wasn't how the knife worked. It might hurt the thing that way—obviously it *was* hurting it—but he had to stop it from regenerating the damage as fast as he could inflict it. And he'd have to do it now. Already his hands shook on the hilt, the strength in his arms dwindling as his leg continued bleeding.

It had to be now.

Focusing once again, he concentrated on the knife, on pouring energy into it. He didn't practice black magic, but in his insatiable curiosity to know everything there was to know about all types of the Art, he'd spent enough time studying it to know how it worked. If he couldn't pull life force from other humans to power the effect, he'd have to power it with his own. And there wasn't much of that left.

"Die, you bastard," he breathed through gritted teeth. Power flowed from him, through his hands, through the hilt, down through the blade, and into the ghoul.

The effect was immediate, as if the creature had been hit by a live electrical wire. Its body went rigid, its arms stretching out, its neck jerking back until Stone could see its wide-open, panic-stricken eyes. It tried to reach him again, but it was too far gone for that now. Stone gripped the knife's hilt and kept at it. He had to make sure it was dead. If he passed out before it died, it could go after Imogen again. He couldn't let it do that. He focused on that thought above all others as consciousness slipped away.

He heard someone scream behind him again, and then the grayness became blackness, and the blackness became nothing.

| CHAPTER FORTY-NINE

STONE AWOKE IN DARKNESS. For a moment, he wasn't even sure he *was* awake. He lay on something soft and he didn't know if he could move.

Memories flooded back: the house, the ghouls, the fire—

"Imogen..." His voice came out as a rasp, barely audible, followed by a fit of coughing that took what remained of his energy.

"Shh..." a soft voice said. "It's all right. You're safe."

A cool, wet cloth settled over his forehead. It felt wonderful. He risked opening his eyes.

A figure sat next to the bed. He couldn't make out features in the room's near-darkness, but he didn't have to. He knew her silhouette. "Imogen..." he whispered again. The room smelled like clean linens and antiseptic. "Where...?"

"Shh..." she said again. "Everything's fine. Just rest. I'll be right back."

Before he could do anything to stop her, she hurried from the room. He might have drifted off again, but awoke when someone switched on a dim light.

Imogen was back in her chair next to the bed. He blinked a couple of times to focus, and saw that she was wearing unfamiliar clothes that were too big for her.

Another figure stood next to her: Dr. Lu. "How do you feel, Dr. Stone?"

"What happened?" he rasped. "Where—?"

"There's time for all that," Lu said. "Tell me how you're feeling. Does your leg hurt?"

He thought about it, and discovered that it didn't, though he felt something wrapped snugly around his calf. "Not...at the moment."

"Good. I gave you something for the pain. You lost a fair bit of blood, which is probably why you feel so weak. Aside from that the wound wasn't bad. I stitched it up, but you should try to keep weight off it for a few days until it heals."

Now that the lights were on, Stone saw that, contrary to what he'd first assumed, he wasn't in a hospital. This looked like someone's bedroom. All he wanted to do was go back to sleep for about three or four days, but he had too many questions for that. "Tell me what happened."

"They're all dead," Belmont said. He'd entered the room as Stone had spoken. "You got the leader, we took out the two in the garage, and the others chucked the last one into a wood chipper. They won't be back."

Stone closed his eyes. The ghouls were dead. Imogen was alive. It was over. "And our side?"

Belmont's expression sobered. "Zeke's dead, like we thought. So is Connell. Everybody else got out."

"Tell me what happened. Last I remember, the house was on fire—" Stone tried to raise up a little, but gave it up as hopeless. Lu didn't realize—couldn't realize—that it wasn't just blood loss that had laid him low. He didn't know how long he'd been out, but it wasn't only his body that felt weak. That knife had taken more than physical energy from him. He suspected it would be quite some time before he was back to anything close to his normal strength again.

"Yeah," Belmont said, pulling up another chair next to the bed. "Once we knew all four of them were dead, we got out of there fast. Wouldn't be good for any of us to get caught on the scene. Somebody must have seen the flames and called it in. I heard on the radio they got the fire out before it did too much damage to the surrounding area, but the house and the garage were a total loss."

Stone tried to pummel his sluggish brain into following all the implications of that. "So...they're unlikely to find evidence that we were there?"

"Grider says probably not. Says they'll find the burned bodies of the owners, but that's it."

Grider. Stone realized he hadn't seen the detective in a while. "Where is he?"

"He's...here." Belmont's voice held an odd tone, but Stone let it go. "He'll talk to you later. Right now, you should rest. We're safe here—it's the home of one of our people, a few miles away. We didn't want to move you too far until we were sure you weren't gonna die on us."

"No such luck," Stone said, attempting a smile.

Belmont stood. "Hey, it was a little touchy there for a while. C'mon, Lu. Let's clear out and let him rest." To Stone, he said, "We can't stay here too much longer. We're heading back over the hill in a couple of hours. Rest till then."

After he and Lu closed the door behind them, Stone turned back to Imogen. "It's so good to see you," he said. "When I got back to the house and you were gone—" He narrowed his eyes. "How did they take you in the first place? Did they get past the wards?"

She ducked her gaze. "I was an idiot," she said. "You'd told me that a thin, blond man was coming—a friend of yours who couldn't get through them. So when I saw the van pull up and a thin, blond man got out, I thought—"

"Bloody hell…" Stone whispered. "I didn't realize one of them was…" His fists clenched around the bedcovers. "I'm sorry, Imogen. It was my fault, then. I nearly got you killed."

"Don't be daft," she said, and closed her hand around one of his. "You told me he'd wait. I didn't have to go outside. You said not to go outside the wards, and I did."

Stone wasn't convinced, but he didn't have the energy to argue with her. "I'm just glad you're safe," he said. More memories came back and he grinned. "And in any case, *nice* job getting yourself out of there. You didn't need rescuing—you rescued yourself."

"They said they were going to eat me," she said. "That's fairly motivating."

He chuckled, then frowned. "But why did you come back? Why didn't you just get the hell out of there?"

Again, she looked away. "It's a bit embarrassing, actually."

"Oh?"

"I…got lost," she said. "I'm not exactly great at woodsmanship. When I got out, I just ran for it, into the forest. Somehow I got myself turned around trying to get back to the road. I saw lights so I headed toward them—not realizing I was going right back the way I'd come. By the time I worked it out and got to the road, I heard the commotion—and I heard your voice."

"So you stole a van and tried to run them down? Imogen, I had no idea you were such an adventurer." His words were light, but a chill gripped him as he remembered the chain of events, and how many times she had been in danger. "But you could have been killed, running into that garage like that."

"That wasn't on purpose," she said. "The van was theirs—they'd left the keys in it. I was just going to take it and leave until I heard you. Then I knew I had to try to help. The road down was steeper than I thought, though, and I've never driven a left-hand drive car. I accidentally hit the gas instead of the brakes and nearly hit you and your friend, so I panicked and spun the wheel hard so I didn't. That's why I crashed."

"Were you hurt?" He studied her more closely, looking for bruises or other signs of injury.

"Few cuts and bruises. Probably I'll be stiff for a few days. But I'm alive. I'd call it a fair bargain, all things considered." She picked something up off the nightstand. "This is what you killed that thing with. It's magical, isn't it?"

She was holding Kolinsky's knife. It was back in its sheath now. "Careful with that," he said. "And yes, it's magical. I need to return it to its owner."

She set it back on the nightstand and stood. "I should let you rest for a bit before we go. We can talk later, when you're feeling better."

Stone nodded. "If you see Grider, can you send him in? I have a couple of things I want to ask him."

"I'll do that," she said.

He must have drifted off again; when he awoke, pale sunlight streamed in through the room's thin curtains and he heard signs of activity in the front part of the house. He was about to see if he could get up and stagger out to see what was going on when another familiar figure appeared in the doorway.

"Well, you look like hell," Grider said.

"Good morning to you too." Stone tried to sit up; it was a little easier this time. His energy was coming back slowly, but at least it was coming back.

Grider propped up a pillow behind him and dropped heavily into the bedside chair. "You don't do anything easy, do you?"

"It's over, though. That's the important thing." He studied Grider; there was something off about the man, but he couldn't put his finger on what it was. "Belmont says the police aren't likely to come after us."

"Nah, I don't think so. Been listenin' to the police radio. The place burned to the ground before they could get the fire out. Only reason the surrounding forest didn't go up like a tinderbox is that it's been rainin' recently." He paused. "Also, I called in a couple favors and did a lot of fancy dancin'. By now the right people know that the Cannibal Killers died in that fire. That'll be worth enough to 'em to keep the investigations away from you and the rest of this bunch."

"What about you?"

"Me, I could use a good stiff drink or three."

Stone frowned. "I'm sure we all could. But what will you do?"

Grider's gaze shifted away. "I figured I'd prob'ly take early retirement, y'know?"

"There's something you aren't telling me, Lieutenant, isn't there?"

The detective sighed. "You don't miss much, do you?" When Stone didn't answer, he shrugged out of the unfamiliar jacket he wore and held out his left arm.

Stone stared, his breath catching in his throat. Grider's forearm was swathed in a white bandage; a little blood had seeped through and stained the middle of it. "Grider...you didn't—"

"'Fraid so," he said. "Happened when I was dealin' with that guy you killed. He got me a good one before I blew his guts out. Time he got himself back together I'd made myself scarce, but the damage'd been done."

Stone gazed at the bandaged wound as if hypnotized. He had no idea what to say, so he said nothing.

"Been talkin' to Belmont and Lu," Grider said. He shrugged back into his jacket. "They're gonna take care o' me. Make it so if it happens, I won't turn into one o' those monsters."

Stone didn't say it, but he was surprised to hear that. His mind went back to the conversation he'd had with Laura Phelps, where she'd told him that the temptation to kill herself, even with her strong faith, had been so overpowering that she'd actually tried it. "You're...taking this rather better than I'd expected," he said finally, with care.

"You mean why didn't I just decide to blow my brains out when I found out?" Grider snorted. "Don't need to sugarcoat anything, Stone. I'm a big boy."

"Well," Stone said, "not that I'm advocating it or anything, mind you, but—"

"Yeah." Grider nodded. "I get it. But you know, life's funny sometimes. Fuckin' hilarious, in this case."

Stone raised an eyebrow. "Oh? How so?"

"Remember I said I was talkin' to Lu? He's a doctor. When I told him I should just off myself before it takes hold since I ain't got much time left anyway with this thing eatin' my brain, he set me straight." His voice roughened, and Stone was surprised to see his eyes glitter.

And then he got it. Shocked, he said, "You're telling me that the tumor—"

"Lu thinks it'll be gone by the time the transformation finishes up," Grider said. "It's not part of the original equipment, so the regeneration'll take care of it." He laughed, a harsh little sound that held no humor. "So becomin' a fuckin' cannibalistic monster's gonna save my life. I told you it was hilarious."

Stone let his breath out. He couldn't help thinking about what might have happened if it had been Imogen instead of Grider who'd been scratched. He was about to say something else when Belmont knocked and pushed open the door.

"Time to go," he said. "Grider, can you help me get Dr. Stone out to the car?"

"I can walk," Stone grumbled. He sat up the rest of the way, and another wave of grayness flooded over him. "Or...perhaps not yet," he said faintly.

"Easy, there, slugger," Grider said with a grin, and took hold of his arm. "Hey, if I can deal with becomin' a flesh-eatin' fiend, you can deal with somebody helpin' your ass out to the car."

"I can hardly argue with that," Stone said. He picked up the knife from the nightstand and let Grider and Belmont half-carry him out to the waiting car.

| CHAPTER FIFTY

Holmbury St. Mary, England, Christmas Eve

"YOU LOOK LIKE your mind's a million miles away."

Stone turned from the window. He'd been staring out into the darkness, watching the steady, sleety rain that had been coming down for most of the night. No white Christmas this year, but then, it didn't usually snow in Holmbury until at least January, if at all.

He hadn't heard Imogen come up behind him, but she stood there now, watching him with a wistful smile. She looked quite festive tonight in a dress of deep red, and held the thin stem of a half-full wineglass between her fingers.

"Sorry," he said. "I think it might have been." He followed her back over to the sofa and sat down in front of the fire, retrieving his own wineglass.

It was after eleven o'clock; Aubrey, pleased that Stone had come home after all even if it had been a last-minute decision, had put together a modest but delicious meal topped off with a brandy-doused Christmas pudding he'd made months ago ("I thought I'd have to save it for next year," he told them.)

The three of them had spent a pleasant evening presided over by the towering fir tree that the caretaker had put up at the last minute and decorated in an attempt to make the large drafty hall seasonally appropriate. Half an hour or so ago, he'd discreetly made himself scarce and retired to his spacious apartment over the garage, leaving Stone and Imogen to carry on their evening.

"I'm so glad you were able to come after all," Imogen said. "I was afraid you wouldn't feel up to it."

"So was I," he said. In truth, it had only been in the last couple of days that he'd started feeling like himself again. He insisted that Imogen catch her return plane home the previous Monday; she'd almost refused, but he managed to convince her that he was not only capable of taking care of himself, but he preferred it that way. He promised he'd come home for Christmas if he felt up to taking the portal, and had given her a call before showing up that morning. Aside from a slight limp from the leg wound that hadn't quite healed up yet, he was mostly back to normal at this point.

"How long can you stay?"

He shrugged. "I have to be back for the start of the quarter, a little after the new year. Aside from that, no obligations."

She smiled, but didn't reply. After a moment, she said, "Is everything all right back there? Belmont and Grider and the others?"

"They're fine," he said. "Grider's making it through the transition fine so far with the help of Lu and the rest. Lu checked him out and he was right—his tumor's already shrinking. He thinks it will be gone by the time the transition's complete."

"So what will he do? Retire from the force? And was he able to fix it so you don't have to worry about anyone coming after you for—what happened?"

"He came by a couple of days ago, and told me that they bought his story—that he'd gotten a vague lead he wanted to pursue, ended up locating the house they'd taken over, and in the ensuing battle the killers died in the fire."

"Really?" Both her eyebrows went up. "Seems fairly farfetched, doesn't it?"

"I'm sure it is, and I'm sure everybody knows it is," he said. "But the Cannibal Killers are dead, and Grider's friends are fairly high up the food chain. They'll smooth over the whole thing, he says. I won't worry about it unless something comes back to bite me."

He studied her again; he'd been doing that a lot today, using both mundane and magical means, trying to spot any signs of lingering trauma from what she'd experienced. He forgot sometimes—while the whole business with the ghouls hadn't exactly been something he was used to dealing with, his many years of magical study had prepared him for at least accepting supernatural threats. Imogen, despite the time she'd spent over the years with her father and Stone himself, had little actual contact with magic. She'd always heard about it more in the abstract. The events of the last few days had been anything but abstract, and certainly enough to affect even the most mentally grounded. He'd avoided bringing up the subject so far, trying to keep the mood festive, but since she'd mentioned it, he figured she was ready to talk. "Are you...all right, Imogen?"

She leaned over to rest her head on his shoulder, her shimmering brown hair falling over his eyes. He felt her own small shrug. "I guess," she said. "Been having nightmares a bit, but they're getting better. It's not like I can exactly go talk to a therapist about it or anything, is it?" She chuckled. "Right, then, Doctor: I'm having some trouble sleeping because I was kidnapped by ghouls who planned to make a meal of me if my b—" She paused suddenly, stiffening.

Stone closed his eyes. He knew what she was going to say: *if my boyfriend...* He also knew why she couldn't say it. It was the same reason he'd been carefully avoiding the discussion of anything beyond a few days' visit back home.

"It's not going to work, is it?" he said softly.

He felt her head make a slow shake back and forth once on his shoulder. "I...don't think it is," she whispered, barely loud enough for him to hear.

Gently, he took her shoulders and drew back so he could look into her eyes. They were big and glittering, but her pale face didn't look childlike. She looked sad, and resigned, oddly calm. "I love you, Imogen," he said. "I have for a long time. I'm sure you know that, but I don't think I've ever said it enough."

She smiled a faint smile. "I love you too, Alastair. I have almost since I met you. I made a mistake with Robert...I thought I knew what I wanted, but I realize now that I was just running away from something, and that's never a good way to start." When he drew breath to speak, she held up her hand. "But I also realized that I wasn't wrong about *why* I did it. Not wrong, but I didn't take it far enough."

He frowned. "What do you mean?"

She took a sip of her wine and set the glass down. "I was just thinking about myself. About how hard it would be to live a life surrounded by something that I couldn't participate in, no matter how much I wanted to. But I didn't think about you." She took his hand and squeezed it. "I'm not making a lot of sense, but...I hope you understand what I mean."

"I do," he said. He'd never been good at thinking about his feelings—his introspections usually ran more toward trying to solve problems, or pondering the darker corners of his mind—but he'd had a lot of time alone with his thoughts over the last few days while he'd been lying around in his townhouse rebuilding his energy.

"We've just sort of...fallen back into old habits," he continued. "Expectations about the way things are supposed to end up.

And you deserve better than that." He sighed. "I'm not going to change, Imogen. I'm not proud of that, but it's true. It's probably going to bugger up my life in all sorts of ways as time goes on, but there you go." He reached out tentatively toward her, and when she didn't pull back, he drew her into an embrace. "I do love you. I'll always love you. And I'll always hope that you find someone who'll make you ecstatically happy."

She tightened her grip and made a little noise that was half-laugh, half-sob. "Someone Dad won't be tempted to turn into something small and helpless if he puts a toe out of line."

"Baby steps," he murmured.

She pulled back. "And what about you? I want you to be happy too. You could come back, you know. Your life's here. Don't let me drive you away from your home."

He'd thought about that over the last few days, too, and the conclusion he'd come to had surprised him. "I'm not so sure it is," he said slowly. "I thought it was…I honestly wasn't sure whether I would take the offer, go back for next year. But…" He shrugged. "It's not like I can't come back whenever I like, now that I've found the portal."

"You *like* it over there," she said, eyebrows going up again. She had very expressive eyebrows, but she'd always been jealous of him because she'd never been able to raise them one at a time. "You've gone over the wall."

"Maybe I have," he said, chuckling, but then he sobered. "I think I need it, though. I think we both do. Especially since I doubt your father will give it a rest if we stay that close together."

"True," she admitted. "He's been dropping hints the size of boat anchors ever since he worked out that we fancied each other."

He leaned in and gently kissed her. "What about it, then? Friends?"

"Friends," she said. Then she smiled, a wicked gleam in her eyes. "But…"

"But what?"

"Well…Aubrey's gone and left us alone in this big, cold house. Do you think that perhaps we could start being friends…tomorrow?"

He matched her wicked smile. "I think that's a brilliant idea."

| EPILOGUE

Six months later

Dear Dr. Stone,

I hope you're well, and that the new year has been good to you.

I apologize for taking so long to write, but it's taken a while to get everything organized and settle in here. I won't tell you where we've gone—Christopher thinks it's best for all of us if we try to keep it a secret. I think if you ever really need to find us, though, you have your ways, right?

I thought you might like to know this: I've always believed that the Lord works in mysterious ways, and this is a good case of it: Frank (did you ever even know that was his first name?) and I have become good friends over the last couple of months. He was able to retire early and get almost his full pension, so he made a clean break from the force before we left. I still miss Douglas every day, but I think he'd want me to move on. I'm so grateful to Frank. He really is a kind man under that gruff exterior.

I've told Sarah and Cory about where I am (and swore them to secrecy), but not about what's happened. I don't think they can deal with it. I've bought a nice little house with the money from selling the place in Palo Alto, and put a good nest egg away.

I won't say that life is "good," exactly, but it's getting better, and I'm feeling a lot more hopeful about the future than I was when Douglas died. Even though I don't like certain aspects of what my life's become, I'm learning to deal with them.

Thank you again for everything you've done. I wish you all the best, always.

Much love,

Laura Phelps

Read on for a preview of

THE INFERNAL HEART

Book 9 of the Alastair Stone Chronicles

Coming in March 2017!

| PROLOGUE

DENNIS AVILA HATED HIS JOB.

To be fair, he didn't hate the job in general—the construction industry had been good to him, he got along okay with the other guys on the crew, and he liked the fact that he could knock off at quitting time and stop for a drink without his boss being on his case to take a big pile of work home. Those computer wonks might make the big bucks, but Dennis made enough to keep him in beer and cable TV, and at least he got some exercise instead of letting his ass spread out till it was shaped like one of those stupid five-hundred-dollar ergonomic chairs.

No, what Dennis hated was the crop of oversized, overpriced monstrosity houses popping up all over the Silicon Valley as more and more computer wonks moved in with their stock options and their startup companies. "Fucking McMansions," he liked to call them, and, while he didn't think of the situation in exactly these words, he considered them a blight on the area where he'd grown up. His words were more like "they're fuckin' money-pit disasters for fuckin' rich assholes, is what they are," but the sentiment was the same.

Take this current job, for example: this area used to be an orchard, and following that it languished as a weed-strewn, vacant lot for years after some faceless holding company bought it, had all the trees razed, and then gone bankrupt. By the time the legal snarls got untangled and some development company picked it up on the cheap, land in the Silicon Valley—even out here in East Bumfuck, Milpitas—had taken a jump for the stratosphere and everybody involved wanted to milk every stray plot of dirt for every penny it was worth. So instead of a nice little neighborhood full of small, affordable houses, they repurposed it to a collection of mini-mansions twice the size and three times the price of those originally planned. And every last one of the damn things was already spoken for, with deposits secured and preliminary papers signed, before the developers even broke ground.

Dennis swiped sweat off his brow, took a long slug from his oversized water bottle, and lowered the boom down again, dragging up another bucketful of dry earth. It was four-thirty, almost quitting time—he was already thinking about heading to Santana's to hoist a few cold ones with the guys and see if the Giants could get their shit together enough to break their current losing streak. Just a few more loads and he could hang it up for the day.

Something in the bucket caught his attention.

Narrowing his eyes, he pulled a lever to stop the bucket in mid-swing, then adjusted his Ray-Bans for a better look. It was probably nothing—a trick of the sun, or the glint of light off an old beer can—but he thought he'd seen a gray object in the middle of the light-brown expanse of his latest load of dirt.

He shifted the backhoe into neutral, engaged the brake, and jumped down, glancing around to make sure Carl, his boss, wasn't watching. As he hurried around toward the end of the boom where the bucket hung like a scraped-up yellow lobster claw, he noted that he wasn't seeing things: there *was* something there, and it wasn't a beer can or a dark-colored rock.

In fact, it looked like some kind of gray box, about the size of a kid's shoebox.

He glanced around again—the backhoe was between him and the other guys he could see—and quickly plucked the item from the bucket. It was a lot heavier than he expected it to be. He didn't take a good look at it until he'd scurried back around and jumped back into the driver's seat.

It was indeed a box—but not a shoebox. It seemed to be made out of some kind of weathered stone, which must have been why it was so heavy. Dennis turned it over in his gloved hands, examining the carvings on it. Looked like something religious—a big cross in the middle, surrounded by scrollwork and what looked like the images of angels. He tried to pry it open, but it was sealed tight.

For just a moment, a few seconds, he thought about showing it to Carl. It was probably something important—something that belonged in a museum. It was down way too deep for it to be buried by kids, at least not any time recently. In these days of increasingly stringent earthquake codes, they had to dig the foundations deeper than they used to, especially for monster houses like these.

He should hand it over to the authorities, so they could figure out what to do with it.

He should, but he didn't want to.

He studied the box again, his hands tightening on it. He glanced around once more to make sure nobody was looking.

Whatever this thing was, it was interesting, and he *wanted* it. Or at least wanted to see what was inside it before he gave it up.

Dennis reached down and grabbed his battered, dusty backpack from next to the backhoe's seat. He unzipped it, and with one final, furtive check, shoved the box inside and zipped it back up.

Maybe he wouldn't go to Santana's tonight after all, he decided.

❖

An hour later, he stopped off and grabbed some Burger King from the drive-thru, then headed straight home. If the guys asked him tomorrow where he'd been, he'd tell them he was beat and decided to catch up on some extra shuteye.

His apartment was on the second floor of a dusty, thirty-year-old complex off Senter Road in east San Jose. He had the money to move if he wanted to, but it always seemed more trouble than it was worth. This place had everything he needed—it was close to the freeway, the supermarket, and several liquor stores—and the manager was a pretty good guy for a pothead. Dennis even picked up a few extra bucks sometimes doing repairs, because the pothead was too cheap to call a pro and would probably slice his own hand off if he tried to do them himself.

As soon as he rattled his key in the door he heard scratching noises coming from inside, and when he shoved it open, a furry gray-and-black striped missile hurled itself into his legs, tail pointed straight up.

Dennis grinned and leaned down to pet the cat. "Hey, Raider. You have a good day, buddy?"

Raider wound around his legs, following him out to the kitchen as he dropped the Burger King bag on the breakfast bar, his backpack on one of the stools, and grabbed a cold Bud out of the fridge. He jumped up and head-butted Dennis as he sat down.

"Hang on, hang on, you're so impatient!" he growled, but he was grinning. He'd never admit it to anyone, but he looked forward to coming home to Raider. Sure, he was a cat and not a big tough Rottweiler or Pit Bull like some of the guys had for pets, but Dennis spent so much time away from his apartment that keeping a big dog cooped up all day wasn't fair to the dog or the apartment. Raider was self-cleaning, did his business in a box instead of needing to be walked, and seemed quite content to sleep the day away while Dennis was gone. The cat also—and Dennis would have cheerfully punched out anyone who suggested it might be true—loved to snuggle up next to him at night. Until he managed to find himself a girlfriend, Raider was the only warm, affectionate body he was likely to have in his bed.

He pulled out his food—a double Whopper and large fries for him, a plain hamburger for Raider—and spread it on the counter. As he did, his gaze fell once again on his backpack. He unzipped it and took out the mysterious stone box, setting it down to examine it as he ate.

Raider glanced at it, hissed, and immediately leaped off the counter, ignoring his hamburger.

"What's up, bud?" That was weird. Raider *never* passed up a burger.

The cat stopped about six feet away, eyeing both Dennis and the box with wary green eyes. His tail was puffed up like a bottlebrush.

Really weird. Last time Dennis had seen him do that, the neighbor's big goofy Rottie had gotten loose and was peering in the window at him.

Ah, well. Who knew what went on in cats' minds? He put the burger on a plate and set it on the floor. "Fine. You don't wanna hang out, you can eat it later."

He turned his attention back to the box. Under the kitchen light, it looked even older: chipped, dusty, somehow faded. The carvings looked like they'd been elaborate at some point, but being under all that dirt for so long had dulled their edges. He brushed at it with a napkin, knocking some of the dirt off onto an old newspaper, and eventually revealed the thin line of a seam. No sign of a catch or a lock, though.

I really should take this to somebody, he thought again. If not Carl (who, he had to admit, would just as likely try to pawn it for a few bucks as hand it over to the proper authorities) then maybe to Father Rivera, the priest at the Catholic church Dennis attended twice a year (Easter and Christmas) to make his mother happy. After all, it did look religious, and if it was old, it was probably related to the Catholics somehow. Maybe they'd want it back.

That was a good idea. He'd do that, he decided.

Just as soon as he checked out what was inside.

After all, if there were gold coins or something in there, that might change things. The Church was rich enough—if he handed over most of the coins like a good boy but kept a few for himself, who would know? Finder's fee, right?

He finished off the Whopper and grabbed a steak knife from the rack on the wall. Just to be safe, he donned his heavy work gloves from his backpack, then carefully slipped the blade of the knife into the seam on the box. His heart rate increased—he felt like a kid again, looking for buried treasure.

It took him a while of prying, but eventually the knife slid in far enough that he was able to pop the lid off the small box. "That's it!" Dennis cheered as it fell onto the newspaper, revealing the interior.

There weren't any gold coins inside. When Dennis plucked up the dull red cloth covering the contents, all he saw at first was a large wooden cross, simple and unadorned with any fancy scrollwork or metal inlays. Its only decoration, if you could call it that, was a few strange, swirling figures carved crudely into it, as if someone had done it with a pocketknife. It took him a second to realize it was resting on something underneath, but he couldn't tell what the hidden object was without moving the cross.

Dennis crossed himself (he was still enough of a good Catholic to respect the symbols of the faith) and pulled off his heavy gloves. Gently, afraid it would crumble in his hands, he lifted the wooden cross free of the box and set it on the cloth.

Beneath it was—what? He couldn't tell. Some sort of shriveled, desiccated object about the size of a child's fist, blackened and dry.

Some kind of seed pod, maybe?

But it didn't look like a seed pod. It looked—

Alive.

And then it began to glow, a faint red gleam that throbbed with slow, steady rhythm against the box's slate-gray sides.

Pulsed.

Like a heartbeat.

Dennis stared at it, transfixed. Barely realizing he was doing it, he reached out and scooped the object from the box. Lying there in his palm, it continued to glow and pulse. With each beat, it seemed to grow, to plump up, as if something were rehydrating it.

The more it grew, the more it became clear to Dennis what it was—and by the time it finished and lay there, quivering and glowing in his palm, he knew.

It was a heart. A human heart.

Except instead of red, it was solid black. The only red was the glow around it.

It felt warm in his hand.

It began to speak to him.

And he listened.

After a few moments, he picked up the steak knife in his other hand. He gripped it tightly. If his hand shook a little, it didn't stop him from doing what he needed to do.

Calmly, deliberately, without taking his eyes from the thing in his other hand, he brought the knife up and sliced it decisively across his own throat.

As the knife dropped from his hand and clattered to the floor, he neither moved nor screamed. Instead, he leaned forward, holding himself up with one shaking arm.

The last thing he saw before he died was the bright red blood gushing from his slashed throat, spraying and splattering over the box, the cross, and the thing in his other hand, bathing them in hot fluid. The thing was shriveled and desiccated again, but as his vision began to fade and his arm gave way, he saw that it had begun to grow once more.

From across the room, hidden beneath a chair, Raider the cat watched his human die. He knew he was dead—he could smell it from here. He could also smell something else, something infinitely *wrong* in a way that his simple feline brain could never articulate. The feeling was a deep-down instinct: *this is bad. Stay away from it.*

Raider didn't run. Something told him not to. He merely crouched beneath the chair and watched as—*something*—began to form around whatever the badthing in the human's hand was. It continued to rise until it too was shaped like a human.

But it wasn't a human. It didn't smell like a human. It was a thing made of darkness and wrongness and fear. As Raider watched, it seemed to get its bearings for a moment. It stood still, regarding the box and the crucifix on the counter. Without touching either, it turned and crossed the room to the door. Even its movements were wrong: old and jerky and careful. It didn't even glance at Raider as it passed, but only opened the door with a bony hand and left the apartment.

It was many hours before Raider was brave enough to venture out from beneath the chair. When he did, creeping carefully over toward the huddled lump of dead flesh that used to be his human, he noticed that whatever the badthing had been in the human's paw, it wasn't there anymore. The black figure hadn't taken it—Raider had watched the whole process—but it was gone now nonetheless.

The cat pondered the scene for a moment, taking it all in, evaluating one last time to make sure the threats were gone. Then he licked himself, rubbed one last time against the dead human's dangling leg, and went over to finish his hamburger.

If you enjoyed this book, please consider leaving a review at Amazon, Goodreads, or your favorite book retailer. Reviews mean a lot to independent authors, and help us stay visible so we can keep bringing you more stories. Thanks!

If you'd like to get more information about upcoming Stone Chronicles books, contests, and other goodies, you can join the Inner Circle mailing list at **rlkingwriting.com**. You'll get a free e-novella, *Shadows and Stone,* that's not available anywhere else.

ABOUT THE AUTHOR

R. L. King is an award-winning author and game freelancer for Catalyst Game Labs, publisher of the popular roleplaying game *Shadowrun*. She has contributed fiction and game material to numerous sourcebooks, as well as one full-length adventure, "On the Run," included as part of the 2012 Origins-Award-winning "Runners' Toolkit." Her first novel in the *Shadowrun* universe, *Borrowed Time*, was published in Spring 2015, and her second will be published in 2017.

When not doing her best to make life difficult for her characters, King is a software technical writer for a large Silicon Valley database company. She enjoys hanging out with her very understanding spouse and her small herd of cats, watching way too much *Doctor Who*, and attending conventions when she can. She is an Active member of the Horror Writers' Association and the Science Fiction and Fantasy Writers of America, and a member of the International Association of Media Tie-In Writers.

You can find her at *rlkingwriting.com* and *magespacepress.com*, on Facebook at www.facebook.com/AlastairStoneChronicles, and on Twitter at *@Dragonwriter11*.

Made in the USA
Las Vegas, NV
09 September 2024